A CORNISH AFFAIR

A CORNISH AFFAIR

LIZ FENWICK

LARGE PRINT

Oxford

First published in Great Britain 2013
by
Orion Books
an imprint of The Orion Publishing Group Ltd.

Published in Large Print 2015 by ISIS Publishing Ltd.,
7 Centremead, Osney Mead, Oxford OX2 0ES
by arrangement with
The Orion Publishing Group Ltd.
an Hachette UK Company

CIP data is available for this title from the British Library

ISBN 978–1–4450–9992–7 (hb)
ISBN 978–1–4450–9993–4 (pb)

Printed and bound in Great Britain by
T. J. International Ltd., Padstow, Cornwall

For Sasha

Not of the land
Not of the sea
Visible only
When August Rock sees

CHAPTER
ONE

Osterville, Cape Cod, Massachusetts

I stood in front of a full-length mirror and didn't recognise the woman who appeared there.

"Breathe out." Sophie, my best friend, instructed. "How much weight have you lost since the last fitting?"

"I don't know." The dress hung on me. "Can we stuff something in it to fill it out?"

Sophie reached into her dress and pulled out two gel objects. "Here, use these."

I waited while she undid the buttons at the back of the dress. I was not a pretty sight, and not how I ever imagined I'd look on my wedding day.

"I just don't understand why you are in this dress."

"Don't go there. Mother wanted this one."

Sophie rolled her eyes. "I was there. This dress would have suited Rose, or even your mother. It's not you at all."

I took a deep breath and shoved the inserts into the corset. My boobs popped up but not really out. Sophie buttoned me up again. I knew exactly what she meant about the dress. It was fussy, and I looked like a coat hanger wearing a meringue.

"Sorry to mention Rose."

"It's OK."

Sophie gave me a swift hug, both of us blinking away emotion. I was wearing far too much mascara to cry.

"Are you ready?" My mother, Jane, walked into the room without knocking. She studied me from head to toe. I held my breath.

"You look . . ." Mother came up to me and adjusted the neckline of the gown over the bolstered curve of my bust. "Perfect."

"Thanks." Another glance in the mirror confirmed her words were a lie. Mother stood beside me, gazing at our reflections. I towered over her delicate frame. Her lilac dress set off her blond hair. The only similarity between us was our mouth; I had her full lips. Rose had been the image of Mother, where I was gangly and dark.

"I knew I was right about the dress. It's far better on you than the one you preferred."

I nodded. There was no point in disagreeing at this stage; I'd left it too late.

The leaves on the birch trees surrounding the church were still. It was as if time had stopped, yet I heard the chatter inside. I stood at the porch and tried to breathe. The air was heavy, threatening. Despite the haze, the temperature was over a hundred degrees. How could it be so hot on Cape Cod in early June?

"OK?" Dad asked as he appeared from behind and took my elbow.

I frowned, but then turned and gave him a grin.

2

"Nervous?" He glanced at his watch. It was three o'clock. Any moment now the music would change and I would begin my last walk as a single woman. I looked through the door and down the aisle. The church was filled with pink flowers — hundreds of lilies, to be precise. The altar was barely visible for all the massed blooms in every shade of the wretched colour; particularly pale pink. I've always hated pink. I should have said so, but I hadn't.

Beside the altar stood my fiancé, John: tall, blond and gorgeous, but even he hadn't escaped the colour. His waistcoat matched the flower girls' dresses. Like dolls, they spun around my knees with pink, stinking lilies clutched in their fists.

I held my bouquet away from me. The scent of lilies was overpowering at any time, but in the heat it was worse, unlike the fragrance of some other flowers. I looked up into Dad's eyes.

"What's on your mind, Jude?"

I leaned over and rested my head on his shoulder for a second. "The garden we created in Abu Dhabi."

"It was this hot too."

"Yes, it was." Abu Dhabi had been special. Rose had still been well when we'd lived there, Mother less frantic, and the garden was sublime. The fragrance of frangipani and night-scented jasmine came to mind. "I loved that garden."

"Me too." Dad straightened his waistcoat. The heat was bad enough in my dress. It must have been unbearable in a morning coat.

"It was the first one we made from scratch."

3

"A long time ago now." He put his hand on my arm.

"Almost twenty years." The music stopped. I felt the pressure of Dad's grasp increase on my arm. My mouth went dry.

"Ready?" he asked.

I nodded, but then I saw Mother signalling to the choir loft.

"False alarm." Dad took a hankie out of his pocket and wiped his brow. The rosebud in his buttonhole had gone limp. I touched it.

"Not made for this heat, me or the rose." He put his hankie away.

"I love roses, though." A lump formed in my throat.

"She'd love all of this." His glance made a broad sweep of the church. "She's with us in spirit." He found my hand and gave it a squeeze. "Your mother's walking back down the aisle. I'd better go see what the delay is."

He moved quickly and led Mother back to her seat. The church was packed with five hundred people all in their finest. Between John and me we might know half of them, but only a hundred could be called friends. My parents had splashed out, and I hadn't the heart to rein them in. After all, this was their one chance. I was their only child now, and had been for eighteen years. It was all I could do. They would never see Rose's wedding day, so mine was their only chance to throw a big party.

My parents stood beside the front pew with their heads together. Around them the congregation buzzed with hushed discussions. The simple lines of the church

4

were obscured with all the decorations. No detail had been too small for Mother's attention.

I closed my eyes, wondering what was up. I fiddled with my charm bracelet. The hump on the camel should have been worn off because of all the times I had rubbed it, wishing that Rose were still with me. Seven years my senior, I had adored her. If she were here, if the kidney disease hadn't killed her, I wouldn't be nervous and Mother wouldn't be fussing.

The music changed and I opened my eyes. Where was Dad? Shouldn't we be walking down the aisle? Searching the church, I found him settling Mother. He pressed a kiss to her temple and began to pull away.

A car drew up to the bottom of the church steps and I recognised the thick ankle that was emerging. I dashed to help Great-Aunt Agnes out of the car. She batted me away with her walking stick as her driver came round to help.

"I'm pleased I'm not late." She grabbed the other stick from the driver and made for the steps. I walked beside her, ready to steady her. She was ninety-four and still lived independently, despite everyone except me trying to push her into a home.

"No need to fuss, Jude." She turned to me. "I've managed to stay alive until your wedding day, so I can damn well make my own way into the church."

I loved her spirit. Despite Agnes' insistence on walking in alone, I glanced about for one of the ushers. It wasn't tradition for a bride to seat her guests, but Agnes was special, so I might risk Mother's ire and do just that.

We reached the church door and she took a few breaths while she studied me from head to toe. "Nice shoes. Ghastly dress. Your mother's choice, I expect. She's always got hcr own way."

I opened my mouth to reply but then shut it.

"You're a dear girl, but have always been too biddable for my taste. Keep wondering where the Warren backbone is in you." Her voice rang out, and I wondered if she had forgotten to turn on her hearing aids. I placed a hand on her arm. "Mind you, your father seems to be missing it too. Your mother's always had him by the balls, from what I can tell."

I glanced around, hoping that no one could hear her over the organ. Clasping her elbow, I began to lead her into the church when Sophie's boyfriend Tim came to my rescue. "Handsome boy." Agnes took his arm, then turned to me and winked.

I back-stepped to the lobby, feeling Mother's wrath as her gaze burned into me. A drop of sweat trickled down my bolstered cleavage. A breeze swept past, stirring the delicate birch leaves. Only a thunderstorm could relieve the oppressive atmosphere.

Peering down the aisle, I caught a glimpse of John standing with his best man. He looked so distant, so formal. His glance met mine and he smiled. It would be all right. Nerves were normal.

"Hasn't Jane done well with Judith marrying John? This is what she's been trying to achieve for years." A woman spoke over the music.

"I know. The Stewarts are such a good family, and he's already a partner in the firm. But I have to say I

6

still wonder what he sees in the Warren girl. She's nothing like Jane, has none of her style. Jane did well to marry her off." They looked at my mother as she resumed her seat at the front.

I didn't know either woman, but they knew me, or more precisely, Mother. Mother had been over the moon when I had begun dating John, and thinking about it now, moving me towards this day from that moment. Was John my choice or hers?

The bouquet I held reached the floor with its cascade and, almost as if I weren't really there, I watched my hands tremble so much that I dropped the candyfloss mess. One of the flower girls dived to retrieve it and I extended my hand, looking at the artful design of the arrangement. It wasn't right. It wasn't *me*. This whole thing was wrong. I dropped my hand, then I ran as fast as my shoes would let me, never looking back.

The incoming tide lapped over my red toenails and wet the brilliant white froth of my wedding gown. Tears caused it all to blur to pink, reminding me of the wretched lilies. That was hours ago, and now the salty water of the Gulf Stream had removed the stiffness from the skirt so that it collapsed against my legs. Finally I felt at peace with the damn dress.

A seagull dive-bombed into the water. I wiped my eyes so that I could see if it was successful. It was, and I smiled. At least someone had gotten what he wanted. But then, the gull knew what it wanted, and I hadn't. Big difference. I had only discovered what I hadn't wanted at the worst possible moment.

It was an effort to stand. My legs had gone a bit dead. I'd lost count of how long I'd been sitting staring at the water. It didn't hold any answers, and now I had to go back and face everyone. The sun had set, and by rights I should be on my way to Boston for my wedding night, then onto Maine to start my honeymoon, not standing by an empty lifeguard tower.

Looking at the sea again, the enormity of what I'd done hit me. I needed to talk to John, but I had no words, or none that could begin to make amends for what I had done to him.

I brushed the sand off as best I could, wishing I had a phone. All I had was a soaking dress, a veil and a useless pair of high-heeled shoes. My progress across the beach was slow. The dress hindered my movement. It hadn't been light to begin with, but Mother had been so excited, and I'd wanted to make her happy if I could. In a way, this was to have been her day as much as mine.

My legs ached. The walk felt endless. A car's horn sounded as it whooshed past me. I knew I looked a sight, and the sooner I could change the better. The house came into view and I stopped.

The flowerbeds at the front of the house were a riot of colour with the orange Hemerocallis, or daylilies, shouting for attention over the soft tones of the white peonies. Dad had thrown his heart and soul into making sure the garden would be beautiful for my day. My day . . . I squeezed my eyes shut. Those happy moments when John and I had worked with Dad seemed ages ago, but it was only a few weeks.

Caterers came out, and I hid in the shadow of a large pine. Once they'd gone back inside, I limped onto the lawn and studied the one constant in what had been my peripatetic life: a weatherboard house with dark green shutters. We had come here every summer, and when Dad retired it had become our permanent home. I didn't want to go in. Mother would be in a state; and why wouldn't she?

Standing by the house, it appeared so peaceful, but that could be deceptive. It didn't look as if it was on the water from this angle, but it was. From here it could be in the woods, but walk through the door and the house opened out to reveal Eel River. It was originally built by my great-grandfather as a summer cabin in the 1920s when summer cabins were ambitious, with room for servants, and you came to Cape Cod on the train with steamer trunks.

I had let all of them down, past and present, by not walking up the aisle. Everything was so clear in my mind, but how could I explain to everyone without hurting them more? Now, hours later, I was facing what I'd done as lights shone out of all the windows of the house. It looked happy. It was dressed for a party, my party, and I hadn't turned up until it was over. The cost of the whole thing made my eyes water.

Pushing aside these thoughts, I knew that what held me in the shadows was not fear of Mother's huge displeasure, but of Dad's disappointment. How was I going to explain to my rock why I had bolted?

I moved towards my car. It was parked out of the way, waiting for my return from honeymoon. What was

John doing? Getting drunk, I should imagine. That sounded appealing, but before I could do that, or anything else, I needed to get out of this damn dress. As quietly as I could, I moved to the side door where the sounds of chairs being stacked and orders given almost drowned out my mother's voice. I stood still and listened.

"What was that child thinking?" Her English accent was always more pronounced when she was angry. Her words carried on the night air.

Child? Thirty is not a child. I began to walk out of the shadows, but stopped as she continued.

"Such stupidity."

"Jane." Dad cut her off.

"Leaving John at the altar was such an overdramatic, asinine thing to do." Mother paused. "Did you see Mary's face? There was her beloved son, standing at the altar looking like a fool and our daughter was the cause. I doubt they will ever speak to us again."

"It was terrible." Dad's voice broke.

"I've never been more embarrassed in my entire life." Jane sighed. "I don't know how I'll ever be able to show my face again."

I couldn't see my father, and whether he agreed with her or not. "You're tired. You put so much work into making this day wonderful for her." His voice trailed away. "Where the hell is she?"

Jane sighed. "I'm sure she's fine and thinking only of herself, and not of John or his parents or even us. Hasn't that always been the way with her? I'm so disappointed."

"Me too."

"Rose would never have done this. She was so thoughtful, and not at all selfish." Jane sobbed.

I remained in the shadows. I couldn't move. Mother's words echoed in my head. She was right. Rose would never have done this.

CHAPTER
TWO

The lawns lining Long Beach Road were still covered in dew as I parked my car. The air was sweet with the scent of sea-spray roses. I closed my eyes and accepted that I was a contrary being. These *Rosa rugosa* were pink and I loved them. That much I knew, but not much else. I glanced at the phone in my hand. It kept beeping at me because its memory was full. I didn't want to read the hundred-plus messages all asking questions. I had read only one, John's. It simply said, *Meet me at eight AM. You know where.*

There had been no X or O or even a "luv". Not that I deserved any of that. I scrolled through the other messages, clicked *Delete all* then shut the phone off. The rest of the world could wait.

Tall grasses scratched my bare legs as I followed the path through the small dunes to where it opened up onto the beach. The sand that covered the long strip of land separating the Centerville River from the ocean seemed to have made its way into my throat. No matter how many times I swallowed, the dryness wouldn't recede.

The sun warmed my back as I slipped off my flip-flops and began to walk to the water. I'd lain awake for hours revisiting what I'd done and trying to put it into words, but all I got were dark circles under my eyes. How could I say that we never should have been anything more than friends? Years of summers and weekends at our parents' houses on the Cape rolled through my mind, along with drinks after work in Boston, skating and skiing. So much joint history woven together.

John sat near the water throwing shells into the sea. His shoulders were hunched while the morning light caught his blond hair. My legs refused to move. Everything inside me contracted. The first time we'd kissed had been here on a moonless night after a dare to go skinny-dipping. I licked my lips, remembering the taste of salt on his mouth and the pure thrill of that embrace. That had been ten years ago, long before we had begun dating. For years our lives had been entwined, as friends. How long had I loved him, and had that stopped? I didn't really know any more.

I counted to ten for courage, then sank into the sand beside him. My arm pressed against his. His warmth travelled through his linen shirt to my heart. He pulled away.

"Hi." The strangulated tone that emerged from me didn't sound normal. "Sorry." Never had a word felt more inadequate.

"Jude, why?"

"I . . ." I didn't know what to say. "I wish I knew." I lied. I couldn't hurt him more than I had already.

He turned to me. His blue eyes were filled with tears. He pushed them away, then threw another shell into the sea. "What the hell's that supposed to mean?"

"John," I began, but stopped when he stood.

"How could you do that to me?" He turned from me. "To us?"

I looked at the water running over the sand. I deserved this, and more. "I don't know." But I did. I just couldn't say it.

"That's not good enough."

"I know." I stood.

"That doesn't help." He turned away. "It's not giving me answers. It doesn't stop me looking like a fool."

"John, you're not the fool. I am."

"Why?" The look of pain in his eyes filled me with remorse. He walked down the empty stretch of beach and I chased after him. I couldn't leave it like this. He stopped when I put my hand on his arm.

"I only want to know one thing." He picked my hand off and looked at his ring still encircling my finger. The solitaire sparkled in the sunlight, reminding me of all the excitement when he had placed it there a year ago. "Do you still love me?"

My heart shrank. His face was drawn. "Yes." My voice was little more than a croak. It was true. I did, but not the way he meant.

"Then why, Jude?" I saw all the hurt and anger in his eyes. How could I have run out on him like that?

"I . . ." He was so expectant. I couldn't tell him the truth. My shoulders slumped. How could I say that I realised he was like the dress, the flowers and the whole event — my mother's choice and not mine? I couldn't. Before I could say anything else, he turned and walked away down the long stretch of beach.

14

Pulling into the drive, I counted three cars and recognised them all. Just for an instant I thought about changing direction and driving away for ever. These vehicles belonged to Mother's golfing partners. I didn't wonder why they were here. Mother didn't play golf on a Sunday, but Dad did. They'd come in search of the lowdown on the bolting-bride saga and to support my mother, who was beyond humiliated by what I'd done. I opened the back door and hoped I could slip past them and up to my room.

"Judith?"

I winced. "Yes."

"There's a list of people who rang for you on the kitchen table. Come and say hello."

As I walked to the sunroom, I wondered what I was going to say. I had no desire to see anyone, and these women would make me feel worse, if that was possible, than I already did. I stopped at the door and four sets of eyes stared at me.

"How are you?" Pat tapped the seat beside her.

How was I supposed to answer that? "Been better." I shifted from one foot to the other.

"Nerves are a terrible thing." She smiled and I nodded. Nerves hadn't helped.

"If you'd had doubts, you could have sorted them sooner, dear." Pat smiled at me, and I wanted to scream that I already knew this and they didn't have to tell me, but of course they did. She was only saying what everyone was thinking.

15

"And your poor mother had gone to all that work to make your day perfect." She looked at Mother, and I could see this was helping her. She needed them and their support to face the gossip.

I began to speak, but Pat went on: "And all that money your father spent."

My mother smiled. This was the public face that she had been wearing rigidly since last night. It was a smile that said it was all right even when it wasn't. I knew it well from Rose's illness. She hadn't wanted people to know how bad things were, how our life had fallen to pieces.

"If you'll excuse me, I have phone calls to make." I copied my mother's smile, then dropped my head and left the room. There was no other way. Everything Pat said was right. I was the hot topic everywhere, and I'd have to get used to it.

In the kitchen, I thought about the breakfast I hadn't eaten before seeing John. I still couldn't face food, but another cup of coffee might help.

While I'd been out, Mother had been busy. There was the full list of presents John and I had received. A note would need to be sent to everyone. I would have to create something that explained my actions yet said nothing at all. Sinking onto the chair, I put the mug on the table. The neat pile of pages tormented me. I had been blind. I couldn't make it right, but I could apologise.

My conversation with the realtor confirmed what I suspected. Until the first year was complete, there was no break clause in the rental agreement for my condominium in Boston. I'd thought that was a good thing when I'd signed it. After all, we had planned to move to London with John's job, and the rental income would pay the mortgage. He had done the same with his apartment. It had all worked out so well, but now I needed a place to live.

The phone rang. It had been ringing non-stop. Everyone wanted the story.

"I've finally reached you." It was Sophie. "Why haven't you returned my calls?"

"I . . ."

"How could you do it? I mean, everyone was there waiting for you. One minute you were there by the door and everything was cool, then they started the wedding march and you weren't."

I'd forgotten the wedding march. Mother and I had argued about this endlessly. She'd wanted it, and I'd wanted Bach's Double Violin Concerto, Second Movement. However, Mendelssohn turned out to be a surprisingly good tune to run to in heels.

"Sophie, I . . ."

"Seriously, what were you thinking, leaving John standing there like an idiot?"

"I . . ."

"We've all been asking what got into you, and you haven't called any of us." She paused for air. "I sent you text after text, and eventually you replied 'Am alive'. What sort of answer is that?"

"Possibly the only one that should matter?" I said, but Sophie didn't hear me. I spun a pen around on the table. What was I going to do?

"Jude, are you listening to me?"

"Um, no." I stilled the spinning pen.

"Thought not. All a bit much? Sorry to rant."

"You are right to." I walked around the central island in the kitchen.

"No, what you need is a hug and a bottle of wine, or maybe a margarita or five."

I laughed.

"That's better. Now, tell me what's happening. Have you seen John?"

"Ah, yes." I stopped walking.

"Didn't go well?"

"I wouldn't say well, but it went."

"Oh dear, I can imagine he wasn't too pleased."

"You could say that." I frowned.

"Right, what are you doing now?"

"Looking at Mother's list of gifts to be returned, and wondering where I'm going to live and how I'm going to support myself." I poked the list, wishing it would disappear.

"Yes, that's a bit of a problem. Have you called work?"

"Not yet, but," I sighed, "you know I practically begged them to give me a sabbatical so that I could move to London with John?"

"God, I'd forgotten that."

I took a deep breath, wondering if it really was just two months ago that we had been apartment-hunting in London. After a few days of meetings in New York City, John would be opening his law firm's office in London next week. We had it all planned. A short honeymoon in Maine, then we would fly to London, where our new life would begin. "I doubt they can help, as they've hired another archivist to do my job for two years. I won't be able to have my job back until my two-year sabbatical is over."

"True. Well, something will work out." Good old Sophie always looked on the bright side, and always had. Her positive attitude had gotten me through boarding school and my bachelor's degree in history at Mount Holyoke.

"I hope so."

"When am I going to see you?"

"Soon. When are you back on the Cape?" Like so many twentysomethings who lived and worked in Boston, Sophie decamped to her parents' house on the Cape every weekend to make the most of the summer.

"I'll be down on Saturday."

"See you then." I put the phone down. Maybe I should drive to Boston. Sophie lived in a studio but I could sleep on the floor for a night or two. I turned to the kitchen table and the gift list. It would take me the week to write to everyone. I picked up the pen and paper, then began. I wouldn't be able to do anything until I'd completed this task. One note at a time was the way to go . . .

Dear Mrs Smith,

Thank you for the thoughtful and generous gift of the silver chicken-breast fork. Your kindness is greatly appreciated.

I paused. What the hell could I say? A silver chicken-breast fork? I hadn't known what it was, and had to look it up. John thought it was a mini pooper-scooper for a pet. We'd laughed for ages.

As you are aware, the wedding did not go ahead, but . . .

But what? I hadn't a clue what to put next.

thank you for coming.

No. I tore the note up and began again.

The walls of my bedroom in my parents' house were still pink. We'd never changed it because Rose had chosen the colour. She and I had shared the room. Not that we'd needed to: Eel River Cottage was far from small, but I was prone to nightmares and Rose had volunteered to be with me to keep the dreams at bay. The nightmares hadn't gone away, but Rose could just put out a hand and settle me. When she became ill it had been my hand to comfort her. I'd never been able to do more than hold her hand. So damned useless. I took a deep breath. We should have redecorated years ago; keeping the room unchanged hadn't brought her back.

The shelves were lined with books and photos of the two of us. I picked up one taken on holiday in the Caribbean. Freckles were scattered across Rose's nose, and I was as brown as a nut. Putting the picture back on the shelf, I touched the frame wishing she were here for me to talk to. This family hadn't been the same without her, especially Mother. Her companion had gone, and no matter what I had done I'd never been able to fill her shoes.

"Judith, there you are. Now that you'll be staying, maybe we should redecorate your room." Mother stood in the doorway. She was dressed for golf in her bright skirt and top with her sun visor in her hand. "It looks a bit young for a thirty year old. See you later. You'll get those notes finished, won't you?"

I sank onto the bed repeating her words: *It looks a bit young for a thirty year old.* What was I going to do? I couldn't live here until my sabbatical was finished and my condo became available. It was fantastic that they were willing to have me, but . . .

I stood and headed to the kitchen. I'd really made a mess of things. It wouldn't be so bad if I was the only one affected, but my parents had to face the gossip and possibly the burden of supporting me again. I shuddered at the thought.

It would be great if I could just go to work and get lost in it. I adored my job. It was perfect. Books, gardens and academia all rolled into one. Leaving it had been the difficult part about agreeing to move to

London. Now I didn't even have London to look forward to. Ahead of me was living with my parents and being talked about by everyone.

Out of the window I could see Dad working at the far end of the garden in the rose bed. The roses were about to come into their peak. I should go and help him. I straightened the pile of envelopes waiting to be filled with those damn notes.

The notes could wait, but trying to make some kind of peace with Dad wouldn't. Mother had been behaving as if nothing had happened, her English reserve evident in every move. But Dad and I hadn't spoken. I'd thought he might understand, but thus far I'd been wrong.

Picking up my cell and my gardening gloves, I walked down the lawn, watching Eel River shimmer in the morning light. Dad looked up, then swiftly went back to pulling off diseased leaves. Kneeling two bushes away, I began the same task. This year the black spot wasn't too bad. I moved down two roses ahead of him. Each time I heard him pause, I tried to speak, but rather than the words I wanted to say, like sorry for ruining everything, other words kept jumping in front. Instead of talking, I plucked leaves off and recited the Latin names of the different roses as I went along. The garden had been a very basic one when Dad had inherited the house. My grandparents had not been gardeners. A simple garden had suited them, but not Dad. Each summer when we'd returned, Mother would adapt the inside of the house and Dad would add his mark to the garden.

After Rose's death, we had created this bed. Together we'd pored over catalogues, choosing them — the clove-scented Souvenir de St Anne to remember our time on the Arabian Peninsular; the David Austin rose William Shakespeare because of her love of the bard; and Grace because that was her best friend's name. This had been our way of mourning her together. Was he working here now because he was missing her and I was such a disappointment? I turned to him.

"Sorry for everything, and the money wasted."

His head came up and I could see his eyes were filled with tears. "You've made such a mess of everything again."

I sat back on my heels, squeezing a stem in my hands. Blood trickled through the glove where a thorn pierced my palm.

My cell phone rang. It was Mother. "Judith, Pat's niece is stuck at the Hyannis Mall and we've decided to play eighteen." She paused, and I knew what was coming next. "Go and collect her. She'll be at the North entrance at twelve. You'd better get moving. Oh, and stop at the farm stand on your way back and pick up some salad things for tonight."

"Go." Dad put his head back down and continued with his task.

It was three days after the non-wedding, and my wrist ached. With the half of my brain that wasn't writing meaningless words on a page, I concocted a plan. I glanced at the one-way ticket to London. It had been purchased with a completely different goal in mind, but it provided me with an exit strategy. I couldn't continue to live in my parents' house; it was like being a seventeen year old again at Mother's beck and call. I would do as Dad had asked and go.

If I left then, the scandal would die down and I wouldn't be the subject of every conversation. Even strangers at the farm stand were discussing the bride who fled. My options at the moment were limited. I had no job and no apartment, but I did have a one-way ticket to England. John would be in London with his new job, and I could begin again in Oxford. I'd done my postgraduate degrees there and it was where my godmother Barbara lived. It was the beginnings of a plan. I had some savings, I could live cheaply and if I was lucky, I could find a job.

The flight was tomorrow, unless I could change it. Flying to London with John would be too much. I picked up the phone and hoped the airline would help. Chewing the top of my pen, I worked through the automated system to reach a person. The view outside the kitchen window showed clouds building up on the horizon. A storm front was moving in.

At least the ticket change happened without drama. The woman had been very sympathetic. I just hoped everyone else would react as well.

That gave me only a few hours to sort everything and tell those who needed to know. Hopefully my parents would be relieved. Without me, they could resume their lives. I'd email Barbara now. The bigger problem was what I was going to say to John. This ticket was supposed to bring me to the start of our new life together, and now it was the beginning of our life apart. It would be tricky. We hadn't spoken since the morning, on the beach. He didn't want to talk to me, and I couldn't blame him.

I picked up the phone and dialled Aunt Agnes' number. "Hello, Aunt Agnes."

"Jude. I'm glad to see you do have a backbone after all."

"I suppose you could say that." I laughed.

"I do. How are you?"

"OK, and I just wanted you to know that I'm off to Oxford for a while so that," I paused, "the dust can settle a bit."

"A good idea. Keep in touch."

"Will do. Stay well."

She laughed. "At my age just being alive is well." We said our goodbyes, and I hoped that she would indeed stay well. I put the phone down, fighting a sadness I couldn't explain.

"There you are." Mother walked into the kitchen. "I just had Pat on the phone. She received your note with the returned present."

This wasn't going to go well. Mother's lips were pursed and she had a pencil behind her ear. She was definitely not happy if she had forgotten the pencil was there. I stood.

"She tells me that you didn't explain why you didn't go through with the marriage. That you avoided the issue altogether."

"That's correct." I closed the lid to my laptop carefully.

"I have been more than patient waiting for you to tell me what happened. People, especially your own parents, deserve some explanation for your irrational actions." She put the kettle on, and her voice remained as smooth as if she had been instructing me on how to make a cup of tea.

"It's none of their business."

"Judith, you made it their business with your behaviour."

I took my glasses off and placed them on the table. "I've said I'm sorry and will continue to do so, but there's nothing else I can do."

"Explain is what you can do. Everyone keeps asking me why. It was the perfect match. John's handsome, successful and from a good family." She turned and stared at me. "You're a fool. You'll never find anyone else who will take you on."

"Take me on?" My voice rose sharply. "Take me on? What? Am I some loser? I don't need someone to *take me on*. I have a career. I can look after myself."

"Really? You think the measly salary you receive as a librarian is going to support you in the lifestyle you lead?"

"I'm an archivist, and I work for Harvard."

"Then why aren't you teaching, instead of off in some garden library?"

I gritted my teeth. She was right to be angry about the wedding, but I wasn't going to let her undervalue my work. "I do teach, but my main focus is maintaining the important collection of the arboretum."

"It's just bloody gardens! It's not saving the world." Mother poured water into the teapot. From her manner you would think we were discussing the weather, not having a fight. "Rose would never have . . ."

"No, Rose was perfect." I clenched my hands.

She put the kettle back onto the stove with a thump. "You've been behaving like a spoilt, ungrateful brat."

"If that's how you feel about it, I can't change that. I've apologised about the wedding, and I'm sorry I'm such a disappointment in every way."

"Don't be ridiculous."

"I'm not. It's what you just said."

Mother spun around. "I don't want to hear any more nonsense."

"Sorry, but sometimes things need to be said. You want me to spill my guts about why I didn't marry John, so what's different about this? Rose was perfect. I'm not. Just say it." I felt my face flame.

Mother slapped the teacup onto the table, shattering it. "Judith, I said enough. I don't want to hear another word."

"I'm leaving, which should make that possible."

"Good riddance." Mother muttered. As I left the kitchen, wishing that things were different between Mother and me, I caught sight of my father standing by the back door with a bunch of roses in his hand. He'd heard every word. This was not how I'd planned to tell them, but it was done now, and from the look on Dad's face, I might never be allowed back.

27

"What? Leaving? Are you mad?" Sophie studied me over the rim of her coffee cup.

"Clearly I am. I didn't marry the most wonderful man in the world, and I'm walking away from all of this." I glanced round the coffee shop, avoiding the eyes of the people who were staring at me. One was even pointing.

"What are you going to do?"

"Stay with Barbara until I get a job."

"Can you work there?"

"Dual nationality."

"How could I forget, the passport juggle." We both smiled at the memories of flying to far-flung destinations to reach our parents. Hers had been based in Hong Kong, while mine had moved around a lot. "Well, I suppose I was going to lose you to London anyway, so this isn't really any different. Does John know what you are doing?"

I felt for the envelope in my bag. In it was my engagement ring, which I needed to return to him. "No, I haven't told him yet."

"He may not like it, but then again he may. He's still in love with you, you know."

I nodded. My left hand looked naked without the ring, only the slight indentation remaining where it had once been. "I'm going to drive by his parents' house now and see if he's there."

"He's been staying with them this week." She put her hand out and grabbed mine. "Don't envy you."

I laughed. "Well, I got myself into this predicament, so I need to find a way out."

"Yup, but let me know if I can help."

"Thanks." I sighed. "I have to go. Don't let Tim slip away. You two are great together." I stood and kissed her cheek. "I'll be in touch."

"Thanks." She smiled. "Why do I get the sense that after all these years you are finally rebelling? It's a bit late, isn't it?"

"Good question, and I don't know." I walked towards the door.

"A tattoo would have been easier!" Sophie dashed over and gave me a hug.

"True." I looked down at her. "I'm going to miss you, short stuff."

"You bet. Be good." She stopped. "Nah, be crazy, for once!"

"I just may." I waved and went to my car.

Red impatiens filled the flowerbeds beside the front door of John's parents' house. I played with the phone in my pocket. He hadn't answered my calls or replied to my texts. I needed to see him and not his parents. I had tried to call them earlier in the week, but only reached their machine, so I'd written to apologise. John's mother frightened me a bit. Whereas my mother was tiny and controlling, his was large and expansive. She was well meaning, but I had hurt her son and she had every right to hate me.

The screen door gave a glimpse into the house. No one was visible, but John's car keys were on the table just inside. I knocked and waited. When I heard footsteps over the sound of my heart, I knew they weren't John's but his mother's. My throat went dry.

"Jude." She stood on the other side of the screen door. There was no smile of welcome, and I hadn't expected one.

"Mary. I'm here to see John, but first let me say —"

"Don't bother. I got your letter."

"Sorry." There was that word again.

"You've broken his heart."

"I know."

"I can never forgive you for that."

I nodded. "May I see him?"

"What, so that you can hurt him some more?"

"Mom." John touched his mother's shoulder, then walked to the door and came out. "Let's go for a walk."

"OK."

He set off quickly towards the beach. Before long we were on a long strip of sand, which, thankfully, was empty. I didn't want witnesses. John only stopped walking when he reached the water's edge. I rolled up my jeans and waded in the shallows. Each little wave stirred up the sand and clouded the water around my feet.

"John." I took a deep breath. "I'm going away tonight."

"What?" He turned towards me.

"Look, I think it's best if I go, and give everything time to die down." I turned away and studied the big houses that lined the shore across the Centerville River.

"Where are you going?"

"To Barbara's."

"You'll be in England?" He stood in front of me. I could see hope in his eyes.

"I won't be in London."

"Jude, I have spent the past few days, days in which we should have been making love night and day, trying to hate you."

I winced.

"It almost worked." John took my chin in his fingers and forced me to look him in the eye. "The problem is, I still love you. I've spent years loving you, and it took me ages to convince you that you loved me too."

"Don't." I bit my tongue. "I don't mean it that way. I . . ."

"These past two years together have been everything I've ever wanted. You're the only one who gets my jokes." He gave a bitter laugh and let go of my chin. "You and your damn books have lit up my life." There was so much longing in his voice.

"Forget me." I thrust the sealed envelope with the engagement ring in it at him. How could he still feel this way after how I'd behaved?

"I can't, and I don't want to." He took it and grimaced. My fingers moved and I wanted to smooth away his frown, but I held them by my sides. He didn't understand, and I'm not sure I did either. Touching him again would make it more difficult for us both. He reached for me.

I stepped back. "Don't, don't make this harder."

"Jude, that's so unfair."

"Yes, it is. I've been unfair to everyone in this whole thing, but mostly to you." I blinked away tears. "Forget me. Go and find the woman you deserve." I turned and ran from the beach, leaving him standing alone.

CHAPTER
THREE

Oxford

Dust motes took flight from the shelves lining the walls of the sitting room. They glowed in the late-afternoon sunlight like fairies. Fairies? Childhood fantasies. They were long gone.

Before walking outside, I hesitated and scanned the book titles. Being in Oxford brought back so many memories. Even good memories might allow the less pleasant ones to fight their way to the surface. Nothing was the same, except, of course, my godmother.

With a lurid sun hat shading her face, Barbara was stretched out on a lounger in the middle of what pretended to be a lawn. The overgrown state of the garden had become wilder since I'd been here as a student years ago. I'd been surprised that my front-door key still worked, but then things around here never seemed to alter. Students came and went; more books were written, yet somehow the woman remained true to herself.

Pulling my shoulders back, I crossed the threshold. Barbara's hand reached for the jug beside her and topped up what I suspected was a rather large gin and tonic. "Is that you, Jude?" She peered at me from under the floppy brim of her hat. "God, you look like you need this more than me. Shall I pour you one?"

She waved at the seat beside her as she dashed off to find another glass. I sank into a lounger while staring at the honeysuckle that had taken over the garden wall. While I'd lived here, much of my spare time had been spent trying to tame this wilderness, but no evidence of my hard work remained.

"I wondered when you'd appear." Barbara returned with a glass and filled it.

I sniffed the drink she handed to me, enjoying the scent of the juniper.

"Your timing was immaculate. Full marks for achieving maximum effect."

"It wasn't like that."

Barbara raised an eyebrow. "A few months or even days earlier would have been a bit more convenient. However, it's a blessing you didn't go through with it. Once you've stopped savouring the aroma of your drink and swallowed some, would you care to tell me just what happened to the all-pleasing Judith? Why the last-minute rebellion?"

The alcohol hit the back of my throat and I coughed. Rebellion? That's what Sophie had said. "Where do I start?"

"Do you love him? Did you love him? He was a bloody star, by the way."

I flinched. Even Barbara's light-hearted tone couldn't disguise the reprimand. Never one to avoid the issue, Barbara marched where few dared to go. How she and Mother had remained friends all these years was a mystery to me. Maybe their years at school together had created a bond that couldn't be broken. I didn't get it. Mother's life was all show, and Barbara's was discreet disdain for society and all its trappings.

"Was he a star?" I didn't want to talk about John and how I'd hurt him. But I knew I wouldn't be able to shift Barbara off the subject.

"Yes, he damn well was. Your mother screamed and then fainted. His mother turned white. Did anyone tell you any of this?"

I cleaned my glasses. "No."

"It was quite amusing, if I'm honest, but your mother may never recover. As for his, well . . ." Barbara trailed off.

"No, you're right."

"Now, shall we start again?"

While birds chirped in the afternoon heat, she waited for my response.

"Yes." I gave in, knowing she wouldn't drop the subject until she'd had her say.

"Why did you agree to marry him? Do you love him?" She stared at me.

"I . . . Well, I suppose I do. I've known him for ever. He's funny and handsome."

"That doesn't answer any of my questions."

"No?" I bit my lip. "He's my friend. I love him. I always have. He's safe, and I . . ." I paused, then rushed on. "Everyone was expecting us to, and it seemed the right thing to do."

"Really? How's that supposed to work? Getting married because it was expected of you?" Barbara placed her glass down with a thump.

"I didn't think of it that way."

She stretched out in the lounger. "No wonder you bolted. When you walk down the aisle you should only be doing it for love, not for convenience. Not in this day and age." Barbara adjusted her hat. "Well, my girl, you've done the right thing and saved yourself and John from a divorce a few years down the line."

"Yes, I know." I downed the rest of my drink. "But it sure as hell hasn't made life any easier."

Barbara snorted. "Who told you life would be easy? It's never easy, but you're certainly doing a brilliant job at making it more complicated."

"True." But just when I'd needed her support, my only hope had been on the first flight back to England. "Why did you leave so quickly?"

Barbara turned and looked me in the eye. "I wasn't going to stand between you and Jane. I love you both. Nothing I could have said or done at that point would have helped, so I left and thus avoided an awkward situation."

My lips twitched. Typical of Barbara to look at it in a completely different light — that was why I was here.

"What's going on in that clever head of yours?"

"You've got to be joking. I've gone and done something so stupid, and you call me clever?"

"Yes, I do. You were smart enough to pull the plug before permanent damage was done. You're intelligent and beautiful, but you need to find that out for yourself. Have you made amends with John?"

I looked into my empty glass.

"Yes, you do need another one." Barbara filled it. "So, it was that bad?"

I closed my eyes. "No, not really." I could still see him standing on the beach, alone.

"Hello? Jude?" She tapped my arm. "Is this silence jet lag, or are you on a different planet?"

Opening my eyes, I took a sip of my G and T. "I was a world away."

"You were going to tell me about John."

I looked away. "Yes, well, John's OK."

"Jude, that's a load of crap. You've broken his heart."

"Thanks, that's just what I needed to hear again."

"You didn't come here for me to lie to you."

"No, but it might make a nice change."

Barbara tipped her head back and laughed. "There's no changing an old bag like me."

"You're wonderful."

"Why, thank you, but this isn't about me."

I sighed. "I don't know what I'm going to do."

"Let go and move on."

"More easily said than done."

"True, but you've taken the first step and you are here. This is where the new Judith Warren begins to live and leaves the past behind."

I laughed. She made it sound so simple.

Jet lag and gin don't mix very well. It was noon as I made my way downstairs. Looking into Barbara's study, which was piled high with books and papers, I wondered if the course of my life was now set. Would I continue life alone, as Mother had implied? Barbara's solitary life looked good to me, and I felt that involvement with men should be avoided for the foreseeable future.

Moving on, I made my way to the kitchen. Everywhere I turned I saw books. Neatly stacked on tables or tucked into chairs. The woman lived and breathed them. Even the kitchen wasn't immune. Barbara didn't often cook, but that didn't inhibit her love of cookery books.

With the kettle on, I pulled out my cell phone. I didn't want to make the call after the way my parents and I had parted, but I felt I should. I glanced at my watch as the number of rings increased and eventually the answerphone kicked in. I swallowed as I listened to Dad's voice telling me to leave a message.

"Hi, are you there? It's me. I just wanted to say . . ." What did I want to say? "I'm at Barbara's and, umm, sorry again." That was dire. God knows what they would think when they got that message.

My stomach growled and I looked into the fridge. Stupid gin was making everything harder than it needed to be. The kettle clicked and I pulled my head out, banging it on the door.

"Shit." I rubbed my head.

"Good afternoon to you too." Barbara dropped some books on the table.

"Ouch."

"Head a bit tender?" Barbara chuckled.

"Yes."

"Lightweight."

"Out of practice."

"Well, you're back in England, so time to begin training again." She paused. "Let's go out to lunch, and you can have a hair of the dog."

I grimaced. "No thanks, but food sounds good." I followed her out the door, grateful she didn't demand conversation as we walked. Multitasking wasn't going to work well today. In fact, walking was an effort, and I was grateful when the restaurant appeared and we were seated immediately. Once drinks were on the table, Barbara raised her glass. "Here's to Jude Warren and her new life."

Our glasses clinked, but I didn't feel the optimism she was expressing. I downed the water in my glass. There was no way I could face the wine she was enjoying.

"What are your plans?"

I rubbed my temples. "Hadn't got that far."

"Thought that might be the case."

Looking up, I found Barbara studying the menu. "I've always thought Spaghetti Bolognese has healing powers, and is therefore excellent for hangovers."

"Really? Is it brain food too?"

She grinned. "Yes, and I've been thinking."

"That worries me."

"It should." The waiter arrived and I let Barbara order for me. "To start this new life, I think I may know of the perfect job for you."

"A job?" My eyes widened and my head throbbed.

"Yes. Were you planning on lounging around?"

"No, but the idea had some appeal."

"I bet it did. Now this job."

"Doing your research?" I propped my head in my hands.

"No. Elsewhere, and not for me."

"OK. Where?" Fear gnawed at my stomach. I was going to have to begin all over again, and do it alone.

"Cornwall."

A spark of excitement rose in me.

"Petroc Trevillion is an old friend of mine." Barbara sipped her Sauvignon Blanc.

The name was familiar. "*English Gardens* and . . ." I peered over my glass at her and it came to me. "He wrote *Medieval Gardens?*"

"Yes, that's him."

"I love his work! Quite brilliant."

"Good. That helps, as you'll start on Monday." Barbara signalled to the waiter.

"Start what in two days' time?"

"Your new job. Petroc, after years of bullying by me and others, has accepted that he needs help organising his papers and probably himself, unless he's changed since he was an undergraduate."

"His papers?" I squinted.

"It's perfect for you with your love of gardens, on paper and in person. It's a good and absorbing task, away from the world. Cornwall is divine."

I smiled. Things were beginning to look up.

CHAPTER
FOUR

Pengarrock House, Manaccan, Cornwall

Granite gate-piers stood like sentinels guarding the entrance to Pengarrock. I stopped before I passed between them and waved at the farmer who had led me here, albeit slowly, through the tortuous lanes. Pushing the little car into gear, I travelled into another world, or so it felt as I passed a gatehouse with gothic windows. In the distance *Pinus radiata*, Monterey pines, filled the skyline. A legacy of Victorian travels, they stood out in the landscape, towering above the native oaks, and I wondered if the plant collectors had envisioned what their souvenirs would look like full-grown and in situ. Not that I didn't like them; they just weren't native. I made my way down the sweeping drive lined in places with rhododendrons and hydrangeas — more foreign imports. They had been here about a hundred years and had earned their place, as had the pines.

Past the stable courtyard, I followed the drive to the house. Although I'd researched it, nothing had prepared me for Pengarrock in its situation, large, solid and proud above the river. The outline of the structure displayed different periods, reminding me of an embroidery sampler. Someone had even added crenellations on one wing. Pretension, or protection?

Tears pricked the back of my eyes. It must be the frustration of being so totally lost, and that was not ideal. I wanted to make a good impression. During my undergraduate years, Petroc's books had been pinnacles I'd aspired to. I'd admired the way he got to the heart of the matter, and so succinctly. Everything was meticulously researched. He had been a hero to me. I'd tried to model my work on his, but had failed. Crafting words had never been my forte. I just wasn't smart enough to be the historian that he was, but in the process of trying I discovered that research and organisation had become strengths, making my career choice easy.

A deep breath helped to calm my circling thoughts while I parked the car next to a battered four-by-four. The years of self-doubt threatened to swamp me. I might not be a model daughter or even a perfect scholar, but I'd absolutely no reason to be nervous about this job. The task was ideal. Petroc Trevillion's papers were being put into qualified hands, although I couldn't quite believe Barbara's assertion that Petroc was hopelessly disorganised. He couldn't have written those books if that were true.

I just needed to keep my nerve when I met him. Our phone conversation had been awkward at best. My awe of his work had made me tongue-tied, which hadn't helped. In my mind I'd drawn a picture of a dry academic with no social skills. When I'd expressed this to Barbara, she practically rolled on the floor with laughter. She wouldn't explain her behaviour either, which rankled but was typical.

Silently lecturing myself, I stepped out of the car and caught my breath. The late-evening light cast the headland opposite in a molten glow and made the rich blue of the river almost iridescent. Bedazzled, I steadied myself by holding onto the car. A tall man strode in my direction.

"Judith Warren?" He stopped a few feet from me. His hair was thick and grey. He stood well over six foot. Now I knew why Barbara had laughed. She could have warned me, but she would have said I needed to experience things for myself. Petroc Trevillion could have been a film star. When I'd searched the Internet for details on him, there had been no pictures. I'd wondered if he was a recluse of some sort.

"Yes." I wiped my sweaty palms on my jeans.

"Petroc Trevillion." He extended his hand. "We've been a bit worried. You were due hours ago."

I shook his hand. "I'm afraid I got lost."

"It happens frequently." He smiled. "You must be tired."

"Yes, it's a long drive." I reached into the back of the car, feeling pain in my shoulders from the tension of the journey.

"Allow me to help with your bags."

"Thanks." I handed one to him. "The view is stunning." I glanced at the landscape again. "It makes me want to paint it, or capture it in some way." My fingers stirred, trying to grab hold of the intangible, and I turned to him. "Do you find yourself staring out the window all the time? I'm not sure I'd be able to concentrate with that . . ." I waved my hand in the direction of the river. I was babbling like a schoolgirl.

"It's magic, and concentration can be difficult unless that's what you are working on." He laughed. "Welcome to my bit of paradise." He strode off in the direction of the massive house.

A stout woman emerged from the front door and held out her hand. "Hello, you must be Miss Warren. I'm Helen Williams, the housekeeper."

"Hi, Mrs Williams." I winced at the strength of her grip, but her smile left me in no doubt of her welcome. Again I glanced up at the front facade of the house, where wisteria climbed to the first-floor windows and still carried blooms.

"Helen, please." She noted the direction of my gaze. "Just finishing. Wonderful fragrance."

"Heavenly, but isn't it late?" I followed the tendrils upwards over the granite surface. The sun was catching the windows and illuminating the interiors of the open ones, providing glimpses of paintings and fabric.

"The cold wet spring has delayed everything, but with the hot weather we've been having recently, it will all speed up." Petroc put my bag down.

Helen took the other one from my hand. "So, you're American. Welcome to Pengarrock."

"It's that obvious?" I tilted my head to one side. Everyone at home had said I sounded more mid-Atlantic because of Mother's influence. "Pengarrock is so lovely."

44

Helen beamed. "It is indeed. You must be tired after your journey."

"Sorry again to be so late. I'm afraid I was totally lost, and if it hadn't been for a farmer I'd still be driving. It might be jet lag, but I'm beginning to suspect that whoever put the signposts up was drunk, or taking the mickey. I can't quite figure out where I went wrong."

"You missed the main turning to Manaccan and Helford, and took the next one. Seen it before," said Helen.

"Pleased to know I'm not the first."

She chuckled, and I began to relax. Two dogs raced down the lawn towards us.

"Meet Gin and Rum." Petroc's face lit up as he watched them.

They eagerly sniffed around me and I bent to stroke them. "Which is which?"

"The labrador is Gin and the spaniel is Rum," he said.

"Let's get you settled so that you can rest after your journey." Helen led the way into the house, and I fell in behind. "I've put you in the Green Room."

"I thought you said Blue, this morning." Petroc entered the hall.

"No, the Green."

He shrugged, then went up the grand staircase. Dashing after him, I didn't know where to look — the large window on the landing, which framed the view of the river, or the portraits that lined the walls.

"Surely there's no rush! You'll wear the girl out with your hurry." Helen called.

Petroc stopped and I bumped into him.

"Sorry." His hand reached out to steady me.

"No, it was my fault. I should have been watching where I was going." I caught my breath and tried to smile. He was certainly not the dusty academic I'd imagined him to be. He was fit, unlike me, who was breathless.

"The Green Room is just this way." He led me to the right. The hallway was wide and windows lined one side, the evening sun streaming through them. I tried to take in the details. Marine watercolours hung on the walls between the windows. I looked forward to examining them in greater detail.

Petroc pushed open a door and stepped aside. "After you."

"Thanks."

He followed me and placed the case on a footstool at the end of a large four-poster bed. It had a plain canopy above it. Furniture periods were never my strength, but at a guess the bed was gothic revival.

"I'll leave you to settle in. See you later." He left the door ajar as he departed. I spun round with eyes wide open, reminding myself that I was here to work and not on vacation, despite the plush surroundings.

The Green Room was on the north side of the house, and the views from the windows encompassed both Falmouth Bay and the river. I turned around, noting the details of the beautiful room, but the view drew me back to stand and simply stare. A spell was being cast on me. I was aware of it but powerless to stop it.

The landscape reminded me of home in some ways, yet in others it was foreign. Both aspects grabbed hold of my heart. Despite leaving home, I couldn't deny that I longed for it, but it was now as foreign as, if not more alien than, what was spread out in front of me. I still wasn't sure how a landscape could change so swiftly in my mind. As I'd driven away from what had been home, past East Bay, I'd distanced myself from it. The grey skies hadn't helped. Rain had begun to fall on my journey to Boston, and my mind kept reviewing how my life had altered and not in the way I had planned.

"It's a beautiful view." Helen spoke from behind me.

I jumped. "Utterly."

She came and stood beside me. "I'm sure you'll want a bath or shower after that long journey." She waved her hand towards a door to the left of the bed. "It's such a glorious evening. You and Petroc will eat outside on the terrace. He's a creature of habit, so he'll be having a drink at six-thirty with dinner to follow at eight."

Even from our brief acquaintance, I felt Helen's statement about Petroc was true. Although I knew he was sixty, he seemed older. Not so much from his appearance but from his mannerisms. The only thing that belied his age was the glimmer in his eyes. They held humour and, well, mischief.

"Thank you for your help, and thank you for choosing this room. It's amazing." I looked around again. The walls were covered in paper adorned with trailing vines, and the bed was positioned against the far wall to take advantage of the view.

"I had a feeling you might like it. Give me a shout if you need anything, my lover."

I turned around but Helen had gone into the hall. That was an expression I'd never heard before. Her accent was delightful. I sank onto the bed. If I just closed my eyes for a few minutes, maybe I would feel a bit more alert this evening.

I was pulled from a dream, a dream of wild waves beating against rocks in a storm, by a caress across my cheek. Lightning had filled the sky, illuminating the scene in bursts. I sat up and rubbed the goose bumps on my arms. A cool breeze blew in through the open window.

I stroked my cheek where I could still feel the light touch. It must have been an insect, and I searched the room for the culprit. Finally I spied a daddy-long-legs on the ceiling above the nearest window. There was the guilty party. The lore from my childhood said that daddy-long-legs were always harbingers of good luck. A little help from fate might not be such a bad thing.

With that thought, I rose and glanced at my watch. There wasn't time for a bath or shower. If Petroc was a man of habit, I'd better get moving. Racing down the stairs, I wondered how to get outside. In the middle of the hall I turned around. Doors led off in different directions, and to one side the hallway made a sharp bend to the left of the front door.

"Ah, there you are, Judith. Barbara rang about an hour ago to see if you'd made it." Petroc emerged from one of the many rooms. "I said you were fine, but to be honest you look a little peaky."

"Made the mistake of falling asleep." As soon as I finished speaking, a yawn began and I hastily covered my mouth.

"Well, a drink should put some colour back in your cheeks. I believe Helen has set a tray outside. Shall we go?"

Trying to get a feel for the house, I trailed behind him. A map or plan might be helpful. Petroc walked into what I assumed was the drawing room. French windows lined the two outside walls, giving the room a sweeping vista of the lawns to one side and to the other, glimpses of the river. When the house had been extended or altered in the Georgian era, I imagined that this room would have had clear views to Falmouth Bay, but trees now partially obscured it.

Stepping out through an open French window, Petroc turned to the left onto a stone terrace, which was flanked by three cannons. They pointed across the river.

He noted my interest. "Two are a legacy of the days when the river was not so peaceful, and one is a war trophy, from Waterloo, I believe."

"Makes for interesting garden ornaments." Aside from a few large tubs filled with fuchsias, this aspect was devoid of flowerbeds. The view stole the show.

"Indeed."

My eyes grew wider as I watched him pour gin into the glasses using three fingers as a measure. I'd need to pace myself.

"As you're American, I suppose you would like a lot of ice with your G and T."

"'Fraid so." I smiled.

"We'll have you out of the habit before long." He handed me a glass. "So, are you going to tell me why someone with your experience has come to Cornwall to sort out an old man's papers?"

I opened my mouth, then shut it.

"Yes?" he prompted.

"Barbara didn't say?"

He laughed. "Dear Barbara says only what suits her. She knew I needed some assistance, and she had the solution. It was a short conversation."

"I know how that feels. The short answer is that I was unexpectedly at a loose end."

Petroc strolled over to some chairs and indicated that I should take a seat. The cool breeze that had chilled me earlier blew in from the east and disturbed the surface of the river.

I coughed.

"I see."

And I was sure those eyes saw a lot more than I was saying.

"My gain, I expect, but we won't talk work tonight. Instead, let's enjoy this glorious weather and discuss politics."

I blinked. "Work might be easier."

"It might indeed, but who knows — we may agree, or better yet we may disagree, and then we can both learn something."

I laughed. "Before we move on to contentious subjects," I paused and scanned the horizon again, watching a boat skirt a buoy, "what's that marker out there?"

"Ah," Petroc sighed. *"Not of the land. Not of the sea. Visible only when August Rock sees."*

I turned to him. "A riddle?"

"That is the buoy for August Rock, a mostly submerged reef."

"A riddle about a reef?"

"Yes; it tantalises with a hint of lost jewels. It is a riddle of false hope, hidden treasure that has caused heartache and death. Generations have been tempted by its promise."

"Including you?"

"Yes, me, of late." He ran a hand through his hair, setting it rakishly askew. "I had all but forgotten about it until recently."

"You have my full attention."

He laughed. "Well, as my son would tell you, I am a fool, and there is nothing worse than an old one, as they say, but," he paused and sipped his drink, "what is life if not an adventure, a quest?"

I shrugged, waiting.

"Back in the late 1600s, a man fell in love with a woman." He had a faraway look in his eyes, and I imagined he was seeing it all. "But he was the second son, and therefore had nothing to offer the fair lady."

I thought I knew where this was going.

"He left for far-off lands and made his fortune. A few years later, he returned to woo his lady with a sapphire of great size and beauty, the like of which had never been seen before."

"Why do I think this is about to go horribly wrong for our hero?"

He chuckled. "Because you loved a good fairy tale when you were a child?"

"Yes." I smiled.

"Upon his return to Pengarrock, he found his lady married to his older brother."

"Oh no."

"Oh yes. So our hero presented her with the sapphire as a symbol of his enduring love, and then left for the Continent."

"So sad."

He nodded, then sipped his drink.

"Do you know what became of him?"

"Unfortunately no, but he left the family with some amazing jewels."

"What on earth did you do with them?" I turned to him.

"Sadly I didn't. They are lost, and have been for over a hundred years." He sighed. "But enough of that. Tell me a bit about you."

"Oh, I'm boring. Instead, tell me about what you are working on at the moment."

"I doubt you are boring, but I won't push." He frowned. "A book on the Helford River."

"Not gardens?" I looked at the river again, then towards the vast sweep of lawn.

"No, the river has been calling me for some time, and I want to pull all the research together."

"A history?"

"Not in the traditional sense, or like my past work. I described it to my publishers as a memoir of sorts, a bit like the Victorian travel journals, more conversational than academic." He smiled. "Shall we see what Helen has left us for dinner?"

I nodded, and followed him around the outside of the house to the kitchen, trying to look at everything. Sensory overload slowed my tired brain further. Pengarrock was incredible, and so full of history. I was going to enjoy learning all about it.

CHAPTER
FIVE

My heart raced. The low light played havoc with my eyesight. Switching on the bedside light, I confirmed what I'd known: I was alone. How could I be anything but alone? It was four in morning and I was in Cornwall, not in London and not married. I was still jet-lagged, and it was not doing what it was supposed to, forcing me to sleep late. Quite the reverse; it was making me see things that weren't there.

Lying motionless, I listened to the dawn chorus and abandoned all hope of sleep. I threw the covers off and walked to the window. Colour was just creeping into the sky over Falmouth Bay. There wasn't a cloud to be seen, and it promised to be another glorious day.

Somehow I knew I was in the right place, even though a sense of familiarity in the view caused a twist in my stomach. I was far enough away that that world couldn't reach me. I was simply Judith Anne Warren. That was all, and it was just a bit scary, with no guidelines or expectations.

Thinking of Cape Cod, I switched on my phone. The charges would be painful, but I wanted to check in. The more time passed, the more I regretted the way I'd just left. While I waited, I studied the room again. A fireplace, which looked as though it still worked, was in the centre of the wall opposite the bed. What would this house have been like in the days before they put in central heating, when the winds off the ocean brought in storm after storm? The warmth from an open fire wouldn't have carried very far in this big room. Of course the bed would have had curtains then, which would have helped keep out the cold draughts.

I wanted to describe it all, but who could I tell now that I'd done what I'd done? Sophie was brilliant, but old houses weren't her thing. Under the window I spied a writing desk. I'd write to Aunt Agnes, like I had in the past.

Pulling out the chair, I turned on the small desk lamp. The top drawer contained fine white paper and several pens.

Dear Aunt Agnes,

I hope you are well, and the heat of the city isn't too much. Have you made the trip north to Maine to see your niece?

Pausing, I wondered if I should mention the wedding again. I'd already written and returned the generous cheque that she had given us.

I know I told you that I was going to Oxford, but I'm in Cornwall working with Petroc Trevillion at Pengarrock. I'm so excited about this because I love his books, and Cornwall is amazing. You would love it here. It's a bit like Cape Cod and Maine rolled together. Have you ever been?

I yawned and looked at my watch. It was now five, a more civilised hour. I'd finish the letter later. Coffee was essential. The challenge would be to find the kitchen without getting lost. I threw on some clothes and looked at my phone. There was no signal, so I put it in my pocket and set out.

Once in the hallway, I tried to envision the house in its heyday filled with the Trevillion family and a full retinue of servants. At this hour, they would have been the only ones about, making the house ready for the day. Now, at dawn, there was a ghostly silence. In this great mansion of a house there were just two of us, and it didn't feel right.

In the dim light, I couldn't make out the faces of the portraits that lined the staircase. I was sure each one could tell me quite a tale, stories of gain and loss and, most importantly, survival. Putting my glasses on, I peered at the faces and wondered who had married his brother's love. I stopped in front of a Cavalier, the white plume on his hat almost glowing in the near darkness. "Was it you?" The subject looked down his long nose at me. Each one of these faces represented a phase in the estate's history.

At the bottom of the stairs, I turned to the right and walked past several closed doors. The physical structure of the building changed, and the walls further down the corridor were not smooth but held gentle undulations. The coffee I longed for would be beyond the arch three-quarters of the way down the hall. I wished I knew this because I was paying attention to the changing architecture, which showed me that this corridor led to an older part of the house, and of course that would be the kitchen. But in truth it was the smell of freshly brewed coffee. Petroc must be up. I opened the heavy door.

"Good morning." Petroc looked up from a notebook, pen in hand.

"Mmm. Don't suppose there's any of that coffee left?"

He smiled and stood. "Of course. I thought we wouldn't see you for hours."

"Me too, but no such luck."

"Milk? Sugar?" He poured the coffee.

"Black, please." I took the mug he offered me and moved out through the tall doors in the end wall. It opened west onto a terrace and then a small kitchen garden, which was filled with herb beds lined with rosemary hedges. The air was fresh and dew covered the slate slabs beneath my feet. The sun had risen enough for me to see colour returning to the world. The fields on the opposite side of the river were no longer shades of grey but green.

"Careful you don't slip." Petroc spoke from the doorway.

"You are so lucky." I was totally seduced by the view. Whenever I wanted to look elsewhere, I couldn't; its enchantments kept luring me back.

He joined me. "Yes, I am. I only wish . . ." He stopped and I turned to him.

"Only wish what?"

He shook his head.

"You can tell me." I smiled. "Promise it won't go any further."

He laughed. "I suspect that's true, Judith."

I tried not to flinch at being called Judith. "Well, then, trust me."

"I only wish that Tristan felt the same way."

I pursed my lips. "Your son?"

Petroc nodded.

"Doesn't like paradise?"

"No."

"To each his own, as they say, but I can't help thinking he must be blind." I looked at the view again.

"In that, you may well be right." I saw a grimace of pain cross his face. I placed a hand on his arm.

"The young just don't understand what they have." Petroc coughed.

"No, they never do." I bit my lip, knowing that my parents would probably say the same about me.

"Now that you've had some breakfast — although I do not consider a slice of toast breakfast, and neither will Helen," Petroc held open the kitchen door, "I'll show you around the house and, more to the point, my study." As we left the kitchen, the silence of the house hit me as if it were a physical barrier. The hum of the refrigerator and the birdsong from the garden evaporated in the cool, still air of the hallway. Only the sound of our footsteps on the slate flagstones echoed in an environment that was strangely reminiscent of a deserted church. All that was missing was the scent of extinguished candles.

"This door leads to what I call the estate office. It technically houses all things to do with the workings of Pengarrock. Thomas, the manager, uses it as his base, but mostly it sits empty, apart from piles of bills for filing." He sighed. "I have never excelled at paper management."

"In all things, or just to do with practical matters of the estate?" The desk was buried in paper. I couldn't miss the final-notice demand in big red letters sitting on the top.

He glanced over his shoulder. "All things, I'm afraid. The evidence will be visible when we reach my study. I do hope Barbara warned you."

"A bit." I could only hope that his study was better than the estate office.

"That's a relief." He stopped in front of a door on the north side of the house. "This is the dining room."

Like the drawing room, French windows, four of them, faced the river but, unlike the drawing room, the view remained here as the treeline began much lower down. A long table that would easily seat sixteen occupied the centre of the room. The walls were panelled and stained dark, almost black. It was striking, and made the paintings which hung there appear to jump out from the wall. I was struck by one life-size portrait.

"Ah, yes, Mary Trevillion. Ugly as sin, isn't she?"

"I wouldn't go that far."

"I would. It's a damn shame that the one Gainsborough we have is of the homeliest chatelaine of Pengarrock."

How awful to be remembered simply as the ugliest. Had she faced that all her life? I hoped that her husband had loved her, and didn't focus on the overlarge nose and bulbous eyes, but saw a warm heart and elegant neck and shoulders. The realistic side of me wondered if maybe she had been a wealthy woman and Pengarrock needed the money. Running an estate of this size, or the size it must have been then, would have been very costly.

"That's quite a brooch she's wearing." I approached the painting to study it.

"Yes, the Trevillion sapphire. The one I spoke of last night."

"I thought you were just spinning a tale to keep me entertained." I stepped closer.

"Oh, no. The sapphire was very real. It was reputed to have been over four-hundred carats. It should have been seen on kings, queens and maharajas, not on landed gentry."

"Wow! That's quite an heirloom."

"It would be."

"Yes, you said it's been lost. It's a bit large to misplace." I turned to him.

"True. I'm trying to get to the bottom of what happened to it. Disappeared, lost, stolen or gone down with a boat on August Rock — who knows? It's become part of the lore of the area."

"A great mystery." I turned to him.

He nodded.

"You've looked?"

He laughed. "Not yet, but many others have."

I stared at Petroc. I knew his academic work, and it was sound. He didn't strike me as a person to chase rainbows, but here he was by his own admission saying just that.

"Should we leave the study for last?" Petroc looked hopeful, but as much as I wanted to see more of the house, I was here to work.

"The study, please."

We took a short walk towards the main staircase, then Petroc opened a door. I blinked. Sun streamed through the French windows, but it wasn't that. The floor and every surface in the room were covered with books, papers and photographs. Petroc took a long stride and hit a bare space on the floor and didn't stop until he had reached the window, which he opened. Noting his path, I saw small patches of carpet. It was as if he had left a crumb trail for me to follow him in the chaos.

"Terrible, isn't it?"

"Um, yes." My heart sank. There was no way that anyone could work here, let alone produce works of near genius. Three of the walls were covered in bookshelves, and I could see that they were packed two or even three books thick in places. Papers protruded from them. One of the filing cabinets next to the desk was in danger of tipping over from the weight of the open drawers, with notes tacked on it.

The desk was no better. Piled high with such a mishmash of stuff, I wondered how he could function at all in here. I didn't mind a bit of disorder, but this was beyond workable. In the centre of the desk sat a fountain pen and a pad of lined paper filled with writing.

"Speechless?"

I nodded, and Petroc laughed.

"Now you can see why I was looking for help."

It was verging on too much to take in. "You may need more than me, though. Maybe you should call the marines."

"Don't worry, there is some organisation here."

I tipped my head to one side and stared at Petroc. "Really?"

"Yes. On this side of the room are papers for filing." His hand swept to the left. "And this side contains the things I'm currently using."

"If you say so."

"I do."

"Where do you want me to start?" There was no place I could see to walk, let alone sit and work. "And what exactly do you want me to do?"

Three long strides took him to the desk. "Good question."

"You don't have a preference?" I glanced around me again, hoping for inspiration.

"No." He stood at the desk and collected his pad and pen. "I leave it to you."

"In which case, it might be best to begin at the doorway and work to the left, your filing side."

"Good plan. I'll be in the library if you need me." He was gone before I could ask where the library was, and exactly what he wanted me to achieve.

I hadn't felt proper hunger in weeks, and I was surprised when my stomach rumbled. Eating was a necessity, simply fuel. Today the need was touched with a bit of desire for something more. I glanced at the files — no, the chaos — around me. I hated to call it mess, but it was in such disorder, I had to. I'd been working since Petroc left me and I'd managed to clear enough space to sit down on the floor. That alone had taken two hours. During that time I'd questioned Petroc's sanity more than once. It was a mystery how anyone could work like this.

Now with room for my laptop and a notebook, I felt as if I could begin, but the problem was that everything was too interesting. It was hard simply to list an article. Each thing I picked up called for more than just a few descriptive words on a page and a filing number. Every item seemed to lead down a partially explored path that begged to be taken further. Picking up the nearest sheet of paper, the words on it gave me a tantalising glimpse of a garden near Truro, which had been uncovered when the owners had begun to build a swimming pool. All digging had ceased until the remains of a monastic garden had been properly recorded. But Petroc hadn't noted what happened next. Frustrating.

The main problem now that I had begun was what to do with the items once I'd noted their existence. I had no boxes to file and store. The cabinets were full, as were the bookshelves. Initially I would create a simple index, but then it would need to be thoroughly sorted. What did Petroc intend to do with the collection? That answer was the key to how I really needed to work. Some of the items I'd recorded thus far were in need of conservation in acid-free boxes before they deteriorated any further. Plastic sleeves for the photographs would be helpful so that they could be viewed without damage. To do this job properly, Petroc had to tell me what he wanted me to do.

I stood and admired the view while the blood flow returned to my legs. Bees moved from one small white bloom on the clematis *C. uncinata* to the next. Their industry was impressive, and just watching their activity made me even hungrier. Reluctantly I left the study to find food.

Wandering down the hall, I thought about the development of Pengarrock. The hallway could double as a time tunnel. First there was a butler's kitchen, then a pantry or scullery, a game room for all the pheasant on the estate, I imagined, and then finally the old kitchen with the huge hearth and a big stove. A table filled the centre, which functioned as half worktop and half dining surface.

"Hello, Judith." Helen looked up from the ironing board as I came in.

"Morning, Helen. Please call me Jude."

"But Judith is such a beautiful name."

"Yes, it is, but whenever I hear it I think I'm in trouble."

"That's how it is, is it?"

"Yes."

Helen put her iron down and gave me a look. "Finally hungry?"

I relaxed. Helen, clearly astute, wasn't going to question me further. "You bet! I'm starved, and something smells good."

"Help yourself. There's mackerel poached in wine, a bit of salad, a cold soup, some crab and cheese . . ."

"Stop! This can't be true. Have I walked into the local gourmet restaurant?"

Helen laughed and rubbed her hands on a dishcloth. "I just felt you might need a little feeding, that's all, and I didn't know what you liked."

"Let me put your mind at rest. I like everything except anchovies." My nose wrinkled.

"I'm so glad to hear you're not one of those silly types who don't like their food." She looked at me from head to toe, but her eyes rested the longest on my wrists. Bones and veins seemed to be the only things visible.

"You don't have to worry about me, but I may have to worry about you if you're going to cook like this every day! I don't know where to begin." The offerings were wonderful. I started with a bowl of soup and some fresh bread, noting Helen's approving glance. "Helen, have you always lived here?"

"I was born in the gatehouse. My father was the gamekeeper until he retired."

"Is that where you live now?"

"Yes. Me and the husband." She smiled.

"Does he work on the estate?"

"No, he's a fisherman."

"Oh." I stopped, my spoon in mid-air.

"That surprises you?"

"Not really, I guess."

"Where'd you think the mackerel was from? Have you tried it yet? Fresh this morning."

I put my empty bowl in the sink and began to wash up.

"Leave it and try the fish."

I tucked into the cold mackerel with some salad. Mackerel had never been high on my list of fish, but this was different. It was light and melted in the mouth with a slight hint of onion and something else.

"Helen, that was divine. Thank you."

"Now you'll have the energy for a good walk while it's so lovely." She looked out the window. "It's too beautiful to stay in with paperwork all day. Why don't you walk down to the beach?"

"Beach?" I envisioned Craigville with its long stretch of white sand.

"Yes, the beach. Cross the lawns and follow the garden down. You'll come to it eventually."

I paused in the doorway. "Thank you for a delicious meal."

"A pleasure. Go and get some fresh air. You have all the time in the world to sort out Petroc. Mind you, it may take all that time too." Helen chuckled as she resumed her ironing.

I went in search of Petroc. Before I did anything else, I needed to talk to him. He was in the estate office when I tracked him down. He looked up from the chaos on the desk. "How is it going?"

"OK, I think, and I've just eaten the most enormous lunch."

"Excellent. You should go and stretch your legs."

"That's what Helen said."

"Wise woman." He dug around on the desk, dislodging a pile of papers.

"Can I help?" I bent to pick them up. They looked like overdue bills. Was this just poor paper management, or a sign of money troubles?

"I doubt it, unless you can work miracles. I left a notebook in here the other day when I was chatting to Thomas."

"Petroc." I paused, watching him continue his search. "We need to talk about what you want me to achieve, and also, do you have any archive boxes or other storage items available?"

"No, I don't have any, but I'll see what I can do." He continued to dig through the paperwork.

"And I need to ask a favour. I can't seem to get a signal on my cell phone. May I use your phone quickly to call my parents, and can I give them Pengarrock's number in case they need to contact me?"

"Of course." He waved at the phone on the desk and then disappeared out of the office. I picked up the handset and dialled. It rang, then went to answerphone again. But they should have been home at this hour. Was Mother in the bath and Dad already in the garden? I left another garbled message and the phone number. I resisted the urge to make one more call. Despite everything, I was missing John, and longed to tell him how exciting it was to be working with Petroc, even though Petroc was hopelessly disorganised.

Coming out of the office I stood and listened, wondering where I'd find Petroc, but heard only the buzz of a lawnmower in the distance. Before I began again in the study, I needed to pin him down to a course of action. I don't know why, but I felt he was being evasive, and if not evasive, that he was totally absorbed by whatever he was working on. This morning he had had an almost haunted look about him as he searched for the notebook.

The hall was the central hub of Pengarrock and everything branched off it. Aside from the staircase and the hallway, which led to the kitchen, there were three doors visible across the hall and a corridor that went out of view. One door was open, so I decided to begin the search for him there. The unpaid bills in the office bothered me. If he couldn't afford to pay the bills, how could he afford to pay me? My task was not essential to the estate, like Helen's or Thomas'.

I tapped on the door frame.

"Come in." Petroc looked up from the map he was holding. Papers and photographs were spread all over what I thought was a billiard table. In fact, every spare surface was covered. It was as if the contamination of the study had spread in here.

"Is this the book?"

"Some of it."

"And the rest?" A quick glance at the floor gave me no clue.

"Research on the treasure."

I frowned. "Are you including it in your book?"

He lifted his head and looked towards the ceiling. "Not sure. Why do you ask?"

"Well, you are in the middle of writing a book, but you seem to be spending a lot of time and energy on this lost treasure."

"Well, I only found the information while I was researching the book, and some things seem more urgent."

I took a deep breath. "Urgent? Finding the treasure, or the deadline?"

He laughed. "I've already passed the deadline."

I didn't know what to say. "OK, I won't ask any more, but I do need to know what you want me to do."

"Organise me." He looked back down at his map.

"You need a plan, and I need to know what you intend to do with the documents."

"As you see fit." He didn't look up.

"That won't work." I sighed. He was a brilliant scholar, and I had to tell him what to do? This was all wrong. "As I go through your papers, I need to know if you will be using them regularly, or if they should be stored, and so forth."

"File it alphabetically." He remained focused on the map he held and I felt dismissed.

"Fine, but where do I put the documents, once catalogued?"

"Ah, you have a point. I'll get on to it." He smiled, then went back to making notes on a piece of paper.

"Thank you." I was dismissed, so with one last glance around the room I left and headed back to the study, exasperated.

My hamstrings ached from the walk to the beach I took after work yesterday. The journey back up to the house was steep, very steep, and I was out of shape. Muscles complained with each movement now. I should have stretched. On each step down the stairs, I wondered if my legs were going to give way. However, the slow descent allowed me the time to admire the portraits instead of passing them in a rush. My cavalier on the landing surveyed his domain, peering out over the river as he watched for signs of foreign ships and other activity that could affect the inhabitants of Pengarrock. I needed to quiz Petroc more on the family history.

On the opposite wall, a pompous man appeared far too pleased with himself. I didn't like the look of him. Moving along, the only portrait of a woman on the stairs was at the very bottom. She was stunning, and had such delicate features, unlike poor Mary in the dining room. Mesmerised, I walked into Helen.

"That would be Imogen, Petroc's wife. She was a beauty."

"Yes, without question. When did she pass away?"

"Oh, many years ago now. It was a sad thing. Never mind, though, it's in the past and there it stays." Helen turned away and bustled into the kitchen.

Right; there was something here that wasn't spoken about. All families seemed to have these things. My family had worked that way. After Rose passed away, we never really spoke about it and the hole in our lives just got bigger, not smaller. I was doing the same thing now by not saying why I'd fled. Even if I wasn't ready to talk about what had happened, I should write to John. I owed him that. It was just a question of how to phrase it without hurting him further.

A bowl full of roses from the garden sat on the round table in the hall. For years, night after night, I'd dreamed that I'd given my kidney to Rose and she was still alive. I would wake happy until reality would hit. Looking back now, I can see that each day I withdrew a bit, holding back more of myself and spending more time in books. I watched my parents' grief and believed I'd caused it because I didn't save Rose. I was a match, but I was too young. Dad was a match too, but he had given a kidney to his brother. Mother hated him for that, and hated herself because she couldn't help. I found myself wondering whether, if we'd talked about it rather than letting it fester, things between Mother and me might have been better.

Instead of having breakfast, I went straight to the study to pick up where I'd finished off last night. Yesterday Helen had brought in plastic storage tubs saying that Petroc had found them for me. They were far from ideal, but as a temporary measure they would work. I'd filled two so far with the things I'd managed to catalogue.

A small black leather notebook was the only item that remained in the square foot that I'd cleared on the filing side of the room. I opened it. Petroc's handwriting covered the pages. It looked like a journal.

I put it to one side so that I could ask him about it, then picked it up again to place a note in it. My memory might let me down with the size of the task. I glanced at the floor, trying not to acknowledge the despair that filled me. How could he have let it get so bad? His research was meticulous and his writing superb, but I just couldn't see how it could have been created out of this bedlam.

Closing the book, I enjoyed the feel of the textured leather. It was supple, not rigid like many notebooks. I flicked through the pages, which were edged in gold, and it fell open to a passage.

She stood on the path above those cruel rocks. She just kept staring. Her beautiful face was etched in grief and longing.

I snapped it shut. The hair on my arms stood erect and the image saddened me. Who was he talking about?

Petroc was a bit of a puzzle. He was a widower of long standing and had never remarried. That seemed odd, considering his looks and his charm. Had he loved Imogen that much that he couldn't move on?

Closing my laptop, I stood and looked out at the glorious weather. I could make out the buoy marking August Rock. What were the lines Petroc had quoted?

Not of the land
Not of the sea
Visible only
When August Rock sees

It was a short riddle that felt incomplete. What would a reef see?

"How are you progressing?" I jumped as Petroc walked into the study.

"Good question. I still feel like I'm in the dark about what you want me to do."

"Sort me." He smiled.

"I'm not a mind-reader, so can we make a list of your priorities?"

"Do what you think needs doing most."

"No, you're not off the hook so lightly. I'm here for a limited time, and I need to focus my energy because otherwise it will be scattered and nothing will be achieved. The way I see it thus far, you have several needs. The first one is just a list of what you have, then you need a plan to organise it in a logical manner."

"Sounds excellent, and would be a tremendous start, making things easier for those who come after me." He frowned. "Now, if you'll excuse me, I have a meeting."

I opened my mouth to protest, but he was already out the door.

CHAPTER
SIX

The dogs dashed ahead and Petroc walked in front of me as the footpath came to where it clung to the edge of the cliff. The wind hit us once we were out of the shelter of the trees, and clouds blew briskly across the sky so that despite the sun, it was chilly. Petroc stopped walking and waited for me to reach him.

"Petroc?" I took a deep breath, trying to get air back into my lungs. "How far does the estate stretch?"

"Not very far any more, but it includes much of the land you can see on this side of the river, and a few small pieces in North Cornwall." He shook his head and leaned against a gate. In front of him the land dropped away to the sea while waves crashed in the cove below. "It's now two-thirds the size of what it was when I inherited it."

I opened my eyes wide.

"Once the Trevillions owned vast tracts of Cornwall, including tin mines. Now, thanks to poor management, gambling, taxes and the huge cost of running the estate versus its income-generating ability, it's a small echo of what it was." With the utterance of those words I saw Petroc slump in front of me. He loved it so, but the weight of holding it all together was clearly pulling him down. His pace slowed as we walked on until we reached the tip of the headland. "Dennis Head."

"Who was Dennis? An ancestor?"

"You'll need to brush up on some Cornish words." He smiled. "*Dinas*, anglicised Dennis, means castle or fortress. Here, there are the remains of an Iron Age fort and one from the Civil War."

Its position was ideal for defence, but all that was left now were mounds covered with gorse and scrub pine. Closing my eyes, I wanted to hear and feel the echoes of the past, but only the call of gulls reached me.

Petroc's cell phone rang, and I wondered what it was like to be the caretaker of so much history. Cannons on the lawn and ancient sites on your land — it must be overwhelming at times. It had been bad enough that Dad had the Pilgrim Fathers in his past.

Petroc motioned to me to follow while he spoke in an animated fashion on the phone. We walked back at a gentle pace as he tried to resolve some problem on the estate. In the cool, damp air, bamboo vied with gunnera and tree ferns to line the route up to the house. I took the time to enjoy the dappled green light. A stream kept Petroc and I company as we walked through what felt like a hidden valley. Only the sound of the trickling water disturbed the silence. Moss-covered rocks and lichen adorned the lower branches. It felt timeless.

"Petroc, all these tree ferns." I waved my hand at the side of the path.

He stopped. "Yes, in 1880 there was a large shipment of *Dicksonia antarctica*, and the Trevillions pinched some."

"Pinched?" I raised an eyebrow.

"Not pinched, but acquired. Fierce competitive gardening took place on both sides of the river in the Victorian and Edwardian eras."

"The golden age of the plant hunters."

"It was." Petroc began walking again. "Most of the garden you see today is from that period."

"You say most."

"Yes. There are only remnants of the medieval garden."

"Medieval? I love this period." I'd done my undergraduate thesis on it. This was when I discovered Petroc's work. How could he leave it alone? Or maybe this was what had sparked his initial interest in the period.

"Yes, but don't get too excited. I've never had the funds to restore it. It is nothing more than a few dips in the ground and some fruit trees from a later period."

"Have you thought of opening the garden to the public?"

"Yes, but the initial layout would require me to sell off something else, and I'm not sure that, in this remote area," he paused and bent to pull a snail off an agapanthus, "we would get the footfall necessary to recoup the cost, let alone make a profit."

"But gardens across the river seem to."

He laughed. "You've been reading my notes."

"Caught." I spied another snail and removed it.

"They've been successful, but they've made more of their gardens with mazes and adventure areas. Maybe I lack the imagination, or more likely the energy, but I can't see a way to make the garden here an attraction without fundamentally changing its character." He opened the gate onto the lawns and waited for me to enter first. I followed the path next to the long flowerbed that lined the garden wall rather than walk directly to the house. The partially opened lavender flowers were a hive of activity in the late-afternoon sun, while the perfume of the roses hung on the air. The garden was magical. The tight buds of the agapanthus heads held a promise of later summer colour. Did Pengarrock need to have a twist? Wouldn't the beauty of a traditional garden be enough? I had insufficient knowledge about tourism here to make an informed choice, but obviously Petroc had toyed with the idea.

He'd said he didn't have the energy. He seemed vigorous, and he didn't struggle for breath on the way up from the beach — unlike me, thirty years his junior.

"If I could find the jewels, then I would have both the funds and a star attraction." He rubbed the base of his spine.

I looked up from the plants. "Surely you don't think they still exist?"

"They were last known to have been with Lady Clarissa Trevillion, who disappeared in 1846." He stopped to pull a weed.

"Disappeared?"

"Yes; I can't find anything on her whereabouts or her death, but it is clear that the jewels went missing at the same time she did." He shook his head. "There was speculation that she might have been on the yacht *Columbia* which went down with total loss of life after being wrecked on August Rock."

"The riddle." I tried to look out to the river, but there was no view of it from this part of the garden. "It feels incomplete to me."

"I agree."

"In that case, aren't you wasting your time on that one?"

"You are more right than wrong there." He sighed. "I am still convinced they exist, but even if I found the jewels now it would be too late to save Pengarrock. It's on its last legs. A bit like me." He laughed.

"Nonsense." I looked at the house, and although I could see the roof needed some repairs here and there, it was solid. Pengarrock had stood for hundreds of years, and should continue to do so. Petroc was only sixty. I didn't know what he was talking about.

"I'm afraid it's not. Things need to change. It can't continue as it has in the past, not even the garden."

"You can adapt its use. It can move on."

"True, but Pengarrock is struggling for survival. The garden is purely for my pleasure now. It has become a dinosaur, the last of its type and ready for extinction, like me. I'm the last of the Trevillions willing to devote myself to it. It's time I let go."

Everything in me screamed *no*. I looked at Pengarrock; it was an architectural hotchpotch of styles and I adored its quirkiness. "But you love it so much. I don't believe you."

"I do, but I'm coming to the conclusion that it's best to stop holding onto the past. Trying to hold on is not the best use of what time I have left."

78

I put my glasses on so I could examine the *Penstemon digitalis*, loving the flush of pink on the white bell-shaped flowers. I didn't know what to say, and I didn't think he really wanted a response from me.

"I must come out here more and give Fergus a hand. He's wonderful, but it's a lot of work for one man, with only occasional help from some of the boys in the area."

I nodded and thought about Dad. It was summer, and I always worked the garden with him. Why hadn't I heard from them? I knew they were angry, but some acknowledgement would be appreciated.

I stood in the doorway to the study with two mugs of tea. Petroc had been in here a few minutes ago. Helen came down the main stairs. "Can I help?"

"Yes, have you seen Petroc?"

"He's in the chapel."

"The chapel?" How had I missed a chapel? I'd been here almost a week.

"Oh yes, the chapel. Haven't you noticed how the wing to the right of the front door has very different windows and doesn't quite fit?" She smiled.

I nodded.

"Shall I show you?"

"Please." I trailed behind her past the doors to the drawing room, billiard room and another room that I had no idea existed until we reached the end of the corridor. Helen swung the door in front of us wide and stepped aside. "See you later."

I walked in and stopped, taking in the beautiful simplicity of the most exquisite chapel, with clear mullioned windows reflecting the glorious sunshine in riotous angles across the mellow stone and wood. There were no pews, but a single kneeler had been placed before the altar.

"Speechless?" Petroc stood by the rood screen. "Thought you might like it."

"Like it! You could say so." I grinned. I couldn't explain why domestic chapels always lifted my spirit. They spoke of people living in the real world while acknowledging the unseen. I handed Petroc his tea. "You were going to discuss work with me, and then you," I stopped myself from saying *ran away*, "disappeared."

"Indeed. I thought we could have the tea here. I always find it peaceful." He sat on the only seat, a wooden bench along the back wall facing the altar.

"OK, but don't think you are going to avoid this discussion." I joined him on the bench. The walls around us were whitewashed, which added to the airy feel.

"I wouldn't dream of it."

"Good." I took a sip of tea. "Do you want me to group all the general garden history separately from the Cornish gardens, and also separately from the Pengarrock paperwork?"

"Good question. What do you feel makes the most sense?"

"It's not me who will be using the material, so you must tell me."

80

"I don't work in categories."

"I realise that!" I blew on my tea, watching the surface ripple.

"But it would make more sense, so do it that way and keep it separate, as you suggest. I will make every effort to keep it like that."

I raised an eyebrow.

"I promise."

"OK." I looked at the book resting on his lap. I could see sheets of paper stuck into it, like so many I had found. "I love your notes."

"I'm pleased someone does." He chuckled and leaned back. "Now that we know each other a bit better," Petroc turned over the book, "can you tell me why you are here?" He smiled. "That's not meant as a complaint, by the way."

"To sort you out." I frowned.

"Yes, but you are wasted here."

"Hardly wasted. Being here is a gift. I love nothing more than reading about gardens." I stood and looked towards the nave with its stone altar carved with the image of the Blessed Virgin and the Christ Child, and adorned with a simple silver cross.

"Of that I have no doubt, but that doesn't tell me anything I didn't already know."

"True." I walked to a window and admired the hand-blown glass. "I needed to get away."

"Yes?"

"I was . . ." I stopped. I didn't know what to say.

"Something must have happened."

"Well, I was about to get married, and suddenly I felt it wasn't the right thing to do . . . or rather, it wasn't the right person." I fiddled with the necklace I was wearing. "Or maybe I just felt I was doing it for all the wrong reasons."

"I see."

"I'm happy you do." I turned around. Petroc had a knowing smile on his face.

"So you left?"

"Yes, and I don't think I did it very well." That was an understatement.

"Have you considered why you left?" He joined me by the door.

"I just knew that it wasn't right, and that I was merely doing what was expected of me. I haven't worked out if there was anything else."

"And being American, you need to work this out." Petroc drained his mug.

I laughed. "Yes, I do."

"You might be right. Sometimes I don't think I have thought things, no, emotions, through enough."

"Why do you say that?" I turned around, noting the rose window above the altar. A quick glance at the wagon ceiling, and I was pretty sure the chapel was late fifteenth century and therefore early compared to the rest of the house, a large portion of which I guessed to be seventeenth century.

"I don't believe I questioned things enough in the past, or thought of other people's feelings as I should have. I did as was expected of me."

"That was wrong?"

"With hindsight, I think yes."

"That must hurt."

Petroc sighed. "Yes, but the more I consider it, the more I feel there is still time to make some things right."

"Well, that's good then."

"True. And what have you done to repair things?" He held open the chapel door for me.

"Not sure mine are fixable."

"Have you tried?"

I laughed. "To be honest, not really. I think I may still be a bit too close to it all."

"Time does help. And what of this poor chap, who I'm sure is devastated without you?"

"I don't know. He says he still loves me." We began to walk down the corridor.

"I'm sure he does. He'd be a fool not to." Petroc smiled.

"Thanks for the vote of confidence." I laughed.

"Sometimes it's good to go away, in order to gain the perspective you need so that you may go back."

"I'm not sure I want to go back, or that I'd be welcomed."

"I wonder." Petroc stopped and put his hands in his pockets.

"Me too."

"No, I wonder if one can truly move on if one hasn't faced the demons of the past."

"I wouldn't call my parents demons."

He laughed. "I was talking about my own life, not yours."

I frowned. Somehow I felt he and I were talking at cross purposes. I pointed to a closed door. "What's this room here?"

"The library."

"May I look?"

"Of course, you've the run of the house. Look where you will." He stopped with his hand on the doorknob.

I raised my hand. "Don't open it. If I go in there I won't get anything else done."

He laughed. "Fair enough. Take a look this evening. Now, if you'll excuse me, I realise I have left my book behind."

Barbara was right. Petroc hadn't an organisational gene in his make-up. The space I'd cleared on the floor the day before was again covered. He must have worked late into the night, and in a frenzy. It appeared the man never filed anything, yet the cabinets were full and Helen let slip at breakfast that there were boxes of papers in the attics too. I'd considered leaving at this point, but the sun was shining and I had no place to go. Besides, I liked it here.

This morning Petroc had left for London to see his son, Tristan. So I had a few days without distraction to make progress. The floor seemed the obvious place to begin again. I would bring order to this chaos, I told myself, and the only way to do this was one file, or even one piece of paper, at a time.

I grabbed the nearest stack of loose sheets. On the top was an estimate to replace part of Pengarrock's roof. The cost was enough to make my eyes water:

£100,000. The figure for a simple repair was £20,000. The sheer size of Pengarrock must put seemingly small things on a much bigger scale.

Photographs slipped from the pile, faded black and white images capturing Pengarrock and the River Helford. With no people in them, the scenes were timeless. Then I came to one of a two-mast schooner pulled up to a quay. Even without the pencilled-in writing at the bottom, I could guess the date, but I didn't have to. It was in a Cornish village, Gweek, c.1860. The water was mirror-still and the men stood in the small tender beside the larger vessel in their shirtsleeves and waistcoats. Women looked on from the shore in full-length dresses. I scanned the hillside and noted the scrub oak and a few tall trees proud against the sky.

Something stirred behind me and I turned, expecting to see Helen, but no one was there. Weird. Nothing moved on this still morning. I picked up the next item, a book on orchids in Cornwall by W. Trelawny and I. Rowse. A quick scan through revealed data on the various species and their habitats. Next was another black leather journal. I hesitated before opening it, but then I noted the dates that Petroc had inscribed on the opening page. The journal from the other day had disappeared from my "Query Petroc" pile. I sighed, and rotated my stiff shoulders.

Helen popped her head through the door and I looked up from some information on commercial activity on the Helford, which must be connected with Petroc's current book.

"How are you doing?" Helen glanced at the mess.

"More than a bit stymied by Petroc's methods." I laughed.

"I can see why. Come and have some lunch."

I frowned but followed Helen into the kitchen. "You know, I'm more than capable of making my own lunch."

"I'm sure you think you are, but I know differently. You're all skin and bone! You need a bit of help in that department."

"So you mentioned."

"And I will continue to do so until I see a healthy bloom on you. You've got a nice bit of colour back. Now all we need is to put a bit of flesh on you. A body needs it to survive and thrive. What you need is fresh food and good Cornish air." She looked at me hard. It was plain that she'd drawn some conclusions about me, but I didn't know what they were.

I pulled a chair close to the door where the breeze was blowing in. "Helen, I know you've lived on the estate all your life, but how long have you worked here?"

"All my life." She wrapped a tea towel around her hand. "I've been working on Pengarrock Estate in some way or other since I left school. Since before, if you count picking the daffs."

"Picking the daffs?" I frowned.

"Daffodils. They're big business round here, or more likely were. The demand has dropped now that there are other markets providing the early ones. Mind you, there's still money to be made." Helen moved about the kitchen putting plates away. I was trying to guess her age. She might be sixty, like Petroc, but she looked younger with her fuller features.

"I'm off home to sort out food for JC. I've left yours in the fridge. You'll just need to warm it." She stared at me and I sat straighter. I think she'd missed her calling as one of the old nuns who'd taught me in Paris. "Make sure you eat it."

"Yes, ma'am."

Helen chuckled as she left.

I picked up a scrap of paper and pencil and made some notes on things I needed to ask Petroc:

1. Personal notebooks. What do you want me to do with them?
2. Have you compiled a history of the house and garden? If so, where is it? If not, why not?
3. Where should I temporarily store the filled boxes? Because once the cataloguing is complete, they will need to be redone in proper order according to subject and date.

I looked up and was surprised to find I'd eaten all the food on my plate. Helen would be pleased. I went back to the study, where I immersed myself in the chaos on the floor.

Where had the time gone? I glanced at my watch. It was six o'clock on a Friday night. At home, John and I would be driving to the Cape right now and once there, we'd be joining friends at a local bar. Now the whole evening stretched out in front of me, alone, but that had been my choice. What was John doing in London? How was he coping? I took a deep breath. It was a beautiful evening, and a long walk was just what I needed to clear my head. On the floor I unearthed a local map and decided that Frenchman's Creek sounded interesting.

After locking the house, I strolled towards Helford village with the two dogs. They hadn't been a part of my original plan, but they had other ideas. The sun was warm and the breeze moved the grain in the fields in gentle waves. I couldn't see the river, but could smell its proximity as I emerged onto the coastal path. It was lit with the setting sun, which coloured the sails of the boats a soft gold as they made their way home.

I laughed as I watched the trials of someone trying to get up on water skis. My summers had been littered with similar failed attempts. John had endlessly circled the boat as I tried again and again. I'd been the only one of my friends who never got it right. John's theory on my lack of success was that I was all legs, and therefore my centre of balance was off. He just wouldn't accept that I was clumsy and inept in most sport-related activities. Mother had despaired at my lack of ability on the tennis court or golf course. She took no pride in the one thing I had excelled at in the physical arena — rowing. It had been something Dad and I had shared. He'd rowed for Harvard and then Oxford, which was where he'd met Mother. I always felt she'd been jealous of that bond between Dad and me.

The spaniel, Rum, kept close to me as we approached the village, but the labrador, Gin, was well out in front. I walked down the road past the whitewashed cottages thinking I'd seen postcards that looked like this, but never believed that they existed. The tide was in as I crossed the footbridge over the creek to the other side. Swans and their young swam peacefully until they saw the dogs, who began barking at them.

"Rum, Gin, here," I shouted, but they ignored me. My childhood had been seriously lacking in the pet department, thanks to the frequent moves. You don't have to train fish. The only experience I had of dogs, as much as I enjoyed them, was with John's family's dog. Clearly I'd never paid enough attention because these two took no notice of my commands. Maybe if I walked on they would follow. That proved to be a fruitless exercise. They paid no heed to me, and were totally focused on the swans. Knowing that swans could be vicious, I wondered who was more at risk.

"Gin. Rum. Here." I clapped my hands. They continued to bark. I couldn't whistle. "Rum, here, girl." Rum's ears pricked up, but no action followed. A whistle sounded, and both dogs stopped and came to heel. I looked up to see a tall man grinning at me.

"You must be the American."

My eyes opened wide. Did I have a sign on my back declaring my nationality?

"I'm Mark Triggs." The dogs sat peacefully at his feet now, looking a picture of innocence.

"Jude Warren, the American."

"Welcome to Helford." He began walking down the road and the dogs followed.

"Thanks." I had little choice but to match my stride to his. It was apparent that he knew the dogs well, and soon had them whipped into shape. "Where were you heading with these two?" He looked at the culprits.

"Frenchman's Creek."

"They'll enjoy that."

"I bet they will! They weren't invited but just joined me."

"Well, I can't say I blame them, a walk in one of the most romantic places on earth with a beautiful woman." He gave me a sideways glance and I stepped back. He was a bit of a heart-throb, with broad shoulders and a warm smile. But I didn't want involvement with any man, no matter how attractive.

"Lucky them, to have you all to themselves."

I smiled but I wasn't going to play. "Thanks for the help."

"A pleasure." He waved, then ducked into the Shipwright's Arms. The sound of voices spilled out before the door closed. I walked on, barely noticing the scenery and trying not to think of loneliness. Much to the dogs' displeasure, I cut the walk short to head back and finish the letter to Aunt Agnes.

CHAPTER
SEVEN

It was eight in the morning, and Helen hadn't arrived yet so I had the kitchen to myself. Once the kettle was on, I opened the back door and took a breath of the damp morning air. Although clear on the north side of the river, mist hung over the water, filling the valley and climbing up its banks to the kitchen garden in front of me. It blunted the edges of the buildings, and time stopped. With birdsong drifting in, it felt mystical. Only the click of the kettle broke the spell. Low cloud swept in waves across the terrace. In the beauty of the cool morning, my skin felt as if it had been touched. I shivered.

With a cup of coffee in hand, I walked to Petroc's study. With pleasure I noted there was a three-foot-wide path from the door to the desk and then to the French windows. In clearing that space, I'd glimpsed bits of the estate's history: a garden in Yorkshire, the household accounts of a country house in Devon and some notes for his book on the Helford river. Also, there were catalogues with various gems that had gone to auction and a note of what they had sold for.

No sooner would I immerse myself in one piece of research than it was gone, and I was left hanging. At first I found this very frustrating, but I was beginning to feel I understood Petroc's mind and the word "magpie" summed it up quite well. He may well jump from shiny project to shiny project, but I was becoming awed by his insights and his gift with words. Through the latter I was transported not only back in time, but also to gardens all over Europe. But what was clear was that his true passion was Pengarrock and the Helford river.

From what I'd seen so far, he had enough information and photographs to open his own library on the history of gardens. Some of the books were ones I hadn't even known existed. I would need to follow up to discover why I hadn't seen them before, and why they had been left out of other collections or reference lists.

Leaning against the window, I watched fishermen collecting the lobster pots. The mist still lingered but it wasn't as dense. The sun would soon burn through it and it would be another scorcher. Well, one for this part of the world, anyway.

Before settling down to work, I roamed the ground floor of the house. Walking into the billiard room, I looked at Petroc's mess — no, work. There was the journal that had disappeared from the study. It lay open.

The daffs are ready for picking and the crews have arrived. I just hope we are in time.
As I stood and looked down the river there she was, unchanged.

I backed away. This was far too personal. Closing the door, I looked down the hallway where the door to the chapel was open, inviting me in. Life here in the late 1400s must have been challenging, as Pengarrock was so remote. The isolation must have been a blessing and a curse. Even in the modern world with planes, trains and automobiles it was still far away.

A butterfly flitted around the ceiling and candelabra. Its large white wings almost blended into the recesses of the ceiling. The roof bosses were carved with flowers and the insect sought them out as if for nourishment. It needed to escape. I opened a top vent in a side window in the hope that it would seek the fresh air.

So much history in one place, and this space felt little altered since its beginnings. I leaned against the wall. The butterfly continued to move through one ray of light to the next in search of a real flower. Was it indeed, as the Irish said, a soul waiting to go through purgatory? Turning away from the butterfly, I found myself saying a prayer for the soul that was caught here.

There were places far worse than Pengarrock to be stuck in. But what about heaven and hell? I thought of Rose, and how she'd been taken from us too soon. In Sunday school a teacher had described hell as being able to see those you love, but never being able to speak to or touch them again. They'd told me Rose was in heaven and was happy with God. But each day without her was a form of hell for those of us left behind.

The telephone rang, and I ran from the chapel and picked up the handset in the hall. "Pengarrock?"

"How are you getting on?" Barbara sounded chirpy for this early hour.

"OK. You?" I looked up at Imogen's portrait and wondered again what had happened to her.

"I was just chatting to Jane."

"Oh." I walked around the table.

"No 'oh' about it. She asked after you."

"That surprises me. I've left several messages but have heard nothing."

"What happened between you?"

"She didn't tell you?" I stopped and looked up at the blue sky out of the large window on the stairs.

"No."

I sank down onto the bottom step.

"Judith."

"Please don't call me that."

"It's your name."

"I know, but that doesn't mean I like it." I wrinkled my nose.

"You prefer Jude of the Lost Causes."

"Well, we might have need of him if you think there can be a reconciliation between my mother and I."

"Nothing's impossible. Call her."

I stood. "I have."

"Try again."

"Yes." I sighed. "How are you?"

Barbara chuckled. "I get the hint. You don't want to talk about it, but you will at some point. You can't hide in Cornwall."

"You sent me here."

"Not to hide but to work."

"Well I am, or would be if I wasn't on the phone with you."

"Fair enough."

As I put the phone down, I wondered what was happening with my parents. I should have asked Barbara for more information. I dashed upstairs and picked up the letter to Agnes. I needed to mail it. Maybe her reply would tell me what was happening. In the past, she had always been good at keeping me informed.

"Morning, Judith." Petroc glanced up from his desk as I walked past. My heart skipped a beat. He wasn't due back until tomorrow. I stopped and stood in the doorway to the study. "You're back early."

"I have so much to do and so little time. Come and look." His eyes were happy in a way I hadn't seen since I'd arrived.

Thanks to my work of the past few days, it was easy to make my way to the desk now. I stood next to him, and in his hands he held a beautiful Victorian sketchbook.

"I'd forgotten about this little book, and last night when I couldn't sleep I found it again. It's Octavia's, and she had quite a talent."

"Octavia?"

"Sorry, I thought I'd told you about her."

I shook my head.

"Her mother was Lady Clarissa, the last known owner of the sapphire." He pointed to the watercolour on the opening page. It was of Rosemullion Head with August Rock above the surface of the water. In the distance a barque sailed towards Falmouth. The style was reminiscent of Cotman, and definitely not amateur standard. Under the painting were the words of the riddle of August Rock.

"Your riddle."

"Yes. I remember when I found this book as a child, when I was visiting Pengarrock before we moved here. That's when I first saw the riddle written down, although my grandfather Symon knew it well." He turned a page. "A curlew."

"She was very gifted to draw birds with such precision, but also the landscape."

"That's not all." He passed a few pages too quickly for me to see them and stopped at a picture of a tiny orchid. "Her floral work is superb too."

"She's a very talented artist. Does it run in the family?"

"No. There is no evidence that I've seen." He smiled. "Sadly I think it died with her."

"No genes slipped down to you?" I raised an eyebrow.

"None at all, as she never had any children. There is only a distant connection between my line of Trevillions and Octavia's." He paused. "Have I mentioned that everything was done in order to keep Pengarrock in Trevillion hands? Clarissa was married off to her third cousin, Tallan, by her father in order to keep Pengarrock in his line."

I frowned. "It seems an archaic practice now."

"Agreed, but it was commonplace then."

"What happened to Octavia?"

The phone rang and Petroc raised his hand in apology as he took it. From the change in his voice, I could tell it was not a call I should be listening to. I left the study and pulled the door shut behind me, thinking that Petroc's obsession seemed to be taking over everything else.

Petroc filled his pipe with tobacco, patting it down without looking at it. His eyes were on the river.

"It's beautiful." I walked up to the cannon he was leaning against.

"Yes." Petroc turned to me and smiled. "Each time I look I see something I haven't noticed before. The tide goes out and I walk along the footpath at dawn as I have done a thousand mornings, but this morning . . ." The pipe had gone out and he lit another match and began the ritual again. After a few puffs he continued, "As the sun rose, I saw a crease in the rocks that I'd never noticed before."

I looked back at the river and tried to imagine the privilege of walking its banks a thousand times. It had seduced me already. Sunlight had left the water's surface and a stillness descended. Petroc put his hand on my shoulder. "Dinner is on the table."

"How was your son, and how was London?"

"Hot and crowded, in answer to the last part of your question." He pulled out the heavy teak chair for me to sit. A lump formed in my throat. The small gesture made me think of Dad. "Tristan is fine, and busy."

"What does he do?"

"Some sort of investment thing." Petroc sat. "I think."

"You don't sound positive about that, or about the trip."

Petroc smiled. "No, it wasn't the most satisfying visit, in many ways."

"Oh."

"I failed in everything I tried to do, and I'm not sure it's worth trying any more." He poured the wine. "There comes a point when you have to let go and surrender yourself to your fate. I think I may have raged against mine for too long, and my luck has run out."

The weight of Petroc's sadness closed around us. I had to make him smile. "I thought you went to see your publishers."

"Ah, yes, that went reasonably, I think. I am behind, but that is not new."

"How far behind?"

"The book is mostly written, but it's in pieces and there are other things that must be done first." He passed me the salad. "Let's leave all of this for tomorrow, and enjoy Helen's marvellous food."

As I ate the seafood salad, I wondered what had happened in London to make Petroc so melancholy. Until today I would have considered him a positive soul, but something had sucked that from him.

"Now tell me, what you have been up to these past few days?"

"Quite a lot, but I'm filled with questions." I smiled. "Exactly how long have the Trevillions been here? I adore Pengarrock."

"Maybe we can tempt you to stay in this part of the world."

"Don't think it would take much tempting. I think it's stolen my heart already."

"Excellent. What do you love about it the most?"

I paused. "I'm not sure, but I think it has to be the river. The way everything seems focused around it. I know I haven't been here long, but already the first thing I look to is the tide."

"The Trevillions came here through marriage over six hundred years ago, and have practically sold their soul to keep their name attached to it. And now I wonder if it has all been worthwhile." He stood up and cleared our plates. I fought the urge to hug him, and simply laid a hand on his arm.

"Don't listen to the meanderings of an old man. I love Pengarrock, and have tied my fate to its for good or bad."

I collected the remaining dishes and followed him to the kitchen. The cry of a bird stopped us both in our tracks.

"The curlew." He searched the night sky.

"Odd."

He sighed. "Indeed, at night it is an evil omen."

After we had loaded the dishwasher, Petroc wandered off and I went out to the cannons where I'd discovered a cell-phone signal. I couldn't shake the sadness I felt. I wrote a text to John.

Milky Way fills the sky above & I can't help remembering late nights lying on the beach w u.

My finger hovered over the send button but I deleted it. At night the ache of loneliness was the worst, and wine didn't help. I dialled my parents' number. It was six o'clock there, and they should be sitting on the terrace enjoying the view. It would be a good time to catch them.

It went straight to answerphone. I debated not saying anything, but I recalled how Mother hated that so I mumbled a hello and mentioned how I was enjoying Cornwall. As I walked back into the house, I could hear Petroc talking in the study. It was almost midnight, but maybe like me he was speaking with someone across the pond.

Upstairs in my room, I checked my laptop to see if Sophie was online, but I was out of luck. It would have to be another letter to Agnes.

Dear Aunt Agnes

Lightning shot through the night sky. It was unexpected. Not long ago the sky had been clear, but as I looked towards the window I could see the front moving across the bay. Another bolt, and for a few seconds it was as bright as day. Then the rain came fast, pelting against the windows. I ran to close mine, and wondered if there were any others open.

Thunder sounded as I checked the bedrooms and found a few open windows. The lights went off and everything went black. The hairs on the back of my neck rose as I let my eyes adjust, trying not to imagine shapes in the darkness. I flicked the nearest light switch but nothing happened. I felt my way along the wall back to my room.

The lights flickered, then came on again. Silence descended on the house. The storm had passed as quickly as it had arrived. I opened my window, then went back to my letter to my aunt.

CHAPTER
EIGHT

The foxgloves growing in the hedges seemed like happy exclamation marks as I walked back from the post office. I had to remember to describe them to Aunt Agnes in my next letter. I was now completely entranced, and it had taken just a few weeks. No, in truth, a few days with an old house, a pile of books and I was in love. Maybe I wouldn't go back home when this was finished. What was there for me? It wasn't really home; it had been a place to return to. Did it hold my heart? No, and I didn't need to be defined by who my parents were. I needed to be me. And I was just beginning to see who that might be.

As I entered the house a curlew cried, and I thought of last night. Everything inside me tightened as a scream pierced the air. It was Helen. I dashed through to the kitchen but she wasn't there. "Where are you?"

"The study."

I ran and stopped halfway through the door. There was a broken cup and tea all over the floor. Petroc was slumped over his desk and, ashen, Helen stood beside him.

Three large steps took me to her. "Petroc?"

He didn't move. I felt for a pulse on his wrist, and registered the coldness of his skin.

"Have you called for help?" I looked at Helen quivering, rooted to the spot. "You must call someone."

She nodded. "I'll get the doctor."

It was far too late for a doctor. With his head on the desk and his right hand pushed across, still holding his pen, I had a feeling that whatever had taken him was quick. I moved around the desk and looked at his face. He stared out at his beloved Helford. With a heavy heart, I listened to Helen speak while I searched for a pulse on Petroc's neck, but I knew I wouldn't find one.

Helen turned to me with the phone clutched to her ear. "Is he breathing?"

"No, and I can't find a pulse." I shuddered. "He's cold to the touch."

Helen relayed the information. "The GP's on the way over and said to leave everything as it is."

I put my arm across Helen's shoulders and pulled her close to me. She turned to Petroc again. He looked peaceful, and was wearing the same clothes as yesterday. He must have died in the night. Tears spilled down Helen's cheeks. "Shouldn't we do something?"

"I don't think there is anything we can do now."

"Please!"

"I wish we could, but nothing will help." Helen's tears became sobs. I hugged her, and felt a trail of tears spilling down my own face.

"Tristan," Helen managed to say.

"Are you able to speak to him?"

She sobbed.

"Then it can wait. Petroc's gone, and I don't think Tristan needs to hear the news from a stranger."

Helen nodded, and I led her out of the study and into the kitchen, where I manoeuvred her into a chair before putting on the kettle. I would make tea. Why at times of crisis did I become my mother?

"JC?"

Helen shook her head. "Not until five at least, when the tide's back in."

The tides, the power, that was what controlled life around the river. "How long did the doctor say he'd be?"

"She didn't."

The dogs barked, then stopped. I listened for the sound of tyres on the gravel, but it didn't come. Mark Triggs walked through the kitchen door. He looked at Helen and then at me. "What's happened?"

I waited for Helen to answer, but she was still snuffling.

"It's Petroc. He's dead."

"What?" He stood still. "Sorry, I mean how? When?"

"Don't know, but we're waiting for the doctor." I pulled several mugs from the cupboard. He took them from me and made tea.

"Tristan?" Mark put a hand on Helen's shoulder. She was crying again.

"Why don't you call?" I looked at him hopefully.

"I'm the last person Tristan would need to hear the news from."

I frowned.

"Long story, and now's not the time. I can hear a car approaching."

I left Mark with Helen and went out onto the drive. The doctor walked towards me. "I'm Katherine Carr."

"Jude Warren." We shook hands, and I led her to Petroc. He looked peaceful as he gazed out to the river. The memory of Rose lying in her casket came to mind as I watched the doctor work. Aside from Rose, I had very little first-hand experience of death. We were always abroad when the news reached us, and certainly too far to come home for a funeral. I wrapped my arms around myself.

"When did you last see him?"

"We cleared up the kitchen about ten-thirty, and I heard him talking at around midnight."

"Midnight? You're sure?"

"Yes. It may have been eleven-forty-five, but I looked at the time because I was trying to reach my parents in the States."

She frowned.

"Something wrong?"

"Not really."

"Oh." I looked at Petroc's body. "You don't have to answer this, but it seems rather sudden. Petroc was so healthy."

She stood up from the body after closing his eyes. "There's nothing I can say at this stage."

"OK."

"As he hadn't been seen by me in a while, we'll need a coroner's report. I'll sort it." She smiled. "Now, how is Helen?"

"In shock."

"I'd best see her." I took her to the kitchen, then went outside for some fresh air.

The doctor had sent Helen home with a sedative, and Mark had kindly remained with me. I stood in the kitchen clutching a sheet of paper with Tristan's number on it. I had no choice. "Are you sure you can't make this call?"

"I won't call him. Believe me, he doesn't want to hear from me."

"If you're sure." I couldn't put this off any longer, so I dialled. While it was ringing I debated what I'd say if I didn't reach him and had to leave a message. A voice inside my head that sounded remarkably like my mother urged understatement and cool politeness. It was probably right, as Mother usually was on these occasions.

"Dad?" Tristan answered.

I swallowed. That I hadn't expected, but of course I was calling from the landline.

"Look, I'm in a meeting." His voice was clipped. I bristled and pulled myself up to my full height of five foot eleven.

"I'm sorry, it's not your father and it can't wait." Oh God, I sounded just like my mother when she's uptight! It's not the way anyone needs to hear of a parent's death.

There was silence on his end of the phone. "It's Judith Warren, and I'm calling about your father." I tried to soften my voice. Why the hell had I called myself Judith? I sounded like a prim schoolteacher.

"OK." I heard a chair scrape back and a door close.

"I'm sorry . . ." I didn't know how to say this. "Your father."

"Is he ill?"

"I'm afraid to have to tell you that your father died this morning." The bald statement sounded so inadequate, so harsh. I didn't know whether to talk on or keep my mouth shut. "We don't know how or when. Helen found him at eleven-thirty when she brought him a cup of tea." The broken cup was still on the floor and the tea had bled into nearby files. I must go and do something about that before permanent damage was done.

"Dead?"

"I'm so sorry."

"Where's Helen?" I detected concern in his voice.

"The doctor has given her a sedative, and she's now at home."

"I want to speak to someone . . ." He broke off.

"The doctor has left, but I'm sure you could call the surgery, or maybe talk to Helen in a short while." There was silence at the other end.

"Was it Dr Winslade?"

"No, it was Katherine Carr."

"Thank you."

"I am so sorry." I could hear his breathing. This had to be so hard.

"Who are you again?"

"Jude Warren. I was working with your father."

"Right. Thank you."

I put the phone down with unsteady hands and walked outside.

"Are you OK?" Mark joined me, leaning against the wall.

"Think so." I bit my lower lip. "Overwhelmed and suddenly angry, not sure why."

"Tristan has that effect on people."

"I don't think it's him. Not sure how I'd react if some stranger told me my father had just died." Fear wrapped itself around me. Was Dad OK? How would I cope if something like this happened to him? There'd been no warning for Petroc. He was absolutely fine last night. He was worried. He mentioned banks and London briefly, but seemed fine. It was all so sudden.

CHAPTER
NINE

Mark had gone, and I stood on the terrace. Tears blurred my vision. The mournful cry of gulls filled the air as they followed the fishing boat on the incoming tide. The urge to talk to my parents was overwhelming.

Back in my room, I looked at the computer and Skype logo. The terrible image of Petroc slumped on his desk flashed through my head. Tears began again. I blew my nose and logged in. Dad's status was idle. Should I try? What would I say?

"Just stop thinking about it and do it," I said aloud. No more procrastination. I hit the call button. The mechanical ring sounded repeatedly until it stopped. He must have left his computer on. I looked at my watch. He could be in the garden, or even playing golf.

I put my fingers on the keyboard, pulled them away then put them back.

Hi Dad
Hope all is well at home.

Struck out *at home*.

Love
Jude

Before I could change my mind, I pressed send. I walked out of the bedroom, calling the dogs. They met me at the foot of the stairs and I hugged them both to me. There were so many questions in my head. What would happen to Helen? It was her job and her home. The list went on to include the gardener, gamekeeper and others. From the short time I'd been here it was apparent that the whole community was wrapped up in Pengarrock in some way.

I felt so helpless and alone. Barbara hadn't answered when I'd rung, so I left a message. Restless, I picked up some containers and went to the billiard room. Petroc's publishers would want his book, and the billiard room seemed to be where he was working on it. My shoulders slumped as I looked at the task in front of me. Edwardians seemed to stare at me from the black and white photographs that lined the wood-panelled walls. They told me to get on with the job.

The first few papers I picked up were photocopies of newspaper articles on a jewellery sale at a major auction house. The headline shouted, "World's Largest Sapphire Sells for Record Price". Underlined in pencil there was a mention of the Trevillion sapphire but there were no notes, which was not like Petroc at all. His fascination with the lost treasure made no sense. It seemed such a waste of his incredible intellect and time. As I placed them into a box, it struck me that he wouldn't spend his time on something for no reason.

110

Cornish Gilliflower, an apple with clove scent
from the French *giro flier* (clove)
Kea Plum
Hockings Green (Bodmin)

"Gilliflower." I spoke it aloud, liking the way the word sounded. Apples and cloves were a magic combination. Petroc had detailed lists and descriptions of native Cornish species collected in a folder. Next to it there was a crumbly, well-worn book, *A Week At the Lizard* by Rev. Charles Alexander John, dated 1848. Just a quick scan revealed a delightful glimpse back in time. Petroc had revisited each location and added his own thoughts and updated information on sheets of paper tucked into the book. It was easy to lose track of what I was supposed to be doing. I hadn't accomplished much because Petroc's notes were like chocolate to me. Once I'd had a small taste, I kept going back for another sample until the bar was finished.

In fact, Pengarrock was like that too. I kept discovering additional information. I found that it had two orchards, and that dispersed on several farms there were more. According to the notes, there was one quite close to the house, which could be the trees in the remains of the medieval garden, but I wasn't sure. We'd never made it there the other day. There was still so much that I hadn't seen, and now probably wouldn't.

For the time being, I needed to create some sort of order. I looked at the stack of books: *Flowers of the Field* by C. A. Johns, 1853; *Flora of Cornwall* by F. Hamilton Davey, 1909 and, more recently, *A Review*

of the Cornish Flora Pool: Institute of Cornish Studies,
1980. I wanted to read them all, but I placed them
carefully into the box containing reference materials for
Petroc's book and added their names to the list.

The journal I had seen before was on the table, with
a letter tucked into a page. Was it just marking a page,
or was it something else completely?

My dearest love,

How could you doubt me in any way? You know
me, or at least I thought you did. If I have
wandered it is not because I do not love you, and
if I have wandered it was not seeking love at all.

I shivered. The ink was purple, and it was dated 10
August 1984.

I know there is talk. There always is and always
will be, but you must not listen. You have always
encouraged me to follow my dreams, and I am.
But do not worry that these dreams take me from
you or from Pengarrock. I am on a quest, a quest
for us and for Tristan. Do not doubt me, and do
not doubt my love. Trust me, and let me follow my
heart, for it always leads me in the right direction.
Remember, it led me to you.

Always yours,
Immi

The letter was tucked into Petroc's entry for 15 August 1995.

> We had an earth tremor last night. At first I wasn't sure what it was, but this wasn't the first time a landslip along the shore has caused the house to shake. It was farther away last night, which is why I heard nothing, only felt the movement.

Imogen's letter was so intimate, I felt I had trespassed. I folded it and placed the letter into the journal where I had found it. There was no apparent connection, but Petroc must have put it there for a reason.

Stretching, I walked to the nearest window, trying to push Imogen's words from my mind. Was she having an affair? What was it Helen had said when I'd asked about the portrait? *It's in the past and there it stays.* It was nine o'clock, and still light. The air was filled with the scent of honeysuckle. I leaned against the window frame and took a deep breath. My pace of work needed to increase if I was to accomplish anything of value in the short time I'd be here, but the aura of the place seemed to slow me down.

I placed another box in the hallway beside the study. They looked an unsightly mess, which had been fine while Petroc was alive but now, with the funeral in a few days, this wasn't acceptable. Maybe JC could give me a hand moving these to some less obvious place until I knew what was happening with Petroc's papers

113

and what my role, if any, would be going forward. I needed to do some planning again, like where I could live and find another job. I heard a crash and went to investigate.

"Are you OK?" I noted the broken vase Helen was clearing up. She looked drained.

"No, but don't worry." She smiled at me. "I'm just cross with Tristan. I raised that boy, and he should know better."

"Dare I ask what's happening?"

Helen shook her head. "Nothing new. If he'd only settle with a good woman instead of chasing every pretty skirt he sees, things might be better. But I must be thankful for small mercies."

I raised an eyebrow. "Such as?"

"He's dumped the last floozy, so I won't have to deal with some city girl going all feeble here in the country."

I smiled at the image Helen's words created.

"Now, what can I do for you?" She smoothed down her hair.

"Nothing. More the other way around."

"I'm just off to meet with the florists, as Tristan can't be bothered to get down here and do it himself as he should."

"Good luck." I watched Helen march out of the kitchen, thinking she might give Tristan an earful when he did turn up. The phone rang and I answered. "Pengarrock."

"Hello, Jude. How are things?" Barbara asked.

"Good question, but strange is the short answer."

114

"I can imagine. I'm sorry I won't be able to attend the funeral; I have a speaking engagement that I can't change."

"Bad timing."

"Yes." She coughed.

I traced the grain of the wood on the surface of the table. "Barbara, do you think I should just pack up and leave?" I perched on the edge of the kitchen counter. It had been three days since Petroc passed away.

"No. You must stay there until the funeral is over, at the minimum."

I frowned. For no known reason, I didn't want to meet Tristan.

"Jude, you can't run away."

"I wasn't going to, but I can't see my job here continuing." I hopped off the counter and paced.

"Tristan will want his father's papers put in order. And how close was Petroc to finishing the book?"

"I wouldn't be too sure Tristan wants anything to do with his father's papers, or his book." I couldn't forget Petroc's comments about his son's lack of interest in Pengarrock.

"What are you saying, Jude?"

"I'm not sure, but," I paused, "I think he can't be bothered."

"You mustn't judge people."

"I know, but he could show some emotion. He's not of the stiff-upper-lip generation."

Barbara laughed. "Jude, give the man a chance. His father has just died unexpectedly and he's inherited one hell of a big estate, and that might be enough to make him a bit difficult."

I pressed my lips together, then spoke. "You could be right, but I'll reserve judgement."

"Well that means you'll be staying there till the funeral is over, anyway."

"God, you have a way of putting things!" I flopped into a chair.

"Just the way I look at the world."

"True."

"Heard from your parents?" The tone of Barbara's voice altered ever so slightly.

I sighed. "I tried to reach Dad on Skype, but he didn't respond so I sent a message."

"And?"

"And, nothing. I haven't heard anything. I'm beginning to get worried. Should I be?"

"Have you tried again?"

I huffed. "No."

"Do it."

I didn't respond.

"Jude, don't be mulish. It's not like you."

"Ha, I'm not like me any more, or hadn't you noticed?"

"I had, but that doesn't excuse you."

"OK. I'll try again." I twisted a strand of hair around my finger. It remained coiled when I pulled the finger away.

"Good girl."

"Oh lord, Barbara, don't say that, it'll make me want to do the opposite."

"My, you have changed!"

"Yup." I was still thinking about Barbara's comment as I went into Petroc's study. In the past few days I had made rough piles of types of files and papers, now that I knew I wouldn't be disturbing his way of working. Almost all of the floor was visible except around the walls of the room, where the stacks were two files deep and in some spots coming up about four foot high. His desk remained as he had last used it. I'm not sure if it was just my reluctance to touch the place where he'd rested, or if I felt I should leave that part for Tristan. After all, what was there might be personal, or relate to estate affairs, and might not be research.

I was falling and never hitting the rocks below. My limbs wouldn't move. Panic. I gasped and tried to wake up. I flung off the covers and stood up, reminding myself it was just a dream. Dressing swiftly, I knew I needed some fresh air. The dogs were surprised when I walked past them and went out the back door. Eventually they caught up with me. My pace was erratic as I followed the coastal path in the gloom of the early morning. I came out of the cover of the trees and watched clouds sweep across the fields and out onto the river. Although I couldn't see much, I could hear the sea bashing against the rocks below.

I tripped over an exposed root and landed with a thump on my knees. The dogs were with me in seconds. I'd been too busy thinking about Dad and why they weren't calling me back, and I hadn't registered how far we'd walked. I was almost at the headland; in fact, I

117

wasn't on the path any more, but had strayed off and was somehow in a small copse of scrub oak.

This close to the ground it smelt of damp and crushed grass. Peering at the vegetation, I spied what looked like miniature buds close to the barbed wire that marked where the cliff dropped dramatically to the rocks below. I crawled along the ground towards them then I put on my glasses. On closer inspection they looked like orchids, but they were not a plant with which I was truly familiar. Perfect flowers topped leafless stems. They appeared ghostly in the early light.

The dogs stood a little distance from me and waited.

"I'm OK." Low clouds poured over the cliff and my hair moved as if something brushed past me. I stood and walked to the edge. A stone skittered, then fell to the rocks below. I steadied myself, teetering, and tried to look down. Leaning as far as I dared to go, I squinted. The cove was empty, with only the tide retreating from the pebble beach.

The dogs were sniffing the ground now, and Gin set off in search of a rabbit. I clambered carefully back over the fence. How had I crossed it without noticing? I moved well away from the edge of the cliff. The debris and rocks piled on the beach below indicated there must have been a fairly major landslip here at one point. It wasn't recent, and what little I'd seen of the cliff face looked solid and old. It was all a little too close to this morning's nightmare.

Heading back towards the house, Gin dashed in front of me and Rum trailed at my heels. They acted like two bodyguards, one on the lookout and the other close at hand. I glanced over my shoulder and tried to distinguish between the sea and the sky.

Arriving at Pengarrock beach, the sun had just crested the horizon. I climbed onto a rock and drew my legs up close. The funeral was set for tomorrow. A week had passed since Petroc's death, the cause of which had turned out to be a massive stroke. Tristan was due to arrive some time this morning, according to Helen. Her nerves seemed on the verge of breaking. The fact that Tristan had been handling everything over the phone and not in person appeared to be what was disturbing Helen most. She kept muttering, "He should be here," every time she put the phone down. She'd told him that in no uncertain terms too, but it hadn't made any difference. He would be arriving only twenty-four hours before the funeral, and I couldn't shake the feeling that I was the one who shouldn't be here. At the same time, I was reluctant to leave. Whether it was the magic of Petroc's work, or simply the sheer beauty of Pengarrock and the River Helford, I didn't know.

Over the past few days it had become a ritual that I would pull out my suitcases and begin to pack up, and then halfway through I'd stop and undo the process. It was a complete waste of time. Time that would be better spent continuing to work in Petroc's study. After all, I was being paid to work, or at least I thought I would be. I had the letter confirming my salary and start date, so Tristan would have to honour what was set out in it, surely. Hell, I didn't know what to think, except I hated to contemplate anything happening to Pengarrock. I was aware of the rumours which were already floating around. Tristan would sell it. They said it as if it was fact. What I couldn't understand was *why*. I threw a stone into the water. How could he not want to be the caretaker of so much beauty?

The sun was rising over the waters of Falmouth Bay, and I knew that if this were mine I would move heaven and earth to protect it. But it wasn't mine. It belonged to this Tristan Ungrateful Trevillion. TUT. I laughed, but then looked around to make sure it was just the dogs and I.

"Rum." She looked up from the water's edge. I could see it in her eyes. She was going for a morning swim. I sighed. She might well enjoy a dip in the icy waters, but it would lead to an equally cold hose-down when we returned to the house. What would Tristan do with the dogs? I'd become exceptionally fond of them, and lately they had been more inclined to respond to my commands. Tristan lived in London. My mind had him settled in an all-glass-and-steel penthouse with no place for these muddy companions.

I chucked a stick into the water, and Rum dutifully swam for it and brought it to me. I held on to it, and after shaking herself down she followed me up the path. A quick shout brought Gin out of the woods. Maybe some questions would be answered today.

The spray of gravel in the drive along with the sound of a car door slamming warned me that the master of the house had arrived in a rush. It was nearly noon according to the old clock on Petroc's desk. I had taken to winding it every other day. It was the only thing I'd

120

handled on the desk. But for some reason the little carriage clock was like the beating heart of the study, and without its ticking the place seemed empty, so I braved the invisible yellow tape I'd placed around the desk and set the thing going. Instantly I had felt better.

Helen crossed the hall and I heard her open the front door. The next sound was the two dogs. I wondered if I should also go and make it look like a modern-day setting of the scene from a period drama where the servants line up to welcome the master. Frowning, I stood. I didn't want to create that impression, but my curiosity was whetted. Would Tristan be at all like Petroc? As I put one foot in front of the other out of the study, I found myself hoping that he would.

"'Bout time." Helen was holding Tristan tight as I walked outside to the drive into the hall. Her words and actions were a complete contradiction. This past week she hadn't had a good word to say for him, but from where I stood I could see her tears, and she wasn't letting go. And he wasn't fighting it either.

Rum and Gin circled the pair, waiting their turn. Tristan looked up, and I was startled by the intensity of the green of his eyes. They weren't emerald but more the stormy sea green from a nineteenth-century maritime painting. I'm not sure I've ever seen the colour in nature, but I had on many a canvas.

He bent down to the dogs but continued to study me. His expression was unfathomable, and I wouldn't want to face him as my opponent in a poker match. I didn't like him, and I couldn't say why. He was handsome enough, with a strong jaw and a well-built

121

body, a younger version of Petroc, really, but without the soul. Thankfully he turned his gaze to the dogs. It was clear they knew him well. I didn't, and felt an idiot just standing there while Helen wiped her eyes and the dogs slobbered all over the prodigal son. No, that wasn't right. We were not killing the fatted calf for him; he was planning to sell it.

"Judith." He stood and held out his hand.

I took it, and his grip was firm and assured. My hand tingled when he released it. "Tristan." Could this be any cornier, or more awkward? I almost felt as if I should drop a little curtsey. "Please call me Jude."

"Helen tells me you've been a great help."

I forced a smile, and wondered why that comment sounded like an insult.

He turned away from me. "How many people will be staying tonight and tomorrow night, Helen?"

"Not too many. Just your aunts and your cousin. Have you anyone else I should add to the list?"

"Peter Brooks."

"He can use the Blue Room." Helen frowned.

"Fine."

"Then there's nothing to worry about. Everything's ready." Helen turned and went into the house. I looked at Tristan's face. His mouth tightened for a second before he collected a small bag and suit carrier from the boot. I decided it was best if I kept out of everyone's way.

In the peace of the study I could hear a distant conversation. The cadence of Tristan's voice was similar to Petroc's, but there was an impatience to it. Helen was fussing. Tristan's cousin had arrived and added to the level of tension in the house. I was cross-legged on the floor noting down a book's details when Tristan stormed in. He didn't see me. He stood just in front of his father's desk. Then he reached out and touched the little clock. With his back to me, it was impossible to know what he was thinking. Instead, I could see he was in good shape but on the thin side. His hair was lighter than Petroc's must have been before the grey had slipped in. Tristan stood in the same manner as his father, and when he put his hands in his pockets his shoulders sloped in the same way. I hadn't realised I'd noticed these things about Petroc, but I must have.

He walked to the desk and sat down in his father's chair, then looked straight at me. Actually he glared at me. I wasn't sure if it was me he was angry with, or if I just happened to be in the wrong place.

"Sorry. I'll leave you in peace." I quickly shut my laptop and stood.

"Judith, what exactly do you do here?" Those green eyes fixed on me, and I felt ridiculous in my shorts and t-shirt. I didn't look very professional, but I was perfectly dressed to scramble around on the floor sorting papers on a warm day.

"Jude, please. Your father hired me to catalogue his books and papers."

"You mean organise him? A secretary?"

"No, not a secretary. I'm an archivist specialising in gardens."

"You're a gardener?"

He was being deliberately obtuse. "Would you like to see my CV?" My shorts felt too short. I tugged at them, hoping to cover more of my legs. Mother's endless nagging about appearance and how people judge you by it sounded in my head. At the arboretum no one would question my ability or my intelligence, but I wasn't home, and Tristan didn't know who Jude Warren was.

"Possibly, but I doubt it takes a PhD to sort out my father's scribblings."

"They aren't scribblings. His work is of serious academic value. No one understood the development of gardens like your father." I shifted from one foot to the other.

He laughed. "How long have you been helping him?" He looked around at the piles, and then his glance travelled up my legs. If I was kind I'd say he couldn't avoid them, but I didn't feel kind; anything but. I was being assessed as an object, and not as an academic.

"Almost two weeks." I held my computer in front of me.

"And in that time, have you found anything of value?"

"Oh, yes."

"Before you begin to tell me about my father's work and how fascinating you find it, let me rephrase that question. I mean of value to the outside world, in terms of money. You see, Judith, my father was a dreamer and he was broke. The estate is all but bankrupt."

I opened my mouth to speak but Helen walked into the room. "Tristan, your aunts are here."

124

He stood and walked towards Helen. "We can talk about your departure after the funeral, and also where and how I can dispose of all this."

I rested against the wall. All my work and all Petroc's work dismissed because it didn't have any obvious monetary value. I dashed upstairs to my room and packed my bags. I'd be damned if I was going to help him with anything. He could rot in hell.

CHAPTER
TEN

The sea mist lingered, shrouding the church at St Anthony. The tide was exceptionally high, covering much of the beach. Cars packed the small lane, but a few places had been reserved. JC manoeuvred into one of them. I climbed out of the car after Helen, and I had a lost-in-time feeling. A man in a morning coat and top hat was organising the pall-bearers outside the church. Tristan wore a fixed look as he greeted people as they filed in. After our last encounter in the study, I didn't want to talk to him. I'd stayed in my room last night, allowing the family their privacy, and I argued with Tristan in my head. He was wrong, wrong in so many ways. But neither last night, nor today, was the time to tell him. Unfortunately there might not ever be time, and that saddened me beyond words. I slipped past him and went into the darkness of the small church. It was lit only by candelabra; there was not an electric light to be seen.

The church was already full. Helen tried to pull me forward to the reserved seating, but I managed to resist. I squeezed into a pew made to hold three people, but which held five. Yet more people came in and stood at the back. I recognised a few faces from the village store.

I wondered who the rest were. Some I could tell were from academic life. I wasn't sure if it was the age or the tea stains on the ties that gave them away. Looking closely, I recognised a history lecturer from Trinity College. It was a shame that Barbara couldn't be here, and I longed to have someone to discuss it all with.

Tristan came into the church and sat in the front row next to Helen. The organ sounded a few tentative notes, then the church door opened. None of us in the pew could move without the others, so we all turned together. The vicar walked in followed by the casket, held aloft. I recognised Mark among the pall-bearers.

Rather than try and make room to hold up my hymn sheet, I followed along with the woman next to me. As far as I knew, Tristan had left the hymns and readings in Helen's and the vicar's hands. I frowned. I didn't understand why he was so detached, and as the service progressed he remained so. The vicar spoke eloquently about Petroc's life, work and love of Pengarrock. Helen wept quietly while JC looked pretty broken up, but Tristan's face remained a solemn mask.

We all rose and sang the last hymn. The casket left the small church to the sound of muffled bells, and the congregation followed behind. The mist had cleared and the temperature change was marked from the cool damp church to the heat outside. The sun baked my back in the black wrap dress I wore. A trickle of sweat trailed down my cleavage and reminded me of a few weeks ago. I pushed the memory away.

Mourners walked up the stone steps and through the old headstones to the open grave. Mark and the others slowly lowered the coffin. The vicar began the final blessing, and I studied the ancient tombstones around me.

In
Memory of
Ann
The beloved wife of
John Baldwin
Who died in Breage
Aged 70
September 1880

I moved on to the next one, after noting that John followed his wife eight years later.

Sacred
to the memory of
Oliver Edwards.
Late of Condurrow,in the Parish,
who departed this life
July 11th, 1850.
Aged 81 years.

He lived to a good age as well, and his wife followed two years later. The last line saddened me, and yet I smiled.

All flesh is grass.

The sound of earth hitting the coffin brought the present back into focus. Tristan turned from the grave and the crowd began to disperse. The sun glinted off the creek visible through the trees. Helen was chatting to someone with her back ramrod straight. What was bothering her? I'd noticed that she had become almost monosyllabic this morning. I stopped and listened to the conversations around me.

"Beautiful service. The vicar did Petroc proud, especially when he mentioned his devotion to all things in life, but most especially his beloved Helford."

"He's just going to sell to the highest bidder, with no thought of the community."

"It was a blessing it happened so quick."

No it wasn't. Petroc was taken too soon, I wanted to shout, but instead I admired the pelargoniums displayed on some of the graves while continuing to eavesdrop.

"A blessing for him, but I wonder for the rest of us."

"What do you think Tristan will do?"

"Sell. He hasn't been a part of here for so long. Can't even remember his last visit."

"I can. He came with that model. She was something else."

There was no need for me to hear these things, and I moved away from them and towards Tristan. He was speaking to Peter Brooks. "All these people are just here for the free drink at the house."

"Cynical." Peter smiled at the people milling around them.

"Who, me?" Tristan laughed. "Yes, they want to see the house too."

"Indeed, it may be their last chance." Peter looked around. "Tristan, it's time to begin to sort out probate."

"What a nightmare. How quickly can we get it done?"

"These things take time. The minimum is six months, but with an estate of this size it will take longer."

"Everything down here functions in retrograde motion." Tristan grimaced.

The lecturer I knew walked up to the pair. "Hello, Tristan. I haven't seen you for years." I watched Tristan's polite mask fall back into place.

"Yes, years."

"I was so sorry to hear of your father's untimely death."

Tristan nodded.

"I know it's early days, but have you thought about donating your father's papers to his old college?" I suddenly remembered his name — Latimer.

Tristan blinked. "I hadn't really given it any thought."

"They will be quite valuable."

"Academic or monetary?" Tristan's glance picked me out in the crowd. I debated whether I should join them or walk away.

"Both, I should imagine. If you did wish to donate them to the college, I would be happy to liaise for you."

Peter Brooks jumped into the conversation. "He might do that, depending on the value." He smiled. "I'm Peter Brooks, Tristan's solicitor. Do you have a card, so that I may contact you regarding this? Clearly we will need an expert."

"I think we already have one, in-house." Tristan indicated for me to join them.

I walked over the uneven ground.

"This is Judith Warren. She was helping my father."

"Dr Latimer, how lovely to see you again. You won't remember me, but I did my PhD at Trinity." Let Tristan make of that what he would. Secretary. Gardener!

"Yes." He shook my hand. "Excellent student. You are in good hands, then."

Someone pulled Tristan away and Helen called me, so I excused myself from Peter Brooks and Dr Latimer, who had begun to talk about Petroc's work.

"I'm heading back to the house now. I need to make sure the caterers have everything sorted." Helen's hands smoothed down her dress.

"They seemed that way when we left." I noticed her white knuckles as she grasped her hankie.

"I know, but I want it just so." Helen stopped as Mark approached and kissed her cheek. "Are you coming to the house?"

"No; now that the owner has changed, I won't be welcome." Mark glanced at Tristan.

"Mark, you were so good to Petroc." Helen sighed.

Tristan walked up to us.

"I hear you'll be selling Pengarrock." Mark stared at Tristan.

"So the rumour goes." Tristan's stance reminded me of a fighter.

"Yes, it does, but it goes further, saying that you can't wait to get the hell out of Cornwall again."

"Might be right, but I wasn't the only one who left." Tristan's voice dropped.

"True, but I came back." Mark countered.

"And has it improved your miserable life?"

"Immensely." Mark turned away after giving Helen's hand a squeeze, and I longed to know the cause of the hostility between them.

Helen turned to Tristan. "I'll see you at the house." Then she took me by the hand to join JC, who was waiting at the car.

People spilled from the drawing room onto the terrace. The day had turned hot and still. The level of noise belied the solemn occasion of the event. I scanned the faces, but knew so few. I wished Barbara were here, but her speaking engagement couldn't be broken. In the crowd of people, I was lonely. I wondered what Petroc would have made of this. The academics had found their way into the library. Were they admiring it, or dividing the spoils? No, that was unjust. They had lost a colleague and a friend.

I walked back into the house and up to my room. The hum of conversation floated in through the windows. I tore off my dress and threw on some jeans and an old shirt of Dad's. I needed to get out of here and I longed to be on the water. Instead of taking the main staircase, I sought out another route as I followed the hallway down to where it ended in a large room that must have been the nursery once. It spanned the width of the house. I took a quick look, noting the tidy appearance and deserted feel of the room. Books were stacked neatly on shelves, and toys were gathered round the walls.

The last child who played here must have been Tristan. I walked to the table-tennis table and picked up a bat. It was difficult to picture him small and vulnerable. Someone had mentioned that he had been only eight when Imogen died, they didn't say how. I would have to ask Helen, if I'd be around that long. My bag was packed. Tomorrow I would speak to Tristan. I had already begun to put out feelers for other possible work.

I sank onto a window seat and looked upriver towards Helford Passage. It all seemed so peaceful at this time of day. The basin was filled with yachts and motorboats; the summer season was about to begin. The same thing happened at home, but earlier in the year. Memorial Day kicked the season off. It always felt that one day the harbour was empty, and by the end of the weekend it was full. It wasn't true, but in my head that was how it happened.

From the bookcase below the seat, I took out a book. What would the young Tristan or even Petroc have read? It was not a surprise that it was *The Lion, the Witch and the Wardrobe*. Part of me wanted it to be *Mergers and Acquisitions 101* so that I could explain away Tristan's cold manner. I shook my head, and then I noticed a book on the floor. It was very old and almost pamphlet-like, which triggered a memory . . . it was a chapbook. *A New Riddle Book or, a Whetstone for Dull Wits*. I smiled. Dull wits. A child's hand had coloured in the illustration on the cover. Part of me flinched. Here was a book — I touched the pages — probably printed in the late 1700s, and it had been defaced, yet it had clearly been read and loved. The pages were yellowed and slightly torn.

Of Merry Book this is the Chief,
'Tis as a Purging pill;
To carrying off all heavy Grief,
And make you laugh your Fill.

To carry off all heavy grief . . . I wished that it could. I put the books back and left the nursery. My heart was heavy, and my time here was truly limited. I doubted I'd last the week. The back stairs led me straight to the hallway by the butler's pantry. The kitchen was alive with activity as the caterers came in and out of the room. I slipped through their midst and out of the house. The riverside beckoned.

Silence had returned to Pengarrock. I came downstairs and entered the kitchen, which, a day after the funeral, was back to normal. Helen stood at the sink, staring out the window. She looked so tired and sad. I walked up to her and hugged her.

She sighed and patted my hand. "I just don't know."

"I know," I said, but I didn't and yet somehow I did. Everything here was teetering on a precipice, and Helen of all people was affected the most.

"You're a good girl, and you need to stand up to Tristan and make sure he doesn't throw his father's work away. I know that that's what he wants to do."

I stepped back. "There's not a lot I can do."

"Yes, there is. You can try and make Tristan see the value of Petroc's work. I just know you can." Her eyes were filled with unshed tears.

"Helen, I'll try, but I don't think there is much that can be done. In fact, I guess I'll be gone by the end of the week."

"Then you have to make yourself indispensable. You have to make him see."

"I'm not a miracle worker, despite being named after St Jude."

"I hadn't thought about that, but we are in desperate circumstances." Helen poured me a coffee and handed me the cup. Tristan walked into the kitchen. Had he heard the conversation?

"Tristan." Helen looked up from the counter where she'd begun chopping vegetables.

He nodded in Helen's direction. "Helen, we begin reading the will in twenty minutes in the dining room." He turned and walked slowly back through the door then stopped. "Judith, I'll need to speak with you later, as there will be some mention of my father's work, and at the moment you appear to be the on-hand expert."

I blinked. Talk about damning with faint praise.

"Right." Helen still held the knife, but then she dropped it on the table in front of me.

"My aunts want to be on their way shortly, so let's get this over with." Tristan turned and marched out of the room. Helen muttered under her breath.

"Is he always so talkative?" I took a sip of coffee.

"Ha, wouldn't know. He hasn't been here in so long, I've forgotten."

"What do you mean by that?"

"Nothing." Helen stopped chopping. "Tristan left here a long time ago, and has only come back now that he has to." A tear slipped down Helen's cheek.

"I'm so sorry." I didn't know what else to say as I watched Helen's shoulders shake.

"I could kill him at the minute. Selling his heritage. *Our* heritage. His father's love, but poor rascal . . . I'll leave it there." Helen put a heaped bowl of porridge down in front of me with a thud, almost scattering the contents over the table. I leaned back and waited for what she would say next.

"I raised that boy and he should know better, but," she paused, "he should have stayed here and not gone away when Imogen . . ." Helen picked up the bread knife. She shook her head, then looked at me before carefully carving a slice of fresh bread. I waited for her to continue speaking, but she didn't.

My appetite was whetted for more knowledge, not for the food in front of me. Toying with it, I thought over the new information about Tristan. There was something about his mother and her death. It would be awful to lose your mother at any time, but that young, it would be devastating. Eight is still childhood, understanding but not understanding.

I looked at the porridge in my bowl. My stomach rolled over. I rose and walked to the sink.

"Leave it. I'll take care of it." Helen wiped her hands.

"No, Helen, I'll do it." I placed a hand on her shoulder as she went past. "Thank you for a wonderful breakfast. Sorry I couldn't eat it all."

"It's no wonder you're so thin." She frowned.

"I promise to do better." I put my hand on my heart.

"Mind that you do!" Helen laughed. "Don't let Tristan bully you. You need to defend Petroc's work. If we can't save Pengarrock, then at least we can save his work. Please." She squeezed my hand. "I'd better repair my face."

Helen left, and I wondered how I could do anything at all. Tristan seemed set on one course of action, and the only thing stopping him from discarding his father's work was its saleable potential. I just didn't think that it would be enough to make it worth his while, but I hoped I was wrong.

I was in the kitchen to get a glass of water where I found a tray made up with coffee things. Knowing how stressed Helen was, the least I could do was take it through for her. Glancing around to see if there was anything else that should be on the tray, I spied Tristan sitting on the wall of the terrace with the two dogs beside him. The reading of the will must have finished. I headed out towards him to ask about the tray, but stopped when I saw his shoulders shake, and Rum place her paws on his lap and begin to lick his face. He was weeping. I waited to see him push the dog away, but instead his arms curled around her and he held her close.

I backed silently into the kitchen and picked up the tray. If I was quick I could head everyone off and give Tristan some space. I knew grief could come in waves, catching you completely off guard. Even now, after all these years, I could still be knocked sideways by Rose's death. I swallowed the lump in my throat and walked into the hallway. Helen was on the bottom step holding a suitcase in each hand, and Tristan's cousin was at the back of the two sisters as if she were herding them. They were oblivious to how absurd they sounded and looked, as they complained loudly at the injustice of it all. I wondered what had been said that had them angry and Tristan in tears.

Helen caught my glance and rolled her eyes. I pressed my lips together. Families could be so complicated. As Helen led them outside, I took the coffee through to the drawing room.

Today's newspapers were sitting on the table and while I waited for Helen, I flipped through them and settled down with the local paper. It was filled with pictures of summer fairs and the unfortunate story of a boy who had died while he was visiting London. I pulled out the section on property for sale. On the front page was a delightful cottage in Helford village, on the creek. The price was staggering, which cancelled my fantasy of buying a little place here on the water. I was wondering if something inland might be within my range, when I saw a picture of Pengarrock with a caption: *For sale as a whole or lots — price on request.* My hand shook as I put the paper back on the table. Tristan had been busy. His father had been in the ground only a day.

CHAPTER
ELEVEN

The windows of the study were open and the scent of roses filled the room. I closed my eyes and let the aroma embrace me. It was a pure scent, unsullied by anything else. Just like Rose. Would things have turned out differently if I'd had her to share it all with me? Opening my eyes, I saw Tristan, cell phone clutched to his ear, bent over a box of files on the floor. "Tell me as soon as the due diligence is finished." He stood and put his phone in his pocket. "Did my father spend all his time looking at the view instead of filing?"

I leaned against the door frame and tried to assess Tristan. Pushing aside his obvious physical attractions, here was a man selling off his heritage and that of the community around it without giving anyone a chance to grieve. Did he hate it so much?

"I'm sure he did sometimes, but he used the floor as a filing system, and I've been the one to disorder it by piling and boxing it." I stepped into the room.

"Really?"

"Yes, really."

"OK, Miss Warren, we need to talk. I found your CV and my father's letter to you here, which of course was suitably vague." He sat on the corner of the desk.

"What would you like to know?"

"Exactly what were you hired to do?" It was a question I'd asked myself many times, but I felt it would betray Petroc to share it with his son. "Petroc was aware that he needed help sorting through his work. I believe he didn't want you to have to do it."

"If that was the case, then he died too soon."

I frowned. "That is true, but," I paused and wondered how not to sound too weird, "I think he knew he didn't have long, and wanted things in place."

"In your short employment with my father you gathered this?"

"Yes; he wanted others to be able to use his work, and I was his means of making this happen."

"And just what were you doing? It's not stated in the letter."

"For him, I was cataloguing everything."

"You mean, making a list."

"Put simply, yes."

"I like things simple. And he required a PhD to make this list?"

"Yes and no. I was available, and I have the knowledge base to assess the content's importance." I paused, trying to read his expression. "I'm assuming I will finish the week out and depart."

Tristan stared at me, and I saw the glimmer of a smile. "I doubt there can be anything of worth in this mess, but now that it's been mentioned, we have to try to calculate the value so that the taxman can have his fair share." He waved his hand towards the overflowing

140

filing cabinets. "Frankly I think it would be easier to put it all on the bonfire."

"That would be a huge mistake."

Tristan raised his eyebrows, and before he could speak I raised my hand.

"You know your father was a wonderful scholar and writer. He was known to have a vast collection of reference books, records and photographs of gardens, Cornish ones in particular. His book on medieval gardens was one of my main references."

Tristan's eyes widened. "You read his books?"

"All of them." I was clearing some space on the top of a cabinet when I heard him laugh. I turned around and he was smiling. I think it must have been the first time I'd seen a genuine smile on his face. It transformed him.

"Well, Judith, it appears that I do need you. Someone has to sort this stuff out, and it won't be me. I have enough to do with the rest of the estate, and making sure that my own business stays afloat. Will you continue cataloguing all of this, but this time sorting with monetary value in mind? The estate will continue to pay you the salary that my father agreed."

I wanted to say no, but I had no other job so it would have to be yes, even if it broke my heart to think of what I was being a part of. "I'll continue."

"Good. And as I've heard from Father's publisher, can you see what was happening with this book he was writing?"

"I haven't found the manuscript, but I have some of his notes. I'll keep looking."

Tristan just sat on the edge of the desk, staring at me. "One more thing. Just why is someone with a PhD acting as a glorified clerk?"

I coughed. I couldn't tell him the truth — that I'd dumped a man at the altar and needed to escape the fallout. "I was unexpectedly free."

"Just what is that a euphemism for? You were made redundant?"

"No, I'd taken a sabbatical to do something, and that something fell through." I turned away from him. A cold sweat broke out across my brow. Time to change the subject. Did he have a sense of humour? "When are you going to clear out of this wonderful room so that I can sit and stare at the view all day, and pretend to be working?"

"Immediately, if it means that finally something will move forward in this damn place." He walked out through the French windows and spoke to the gardener. They seemed to be sharing a joke as Tristan gave the man a hand lifting a large tub, which from this angle showed off how well he filled out his t-shirt and jeans.

I was left with an odd feeling, but shoved it aside and began to work while wondering how I was going to make an assessment of all of this. Things were still such a disaster. I took a deep breath and began with one empty box and one I'd filled already. If I sorted according to value to the world versus value to the estate or personal stuff, it would at least be a start. Yet I hated separating the material along those lines. Petroc, despite the apparent lack of organisation, had a plan. I just didn't know what it was.

The repetitive sound of a fly hitting a pane of glass brought me back to the twenty-first century. I stretched out my legs in front of me on the floor. They felt dead, and I wasn't sure I could stand. It was three o'clock. I looked at my notes; five closely written pages, which I would then have to transcribe onto the computer. I had been working directly onto it, but today I thought it would be best to change tack and work in a manner that somehow felt more appropriate. Possibly by working more like Petroc I could then discover what he was up to. Almost randomly, amid his work Petroc had jotted down:

> Not of the land
> Not of the sea
> Visible only
> When August Rock sees

Why was he working on that again? He was a sensible man. His work was a testament to that. His writing was meticulously researched, but here he was, chasing down a riddle. There had to be more to it, and I needed to find out what.

Putting my hands to the floor, I turned over and pushed up onto my knees. The tingling was getting to that really painful stage. I should have known better than to sit still for so long. But the information in the box was gripping. There was so much on the shipwrecks of the region, especially one wreck, the yacht *Columbia*, which had gone down on August Rock in 1846. I scanned the contents. It was sad reading. All on her were lost including the owner, Lord Frederick Peters. I stretched then it clicked: Petroc had mentioned that Lady Clarissa might have been aboard. But why would he think that?

I should just be cataloguing, but I couldn't help reading. Petroc's work was amazing, and as uncanny as it was, I felt he was still here because of his notes slipped into the appropriate pages of the books. I felt as if he were conversing with me.

Finally making it to my feet, I took a deep breath. The scent of the roses had faded, but now jasmine perfumed the air in the afternoon heat. The morning haze on the river had cleared. The water looked so blue and the fields so green; each field was outlined in darker colours, with tall pines capping the headland as it rose from the sea.

On the east lawn, I saw Tristan with the dogs. He was a puzzle; a very good-looking puzzle, but a puzzle nonetheless. Rum had tipped her head to the side allowing Tristan better access to her neck, which he was scratching.

I shouldn't judge Tristan. I'd left my home, hadn't I? What was different about Tristan wanting to leave his? It was clear he felt no attachment to the place. His parents were dead. Mine were alive. He wasn't breaking free of them but from the place itself. My home, although beautiful and set on the water, was not a historic home. Pengarrock oozed history from every stone, but did that make it different? Yes and no. Selling Pengarrock and doing it so quickly was wrong. Tristan was being stupid . . . or maybe it was blind.

I flipped through the pages of a beautiful red leather journal I'd found sandwiched between two thick photograph albums. It was Petroc's from two years ago. He'd kept a near-daily record of his thoughts. Most days it was reflections on the beauty of the river and the land that surrounded it. Sometimes it was simple musings, a fragment of a poem or what seemed like a poem to me. Woven through the prose and poetry were his reminder notes to follow up a particular line of research, or something that needed to be done on the estate. All the costs of running an estate and house of this size were apparent in the journal.

"Jude?" Helen came into the study.

I stood.

"A letter arrived for you this morning." She handed it to me, and I knew from the writing that it was from my aunt. It brought back memories of the years she'd encouraged me to pursue my own interests, and not worry about what Mother wanted me to do.

"Thanks. All OK?"

Helen rolled her eyes and departed. I flipped the envelope over. It would be filled with all sorts of news, and I would read it later when I could savour the contents. My head felt fuzzy and my thoughts weren't sharp. A walk would clear my mind. I dashed upstairs to get my sunglasses and found the printout of John's email which had arrived this morning.

Dear Jude,

I've been thinking. I need to see you. It's been hard to think of anything but you. I've really missed you, and we need to talk.

J

I needed to respond, but I'd deal with it later. Picking up my glasses, I bolted down the stairs and out the front door and straight into Tristan.

"Sorry." I looked at his hand on my arm.

"Running away?" His hand remained in place, and warmth spread from his touch.

"No!" I stepped back from him so that he had to drop the hand that had steadied me. I took a breath. "I just didn't expect anyone to be standing there."

"Sorry."

"No problem." I sought my shades on the top of my head, but then realised they must have fallen off in the collision. I swooped down to pick them up.

"Where are you off to?" He frowned.

"To the beach, to stretch my legs and recover from all the food Helen keeps feeding me." I ran a hand over my distended stomach. His eyes followed it and I removed it swiftly. "Don't worry, I won't be long."

"How did you get on this morning?"

"Oh, quite well."

"Is that an American quite, or an English quite?"

"I, oh, American." I grimaced. "I made some progress this morning." I shoved my hands into my

146

pockets. "Now, as I don't want to be gone too long, I'd best set off." Without concentrating on the direction, I strode off, sensing him watching me as I went.

At the end of lawn, I came to a gate and finally took a breath. Why did Tristan unsettle me? I was definitely not interested in men at the moment, no matter how good-looking they were.

Under the green canopy of the trees the air became cooler, and the scent of leaf mould became stronger with each step further into the woodland valley. Before long, blue sparkled through the foliage in the distance and the hum of an engine could be heard. I glanced about me and found I was alone, totally alone. I'd cut myself off from everyone. No one had any preconceived ideas about me. Anything, any action, was a possibility. I didn't have to stay and help Tristan. My contract had been with Petroc. I didn't need to assist in dividing the spoils just because it seemed polite. Mother wasn't here telling me to be a good girl. The footpath was coming to an end, and I could see the beach clearly now. The sound of a child's voice calling for its mother echoed off the rocks. What did I want to do?

"Time to grow up, Jude." I spoke to the trees. They didn't reply.

After three weeks at Pengarrock, I was finally entering the library. The room faced east and three walls were lined from floor to ceiling with books of every type and with no apparent order to them. There was a thriller next to a collection of Shakespeare's poems. I couldn't believe I'd waited until today. Now here, I wondered if

I would ever leave. In the centre of the room was a large mahogany table covered in stacks of papers and books, more evidence of Petroc's sprawling working methods. The other furnishings in the room were a worn button-back leather sofa and two overstuffed chairs. The small tables beside them were also piled high. This room alone would take me weeks; but blissful ones.

I pulled a leather-bound book off the shelves. If there had been writing on the spine it had long since worn away. It was an English first edition of a collection of Henry Wadsworth Longfellow's poems from 1878, and it was signed by the poet. A marbled page slipped out of the book, revealing an inscription to Alan Trevillion on the occasion of his fortieth birthday. I remembered reading Longfellow in eighth grade. I could still recite chunks of *Paul Revere's Ride*.

Putting the book back on the shelf, I wondered how many first editions were lurking in the library. Tristan might need a book specialist. I could search the Internet for rough estimates of values, but I'm not sure that would be the best use of my time.

This room alone would take ages, and I still had so much to accomplish in the study, and then there were other places in the house that I hadn't yet seen. I went back to the table. On top of it was Octavia's sketchbook. Petroc must have come in here after we had spoken about it. Carefully lifting the sketchbook, I looked at the books beneath and the other nearby items. All of it was surprising. The stack consisted of children's books. Had Helen or Tristan shifted anything in here since last week? Maybe Tristan had been searching for something. That made more sense. I picked up the sketchbook and left the library for another day.

Tristan came out of the billiard room with a scowl on his face. He looked me up and down and his glance stopped at the book in my hand. "Surely that old thing doesn't have any value?"

I resisted the urge to clutch it to my chest. Instead I opened it to the first watercolour. "That painting alone has value. I am not an art expert, but I do know that unscrupulous people looking for a quick buck cut this type of sketchbook up and sell the artwork individually, thereby destroying a valuable time capsule. The separate pieces earn far more than the book kept whole."

"Great. How many paintings in that one?"

"No."

"No? Surely you're not telling me I haven't the right to sell what is mine?"

I glared at him, then turned and walked away. He couldn't be Petroc's son, not with that attitude.

Helen looked up from the sink as I came into the kitchen.

"You're a good girl."

I tilted my head to the side and studied her. "That's a funny comment."

"No, you are."

"Well, thank you." Helen looked frail. She'd lost a lot of weight in a short time, and she seemed to have shrunk in height as well as volume.

She put the kettle on. "I'll make us a nice cup of tea."

"Helen, I'll do it."

"Out of my kitchen."

"Yes, ma'am. I'll go and cut some flowers for the house."

"Good idea."

I grabbed the secateurs and slipped out the door. There was the promise of rain in the air, and I hoped that it would be fulfilled. This summer had been too dry for the farmers. I walked along the bed of roses. The first flush was long past, but they were still producing blooms. I snipped a few for the kitchen table.

I stopped when I heard the doorbell ring.

"Judith, can you see who that is?" Helen called from the kitchen.

"Sure." I dashed around the outside to the front of the house, where there was a delivery van. "Good morning. Can I help?"

"I have two items for Pengarrock House. I need a signature."

I opened the front door, walked in and placed the roses and the secateurs on the table. I glanced behind me and found Helen.

"I'll sign for them." She rubbed her hands on her apron.

"Could you give me a hand with these?" the man asked.

We shifted them into the hall and I wondered if they were paintings, as the only time I'd seen crates this shape were when we'd moved house.

150

Helen looked the items up and down. "We'd best leave them here until Tristan reappears. Don't think you and I could shift them alone, and we don't know where he wants the damn things." She marched off. Helen's mood certainly hadn't improved since the funeral two days ago. As each day passed she said less and less, and I was worried about her. Tristan didn't provide much in the way of conversation, either. I was reminded of my last few days on the Cape.

I was in the study when I heard Tristan curse as he collided with the boxes. I turned and looked out into the hall to see him rubbing his shin.

"What the hell is this?"

Helen joined him. "I haven't any idea. I thought you'd been shopping. I was hoping you were thinking of redecorating."

"You wish, Helen, you wish."

Tristan turned his attention to the labels on the crates. Curiosity got the better of me and I went over to them. I couldn't figure him out. In many ways he was the image of Petroc, and I longed to see that same wicked smile appear on Tristan's face, but it seemed permanently frozen in a scowl.

"When did these arrive?" he asked.

"About ten minutes ago." Helen stood with her feet set apart.

"Do you know who Lady Rutherford is? A friend of Dad's?"

"Never heard of her." Stiff-backed, Helen turned and began to walk away.

"Bloody hell, stop, Helen. I know you don't want me to sell Pengarrock, but I am, so let's just be civil here."

"Fine."

I'd never heard one word have quite so much meaning. With a few backward steps I tried to slip out of the hall. I didn't belong here, and I didn't need to be pulled into someone else's battle.

"Judith, don't leave. I'll need your help with these." He placed a hand on the larger of the two crates.

"Sure." I walked slowly back. My glance darted between them. Helen was spitting mad. Everything about her was tense. Tristan seemed cool, but I wasn't so sure as I heard an exasperated sigh when I moved closer to him.

He pushed the top of the largest crate towards me and picked up the heavy end. "I think we'll take them to the drawing room, where there will be enough space and better light."

It was awkward, but we managed to reach the room without any damage.

"I thought you might need these." Helen thrust a few tools at him.

"Thanks." He took them and set to work opening the larger crate. As the hammer hit the screwdriver, I hoped the contents weren't fragile. I tried not to flinch with each strike.

"Looks like a crate for a painting." I strived to look and sound more relaxed than I was.

"We'll know in a second." Tristan wedged the screwdriver in to pry off the front. "I think you're right."

152

A letter dropped to the floor and I stooped to retrieve it, tossing it onto the sofa before I helped him to lift the painting from the box.

"Ready for the unveiling?" He placed his hands on the covering.

"Don't keep us in suspense." Helen came closer.

I noted the change in the atmosphere of the room. Excitement sparked between the three of us. The wrapping fell away and both Helen and I gasped. I wasn't sure if I'd ever seen a more beautiful woman. The painter had loved her with every brushstroke. It was at once perfectly serene and stunningly sensual. Light reflected off the woman's cheeks, caressing them before moving down to the tops of her breasts. I swallowed.

"Who is she?" Helen whispered. "Although I know she must be a Trevillion."

"Why do you say that?" Tristan held the painting upright.

"She's wearing the Trevillion sapphire." Helen said.

"That bloody thing." Tristan ran his hand through his hair.

"Most of the ladies of Pengarrock wear the sapphire in their portraits." Helen stared at Tristan.

I was almost spellbound by the beauty of the woman and the painting.

"Is it?" He leaned in to study the woman with the jewel.

"Haven't you ever looked around you?" Helen grumbled.

"Clearly I haven't." Tristan shrugged.

"You can say that again." She coughed.

I wondered if I should remain silent and let them have it out. It was not my fight, so I ducked behind the canvas. "It's Lady Clarissa Trevillion, 1845."

"The one that disappeared?" Helen took a closer look at the painting.

"I don't think there was another." I searched the back of the canvas.

"Anything else?" Tristan's voice was quiet.

"No. Just the painter's name, Frederick Peters. The other crate must be a painting too." I watched Tristan leave the room while I thought about the name Frederick Peters.

Returning from the hall with the smaller crate, Tristan said, "Well, any bets on who this is?"

"Another Trevillion?" I moved around to the front of the painting of Lady Clarissa to enjoy its beauty. The work glowed. Her eyes were warm and sensual, yet almost laughing. Her mouth was full and hinted at a smile. I felt she was about to share a secret.

"Full marks for your intuition, but is it another portrait of the same woman, or someone else?" Tristan asked.

"Don't keep us waiting." Helen lifted the wooden top with him and pulled the bubble wrap away.

"What incredibly serious eyes she has. They remind me a bit of yours, Tristan, when you were young and delightful." Helen tapped his arm.

"And I'm not now?" He raised an eyebrow.

"Most certainly not now." Helen walked to the back of the painting and bent low to read it. "This is Miss

Octavia Trevillion, 1845. Same painter, Frederick Peters."

"What's wrong with you, Judith? You look like you've seen a ghost." Tristan smiled.

"Feels that way, having seen some of Petroc's research and the sketchbook." I swallowed. Was Frederick Peters *Lord* Frederick Peters?

Tristan glanced at me. "I see — his treasure hunt."

"Well, he has done a great deal of research."

"All a waste of time. However, the sapphire would be a good find."

Helen stepped away from the paintings. "You'd still sell Pengarrock." She strode out of the room.

I turned to Tristan. "What did your father tell you about the treasure?"

"Not a lot or, more truthfully, I wasn't listening. But I gather he thought finding it would solve all Pengarrock's problems." He shook his head while staring at the paintings. "He was such a dreamer." His phone rang.

I opened my mouth to say that Petroc wasn't so much a dreamer as a visionary, but Tristan had answered his phone and left the room. All Petroc's work and the conclusions he had made were founded in careful research. Would his search for the treasure have been any different?

CHAPTER
TWELVE

The light had faded on the river but the sky was still a warm blue as I stood leaning against the wall on the kitchen patio. This afternoon, as I'd worked, I'd lectured Tristan, and myself. It was a shame he hadn't been there to hear what I had said to him. In the course of the argument, I'd decided to leave. I couldn't remain and assist Tristan in what he was doing. Had he no heart? I looked at the house, and I knew I didn't want to leave. And I'd made something like a promise to Helen. Besides, what would I go back to?

Life was good here, despite Tristan. Pengarrock was a beautiful place to be. This evening the air was softly scented with honeysuckle, and a pale sliver of moon was just appearing on the horizon.

"Do you want to eat, or are you just going to stare at the view?" Tristan called from the kitchen.

"Tough choice." I walked inside. "My stomach is growling, so I guess I choose eat."

"Wise stomach." He smiled and, again, I was surprised. He could be pleasant when it suited him.

"Could we eat outside?"

"Well, yes." He frowned.

"Don't you like eating out?" I piled a tray with plates and food.

"Yes, but I haven't done it here in a very long time."

"Good time to start again on such a beautiful evening."

"If you say so." He shrugged.

"I do." I laid the table while Tristan fetched the wine. It looked so intimate; just the two of us, cold chicken and delicious salads with a chilled bottle of white wine. Looks could be deceiving.

"Pass the chicken, please." Tristan held his hand out.

"It's delicious."

"A bit more wine?" he asked.

Could the conversation get much more stilted? "Yes, that would be nice. That rocket salad is lovely."

"Yes." Tristan looked into his glass.

A new topic was required. I was full of questions, but didn't know him well enough to ask them. He had to have some of Petroc in him. Something in his eyes told me that there was more to him than met the eye; he appeared to be a spoilt, successful ladies' man thinking of no one but himself. I longed to know why he was selling Pengarrock.

The phone rang, and I sighed with relief. Sipping my wine, I thought of what we could talk about.

Tristan returned. "That is so typical of here."

"What is?"

"That was a tenant wanting to know when the new drains were going in."

"That's a problem?" I rested my head on my hands.

157

"Yes. I've been through all the paperwork on the estate, and there's no record of new drains being needed anywhere that I can remember."

"Maybe I'll find something in the study on Petroc's desk. I haven't touched that yet."

"No luck. I cleared the desk of the few estate items. The same with the filing cabinets."

"Nothing?"

"Just junk."

"Hey. I resent that remark." I tapped the table with my hand and laughed.

Tristan's green eyes lightened in colour and the creases beside them when he smiled made him seem human.

"The estate manager?" I suggested.

"He hasn't mentioned it."

"New to the job?"

"Only been doing it forty years."

I chuckled. "Still learning, then?"

"Evidently." Tristan's laughter was like a breath of fresh air. He relaxed. Maybe I could ask some of the questions that were on my mind.

"Your family's had the estate a long time."

"From time immemorial."

I raised an eyebrow.

"Well, hundreds of years, and I never paid any attention and clearly they never did, because it is in such a mess."

"Really? Do you think if you'd paid attention earlier you might not be having these problems now?"

"Been talking to Helen, have you?"

"Yes and no."

He gave a dry laugh. "Right now you are bedazzled by the beauty of the Helford River in summer, but let me tell you it can suck the soul out of you. My advice is to leave here as quickly as you can."

I studied him. "That sounds a bit harsh. Care to tell me why you hate it so?"

"No." The smile left his eyes.

"Didn't think you would, but I thought it was worth a try."

"Good try, but no."

"I get the point." I glanced up at Pengarrock, wanting to know its history but Tristan, if he knew, was not going to answer my questions.

He stood up and walked to the low wall surrounding the terrace. I shivered. The temperature had dropped quickly. It reminded me of summer nights on Cape Cod; sweater almost always required. I stood to clear, and Tristan bumped into me, doing the same.

"Sorry."

"Sorry." His glance caught mine. I held my breath for a second.

"Let me." He picked the fork off the ground.

"I was the klutz," I stammered.

"Not at all." He looked at me again and I turned away. Tristan was trouble in more ways than one.

"Let me clear up. I'm sure you're tired, or have work you want to do." As he wrestled the plates out of my hands, his fingers brushed mine. He stopped. I backed away.

"Ah, yes, I'll just grab a few things from the study." I was a bit breathless.

"See you in the morning." His voice followed me to the study, where I picked up Petroc's journal for 2009. I went to my room, and my ineptitude with men came abruptly to the fore. John's email was in my inbox. I needed to set John free, and me too. I just wasn't sure how.

I reached for the glass of water beside the bed. My throat was parched and I felt clammy. The vivid dreams were just fading, and I shook my head to clear them but I couldn't erase the images of John at the altar looking for me. A glass wall stood between us, and I kept shouting and banging on the glass to get his attention and try to explain. No wonder I was exhausted.

Flinging the covers off, I stood and stretched. John's email haunted me. I didn't need to think about it again. I opened my computer and began an email.

Dear John,

Thank you for your email.

Oh, God that was dire. I deleted it.

John,

I love you too, but don't know what I want any more.

That was better, but still sucked. I backspaced.

John,

I'm confused

That wasn't true. I closed the lid and went to brush my teeth. I would try and write after I'd had some caffeine. One glance in the mirror was enough to frighten the life out of me. Dark circles underscored my eyes. Not a good look.

"Nightmares do wonders for the complexion," I spoke to the mirror then left the bathroom. With my notebook and Petroc's journal, I sat by the window. The light was creeping into the sky and the sun would soon rise over the bay. I caressed the soft leather of the journal before I flipped through the pages to assess their professional or academic value.

The entry dated 2 January 2009 began:

Back from London. Christmas spent there never satisfies but Tristan will not come to Pengarrock. Contact made with Lady Rutherford. The work begins on the daffs tomorrow.

So Petroc had been in touch with Lady Rutherford. That might explain the arrival of the paintings, but nothing else. There must be more in his notes or journals. He seemed to have spent a great deal of time searching for the sapphire in one way or another. I glanced down at the notebook.

The twisted branches of the sessile oak
Bare, gnarled
Reached to the water
Still, reflective

I looked up from the page with the image clear in my mind, swiftly to be replaced by one of the headlands on the north side of the river. They were looming less as the sunlight began to pick out their features. A single sailboat made its way out to Falmouth Bay. I hadn't been sailing in ages. The urge to be on the water swamped me, but I reminded myself I was here to work and not on vacation.

Restless, I stood and went downstairs, where I caught Tristan prowling in the front hall.

"You're up early." I smiled at him, noting the overnight bag in his hand.

"Yes." He stopped for a second before going through the door. "Off to London. I expect you to be well on your way to telling me what all that crap is worth when I return."

I tensed, and had no time to reply. Instead I listened to the loud crunching of gravel as he disappeared from view down the drive. Did he think I could assess his father's collection in a few days? He was mad. I closed the front door and wandered towards the kitchen, still clutching Petroc's journal.

"Hi, Helen. Didn't expect to see you here this early."

"Yes, well, I wanted to talk to Tristan, and suspected he wouldn't hang around now that the funeral is over."

"Oh, I hadn't realised he was going away."

"Yes." She disappeared into the garden.

I had sympathy for anything Helen might encounter this morning. I wasn't sure that she was right, though. It was more than money that was driving Tristan to sell his heritage; I just hadn't figured out what it was. Would money be enough to make anyone throw all this away? A woman might, if he loved her enough and she really hated it. Did he have someone? If he did, why hadn't she come to the funeral? Funerals made people behave oddly in my experience. Every emotion is heightened, raw. I thought of how my parents and I were when Rose died. We were all like touchpaper. Helen needed to cut Tristan some slack, and he her.

Last night I'd seen a different side of Tristan, a rather more pleasant one. He wasn't totally devoid of Petroc's charm. I was pleased about that. And he had both his mother's and his father's good looks.

The lawnmower whirred, and I peered out of a window on my way to the study. The gardener was tying up a rambling rose. *Rose*. It was time for me to let go and move on. Her death couldn't remain the defining event in my life.

Unlike the top of Petroc's simple pedestal desk, its drawers were immaculate judging from the quick peek I took into each one. Was this due to Tristan's recent search, or had Petroc gone against type? I sat in his chair and waited. Waited for what, I wasn't sure, but that sense of expectation lingered. The top of faded leather, marked with ink and stained with cup circles, told a story of hours working here. My fingers could

163

pick out indented words. What had his last thoughts been? I looked up to the view. From this angle, the mouth of the river was framed and I could clearly see the buoy for August Rock. That riddle had faced him every day.

I opened the centre drawer and found the usual suspects: ink cartridges, stationery and a stapler. I picked up a sheet of the paper. In the top corner, in clear black print, it read:

Petroc Trevillion
Pengarrock
Manaccan
Cornwall

"May you rest in peace." I put the paper back in the drawer and closed it. The little clock ticked away. I hadn't wound it in a few days. Tristan must have. I left the desk in search of my notebook. Why was I so reluctant to go through the desk? Why did I feel uneasy? I was being stupid. I sat again and pulled out the top right-hand drawer. A manila folder lay on top. When I took it out, a photocopy of a newspaper story from the *West Briton* 1846 fell out.

Severe Sudden Storm Wrecks Yacht and Kills All

31st August, 1846
On Saturday last, a violent and sudden storm caught the yacht *Columbia* as she left the safety of Falmouth. The yacht was smashed against the

Gedges, locally known as August Rock. The storm was so fierce that nothing could be done to save the passengers and crew. For days following the storm, eyewitnesses spoke of its severity and of the lightning that made the sky blaze, illuminating the scene as if it was noon. Bodies and debris are still being found along the shores of the Helford and as far away as the Lizard. Known to be aboard the vessel were her captain, Zachariah Henderson, and her owner, Lord Frederick Peters, a member of the Royal Academy.

I jumped up. So he was the portrait painter. I opened my computer and searched for Peters. Instantly his style was recognisable, but in the list of his works there was no mention of the portraits. Strange. I put the photocopy back into the file and looked at the rest of the contents, which were more articles relating to the wreck. A photo of the memorial stone to the lost souls of the *Columbia* was the last thing in the file. I flipped it over for details of where and when it was taken, but there were none. Petroc had left no notes on the copies or in the file. Flicking through again, I saw that everything was in meticulous date order. This was unusual. All the other papers I'd been through were filed in order of relevance, but this was strictly by date.

The next file in the drawer was all about Lord Frederick Peters, RA. It too was in chronological order, and there were no notations. This was not the way Petroc worked. He would have sorted these cuttings in order of importance, not date. He would have made notes, if not in the margins then on slips of paper, sharing his thoughts. What was all this meticulous research for? Did he really believe the Trevillion sapphire could still be at August Rock? Surely if the boat had gone down in August 1846 and the jewels weren't recovered then, they were lost for ever to the strong tides and currents. I just couldn't see how something could still be there, but maybe I was wrong. I hadn't seen the reef personally.

The next file contained information on the Trevillion sapphire. There were copies of the various paintings with the chatelaines of Pengarrock wearing it. At some point the setting for the stone had been changed from the one Mary had worn. The final article was about large gemstones, especially those that had "disappeared". If a sapphire of that size showed up, then the world would know about it, unless it was re-cut into several smaller stones. The next file confirmed my thoughts. Petroc had researched smaller stones and the timing of their appearance.

Doubt filled me as I noted down the contents of the files and closed the drawer. The pieces of the story as I knew them didn't fit together.

Fog swirled as I set off down the drive to meet Helen and JC. It softened the edges of the stables, and if there hadn't been a satellite dish on the roof it could have been 1846. Lady Clarissa intrigued me. What had happened to her? There had to be more information on her.

The mist muffled all sounds, including the low grumble of a tractor. It felt far away; the whole world

166

felt that way. The trees were just dark shapes against the sky. I knew what they were because I'd seen them before, but what would I have thought if this was my first sight of them? They were threatening, blocking out what little sky could be seen. It was only a few weeks off the summer solstice and there should be daylight until late, yet with the mist it was artificially dark.

I needed to go home. It was the only way to face up to what I'd done. Was I really needed here any more? Did it matter what happened to Petroc's work, or to Pengarrock? Tristan was going to sell the lot, so might I be better off not knowing what happened? And be happier not being a part of the process, instead of aiding it?

With each step towards Helen's house, I knew this was the right thing to do. Tomorrow I would clean up the work I had achieved, contact Tristan and tell him to find someone else to do his dirty work. I would not be a part of the destruction of Pengarrock.

"There you are, my dear, what terrible weather! And who would have thought it would come after such a beautiful day?" By their gate, Helen waited with JC at her side.

"Evening." JC bowed his head and began walking. This was the third time I'd met JC, and the fourth word I'd heard him speak. Living with Helen I doubted he had much of chance to get a word in.

"How was Truro?" I asked as I matched my stride to theirs. For such a short woman Helen moved at a remarkable pace.

"Fine." Helen bit out the word.

"That sounds like not fine." I turned to her and tried to read her expression.

"Hmmm."

JC chuckled. "Made her look at properties."

"Properties?" I frowned.

We came to the crossroads and headed down into the village. "Yes; we'll have no place to live soon, so himself thinks it's time for us to leave and move closer to Jenna and the kids in Devon."

"Truro is not close to Devon." JC picked up his pace.

"JC is from North Cornwall." Helen stated this as if that explained everything.

"Now Petroc's gone, and soon so will Pengarrock. Don't belong here now."

Helen sighed. "He's right, and it makes me so angry." We came to the door of the pub. "Tristan has no right to do this."

"Well, he does. It's his now." I dashed into the safety of the building and out of Helen's aim. I knew what she meant, but it was Tristan's estate to do with as he wished.

"His responsibility, his duty and his right. He forgets," Helen muttered. JC ordered the drinks and conversation switched to the people in the pub. Many faces were familiar now, yet I was still struggling with names.

"Judith, have you met Tamsin yet?" Helen pulled a smiling woman forward.

"Maybe." I held out my hand, trying to remember.

"Not sure if we have," said Tamsin. "What do you think of our corner of the world?"

"Amazing."

Tamsin smiled. "It is."

"Won't be for long, once the developer gets in." I didn't know who had spoken, but the voice was angry.

"Can you blame him? He hates the place, and all that money he'll get for it," said another.

"What about the cricket club? There's no bloody formal arrangement. I checked this afternoon."

"What did the will actually say, Helen?" All eyes turned to her.

"None of your business." She raised her chin and led me to a table. "I may be angry but I won't be pulled into this. I think Tristan is out of order, but he's mine." She'd spoken so softly I could barely hear her.

"He's one of us, but he's forgotten that because he was sent away. Poor Petroc thought it was for the best." She shook her head. "And now it's come to this, the village squabbling and everyone preparing for the worst. Just not right. Not what Petroc would have wanted. Right, tell me what you're having for dinner."

I scratched my head. "I haven't a clue." How could she switch gears like that?

"Fine. I'll order for you." She disappeared back to the bar and JC arrived at the table with a bottle of wine in his hands.

"I'm worried about Helen," I said as JC sat down.

"Me too, but there's nothing we can do to change her."

Before I could say any more she was back at the table. As she sank onto the chair, she appeared smaller than ever. "As soon as probate's done in a few months, life here will change for ever."

Helen was short of breath as we walked up from the village to the crossroads. JC frowned at her and I wondered if she'd been doing too much for the funeral and its aftermath.

"Are you all right, my dear?" JC placed a hand on her arm to slow her down as we came to the signpost at the crossroads.

Helen nodded but then said, "I don't think that curry has agreed with me." She looked clammy. "I'm not myself, all of a sudden. I feel all faint."

JC caught her before she hit the ground. In my head, I ran through the basic first aid that I'd learned years ago when I qualified to be a lifeguard, and I didn't think she was suffering from food poisoning. My instincts were saying only one thing.

"JC, she's having a heart attack. Put her into the recovery position." I helped him lay her carefully on the ground and checked her breathing. "Helen, can you hear me? If you can, can you cough, please?"

There was no air coming from her nose or mouth. I looked at her chest. Nothing. I threw my phone at JC. "Call for help." And I rolled her onto her back and began CPR. Pengarrock was not going to lose another resident if I could help it.

CHAPTER
THIRTEEN

My eyes burned. It had been a long night of waiting for news on Helen. It had all been touch and go. I'd driven JC to the hospital and then he'd sent me home, telling me I should sleep. That proved impossible, but I finally sat down and read Aunt Agnes' letter properly. That provided some distraction, but worryingly it had mentioned that Dad was away. Away? He never went anywhere without Mother. At ninety-four, maybe my great-aunt was getting a little muddled.

News from the hospital was that, although stable, Helen was not doing as well as she should be. They were keeping her in the intensive care unit for the time being. JC sounded exhausted. I was pleased that their daughter, Jenna, had arrived from Devon so that JC had someone with him.

Trying to reach Tristan last night had been an exercise in frustration. His phone was turned off, and when I was able to reach him it was clear he hadn't been alone. I still felt embarrassed by the whole thing. But he had rung several times since and had left messages, sounding truly worried, which redeemed him a little in my eyes. I didn't buy his excuse that his phone had died. It was always with him, and he was always on it. His business was all-consuming.

The feeling that the discussion in the pub about Tristan selling Pengarrock had brought on Helen's heart attack wouldn't go away. It was all too much for her. Her whole life was being destroyed by Tristan's decision to sell. This wasn't just being laid off from a job. It was her life, and Tristan had been her charge. The pain must cut deep.

The dogs were barking, and I followed the sound to the drawing room. A bird had flown in and couldn't find its way out. It kept throwing itself repeatedly at the closed window. The dogs were adding to its distress. I set it free and looked at the damage caused by the droppings it had made. With a tissue from my pocket I wiped the shit off what turned out to be the family Bible. A pile of paper was wedged inside it. A glance revealed it to be a chapter from Petroc's book. The page I opened to showed Tallan and Octavia.

She was the end of the line for that branch of Trevillions. I flipped through the chapter; it traced the Trevillions' involvement with Pengarrock and the river. On the bottom of the last page Petroc had written in pencil:

"What secrets does the Helford hold?
Neither time nor tide reveals them."
August 1849

Where was this from? I took the chapter and carefully closed the Bible before heading back to the study.

172

Where had Petroc put the rest of the book? It wasn't in here, and I hadn't found it in the billiard room.

I picked up the journal from 2009 and saw that Petroc had noted that in 1879 Pengarrock had moved one step closer to his line of Trevillions when Clarissa's husband died without further issue. Petroc wrote so beautifully of the estate, his work and his anguish at the lost relationship with his son. I wondered what had happened. Flipping the pages again, I discovered a folded note. Opening it, I recognised the stationery. It was Imogen's, and she had written in purple ink a list of names.

Lady Rutherford
Frederick Peters
Lady Clarissa
Octavia

And one object, which was circled.

Sapphire

Then, at the bottom of the page, she had written "a quest for Tristan". There was a connection, but I couldn't see it yet.

A sleepless night and a frustrating day were made better by taking the dogs for a walk. Now a long soak in the tub was what I needed. It was later than I thought. These long evenings were deceptive; it didn't feel like ten. The sky was still light out through the bathroom window.

I had so many things to do, but I hated to leave the bath. It was the first one I'd ever found that was long enough for me to totally stretch out. Normally I'd get cold knees or feet or torso, but now I was immersed up to my neck. It was pure decadence, but my hunger would not let me linger any longer.

With one leg in the bath and the other out, I reached for my towel. Balancing carefully, I had my hand on it when the hairs on the back of my neck stood up. I was not alone. I pulled my other leg out of the bath and quickly wrapped myself in the towel. I could see my robe on the bed. But the noise was close at hand. I had no time to grab it.

Scanning the bathroom for a weapon, I spied an old plunger behind the toilet. Grabbing it, I prepared to attack. I raised the plunger over my head as the footsteps neared the door.

"Judith, are you there?"

The door opened, and before I could stop the motion, I had hit Tristan over the head. My towel dropped to the floor with the force of my attack and, catching the look of horror on Tristan's face, I dropped to my knees to collect both it and my modesty. I was blushing from head to toe, which the white towel only served to emphasise once it was back in place.

Tristan backed towards the door, rubbing his head. I'd given him as good a thump as one could with such a useless weapon.

174

"Tristan, I'm sorry. I had no idea it was you. I just heard a noise."

"Do you always greet thieves in the nude with a plunger?" By now he was smiling, and I laughed.

"Why, yes, I find they are so shocked that they can't move and I can run away."

"You've tested this?"

"Oh yes, many times."

"Right, well, that must have been on American thieves, for I think British thieves might react in a different way."

I died inside as Tristan's glance took in all the flesh still exposed by the too small towel. "I'll leave you and go and find a drink and a bite to eat, then."

"Can I join you? I haven't eaten either, and I'm starved."

"Certainly."

"I'll just get dressed."

"Well, you can stay in the towel if you like, but you might want to leave the plunger behind."

I threw it at his retreating form. His laughter echoed around me. Well! That went well. Hitting your employer over the head and displaying personal nudity. *Well done, Jude.*

Dressing in jeans and a light sweater, I debated how I should handle this. No apology could hide my embarrassment, so I decided I wouldn't mention it unless he did. I squared my shoulders and walked into the kitchen.

"How do you feel about an omelette?"

"Sounds good. Can I help?"

"Yes, pour yourself a glass of wine and sit down. You still look a bit shaken."

"Thanks." I filled my glass, but knew my voice said more than I wanted it to.

"You must have been scared out of your wits, thinking there was someone in the house when you knew you were on your own. I should have rung. I was focused on getting to the hospital."

"You've been?"

"Yes."

"How is she?"

"Improving slowly. I was able to visit her with JC and Jenna."

I watched his competent motions as he made the omelettes. His ease at cooking surprised me, as did the fact that he had dropped everything after I'd finally reached him with news of Helen's heart attack. I hadn't thought he would come rushing down. He'd only left for London yesterday.

My glance followed his fingers deftly chopping chives. They moved with ease on the handle of the knife, completely skilful. He had lovely hands. The wine must be going to my head.

Tristan turned and placed a plate in front of me. "One omelette, hopefully to your liking."

"I'm so hungry, anything would be. The last thing I ate was hours ago."

He filled both glasses. Raising his, he looked directly into my eyes. "Yes, you do look voracious."

I blinked. If I was right, he was flirting with me.

My head was full of Latin verbs. I'm not sure what triggered them, but I'd been reading Petroc's journal again last night before falling asleep. Was it the odd Latin plant name that had sent me back to the classroom? With my computer on my lap, I was perched on the wall outside the kitchen.

"Good morning."

"What?" I jumped. "You gave me a start. I didn't think you'd be up for hours after the day you had yesterday."

"Woke with the sun. Is there any spare coffee?" Tristan's hair was still damp. He must be just out of the shower.

"No, don't think so, but it would be cold if there was."

"Is that a not-so-subtle hint that you would like more?"

"Yes, please." I listened to the noises from the kitchen while staring off into the distance. Durgan was just visible on the other side of the river.

"Did you feed the dogs?" He handed me a cup.

I looked down at Gin. "He may be trying to convince you that I short-changed him, but I promise you I haven't."

"Gin has always been a bit greedy when it comes to his food." Tristan tapped his thigh. The dog came over for a scratch behind the ears.

"It still fascinates you?" Tristan looked across the river.

"Yes."

"You've been here long enough to have had your fill."

"I don't think I could ever have enough of this view. Every time I look up from the files it alters, but each glimpse is as beautiful as the last."

"My father has bewitched you."

"You don't feel it?" I looked at him closely.

"No."

I shook my head, then scanned the distant horizon, noting the large tanker in Falmouth Bay. It was the perfect early summer morning. "Your father loved this place. He wrote so passionately about it."

"It's what he lived for."

I noted the change in his voice. "For you too." I paused. "I take it that you and your father did not get on."

"No. We got on in a way. Petroc wasn't too good with children, not until he could have an intellectual discussion."

"He was distant?"

"No, I don't think that describes him. Absorbed would be a better word." He ran his hand through his hair, messing up the slight curls that had started appearing as it dried. Tristan must have been a beautiful child.

"Tough on a small boy. I take it you weren't into intellectual discussions."

"Not early enough to build any real relationship. By the time I was interesting to him, I was at university and I wasn't interested in him."

"Ouch. Did you share anything?" I asked, hoping there was something.

"Oh, yes." Tristan whistled and both dogs came running from the kitchen.

"Gin and Rum?"

"Yes." He paused to pat them. "Their predecessors as well, Whisky and Stormy."

"Stormy not Brandy?"

"No, Stormy as in Dark and Stormy, the rum and ginger-beer cocktail."

"Did it suit the dog's temperament?" I stroked Rum's head.

"Yes, actually it did. Stormy was Rum's mother." Tristan smiled.

"What did you study at university?" I decided to try a different tack.

"Chemistry."

"Really?" I leaned back. He didn't fit my image of a scientist.

"Yes. It was as far from my father's world of history as I could get."

"True. You're not in the sciences now?"

"No. Never intended to stay in them, but I liked the clear-cut subject matter. No waffling around trying to interpret the past. No dodgy old volumes, but chemicals and reactions."

"What do you do now?"

"I have an investment company."

I threw my head back and laughed. "No learned volumes, just cold, hard cash and dodgy deals."

"Yes." He bowed his head, hiding his smile. "It's still taking the right parts and mixing them together to get the correct outcome."

"The new chemistry, then."

"Yes. People chemistry. You need to get the right people together as well as the right money. The deals won't succeed unless all the components fit to make the new venture."

"So you use people like elements." I suggested.

"You could say that."

"You read them well enough to know how they'll react to the others?"

"Yes."

I stood and picked up Petroc's journal. "Funny; I always regarded people as too volatile and unstable. Books were a safer bet."

"Each to his own." Tristan's phone rang and he looked at it. "Far East."

I watched him walk towards the cannons, wondering what kind of life he had.

I parked the car, grabbed the bags of groceries, then walked into the kitchen and wrote down *Boat* on a Post-it note. That way I would remember to ask Tristan at dinner. If the weather was going to stay this beautiful, I really wanted to get out on the water. It must seem a completely different place from the river. As so many boats used it, it must be reasonably safe for sailing, despite the vast number of shipwrecks that were referred to in Petroc's research. The only apparent

180

threat near the Helford was August Rock, and that was well marked.

Each day, walking the dogs, I'd found the beach filled with families. They were a jovial lot. The kids raced in and out of the water. Yesterday it had been so warm I'd planned to take a swim in the early evening, but I only managed one foot. There was no way that any more of my body was going in. The water's icy fingers had grabbed me, and I'd quickly pulled my foot out. Give me the warmth of Nantucket Sound any day.

Tristan would be back soon from Helston. We'd developed a good working routine over the past couple of days. After the dreadful evening when I'd hit him over the head, I hadn't been sure how things were going to go, but it was fine. In fact, it was more than fine. I looked forward to our conversations, and seeing how he cared for Helen made me think there was more to him than I'd first assumed.

I pulled out my notes. Petroc had made reference to a book on the history of Trellowarren as if the book was in his possession. I'd have to make a quick search in the library. Petroc's notes had left me hanging on something that was in this particular book. It must be in the house somewhere, along with his manuscript, which still hadn't appeared.

I bit the end of my pen and flipped through the sheet where I'd been keeping a secondary back-up list. What I'd catalogued so far would be quite valuable to any university, but putting a monetary amount on it thus far would prove difficult. I had yet to get to the books in the study, let alone the library or his bedroom. But I reminded myself that I'd only been here a short time.

I loved how the trees grew tall in the valley down to the beach, and the way the ones on the high ground were stunted and turned by the howling wind. The branches twisted like the pipe cleaners I used to play with as a child. Despite the summer sun, I could tell when the wind came rattling through that the area could be fierce in the face of blasting winds.

The phone rang. "Pengarrock."

"Jude?"

"John?" I sank into a chair.

"Yes."

I'd forgotten his voice. "How are you?"

"Missing you."

This was not good. He must have called Barbara for the number.

"I was wondering if I could come and see you."

Standing abruptly, I banged my head on the lintel above the stove. "Shit." I rubbed the spot and felt a bump forming. "Sorry, it's not you. I hit my head."

"Oh." He paused. "Look, I need to see you." His voice wavered.

"John, I . . ." I paused. John and all the mess I'd left behind suddenly felt a bit too close. "Cornwall's a long way from London. You can't just pop down for a day."

"It's only three hundred miles. I need to see you."

"I don't think that's a good idea." I played with my bracelet. I didn't want him here.

"You owe me this, Jude."

I took a deep breath. I couldn't argue with that. I did owe him. "OK, but I don't think this is a good idea at all."

"Trust me, it is. It will be so good to be with you."

"Don't get your hopes up." I closed my eyes. I needed to be gentle. "When were you thinking of coming?"

"This weekend. Does that work?"

Everything in me screamed no, but I had no plausible reason to refuse. "OK. You'll need to find someplace to stay."

"Sorted."

I sighed. It was far from sorted. As I put down the phone, I hugged Gin to me. I should have written to John when I had the chance. He must have taken my lack of response as a positive.

CHAPTER
FOURTEEN

"Hello?" I called as I came into the hall followed by my faithful companions, Gin and Rum. My hair was wild again, and I kept pushing away the dark curls, which fell in the middle of my forehead. I wished I could wear it short, but that just made it worse.

"In here." Tristan spoke from the drawing room.

"When did you get back? They were waiting for you, but they were far too impatient." I stopped in the doorway as I watched Tristan remove his suit jacket. He turned to me and I was reminded of my cavalier on the stairs. It was the cut of his jaw and the gleam in his eyes. A lump formed in my throat. He was far too good-looking.

"Were they?" He looked at the two dogs and they shuffled towards him with tails wagging.

"Yes. Tonight the beach was empty. However, we did have one companion down there. A seal."

"A seal?"

"I thought I was seeing things, but I went out onto the rocks to get a closer look. It was a seal. A big one."

"Haven't seen a seal in the river since I was a kid." Tristan smiled.

"Well, there was one tonight. He was enjoying the quiet beach, like me. The dogs didn't notice him, thank God. They were more interested in exploring the little caves." I collapsed onto the sofa and looked at my red toenails. It was one part of me I'd kept perfectly groomed. Mother would be proud — not. My jeans were rolled up and slightly damp. I looked a mess, and it was bliss. No pressure. What was required of me here was my brain, not my social skills or looks.

"Tea?"

"Please. Shall we have it outside?"

"Can't keep you from the view, can I?"

"No."

"Didn't think so."

Gin and Rum followed closely as I walked through the French windows. With bare feet I tiptoed along the gravel path to get to a bench, where I sprawled. I could just see the reflection in the window of Tristan, who had pulled off his tie and left it on the sofa with his files.

"How was Helen?" Tristan handed me a mug.

"Looking much better. I'm waiting to have an update from Jenna later. She thinks they may let Helen out this weekend, but I think it may be too soon."

"I'd hoped to get there this afternoon, but I got sidetracked at the bank."

"Success?" I asked.

Tristan coughed. "No, I wouldn't describe today as a success."

"That good?"

He took a deep breath. "It was a day of dead ends. I spent it ploughing through documents to find out that they had never been completed. The finalised ones are somewhere else, but where? The solicitors thought the papers could possibly be lodged with the bank. The bank said they didn't have them, but that they would check again as they had moved their safe deposits from Helston to Penzance a year and a half ago."

I laughed.

"It wasn't funny."

"The expression on your face is."

"Thanks."

"A pleasure." I smiled and studied the activity on the river. "Tristan, do you have a boat?"

"Two, in fact."

"Where are they?"

"Good question."

"Oh."

"Just another thing to resolve. Dad hasn't used the boats for ages, so they're probably in a shed somewhere. Why were you asking?"

"I'd love to get out onto the river. Is there anyplace I can rent a small boat?"

"In St Anthony."

"OK." I remembered it well from Petroc's funeral. It seemed a long time ago, yet so recent at the same time. "You know the riddle of August Rock?"

"What on earth makes you ask about that?" He frowned. "'Not of the land, Not of the sea, Only visible, When August Rock sees'. It's an old children's rhyme, nothing more, and why my father spent any time, let alone money, on searching for lost treasure still angers me."

"Your father wanted to find it to save the estate."

"He could have done that with better management. Less time chasing dreams and more time on good husbandry. This place sucked the life and sense out of him."

The house phone rang and he ran to get it. What had happened to Tristan that he hated it so here? He had smiled when he heard about the seal. Before I could dwell on it any longer, Tristan returned with a slip of paper.

"Oh, by the way, John called. He wants you to ring back."

My heart stopped. "Thanks. I think I'll finish my tea first."

"That bad?"

"Maybe." I fell silent. The real world was closing in. "I'll go and start dinner." I paced the kitchen floor and then opened the fridge before slamming it shut. John was coming here. *Shit.*

Tristan walked through the kitchen door.

"Tristan?" I turned.

"Yes." His eyes became guarded.

"I know it's none of my business."

"But you will ask anyway." His mouth turned up into a wry smile that I rather liked.

"Why are you in such a rush to sell the estate? Why *are* you selling it?"

The light in his eyes went out. "I don't need it." He turned and walked out of the kitchen.

"I don't think you know what you need, Mr Trevillion." I announced to the silent kitchen. I looked at the ingredients in front of me. Well, he'd given me an answer, but it wasn't the answer I wanted. I didn't feel like cooking, and clearly Tristan wasn't coming back. I remembered Tamsin and picked up the phone.

Twenty minutes later I was standing at the bar of the Shipwright's Arms with a glass of wine in front of me. My shoulders relaxed. I'd left a salad in the fridge and a note on the table if Mr Trevillion reappeared, looking for food.

"Bad day at the office, then?" Tamsin smiled.

"You could say that." I made a face.

"Not the office, just your boss, perhaps?"

I started to nod then stopped. I was livid with Tristan, but the world didn't need to know that, did they? Tristan couldn't see the forest for the damn trees, but it wasn't my problem. I was here to work, and that was all I needed to focus on. Mark walked through the door of the pub and smiled at me.

"Tamsin, why don't Mark and Tristan get on?"

"Why do you ask?" She placed her glass on the bar.

"Curiosity."

"The one that killed the cat?"

"Yes, 'fraid so." I shrugged.

"Be careful of that round here, my lover, you never know what you'll dig up." Tamsin's exaggeration of the Cornish accent made me smile.

"Is this the American?" A woman with her hand in a cast came up to us.

"This is Jude Warren, Linda."

188

"How's things up at Pengarrock? Auctioneers arrived yet?"

I opened my eyes wide. "No."

"Bet the atmosphere is weird with Tristan around."

I cleared my throat. "Different."

"I bet." She frowned, then smiled brightly. "Don't suppose you've any experience taking meeting minutes?"

I tilted my head. What a question. "I do. I used to help my mother on one of her charities."

"Wonderful. Would you be willing to give us a hand?" She waved her cast in the air. "Tomorrow is the final meeting before the village regatta, and I can't take notes. Could you fill in for me?"

I looked to Tamsin and she nodded.

"Sure. When and where?"

"My house." Tamsin took a sip of her wine.

Linda leaned forward. "Have Mark pick you up. We start at eight. See you then." She disappeared into the crowd of people standing at the bar.

"What have I just experienced?"

Tamsin laughed. "Experienced is exactly right. Actually the committee meetings are good fun, and you'll meet more people, which can't be a bad thing if you're planning to be around for any length of time."

I liked that idea, and wondered how I could make it happen.

I took the coastal path to St Anthony. I'd called the Chandlers that morning and found they had just the boat I needed to go exploring. The weather had turned cooler and was a bit overcast, but still lovely as I walked through the trees. Gin and Rum were not happy with me when I'd made them stay behind. Tristan was ensconced in the billiard room with the door shut. He seemed to live in there, always on the phone. Things did not seem to be going his way; nothing was moving on the probate, and I couldn't help thinking it served him right.

A regatta of gaff-rigged boats filled the bay. They reminded me of the Cotuit skiff we'd had when I was a child. It had been Dad's. He would love it here. I stopped walking. He would; but how would he know if I didn't tell him? I longed to share it with him. A quick text might break the silence; not that either parent used their cell phones much. Both only switched the damned things on when they wanted to make a call. Oh, how it annoyed me! No matter how many times I'd lectured them, they still kept them turned off. At least he'd get it when he next had the phone on, but would he reply? I hoped so.

I went up a hill and down to a cove, then on through a field, absorbing the beauty. I looked out to Falmouth and could just make out St Mawes. It was not as clear today, and the wind had died down a bit. I found Tamsin's words coming back to me.

Be careful of that round here, my lover, you never know what you'll dig up.

What would I find if I poked around Pengarrock some more? Why were Tristan and Mark so at odds? Tamsin wouldn't be drawn on it. I yawned. All night long I'd lain in bed listening to the howl of the wind moving the leaves on the trees. But it wasn't the sound of the wind that had kept me awake. It had been the late-night phone call from John. He'd booked a B and B, and would be down on Friday evening. Spending time with him was the last thing I wanted to do. I needed space and I didn't want to explain who John was. But I wasn't to be given any choice, as he was arriving soon.

My steps slowed as I tried to figure out how to get across a field filled with cows. They looked peaceful enough, but I wasn't quite sure of where I was going, even though I had walked this way with Petroc. The sign pointed across the field, but that meant going straight through the herd. Another sign pointed to a circular walk, and I decided a quick detour might be a good idea for circumnavigating the cows.

The sun broke through the clouds and lit up the stretch of water in front of me. Light bounced off the gentle waves rolling into Gillan Creek, and I stood on Dennis Head looking to the Nare. A short sail with an instructor would refresh my rusty memory. I'd last sailed eight years ago.

Deciding confidence was the best course of action with the cows, I strode with determination around them and made my way past the church to the waterside. The tide was on its way in and the beach was full of activity. I popped my head through the chandler's door. "Hello?"

A young man came out of the back room. "Can I help you?"

"I called this morning and booked a boat and an hour's lesson."

"You Jude?"

"Yes." I looked at the varied stock. On one wall beautiful nautical clothing tempted me, while the other catered to the more practical side of boating with charts, tide tables and flares.

"Hi, I'm Ollie, your instructor. You reserved a Wayfarer. Do you know them?"

"Well, I used to sail, and the description sounded familiar."

"Where are you from?" He walked to the register and picked up a cell phone while I eyed the cabinet filled with delicious-looking ice creams.

"Cape Cod."

"Really?"

"Do you know it?"

"Heard of it. How long are you here on holiday?"

"I'm not on holiday." I followed him along to the pontoon and watched him flag someone down in a motorboat.

"No?"

"No."

"Where are you staying then?" He turned his spotty face to me and grinned. I wondered if he was giving me the third degree for some reason, but looking at his smile I decided he was just being polite. "Hey, are you the Yank at Pengarrock?"

I paused. It's a small place, and I guessed everyone would know my business. No different from being at home.

"Yes."

"Well done for the quick moves on Helen. I hear she's doing much better."

I grinned. News spread quickly. "She is."

"Great. They're bringing the boat in now."

I was relieved to see it did indeed look familiar. No real surprises visible. No doubt Ollie would refresh my memory as we set off. From the water the headlands looked bigger and the houses smaller. The cliffs fell into the sea with chunks of rock strewn below them. As I studied the many coves that cut into Dennis Head, I wondered which one I had seen the orchids above. Several of the beaches showed evidence of landslides.

We sailed out past Nare Head towards Porthoustock.

"If you look closely, you can see how the geology changes here on the Lizard."

I peered at the rocks, noting the different colours and lines.

"It's what makes the Lizard different from the rest of Cornwall."

"How do you know so much about it?"

"I'm studying geology." He grinned and pointed to a cliff face in the distance. "Most of the rocks over there are schist, but you can see a lot of serpentine."

"Serpentine?"

"Yes, simply bits of the earth's upper mantle."

I raised my eyebrows.

"Mining it used to be big business in the Victorian age. Mostly used for small carvings and stuff."

He had me hooked, and once back on shore I quizzed him some more. I wondered if Petroc had any books on the Lizard peninsula's geology. I'd have to check. I leaped out of the Wayfarer, having spent a blissful time getting reacquainted with the jib and learning some of the quirks of sailing around the Helford. As I suspected, the area looked so different from the water.

"You'll be fine out on your own now. Enjoy." Ollie waved as I went up the road to the house and back to the reality of John coming here. I loved John. He was a good friend. Hell, I'd nearly married him, and up until now it had all seemed so far away.

I stopped to catch my breath at the top of the hill. Dennis Head was now behind me, and Falmouth was getting less visible in the increasing haze. The weather was supposed to remain dry over the weekend. At least that meant I could take John out on the river. It would be better if Tristan was going to London, but he hadn't mentioned it. I didn't want Tristan and John together. My failed wedding was my past, and it didn't belong here. I was different now. People took me seriously here, whereas on the Cape I was the Warren girl. Mother's shadow hadn't reached across the pond.

It was getting late, and I was getting tied in knots. It was Tristan's turn to cook tonight, so at least I didn't have to worry about that before the regatta meeting. But I might have to worry if he really looked in the study. It didn't appear as if I'd done anything.

Each day I thought I'd get through more, but I'd only fully sorted ten boxes. Petroc's mind worked in close detail. Even the smallest item got his full attention. Sometimes this led to great discoveries, but more often than not it led to delightful but insignificant detours.

My phone pinged and my mouth dried. Was it Dad?

Hi Jude
Been away filming. Just got back. Will email later.
Luv Soph x

It was lovely to hear from her, but it was Dad I longed to have contact with. What was going on at home? Their silence wasn't normal, and it wasn't right. How could I find out what was happening without getting on a plane?

I gathered up my purse, and Tristan looked up from the newspaper he'd been reading.

"Heading out?"

"Off to a meeting for the village regatta." I smiled.

"Don't get involved in life here." He closed the paper and stood up.

I ground my teeth before answering. "What I do in my off time is my business."

"True, but don't say you haven't been warned."

"Fine, but maybe you should try getting involved, and you might see a different side."

"There isn't a different side. This place is hopeless." He picked up the paper and walked out of the room.

That was telling me. I left the kitchen and marched up the drive. The setting sun's rays caught the new growth on the yew trees, intensifying its vivid green. A buzzard circled in slow loops above a field. I slowed my pace. Tristan. He had it all so wrong.

I looked down the drive and saw Mark chatting to JC. He hadn't quite refused to come up to the house, but I sensed I shouldn't push it. Yet he might be more forthcoming on why Tristan hated Pengarrock so much. Because they clearly disliked each other, Mark's take on it might not be the best. But it would be better than none.

"There she is. How's my girl?" JC asked.

"Good. How's Helen?"

"Stronger every day. It's the grandkids. They make you young." JC chuckled as a squeal arose from inside. "Duty calls." He waved and walked back into the house.

Mark smiled. "Good to see you. Heard you were sailing today."

"How did you know? No, don't answer that."

"So you've rented a boat. I could have loaned you one."

"You have one spare?"

"Yes. If you want to borrow it, it's there and underused, but it's not as big as a Wayfarer."

"Let's see how this week goes." *And this weekend with John.* "So where's Tamsin's house?" I got into Mark's car.

"Not far." He glanced at me. "Don't let them overwhelm you. They are a rowdy bunch."

"OK." We pulled up to a large farmhouse with light beaming out of tall Georgian windows. The place seemed to be heaving. A few teenage girls left as we walked in.

"Tamsin has three sons."

"Ah." I braced myself, but was enchanted by the beautiful sitting room with large sofas adorned with flowered cushions.

"Welcome." Tamsin came up to me and kissed me on the cheek. "We're all in the kitchen, away from the noise of the TV. They seem to be killing the entire population of the world up there with some game or other." She pointed to the ceiling and took my arm, leading me into a large conservatory off the kitchen filled with people.

"Hi, Jude, really appreciate you stepping in like this." Linda handed me a pen and a pad of paper. "Hopefully there won't be too much to minute tonight."

Tamsin pointed to a seat and I braced myself for the onslaught. I didn't have a moment to think as they all introduced themselves and went through the formal motions of a meeting.

"Well done. You've really earned this." Tamsin's husband, Anthony, handed me a glass of wine. I nodded and flexed my wrist. I couldn't remember when I had last written so much in such a short space of time.

"So, Jude, what do you think of our part of the world?" Linda put her hand on my shoulder.

"I love it."

"Good to hear. So tell us what's happening up at Pengarrock?"

"Not a lot." I stepped back.

"He'll break up the estate to get the most money out of it." Linda frowned.

"Who can blame him? He doesn't want to live here." Anthony handed round a plate of nibbles.

"Leave Tristan alone. He has his reasons, whatever they may be, to sell up and leave Cornwall for ever." Tamsin sighed. "It's his right."

"That it may be, but what he does affects us all. I heard a rumour in Helston that a Hollywood type was interested, and if that's the case the footpaths will be closed. They will want total privacy!" I couldn't remember the woman's name, but she was clearly scandalised and thrilled at the same time.

I spun around trying to see who was saying what, but gave up and let their words run over me. I wandered into the kitchen, which was dominated by a large range in the old fireplace. A few children's finger paintings were framed and hung about the room. It was charming.

"That would be a nightmare in so many ways."

I leaned against the door frame and listened. There was nothing I could add, and they needed to express it all.

"It would kill tourism. No walkers along the coast." Linda emphasised her words by waving her glass in the air.

"That's just the start." A man reached over my shoulder and grabbed a passing sausage.

"Wish Petroc had left the cricket ground to the parish council." Another man joined in the discussion. "The lease for our house is OK for the time being."

"That's a relief." Anthony refilled glasses.

"Jude, is there any way you could stop him, bar poisoning him or something?" Linda walked up to me.

I shook my head. "Sorry, can't help in any way." I wondered if Tristan had any idea of what people were thinking. But if he did, he didn't seem to care.

CHAPTER
FIFTEEN

Tristan walked into the study. "Ready for dinner?"

I glanced at the carriage clock on Petroc's desk. It was six-thirty, which seemed a bit early, but I wasn't going to argue. "Sure."

Tristan came up to the desk and touched the clock. It hadn't escaped my notice that he'd taken over winding duties. "You love that clock."

"It was my mother's." He turned to me. "You'll need shoes."

"For dinner in the garden?" I frowned.

"No, for fish and chips."

"Now you have me intrigued."

"You've been here a month or so, and you haven't had Tuesday-night fish and chips?"

"No." I looked at Tristan. He was wearing a short-sleeved shirt and had somehow acquired a bit of a tan. The tan brought out the colour of his eyes.

"Then you're in for a treat."

I slipped on my flip-flops.

"You'll need something more substantial than those."

"For fish and chips?"

"Trust me."

"OK." I shrugged. "My sneakers are upstairs, will they do?"

He smiled. "Yes, your trainers should be fine, as it's been dry."

As I dashed to my room, I wondered if we were going to catch this dinner rather than buy it, but I kept my suspicions to myself. When I joined him, I noted that he was carrying a bag but no fishing rod. We left the house and walked up the drive.

"My father bought those portraits from Lady Rutherford."

"They are stunning, aren't they?"

"Yes, but that's not the point. I need two more portraits like a hole in the head."

I turned to him. "Your father, I'm sure, had a reason. It might have been to discover what happened to the sapphire."

"Bloody sapphire." He picked up his pace. We turned towards the village at the crossroads, and Tristan only slowed down when a blue van was in sight. A crowd of people stood about it. I couldn't believe my eyes when I saw Tristan walk up and place an order for food.

"Hello, Tristan. Good to see you here." The woman taking orders smiled broadly.

"Thanks. Busy tonight." He looked around after he'd handed over payment.

"Yes, won't have your order ready for a bit." She looked at the slips of paper on the wall.

"No problem." He stood aside for someone collecting their meal.

"How's Helen?" the woman asked.

"She's getting stronger by the day."

"Hi, Tristan," said a tall man with two kids in tow. "This brings back memories, seeing you here."

I watched Tristan's face to see if he would react, and he smiled. I could have fallen over.

"Been a long time. I'm sure I've been healthier without fish and chips."

"Hey, I heard that." The man's voice came from inside the van.

"Hi, Jude." Tamsin came up beside me.

"Didn't want to cook?" I asked.

"Never do on a Tuesday. My night off, and tonight it's glorious. We're heading out in the boat to eat it on the river. Are you and Tristan doing anything special?" She tilted her head to the side.

"No." I looked over to see him deep in conversation with an old man I recognised as a farmer.

"Shame. You should have Mark take you out on the river one evening, if the tides are right." She looked at Tristan, and there was no anger on display on her face. The expression was more one of sadness. "That's my order. Let's have a coffee or a drink again soon." Tamsin grabbed her bags and disappeared.

The sharp smell of the vinegar only increased my hunger as we walked down the road towards St Anthony. I hadn't a clue what our final destination was. We'd been the last people to receive our order, and in the process I think I'd spoken to every person I'd ever met in the area including everyone who'd raised doubts about Tristan the night before. They didn't do it

202

tonight, and Tristan, to my surprise, seemed more at ease. He was lost in his own thoughts now. Spending time at Pengarrock must feel very strange for him. He was here only to sort out and prepare to sell the estate. I didn't find being here a hardship at all — quite the reverse — but I knew it was different for him. This was the place where his mother had died, and I sensed this still troubled him.

"Are you going to tell me where we're going?"

"You'll see." He smiled, and my heart fluttered just a little.

"So this is an adventure?"

He laughed. "For you, maybe."

"Well, adventure or no, I hope we reach wherever we're eating soon because the smell of the food is driving me mad."

"A little anticipation adds to the pleasure." He cast a sideways glance at me, and my breath stopped for a second.

"It does indeed." A light breeze caressed my face as we stopped by a gate. Tristan checked the field before opening it, then held it for me before securing it behind us. Thankfully there were no cows to be seen. I knew we were near Dennis Head, but I wasn't sure quite where or how. I was used to approaching it from the coastal path. We climbed steadily until we reached the top of the field and below us lay Gillan Creek. The sun was about to set behind the hills and the water reflected the clear sky. "Wow."

"Exactly." Tristan put the bags down and pulled out a bottle of wine and some glasses he had brought from the house. As he opened the bottle of Muscadet, I hid my shock. He handed me a glass and poured one for himself.

"For one who was loath to eat outside, I must say you've surprised me."

"Excellent." He raised his glass. "To a beautiful evening, a glorious sunset and good company."

I was speechless. Was this really Tristan, or had some pixie stolen the real one away while I wasn't looking?

"Take a seat." He waved his hand at the ground, and I checked for cow pies before sitting. He gave me my fish and chips, then sat beside me just as the sun disappeared and the sky's colour intensified.

Grease had worked its way through the layers of paper and steam came off the chips when I finally got to them. I was starved. "I don't suppose we asked for any tartar sauce?"

Tristan dug in his pocket and produced a few packets. "As the lady wishes."

"Indeed she does." Fish and chips were something that my parents had always disagreed over. Tartar sauce went some way to soothing the argument over whether the fish should be beer-battered English style, or in the lighter style of New England. I tucked into the fish and had to admit I was siding with my mother for the first time ever.

As I watched a heron rise from the creek, I realised that Tristan and I hadn't spoken a word while we ate. Both of us were famished. Each time he reached for his glass, I could feel the movement of his muscles yet we weren't touching.

204

I turned to him. "Thank you for a delicious dinner."

"The pleasure was mine." He raised his hand and I tilted my head, unsure of what he was about to do. His index finger swept under my lower lip, then he raised it to my mouth. "You missed some."

I looked at the fish and then at his face. I couldn't read his expression, but I sensed a dare. Well, that's all I was willing to acknowledge. Leaning forward, I quickly ate the small piece of fish and sauce. I tried not to think about how intimate it all felt. I looked away.

"Should we head back before we are in total darkness?" Tristan stood.

"Good idea." I picked up the paper from my meal and added it to the bag Tristan held. "Shall we walk the coastal path, or by the road?"

"The road." Tristan's smile disappeared.

"The path would be quicker and prettier."

"The road." He bit the words out.

"OK." I fell into step behind him, looking at the rigid line of his broad shoulders. Where had my charming dinner companion gone, and what was wrong with the coastal path?

I stood in the doorway of the study. I had finished cataloguing everything in the room except for the contents of the desk and filing cabinets. The desk I'd begun but hadn't finished. Now was as good a time as any to continue the task, then I would feel as if I was making some progress.

At the desk, I pulled out the drawer containing the files on the Trevillion sapphire mystery and opened the correct page on the computer. Unlike the other books and files, I wasn't planning to remove these from the desk. That felt wrong. These were the things that Petroc held close to him, or at least had organised in some way. They should stay that way until Tristan told me the desk was being sold. I slumped in the chair. Before long, auctioneers would be trooping through to do a valuation prior to sale. I had vivid memories of visiting country-house sales with my mother on summer holidays. Who knew what she was looking for, but she never missed the opportunity to prowl through the remains of houses that were clearing out.

I dug to the bottom of the drawer and pulled all the files out. Resisting the temptation to look into the ones I'd been though before, I laid them aside. The next file contained some correspondence from Lady Rutherford, and explained the arrival of the portraits. She was downsizing, and had wondered if Petroc would be interested in them. Had Tristan written to her to acknowledge receipt of the portraits? I made a note to ask him, then opened the next file. It was very slim and contained three sheets of paper: Octavia's birth information, a photocopy from the *Western Morning News* and an engagement notice.

Coroner's Inquest:

On Wednesday before last, Richard Hosken, Esq. Coroner on the body of Octavia Trevillion, a single woman of 18 years of age. The deceased resided with her father, Tallan Trevillion, at Pengarrock.

206

On the morning of her wedding day she set sail in a small boat. The remains of the boat and her body were discovered on Parson's Beach the following day. The coroner declared it accidental death.

I shivered. Her wedding day. How incredibly sad. The next photocopy was from an unknown newspaper.

A marriage has been arranged, and will shortly take place between Capt. Kenneth Edward Trevillion, Royal Mariners, eldest son of Col. E. J. Trevillion, V.D., T.D., and Mrs Trevillion, of Hill House, Launceston, Cornwall, and Octavia, only child of Tallan Trevillion, of Pengarrock, Manaccan, Cornwall, and the late Lady Clarissa Trevillion.

She had been engaged to be married to another Trevillion. That didn't sound good at all. It was almost exactly what had happened to her mother. The last piece of information in the file was a sheet of handwritten notes, but not Petroc's.

What was she doing at August Rock?
Was she looking for the treasure?
Was she sailing for Falmouth and running away?
Does her sketchbook hold any clues?

Something teased the back of my brain. I'd seen this handwriting before, but where? I was feeling information overload, and like a computer I'd run out of working memory. But I closed the file knowing that I needed to solve this. She had fled her wedding, and that fact was a little too close to home. The answers must be in the sketchbook. I'd found nothing else of Octavia's. It was the only place to look.

CHAPTER
SIXTEEN

I stood by the car outside Truro train station looking for John as the passengers filed out. I couldn't quell the awful feeling of not wanting him here. It was just wrong. John was my friend. I should be looking forward to seeing him, but it was too complicated for that. I should have written the damn Dear John letter, then he wouldn't be coming. Or would he? I didn't know any more. What I did know was that I was different here, and I didn't want to have to go back to the old me. Did I have to? No. But would I? That was what I didn't know.

His blond head appeared above a group of teenage girls. My stomach dropped in a not unpleasant way. I'd forgotten how good-looking he was. I waved and he nodded, but there was no smile of greeting. What was he thinking, or, more importantly, what was he feeling? He wove his way through the traffic and dropped his bag. I was not sure how I was going to react. Once close to me, John's emotions were clear and that shouldn't have surprised me. He hadn't seen me for over a month, and I had been the woman he'd desired enough to marry.

"I've missed you." He held me close, and I felt his lips move against my forehead.

"Mmmm," I murmured, and hoped he took that for the right response. I'd missed him, but not the way that he had me. How could I have gotten this all so wrong? I pulled away from him and got into the car.

"How was your journey?"

"Good. Saw some lovely scenery."

"You mean, you weren't working?" I glanced at him.

"Not the whole journey." John reached out and touched my hand. "I spent a lot of it thinking about you."

"John." This would be a very long drive back to Pengarrock if I wasn't careful.

"It's true, Jude. I've missed you like crazy. I thought by now we'd be settled in London enjoying our new life, not me sitting alone in the flat we chose together."

"Ouch. Sorry." I bit my lip. This was not going to go well. John had every right to tell me all of this. I deserved to hear what I'd done.

"Jude."

"Yes?"

"You look amazing."

I laughed. "Why thank you."

"This place really suits you."

"Aw." I began to reach out to him, but then grabbed the wheel firmly with both hands. This was going to be a very difficult weekend.

On the short drive from the B & B in a farmhouse near to Pengarrock, I chatted about my work, but John was quiet.

210

"You're loving it."

"Yes." I parked.

John stepped out of the car. "Wow."

I looked at Pengarrock again with new eyes, and remembered how I'd felt when I first arrived. I wished Petroc were still here, and that I was just working with him and not helping to divide the spoils.

John turned to me. "I can see why you love it."

"Thanks." I did love it. More than I wanted to. One shouldn't feel so strongly about a place, a place that I was lucky enough to be in for a short time. It was wasted passion. But it was a passion I had no control over, and that was frightening.

"You say it's all for sale now?"

"Sadly, yes." I led him into the house. I hoped Tristan wasn't around, but hadn't a clue what he was up to today. He hadn't been at breakfast. I was still puzzling over why he hadn't wanted to take the coastal path. There had been enough light, and as pretty as the lane was, it held nothing on the view from the path.

"Are you here on your own now?" John's head was swivelling around.

"No, Tristan Trevillion is around at the moment too, I think." The house felt strangely empty.

"Is he the new owner?"

I nodded.

"I know I'm booked into the B & B, but it would be good to stay with you, or maybe you with me." He stroked my cheek.

"I told you to move on," I smiled, trying to make light of my words, but they still sounded awful.

"I know, but you can't blame me for hoping."

"Oh, John." I placed his hand down by his side. "I know I've hurt you, and it was wrong, but I do know that it was the right thing not to marry you."

John's face went white.

"God, I said that badly. What I mean is, marrying you, or anyone, was the wrong thing for me to do."

"Jude, what on earth are you talking about?"

"I just know that I wasn't being me."

"Not you? That makes no sense."

"Yes, I know it sounds weird, but I finally realised that I'd spent my life trying to be someone I wasn't." I marched up to the door and thrust the key in. "I'm just so sorry that it took me until that moment to grasp it." Now that I'd said it, I knew it was true and I needed to figure out who "me" was. This would be bad enough at twenty, but at thirty it was ridiculous. "Welcome to Pengarrock." I opened the door and led John in.

He turned to me. "Jude, just what are you saying?"

"I don't know what I'm saying, except," I took a deep breath, "that I'm not sure who I am, or I wasn't sure." John pulled me into his arms.

"Jude, you are you." He pressed a kiss on my temple, and I thought of Dad kissing Mother in the church. "Beautiful, loving, thoughtful."

I pulled back. "That's wonderful to hear, but I need to feel those things for myself, not just hear it from others. I need to decide who and what I am, and not fit into what someone else wants of me."

"I never forced anything on you."

212

"That's true, but what you fell in love with was a girl trying to be someone she wasn't in order to make other people happy." I bit my lip. "To be honest, I'm sure I even tried to alter myself to fit what I thought you wanted, as I had been doing for years with my mother."

"That's unfair." John's hands were clenched.

"No, it's not. It's what I did, not what you did." I reached out and touched his arm. "Let's not spoil the evening by talking about my mixed-up head. Just accept you had a lucky escape."

"I didn't, and I don't want an escape."

I took his hand and led him out of the house. Maybe over a good meal and some wine we could move past this. After all, we had been friends for over twenty years, and had only become lovers two years ago. We had walked as far as the crossroads before I felt able to raise the subject of my parents. "Have you seen them? I haven't heard a word from them."

"I've seen your mother, but your father is away."

"Away?" So Aunt Agnes was right. I silently apologised to her.

"Fishing in Canada." John stopped at the road sign. "How do you say Manaccan?"

I smiled. "Man a can. But don't try and distract me. Fishing?"

"I don't know much, as you can imagine — our parents aren't spending much time with each other these days."

I flinched.

"Exactly."

"I'm so sorry."

He looked at me, and I could see all the pain I'd caused him. There was nothing I could say at this point to make it better. "So that explains why Dad isn't answering my emails or messages."

"Have you spoken to your mother, Jude?"

I looked at my feet. "I've left messages and sent emails. She's either not home or not answering."

"Try again."

The child in me cried out that she didn't love me. She only loved Rose. I was and had remained the second-best child, even after Rose had gone. I didn't know where these thoughts came from, all of a sudden. I spun around with my hands in fists, then turned back to face the road down to the village. I walked so swiftly we were at the South Café in moments. John's hand grabbed mine. I didn't pull away, which I wanted to.

"Jude?"

"Yes." I smiled. I wasn't mad at him.

"That's better. Now can we have a peaceful dinner, like we used to?"

I cocked my head to one side. "I'm not sure that's possible. Someone let this genie out of the bottle, and I'm not sure if I can fit back in."

"Take me," I shouted, but the figure didn't move. My eyes were open and cold sweat covered my face as I sat up in bed. Fear gripped me, and I pulled the covers up to my neck. I shook my head and the figure was gone. This was not like the grim reaper of past nightmares who pulled Rose from my grasp. The figure had

214

changed, but was no less scary. Talking to John last night had brought back the nightmares.

A quick shower dispersed the shadowy fears that plagued me. Thank goodness John wasn't staying here. I had overslept, but at least he would have had a massive breakfast at the B & B. I'd grab a quick coffee and then we would head out onto the river, although I was exhausted. Fighting my demons all night long hadn't left any time for rest.

The dogs jumped up and wagged their tails as I came through the kitchen door. I spied Tristan leaning against the counter. "Morning."

"Just." He glanced at the big clock hanging above the fireplace.

"I never sleep this late." I yawned.

"Coffee?"

"Yes, please." I stopped walking when I saw John sitting at the kitchen table.

"Early bird catches the worm." John stood and came towards me, placing a kiss on my cheek. I glanced towards Tristan, who had turned away.

"Toast?" Tristan moved to the sink.

"I'll do it, thanks." I stifled another yawn.

"Judith, how late were you up last night?" Tristan handed me a cup of coffee.

"Oh, we called it a night at midnight, didn't we, Jude?"

I nodded and took a long sip.

"You feeling all right, Jude?" John looked at me closely, which he'd been doing far too frequently since he'd arrived. I felt as if every freckle had been noted.

The stress dreams were starving me of quality sleep and the world didn't feel right this morning.

"Slept badly, that's all." I held up the coffee pot and asked if anyone wanted more before I drained it into my cup.

"I'm going to take the dogs for a quick walk." Tristan disappeared out the back door.

"Tristan seems nice enough."

I wrinkled my nose. The word "nice" made him sound like someone's grandmother. "Yes, I suppose so." I paused. "What time did you get here this morning? I thought the plan was for me to come and get you."

"I woke early, took a walk and found myself here about eight-thirty. Tristan was out by the cars and I introduced myself."

I frowned and imagined all sorts of introductions that could have taken place. "Sorry I wasn't here."

John smiled. "Interesting guy. Any problems working with him?"

"None at all. We really have very little to do with each other. I'm in the study most of the day, and he works from the billiard room. He has no interest in his father's work except for any possible sale value."

"Is there any?"

"Depends on your point of view, I guess. The volume of scholarly work has some, but thus far I have turned up nothing I can see as having any great monetary value. There are one or two first editions that I've found."

"Does that bother him?"

"Quite frankly, I don't think he cares about it at all." My toast popped up and I grabbed it and the butter.

"No?"

"He just wants out of this place, but he does seem to want to do it well, and that includes making sure his father's work is handled properly and anything of value sold appropriately." I plopped down in a chair. I needed to get my head in gear. My plans to go out on the river would be scuppered if I didn't do so quickly. The tide would be out too far and we would have to wait until early evening.

"Is that more coffee?" Tristan came through the kitchen door. Both dogs dropped outside in the sun.

"Of course. Need to open these eyes somehow."

Tristan smiled at me. I sent him a forced one in return, then looked out at the bright blue sky.

"You mentioned the other day that you wanted to go out on the river." Tristan looked at his watch. "It's a neap tide, so you should be fine for another hour or so. What are your plans exactly?"

John shrugged his shoulders. Last night he'd said he was happy to do anything. He just wanted to spend some time with me, and I had to admit that it was good to see him. Despite all my misgivings, it was OK. The sky hadn't fallen down.

"I thought I'd throw a lunch together and sail around to find some beach to explore. Any suggestions?"

"Sounds good, but are you up to it?" Tristan asked.

"That's a good question. Jude, you're wrecked. You've never been good without sleep," said John.

I cringed. If Tristan had wondered what type of relationship John and I had he wouldn't be in any doubt now. "Thanks."

"What do you suggest?" John glanced at Tristan.

"Well, if you knew the river it would be fine, but . . ." Tristan tapped the table with his fingers. "John, do you sail?"

"A bit rusty, but should be OK."

I felt Tristan's scrutiny even though I'd turned my back to him to look out the window.

"Look, it's a beautiful day and I haven't been on the river in years. It might make sense for you to have some local knowledge on board. Mind if I join you?"

"Great idea," said John.

I looked at John in surprise. Well, if he didn't care, I didn't, I guessed. Nothing felt clear this morning.

"Jude, go upstairs and lie down for an hour while we get organised. We'll come and get you." Tristan pushed me out the door. The sensation caused by the feel of his hand on my back startled me.

"But —" I said.

"No buts, get some sleep. Even a little will help." The door was firmly closed behind me.

CHAPTER
SEVENTEEN

The mouth of the river was full of boats setting out. I enjoyed the rush of the wind as I sat back, letting Tristan and John do the work. Earlier I'd fallen into a deep sleep, and felt as if I'd been drugged when Tristan woke me up. I closed my eyes and remembered the look on his face. I must have been imagining it because I could swear there was tenderness, and that emotion didn't fit into Tristan's world from what little I'd seen.

At the moment, he played guide, pointing out the church in Mawnan that used to serve as a marker for mariners. Looking at the river today, filled with pleasure boats, I struggled to imagine that this had once been a busy route for commerce.

"So, tell me, Tristan, how far does the estate stretch?" John asked. His hair was wild in the wind and his blue eyes held such warmth. It was very strange having him here. I sat up and nearly was hit by the boom.

"There's the old customs house," Tristan pointed to a structure built into the rocks. I tried not to look at him, and to focus on the scenery. I must stop thinking, or I'd put myself into a spin. What did I want? Right now I wanted to find out who I was. I didn't want to be what my mother wanted, and John represented all of that. Life would have been simple if I'd chosen that route. My glance strayed to Tristan's dark head. No. That was madness. But now that I'd let the thought enter my brain, it didn't want to leave.

"Jude, are you with us, or have you gone back to sleep with your eyes open?" John smiled at me.

"Only just awake, I think." I looked around and discovered we were out in Falmouth Bay again. "Is that buoy over there August Rock, Tristan?" It looked very different. From the cliffs or the house it looked a small marker, but close to it felt huge, threatening.

"Yes." He gave me a funny look.

John scanned the surface of the water. "Where's the rock?"

"It's there, between the buoy and Parson's Beach." Tristan pointed.

"If you say so." John touched my ankle. He was still in love with me. It was there in his eyes. I closed mine to hide from the longing in his. This wasn't good. He needed to let go.

"I think I read in your father's papers that it might mean 'near rock'. He had written something in Cornish, *Men Ogas*, near it, but I'm not sure if that is the translation." My eyes met Tristan's. Bad move. Something connected. I looked away.

"It makes sense." Tristan shrugged.

"Has August Rock ever caused any problems or wrecks?" John asked.

"One that I know of," I chimed in.

220

"Yes, there was that one, but I don't think there were any others on the Helford." Tristan paused. "Cornwall is notorious for its wrecks and wreckers. Just move round the coast a bit, and the Manacles have caught more than a few."

We sailed close to a quiet beach nestled at the base of a steep cliff face.

"This looks like a great place to have lunch." I peered over my sunglasses. The cove sat opposite to Dennis Head, and gave me a chance to see again how it had been so effective as a defensive fort.

"Thought it might be good, as the rest of the beaches seemed too full. You can tell the schools have broken up for the summer." Tristan navigated the boat in and John leaped into the water to take it the last stretch.

Gingerly I placed a foot in and pulled it back out while I estimated that it would take me three large steps. "It's not as icy as it was the other day, but how people swim in it I'll never know."

"It's no worse than Maine, Jude." John held a hand out to assist me.

"True, but I never liked swimming there either." I made a leap.

Tristan laughed as he secured the boat. "The water's quite warm today. I bet you'll have a swim before the day is out." I made a face at Tristan as he began to set out the food and opened the wine.

I glanced in John's direction. He was just walking up from the boat with the last bag.

"This is yours, madam, I believe."

"Thank you, kind sir." I bowed slightly in John's direction. "Gentlemen, you did well. I can't see anything you've forgotten, bar the kitchen sink."

"We aim to please." Tristan handed me a glass and I relaxed enough to give him a smile.

I rummaged in my bag looking for my hat. The sun was hot now that we were out of the breeze. I tossed bits of a bikini onto the sand. "I don't think I'll need my swimsuit." I pulled my hat on my head.

"You don't still have that old hat, Jude?"

"Never leave home without it! Care for some cheese?" I handed John a chunk of French bread with a thick slab of cheese. "Tristan? Have you got an appetite yet?"

"Hmmm. Yes." He watched me stretch out on the towel. I tried not to notice.

"Cheese, or something else?" I swallowed. That was not what I meant to say. I could feel colour rising in my cheeks. I pulled my hat a bit lower.

"Cheese will do." Tristan grinned.

"What am I looking at over there?" John waved to the distant headland.

"Which one are you pointing to?" Tristan stood.

"The furthest one you can see."

"It's probably Dodman Point."

"I have to say, I didn't expect this." John turned from the water.

"Didn't expect what?" I leaned forward.

"Well, for a start the weather, it's perfect. It's almost too hot here in the sun. I may have to swim."

"Hmmm. I wouldn't go that far." I shivered.

"Chicken. I'm going in." John headed to the sea.

"I'll join you." Tristan followed.

"Good luck, you two. I'm going to read." I watched the two men, admiring them both. John might be just a bit taller, with a slightly larger frame, but Tristan was exceptionally well put together. The sight of his thighs left me breathless.

"Shit, that's cold." John was up to his knees.

"You'll go numb and won't notice." Tristan dived in. I was glad I was on the beach.

"You have a point, Tristan. It doesn't feel too bad once you're in. The water's surprisingly clear, too." Their voices carried in the cove.

"Jude, you should give it a try." Tristan called.

"No thanks." I pulled the sun hat firmly over my face as I lay flat, enjoying the warmth of the sun and a full stomach.

I'd fallen asleep and woke up cold. The sun had moved and I was in the shadow of the cliff. A cliff that, on inspection, looked like it had had a landslip quite recently. From the debris at the bottom, I wouldn't want to be here when the next one happened. I'd had enough seismic shifts in life recently. John's visit kept drawing me back to things I'd avoided thinking about. In fact, I thought I had heard John telling Tristan that I had been his fiancée, but I was sure I was just having a nightmare. Why would John say anything, and why would Tristan be asking? How long had I been sleeping? Sitting up, I looked at my watch. It was three-thirty. I'd slept for two hours. Where were they?

The tide had come in a fair bit. I was surrounded by the remnants of the picnic, but Tristan and John were nowhere to be seen. The boat was still there. The rocks that projected from the cove were almost submerged again. When we'd arrived, you could walk around to the next beach, but that wasn't possible now. The sea still looked fabulous bathed in sunshine, but the cliff behind looked cold and impassable.

My most urgent need was to pee, and there was no place to hide. The whole cove was visible from the sea. I had no choice but to put on my swimsuit and take a dip. The thought filled me with dread, but I couldn't hold off any longer. With a towel wrapped around me, I struggled to get into my bikini. I searched the sea looking for any passing boat that might take an interest in my activities. Maybe I could risk trying near the cliff face, but it could still be unstable, and worse, what would happen if Tristan and John returned from wherever they had gone? I could face the embarrassment with John, but Tristan? No, I'd have to be brave and wade into the sea.

Large hat still placed firmly on my head, I marched down to the water's edge and kicked off my sandals. I stuck my left foot in and quickly pulled it out again. I put my sandals back on and walked to where the sun was still hitting a small patch of sand and repeated the process there. My foot stayed in this time. Carefully I brought the other one into the water and paused. Once both feet were numb, I moved to mid-calf height and waited. I was now wondering why I'd had that last glass of wine. Surely that was what had pushed my bladder to such extremes. Next time I wouldn't be so greedy. I'd know the consequences.

I inched out further so that my knees were submerged. The water didn't seem as cold in this spot. Maybe if I just squatted here? No, it would be clear to everyone what I was doing. But I reminded myself that I was alone. Who would see, or care?

Wading out to mid-thigh, I wasn't going to last much longer either in the water or holding off. I'd have thought the iciness of the water would have convinced my bladder to hold on a bit longer, but it told me it couldn't. With two large steps I was up to my waist.

"Damn, it's cold," I muttered, and couldn't bring myself to go any further. I checked to be sure I was still alone. It was then that I noticed a red mark slashed across my stomach where my shirt must have come up while I slept. As I peed, I caught sight of sun-kissed brown shoulders and arms cutting smoothly through the sea. My heart beat a little faster. Tristan's wet hair looked almost black. John's easy strokes came a few moments later. He smiled when he saw me.

"Forced into the sea, were you?" Tristan's voiced matched the smile in his eyes. I'd been caught. My face coordinated with the angry red mark on my stomach.

"'Fraid so. Where have you two been?" I pulled my hat lower.

"Went walking along the coves."

I made a quick exit as John swam towards me.

"Aren't you going to finish your swim?" Tristan raised an eyebrow.

"Thank you, no." I headed straight for my towel.

"There's some tea in the thermos." Tristan sat on one of the protruding rocks still exposed to the sun. I quickly turned away as I found I was staring at his chest and noting the dark hair that led in a straight line down his flat stomach to the top of his swimming trunks.

"Thanks. Does anyone else want a cup?" I forced my voice to remain even.

"Yes, please." Tristan stretched onto his back.

"Sounds good to me." John left the sea and water dripped from his shoulders as I handed him a cup. My friends had lusted over John for years, jealous that he was mine. Looking at him now, I could see why. This man had been willing to be mine alone for a lifetime. I was mad.

I peeked at Tristan from under my hat. He was stretched out on a flat rock, and I found my glance kept returning to him. I needed to focus on the practical task of getting the tea out to him. With cup in hand, I braced myself for the first blast of cold water. It didn't feel too bad this time. Possibly I was still numb. But numb wasn't what I was feeling as I looked up and saw him studying me as I came closer. I couldn't read the look in his eyes, but I didn't feel cold in the water.

"Thanks." He sat up and I tried not to look at his stomach muscles, but failed.

"No problem."

"You need to get some suncream on your stomach. You've acquired a bit of a burn."

"Yes, the icy water is quite soothing."

"I bet." Tristan smiled. I couldn't be flirting with him with my ex-fiancé sitting on the beach, could I? Clearly

226

I could. It was a good thing the water was so cold, as it was keeping my temperature normal.

"Yes, and before my whole body goes numb I'll leave you to enjoy your tea in peace."

"So you left him at the altar?" Tristan's voice was so quiet I wasn't sure I'd heard. I swung back round, sending a spray of water at him.

"Hey, you don't have to beat me up."

I hadn't dreamed it. John had told him. Why? Had John noticed I was attracted to Tristan? Hell, yes, he was my friend. He'd watched me go through this a thousand times. It must be obvious. Was John trying to scare him off?

"Sorry." I forced the word out.

"Is that what you said to him?" Tristan rolled onto his side, managing not to spill his tea.

"Excuse me?"

"That's one way to put it."

"You're way over the mark here. I don't need to explain anything to you."

"Quite right you don't, but I think John might need a bit more of an explanation, as he's still in love with you."

"You've picked all this up during a walk and a swim in the sea?" I couldn't believe I was having this discussion with him.

"Yes. John isn't exactly trying to hide his heart at the moment."

"No? Look, it's none of your business." I shot round and sent another blast of water all over Tristan, which was exactly what he deserved. He had no right to comment on my relationship with John. Hell, he'd only known me a very short time. I grabbed my towel, wrapped myself up, then stuck my nose in my book.

CHAPTER
EIGHTEEN

I stood just outside Tristan's bedroom. I'd been avoiding him since John left, I'd been so angry. Both men thought they could comment on my life. John might have some right, but Tristan bloody well didn't. Even days later, his words angered me. I had to push that aside. I needed help.

I knocked on his door. "Tristan?"

"Come in."

I saw neat piles on the bed. "Packing. Where to?"

"London, then New York." He stopped folding his shirts.

"When are you off?"

"In a few hours." He looked up and picked up a pile of papers. "I came across this last night. I'm assuming it's Dad's book, but I couldn't make head nor tail of it. The publishers are on my case, though, so could you make this a priority? I need to know if we can salvage it or just return the advance, which Dad has already spent."

I took it from him. "OK."

"What did you want?"

I stood straight. "Sorry, but my bedroom door is stuck."

"Stuck? I thought you were in there."

"No, I've been in the study and the library all morning. Haven't been upstairs at all. I left yesterday's notes on the bed, and I can't get the door open."

Tristan followed me down the hall to my room. I tried turning the handle but it wouldn't move.

"Let me have a go." He gave it a good twist but nothing moved. He used both hands and still no luck. "This is bizarre. Can't even blame it on the wind creating a vacuum, as there's none today." He twisted it again. "Was the doorknob loose on the other side?"

"Not that I can remember."

"I'll grab a screwdriver from the kitchen and see what happens if I take it off."

"Sounds good, but do you know what you are doing?" I stood back.

"No, but I did think about studying engineering. Does that qualify?"

"It's a good try. Shall I make a cup of tea for the handyman?"

"Yes, thanks." He smiled.

Once in the kitchen, I filled the kettle. Tristan didn't seem to have noticed my recent silence. He was smiling as he rummaged in a drawer, looking for tools. Why was he so charming one minute, then so arrogant the next? Before he'd made the comments about my life, I'd seen him enjoying himself, and when he was talking to John about the estate he sounded almost proud of it. Why was he selling? It didn't make sense. Petroc was a kind and loving man. That only left Imogen, or something about her, as the cause of Tristan's mood changes.

"Tristan, I have been meaning to ask you." I stopped.

"This sounds ominous." He turned his attention to me with the screwdriver in his hand.

"That looks a bit lethal," I stepped away.

"It does. You were saying." He dropped his hand to his side.

"Can I ask what happened to your mother?"

His smiled disappeared and the atmosphere in the room changed. "Why?"

"I found another one of your father's journals, and it was all rather sad."

"As well it bloody should be. He played more than his part."

"His part in what?" I ran my hand through my hair.

"Her suicide."

"Oh, Tristan, I'm sorry." I moved towards him.

"Not as much as me." He left the kitchen and went up the stairs. I raced after him. My mind began putting two and two together. Did her suicide have anything to do with the letter she wrote to Petroc? Had her affair gone wrong?

Tristan swiftly had the doorknob off and opened the door. I watched him, feeling worse by the minute about what I'd said. Emotions played across his face that had nothing to do the task in hand. He took the whole mechanism apart and reassembled it. "It should be fine now. It was only a few loose screws."

"Thanks." I took the screwdriver from him.

He looked around. "This place is falling apart." He turned and began down the hall.

"I'm really sorry." I took a deep breath. "I shouldn't have asked you about your mother."

He stopped walking. "It was a long time ago, but even so people still talk. They should look to their own lives rather than focusing on the lives of others." He went into his room and closed the door. I stood there looking at it. He was right, but the world didn't work that way, as I knew only too well.

In the study I listened to the car pull across the gravel. The dog-eared papers of Petroc's manuscript sat on the desk. Tristan had said to make a priority of it, but there was so much to do as I looked around. The phone rang. "Pengarrock."

"Jude."

"John." I looked at the ceiling. I felt terrible for raising Imogen's death, and now I had John on the phone.

"I thought coming for the weekend was a good thing, but I'm sorry you're so pissed off with me."

"I'm not."

"Come on, Jude, I know you too well."

"Yeah, right."

"Jude . . ."

"Yes?" I played with the pencil in my hand.

"Look, this weekend should have shown you that I still love you, and I still think we have a chance."

"We discussed this." I sighed. He wasn't letting go. What did I expect from a lawyer? He kept questioning me about what had happened on the day. He wanted to know what had changed. I refused to be cross-examined.

"I wouldn't call it a discussion, Jude. You bit my head off."

"Sorry. Touchy subject."

"Tell me about it." He sighed. "I know you need time. I think I know what happened and why."

"If you do, then you are one step ahead of me." I stood.

"I always was."

"Ha." I leaned against a filing cabinet and a fresh breeze came through the open window.

"Jude, I know you need time, and I know that being in Cornwall is good for you, but so am I."

"Conceited, aren't we?" I asked, but a smile was starting to appear on my face.

"No, loving. I love you."

"So you've told me." I twisted my bracelet. I knew this should make me feel wonderful, but it only caused more guilt.

"Jude."

"Sorry, that was a bit hard. I love you too, John, but just not the way you love me."

"I think you do, but you don't know it yet," he said.

"Mind-reader?"

"Definitely."

I laughed.

"That's better. Think of me a little bit."

I was silent. I didn't want to think about John.

"I've got to go, but remember what I've said."

I put the phone down and plucked the petals off a flower in a vase. This gorgeous hunk of a man still loved me. I rubbed my head and I knew the pain wasn't going to go away except with sleep, which had been in very short supply.

In the hall my footsteps echoed as I walked up the stairs. I stopped on the landing and watched the fog rolling in, making the early evening unnaturally dark. These heavy dreams were draining me. They were such a jumble of things, with no clear pattern. They weren't exactly stress dreams, not like at school, pre-exam, or work ones before a review. But they woke me up with my heart racing and in tears.

Continuing up the stairs, I nodded to the men in the paintings. The only one I didn't like was Tallan. If Pengarrock were mine, I would replace him on the stairs with Mary from the dining room. She may be ugly, but there was something nasty in his look. No, I was jumping to conclusions, and I doubted I would ever have time to find out if they were the right ones. I turned to my room and wondered if Tristan had done an inventory of the paintings yet. That would take time too. So much work, just to sell it all.

I was so excited about Petroc's manuscript. At last I felt like I was doing something worthwhile. But I knew I wasn't the right person to finish it. On paper I was qualified as a historian and very capable in academic writing, but this wasn't a research paper.

The more I thought about the problem the more I knew that Barbara was the one person who could really help. Between us we could put Petroc's book into publishable shape and do him credit. From what I'd read of it, it was very different from his academic work. This book was meant to appeal to a completely different audience. I would email Tristan and ask if I could bring in Barbara. He would probably say no, but it was worth trying.

Today, I would tackle the taller of the two filing cabinets in the study. Unlike its partner, this one had closed drawers. The top one pulled out easily, and to my surprise wasn't overstuffed, but was filled with neat spiral-bound notebooks. Each one was simply dated in precise violet lettering. They were in chronological order. I scratched my head. A quick look through a few of them told me what I suspected. This wasn't Petroc's work, but the work of a botanist. The writing looked familiar. I'd seen it before. It was Imogen's.

Making my way through the remaining drawers, I discovered that all the notes were immaculately printed in either black or violet ink. All of it interesting, but I didn't linger. It wasn't Petroc's work, and as such wasn't part of my remit. But the last facts I'd read from the notes were on orchids, and that made me smile on my way to the kitchen. Somehow in my education I'd totally missed the fact that *Orchidaceae* is one of the two largest flowering-plant families. The amusing bit was that *orchis* comes from the Greek meaning "testicle" because of the shape of the plant's root. Sometimes I just loved what I learned through my work.

In the kitchen I discovered I wasn't alone, as I'd thought. "Helen, you should be home resting!"

"Nonsense. It's quieter here than at home, and I'm worried you might be a bit lonely without Tristan."

I wasn't going to admit that I was. How could I tell Helen that I adored the rhythm of life here, from my daily walks with the dogs to my work? I was in love with the place; it filled me as no relationship had ever done. I put the kettle on and decided not to share. It was best kept to myself. "Point taken, but you love the grandkids."

"True, but a little silence goes a long way." She sighed and continued ironing. I was pleased to see it was her own clothing she was doing.

"You should be resting. You need to build up your strength."

"My strength is returning. I shouldn't have another one. The heart attack was stress-related. I've let go of my hope that Tristan won't sell."

"That's wise. Not selling was never an option."

"I was foolish to hope, but hope I did." She sighed.

"I get the sense that Tristan left here a long time ago."

"You're right, he did. He left when he was sent away to school at ten."

"Ten? Not a usual age." My mother had gone at eight, as had Barbara. I had gone at thirteen, a year after Rose's death.

"No, but Imogen was gone, and Petroc felt it would be better for him." Helen switched the iron off. "Better to be with other children."

"You didn't agree."

"No."

"How did I guess?" I placed my hand on her shoulder.

"He was too young, and needed to be with people who loved him, not in some uncaring school."

"You still feel strongly about it," I stepped back as she turned around.

"The boy had lost his mother. He didn't need school. He needed love."

"Do you know why she committed suicide?"

Helen stood still and gave me a searching look, then turned away. "She didn't. Where did you hear that?"

"Tristan."

"What?" She pulled out a chair and sat down. "Imogen didn't take her own life."

"Then why does Tristan think she did?"

"She was found upriver on a beach with a broken neck. She must have fallen off a cliff while walking." She spoke very softly. "The coroner said it was accidental death and I believe him, although," Helen paused and wiped away a tear, "there's always talk, and Tristan must have picked up on that. Poor boy."

"So there is no question that it was suicide."

Helen pursed her lips then said, "Not for me to say."

"I see." I wanted to push her, but now might not be the time. Helen didn't need any more stress.

"I just wish Pengarrock were home for him, and not just a burden."

"Some things can't be changed."

"No, but one can hope." Helen sighed.

"Yes, but I don't think there is much of a chance." I leaned against the counter.

"I know, I know, but I can't help thinking that if he found the right woman then he might stay and hold on to his heritage."

"But what if he loves her and she hates Pengarrock? Then he will quite rightly choose love."

"Then she wouldn't be the right woman." She looked around the room and then stood. "I best head back to the grandkids."

I watched her walk away, wondering if life really was that simple.

CHAPTER
NINETEEN

I hadn't had the promised email from Sophie. She would know what was happening at home. Dad going on a fishing trip was so not him; not that he didn't like to fish. But since his retirement my parents had been inseparable. He didn't take trips without Mother. Something was wrong. I'd tried calling a few more times, and still had only reached the answering machine. I looked at the phone on Petroc's desk. My fingers punched in the number and I waited. Six rings, and it went to answerphone.

"Hi, its Jude. I'll call later." I put the phone down quickly and left the study with Octavia's sketchbook in my hands. I hadn't had time to look at it while John had been around, and then Petroc's book had taken precedence. It puzzled me how Petroc could love Pengarrock so much and not pass any of that feeling on to Tristan. How had Imogen felt about it?

Before I did anything I needed lunch. A simple salad would do the trick. I stopped in my tracks when I saw Helen in the kitchen again. "You gave me a fright."

"Didn't mean to."

I put Octavia's book safely away from the working end of the table. "Was there ever a time when Tristan wanted Pengarrock?"

"He did, briefly." Helen sighed.

"Really?" I frowned.

"Yes, he was very young and in love, but she chose someone else."

"That sounds intriguing."

"Mark and Tristan both wanted the lovely Clare, but Mark won."

"And Tristan behaves so badly because Mark won the girl and he didn't." I shook my head. "How foolish to hold on to teenage rivalry into your thirties."

"It was more than that. It's all rather sad. She died when Mark wasn't here." The doorbell rang and I walked with Helen to answer it. A man with a camera stood outside.

"Can I help you?" Helen sounded far from accommodating.

"I'm from the estate agent's, and I'm here to photograph the house."

Helen held the door in a vicelike grip, moving it back and forth. I wondered if she was going to slam it in his face. "Do you have any identification? I wasn't told of your appointment."

"I spoke with Mr Trevillion and arranged this a while ago. Is he not here?"

"No." Helen's mouth barely moved. I ran a hand across her shoulders. She needed to relax.

The man pulled his wallet out of his bag and produced a business card. The company name matched the one in the advertisement I'd seen.

"It's fine, Helen." I stepped forward. "Come in and tell us your plan."

"Thank you." He moved around Helen, who remained blocking the entrance.

"I'll leave you to sort this." Helen walked out the front door.

"Come into the kitchen and you can tell me what shots you need." I was silently cursing Tristan for setting this up while he wasn't here. This wasn't my job. And worst of all, he'd upset Helen again. Did the man not have a brain or, more precisely, a thoughtful bone in his body?

"I need pictures of all the main rooms and of the view, the beach, the gardens."

"Do you want a shot in here?" I watched him look at the range, the stone lintel and the large table.

He looked around. "No, the kitchen won't sell the place."

"It's one of my favourite parts of the house." The words were out of my mouth before I could stop them. I didn't want the house sold, but I didn't want him to dismiss the kitchen either. I hated the idea of anyone making it all fancy. It was old but it worked well.

"Not modern enough." He walked into the butler's pantry and I followed. If he didn't think the kitchen was modern enough, then this room wasn't going to help. He took a picture of the big sink where I had put the flowers I'd cut this morning. I wasn't sure why that would "sell" Pengarrock. But I could see it looked artistic.

I took him to the dining room next. "Too dark." He stopped and looked at the portrait of Mary. "Nice rock."

241

"Indeed." I sounded like my mother. That was the last thing in the world I wanted to do. "Let's go straight to the drawing room. We weren't aware that you were coming today, so some of the rooms aren't fit to be photographed."

I waited in the hallway while he snapped away. He seemed to spend an inordinate amount of time taking shots of my flower arrangement. Surely anyone buying this estate was not going to be interested in those. Arranging flowers was one of the few skills Mother had taught me that was finally useful. It was bliss to have a cutting garden with so much blooming at the moment. Though I still felt guilty when I'd cut the agapanthus.

"Next room."

I led him into the drawing room.

"Great room, but I need to move those paintings."

"Fine, give me a hand." Together we shifted the portraits into the hallway. With each camera click my anger rose. I should be working, not playing photographer's assistant. It should be Tristan here doing this, but I gritted my teeth and got on with it. It was late afternoon by the time he was done, and I was exhausted. He must have taken hundreds of shots, and I hadn't accomplished anything.

In the kitchen, I saw that Helen had made me a sandwich and propped a note up on it admonishing me to eat. I picked up the sketchbook and carefully opened it to the first page before I touched the food. In beautiful script Octavia had written out her name, *Pengarrock* and the year. It was done two years before she died, and a year before she became engaged. She wouldn't have been looking for the treasure on her wedding day. What would the treasure have done for her, or was Pengarrock in dire financial straits even back then?

I swiftly finished the sandwich and put the kettle on. After I'd made coffee and washed and dried my hands thoroughly, I went back to the book. The first page contained the words:

Not of the land
Not of the sea
Visible only
When August Rock sees

Then there was a beautiful watercolour of Rosemullion Head, and the reef appearing just above the surface of the water. The next page was very different in style. It was almost anatomical. A picture of a curlew sat in one corner of the page, and what I assumed to be a curlew nest in the opposite corner. But there were no words. Turning to the next page, it was similar. There was a beautiful rendition of a dove in one corner and then another smaller picture of a dove feeding its young. There was also a small picture of the dove in flight with a flower in its mouth. The detail was exquisite, but really too small to see without a magnifying glass. It was probably the traditional olive branch.

I flipped through to the end, and a sheet of paper fell out. I recognised it. It was the stationery I'd found in my room and had used to write to Aunt Agnes. I held it up to the light, and I could clearly see IMT embossed into the paper. Imogen. As I looked back to the sketchbook and the last page, I could see the words Petroc had written down.

What secrets does the Helford hold?
Neither time nor tide reveals them.
August 1849

So they were Octavia's words. But why was Imogen's stationery in Octavia's sketchbook?

I jumped a mile when I heard footsteps behind me.

"Helen, what are you doing back here? You scared the life out of me!"

"Didn't mean to, but I left the sweetener for my tea up here, and I didn't have any at home." Helen laughed. She picked up the stationery. "I haven't seen this in a long time."

"There's a supply in my room."

Helen looked up sheepishly.

"Why was Imogen's stationery in the Green Room?"

She turned away. "The Green Room was Imogen's."

"Imogen's room?"

"Yes."

"OK, this may be asking for too much personal information, but didn't Petroc and Imogen share a room? Or am I being too American here?"

She laughed. "They did sometimes, but Petroc was a great snorer and, well, they were going through bit of a bad patch, as they did."

"As they did?"

"Well, yes. They more than some. There was an age difference, you know." She stroked the paper. "Most marriages have their moments, but most marriages don't have the extra rooms to allow for separate beds."

"You speak from experience."

"Experience of being married for nearly forty years. There have been times when I've wished I could have my own space, but that cottage is tiny, so whether we want to or not, JC and I are stuck in the same room and the same bed, which has worked quite well." Her eyes lit up.

"Fine. It's a lesson I'll try and remember if I ever marry."

"Oh, you'll marry all right."

I frowned. I couldn't see myself in a white dress at a church door again. "Why did you put me in Imogen's room?" I remembered Petroc's surprise when she had told him.

"It's the second most beautiful bedroom in the house." Her eyes kept darting about.

"Helen?" I raised an eyebrow.

"If you must know, I used to see Petroc just standing in there, sometimes with tears rolling down his cheeks. It had been happening more of late."

A shiver ran up my spine. "So you wanted to stop Petroc?"

She nodded. "I didn't need him becoming disturbed by the past again."

"Was Imogen having an affair?"

She stared at me. "Why do you ask?"

"I found a letter from her to Petroc."

"Did she admit it?" Helen went pale.

"No." I thought of her words and her plea to trust her. "Was she, and with whom?"

"I don't know. She was young."

"Petroc loved her."

"There's no doubt of that, but another man did too."

"Who?"

"Wilf Trelawny."

I frowned. I'd seen the name Trelawny, W. Trelawny, on the orchid book. "What was Imogen's maiden name?"

"Rowse."

I nodded. "They wrote a book together."

"Yes. That's when it all started." She shook her head and stood. "I must get back to the grandkids." She put her hand on my shoulder and gave it a squeeze.

The Internet gave me all sorts of interesting facts about curlews and doves, but didn't shed any light on the mystery. The next painting in the book was of Dennis Head. From what I could tell, it would have been from painted from Rosemullion. It looked very similar to what we had sailed around last weekend, but something didn't seem the same. I couldn't figure out what it was, though. I would need to get out on the water, or take the ferry to the north side of the river and walk to Rosemullion.

The last picture was of a white orchid flower, which might explain Imogen's interest in the sketchbook. But no matter how I tried, I couldn't see any connection to these paintings and the riddle. Had Octavia just liked the sound of the rhythm of it? Was she just practising her handwriting? I stood and placed the book back down. Riddles were very popular with the Victorians, but that didn't mean there was any correlation.

I paced the drawing room, then went to Octavia's portrait, which was now in the hall propped against the fireplace. I could shift hers on my own, but I didn't want to separate the two paintings, so they would have to wait until Tristan returned.

Octavia's gentle brown eyes looked at me. She was so delicate, I couldn't imagine what must have been in her mind to venture out in a boat on her own.

"Come on, Octavia, tell me what happened. Do your paintings reveal where the treasure is?"

I walked back to Petroc's journals in the study to try and see if he had left me any clues. This family didn't throw out anything, from what I had seen so far. Octavia must have left more than one sketchbook. Maybe there were letters. Had Petroc asked Lady Rutherford if there was any correspondence from Lady Clarissa to her sister? I wondered if they were close, and if she might have told her sister of her plans. I would have told mine.

CHAPTER
TWENTY

I walked down the stairs and found Tristan. He was back, and staring at the portraits in the hall. "What on earth are these doing here?"

"Had to move them for the photographer." I silently added *That you organised and left me to deal with*.

He turned to me. "Photographer?"

"The one from the realtor."

He drew back. "I haven't chosen an estate agent yet."

"What? It was listed in the paper just after the funeral."

"Jude, I can tell you that I haven't put Pengarrock on the market."

I bristled. "If you don't believe me, shall we go and check the realtor's website?" As I walked towards the study, my posture would have pleased my old ballet mistress. I was not imagining things. I picked up my laptop from the filing cabinets and placed it on Petroc's desk. The clock wasn't ticking. The atmosphere in the room was stuffy despite the open window. We waited for the computer to power up and Tristan stood with his arms across his chest.

Quickly I typed in the agent's name and waited for the website to load. "Tristan, I am not hallucinating. I'm not the only one to have seen it. If you read the local papers you would have too."

He didn't say a word but stood beside me. My fingers faltered on the keys in my rush. On the second attempt I managed to put in the correct details and a picture of Pengarrock appeared on the screen. I stood back and let Tristan have full access to the computer.

"Bloody hell."

I resisted saying, I told you so.

"How?" He picked up the phone on the desk and punched in the number. I looked at the details. It was still a preliminary listing and no price was shown, but I began to click through the twenty pictures that I had assisted with, and I wanted to cry. It looked so wonderful. It would secure a buyer with no problem, even if the price were astronomical.

"Could I speak to the person handling Pengarrock?" The tone of Tristan's voice was scary. I didn't envy the person he'd eventually speak to.

"Tristan Trevillion." He snapped. The look on his face was one of pure fury, which I didn't understand. He wanted to get rid of the estate, so this shouldn't be a huge issue, even if it was premature. I decided to leave him to it.

I checked my mail and saw that finally I had a reply from Sophie.

Hi Jude,

Sorry I haven't emailed. I've been away for a week with Tim in Maine. I checked with Mom and she said your dad's been gone for about ten days. Your mother is behaving as if this is normal and was planned for ages, but I wasn't convinced. Sorry I can't add more info. Have you spoken to either of them?

Oh, Tim has proposed! I've said yes. I don't suppose I could convince you to come back and be my maid of honor? I hope I can, but I would understand if you couldn't face it. We aren't doing a big thing. I know it's not a lot of notice but it's in three weeks. Will you consider it? Please, please, please!!!!
Love,

Sophie x

I froze. Go back. Go back and stand at the altar. No way. I walked away from the computer. The feeling that I must go home had been taking over my dreams at night. The sense that something was wrong wouldn't go away. Hearing that Dad had been gone for ten days didn't help. He liked to fish, but only for a day.

Going home was one thing, but to be in a wedding was another matter. It was Sophie's wedding, though; my best friend. She had always said I would be her maid of honour. Always. She had no sister. I had only wanted Rose, and I couldn't have her, so I chose not to have one. Sophie totally understood. But now she wanted me. There was no way I could stand in a silly

250

dress at the altar. I sat down and my fingers hovered over the keys.

Oh, Sophie, how brilliant! I'll look at flights. I'm not saying yes. I don't know if I can get the time off work. You must think of someone better for your maid of honor. Everyone will be thinking about what I did, not how wonderful you'll look and how absolutely fabulous it is that you and Tim are getting married. You know I would love nothing more than being there for you in that way, but what I did to John really makes it impossible.

I am over the moon for you. It is so right.

Thanks for the info on my parents. If you hear anything else, let me know.

Love,

Jude x

I pressed send, then closed my eyes, grateful that I hadn't gone through with the marriage to John. It wouldn't have been fair on him. He deserved someone who really and truly loved him, not someone who was just doing what was expected.

I picked up the phone and tried to reach home, but again it went to answerphone. I left another message, pleading for them to answer and tell me what was going on. It was clear something was wrong. I hung up, and then dialled Aunt Agnes.

"Jude, how are you?" Her voice sounded feeble and I didn't like it.

"Good. Cornwall is fabulous."

"Your letters have been wonderful, and reminded me of the ones you wrote to me during your time in Singapore. Do you remember them?" She began coughing and I heard someone's voice in the background offering her a glass of water.

"I do." I ran my fingers over the clock on the desk, loving the ticking sound it made. "Auntie, you don't sound very good."

"No, I don't. Things are finally catching up with me." She cleared her throat.

"What's wrong?" Fear grabbed my stomach, tightening all my insides. I knew what she was going to say.

"The big C." She laughed, but began coughing. "Well, something had to take me. Can't live for ever, you know."

I closed my eyes, wishing I wasn't hearing this.

"I'm fine, or as fine as you can be with this disease."

I wanted to scream, and then I wanted to hop on the next plane, but that would be the last thing that she'd want. "What are they saying?"

"I'm dying." She laughed.

"It's not funny."

"No, but you get to my age and things you never thought you'd laugh at, let alone do or have done to you become funny. It's how you save your sanity." Her voice faded away. "Enough about me. You sound like you are blossoming in Cornwall."

252

"I wouldn't go that far, but I do love it, and the work."

"Sorry you lost Petroc, though. Sixty is much to soon."

"I know." I chewed the inside of my cheek. "Have you heard from Dad?"

"He visited me about ten days ago. He said he was going fishing."

I shook my head. Fishing. "Did that strike you as a bit strange?"

"Yes, and I told him so."

I smiled. "And what did he say?"

"In your father's typical fashion, not a lot, but I gather he needed," she paused to take a few ragged breaths, "me time."

"That's not good."

"Maybe, maybe not, but it's his problem and not yours." She sighed. "You can't fix it. If there is any fixing to be done then he needs to do it himself."

I stretched my fingers out. Dad had always been so good at fixing me. It didn't seem right that I couldn't help him. I sighed. "Auntie?"

"Yes? I can tell you want to ask me how long."

Tears filled my eyes.

"They won't say, but I'm still at home and happy to be here. Don't worry. I'll make sure they let you know. Now go and live your life." She coughed again. "I enjoyed mine."

I sank into the chair behind the desk as I put the phone down. Aunt Agnes was dying, and Dad had gone fishing and she'd told me not to worry about them. The phone rang and I reached to answer it. "Pengarrock."

"Jude."

"John?" Clearly today was the day for everyone from my past to get in contact.

"Don't sound so pleased to hear my voice."

"I hadn't expected to, that's all."

"I bet. You'll be pleased to know that I wasn't actually calling to speak to you but to Tristan. You answering the phone is a bonus."

"Tristan?" I frowned.

"Yes. Didn't he mention that I was helping him with his deal in the US?"

"No."

"No problem. I tried to reach him on his cell, but couldn't get through."

"I think he might be on it; I heard him talking as I came past."

"Can you get him to ring me?" he asked.

"Sure."

"Jude?" John's voice dropped.

"Don't go there. Keep well, and I'll pass on the message." I put the phone down feeling incredibly cross. John was working with Tristan, and neither of them had taken the trouble to let me know. I knew John was a brilliant lawyer, and I knew that Tristan had been in the States, but I felt like they had been doing things behind my back.

I slipped into the billiard room. Tristan was looking out of the window and chatting on the phone. I grabbed a sheet of paper and began to write a note to

254

call John, then I saw plans scattered all over the table. I stopped. *Development*. I wanted to scream. My glance fell to the plans that looked like breaking the house up into flats, but worse followed as I saw more plans to build houses on vast tracts of land. It looked awful. It would ruin what was here, and all for the sake of profit. Every muscle in me tensed and I longed to tear them all up.

Tristan remained with his back to me, intent on his conversation. Couldn't he see he would be destroying something so alive and beautiful? Money must be so damned important to him. I turned and walked out of the room, slamming the door behind me. Childish, I know, but I felt so much better for it. There had to be some way I could help save Pengarrock, or at least slow this mad rush to destroy it.

I sat in stunned silence as I read the leather-bound notebook in my hand. Petroc's handwriting detailed the painful thoughts in his head. He was agonising over his lost relationship with Tristan. I slipped my glasses off and searched for a tissue. From the year on the cover of the notebook, embossed in gold, I guessed Tristan must have been about thirteen when Petroc had written these words. I could see Petroc's pride in his growing son, but despair at the widening separation.

I stood. I didn't need to read this, only to catalogue its existence. Yet I felt compelled to, as if there were answers here, but I didn't know what the questions were. I had found a few journals, but knew there must be more. Petroc was a man of ritual. This much I'd learned from his work. As he wrote daily during those ten years of journals I had found, it was likely that he had always done this, but I'd yet to uncover the others.

The air was still warm despite the steady rain, which unfortunately was coming too late for some of the crops in the fields. I'd had a long chat with one of the farmers when I was walking the dogs last night. The poor man was quite discouraged, but added that they'd been through this before. He was more worried about what a new owner would want to do with the estate. Would he keep the tenant farmers on, and would he increase the rents?

How would he feel when he found out that Tristan planned to make a big holiday complex of the estate?

I turned to look out at the rain again. Even when it was grey, the beauty of this place reached someplace inside me. It aroused my passions unlike any man had. The gentle roll of the hills and smell of the sea had seduced me totally, and I knew my heart was here for ever.

I ran a hand across the fine leather of the 1986 journal. I'd take them, years 1985 through 1996, upstairs and read them at night. Petroc had captured the essence of the place in his unique words. He was so honest, or at least seemed so, in his feelings about Pengarrock, Imogen and Tristan. Strangely, the only references to the sapphire search came in the last few years. It seemed to be tied up with the research for his book. Petroc had known of the sapphire since childhood, so what had he uncovered while digging around for information that had prompted the quest for it? Had it obsessed him, as Tristan implied? What would finding it have meant for the estate?

I yawned. I could hear Tristan on the phone still. He was holed up, working on destroying Pengarrock and, bar killing him, I hadn't found a way to stop him. He was very English. Nothing was ever said about emotion. Mother was that way, and I had the sense that Petroc only showed his feelings in his journal. I wondered whether Tristan knew his father had kept one. Did he? Somehow I didn't think so. Keeping a journal would be too artistic for Mr Scientist-turned-Financier.

CHAPTER
TWENTY-ONE

My little car looked lonely all by itself in the drive as I walked to the kitchen with the dogs. Tristan had left for London late yesterday, and he hadn't been in a good frame of mind. The dark circles under his eyes hadn't disappeared, and I felt, but didn't say, that he was too tired to make the journey. It would be a slow one as Friday was changeover day for many holiday cottages. Helen put the kettle on as I walked through the door. A big sigh escaped her as she pulled the teapot out. Then she sat down on a chair and cried.

I wasn't sure what to do, so I reached out and touched her hand. The poor woman just cried some more. She lifted her head several times, but more tears came. I found a box of tissues and sat down next to her; I felt so helpless. Eventually Helen got up and straightened her shoulders.

"Sorry." She looked at me with red, puffy eyes. "Surprised you, have I?"

"A bit."

"Me too. Didn't know things were still so close to the surface." She reached for another tissue.

"Petroc?"

"Yes, but." Helen stopped.

"But what?"

"Not for me to say. Too much sadness."

"Why sadness? Petroc's death was sudden and much too soon, but he seemed to have had a good life."

Helen gave a dry laugh.

"From your point of view, Petroc had a good life, yes. He was a fine man, a scholar and a landlord, but the poor man had to live with his choices. His loves."

I frowned. "His loves?"

"Love doesn't always make the right choice, even though it tries. The poor man's heart was always trying to make the right choice."

I picked up the boiled kettle and made the tea. "How did he love wrongly?"

"Not wrongly, but . . . Oh, I don't know. He loved, but his choices were the wrong ones, from where I see it."

"Oh." I knew how easily that could happen.

"I'm so worried that Tristan will make the wrong choices, like his father." Helen blew her nose. "It's a shame that Mark won Clare." She stood and poured the tea. "Tristan loved her, and had they married he would have stayed here. She would have kept him close to his roots."

"That wouldn't have changed her death."

"No, I don't think anything would have changed that, but it would have tied him here."

"Do you think so? He might still have run away, from the pain of loss." As I said these words, I realised that this was what Tristan was doing now.

"It's all so sad in so many ways." Helen came up to me and handed me a mug of tea. "I'll be off now to put my feet up."

"Thanks, Helen." My heart felt so heavy. I wondered if Tristan still carried a torch for Clare, which could explain a lot, but not everything.

I had spent a long time last night writing to Aunt Agnes. I realised there was so much I wanted and needed to say to her before it was too late. All the frustration of the years of being away from home when things happened had finally hit me. But, unlike in the past, when Dad's job had been the reason we didn't make it to weddings and funerals, it was my job and my self-imposed exile that was keeping me away from my aunt. She was the third reason to go home. I could say goodbye to her in person. The first was my parents. The second was Sophie and Tim's wedding. As I walked through the lanes after mailing the letter, I made the decision to go to the wedding. I could stay in the background and just be there to support my best friend.

Walking into the kitchen, I found Helen there again. I looked around for evidence of what she'd been up to. The last thing that was needed was her trying to do too much again. "Morning, Helen."

She looked up from the paper. "Morning. Just catching up on the news. Seems a waste to buy a second paper."

I smiled and wondered whether this was a cover or the truth. But there was no evidence of cooking or ironing. "Do you think Tristan would mind if I had a look through Petroc's room?"

"No. As you would expect, there are hundreds of books up there."

"Thought there might be." I leaned against the table and scanned the headlines.

"Anything in particular you're looking for?" Helen sat back. I thought she was looking much better. Her colour had returned, and she was gaining a bit of weight.

"I'm looking for Petroc's most recent journal. Last night I was reading his manuscript and a few things are unclear. I'm hoping his journal might shed some light on it."

"Oh. Didn't know he kept one."

I raised an eyebrow. "Really?"

"Yes."

"Well, I've found about fifteen volumes so far. I've a batch of ten years together, and then one from his teens and another from two years ago. It makes me think he must always have kept one."

She stood. "What do they look like?"

"Well, the early one is just a small black book, but the later ones are lovely leather-bound books."

"They don't sound like anything I would even notice, and obviously haven't. You'd better go and have a look. I'm sure it won't bother Tristan in the least." Helen rolled her eyes.

I waved at Helen and took the back stairs. The door to the nursery was open. Again I went in and looked around. There was a desk at the end of the room. I pulled down the flap and looked through the pigeonholes at the back filled with writing paper, pencils and a stapler. Nothing looked very significant. I closed the top and looked in the drawers below. Here I found a delightful collection of children's drawings including several by Tristan. My heart stopped when I saw one he had drawn of his mother and father. His mother was holding a flower in her hand. He had signed it in large wobbly script.

I put it away and did a quick check of the rest of the drawers but found nothing. There was so much to do, and so little time left to do it. I stuck my nose in several other rooms on my way to Petroc's. Each one had a desk and bookcases. It would take me ages to do all this on my own. I knew Tristan was trying to move quickly, and that everything I was doing would get pushed aside in the rush to complete.

Outside Petroc's room I stopped and closed my eyes. Hopefully there would be something, or even several things, in there that would unlock some answers. I needed help; time was running out. In the room, I was confronted by a massive four-poster bed. The dark wood was beautifully carved and I ran my fingers over the surface. This room was twice the size of the one I was in, and faced both north and east with views sweeping up the river and out to Falmouth Bay. As I would have expected from Petroc, the walls were lined with bookcases. I walked to the bedside table. In a silver frame was a black and white photograph of Imogen and Tristan. This was the only family photograph I'd seen on display in the whole house. It struck me as odd.

In it, Tristan must have been about seven and his arms were thrown about his mother's neck. I tried to find him in his mother's features, but he was a Trevillion except for his eyes. A lump rose in my throat. It must have been so hard to lose your mother. And to think that all these years he had felt she had taken her own life and left him by choice. I ran my finger over the photo and hoped that Helen was right, and that Imogen hadn't committed suicide. I hated the thought that she might have been in despair.

Then I spotted some books under the bed. When I was halfway under the bed with a pile of books around my legs, I could see a few more that would be easier to reach from the other side.

"Jude?"

I stopped moving as soon as I heard Tristan. It could not possibly be a flattering view of me that he had. "Hi. When did you get back?" I could see his feet beside me.

"Just now. What on earth are you doing?"

I shimmied out from under the bed and my wiggling backside knocked over one of the stacks of books.

"Sorry, what did you say?"

"What are you doing?"

"Oh, your father had a stash of books here under the bed. Some quite interesting ones." Sitting back on my heels, I pulled a book out from the pile still standing. "Here, look at this. It's a first edition. It's in very good condition, and could have some value."

He held the leather-bound book in his hands and opened the cover. "Alan Trevillion." He ran his fingers over the writing.

"There's more. I just need to get at them from the other side." I scrambled over, aware I must look a sight covered in dust bunnies.

"Can I hand these to you?" I called from under the bed.

He knelt down. "Ready when you are."

I passed him five books. Once out from under the bed I scanned the pile. "A-ha. Just what I was looking for."

"And what would that be? A pot of gold?"

I pushed myself back out and got to my knees beside him.

"No — definitely better than a pot of gold. Two more of your father's journals."

"What's so great about them?"

"They are magic."

"Magic? He writes about spells, does he?"

I rapped his knuckles, then thought, *Oh God, what have I done?* but he laughed.

"No, his journals thus far have captured daily life here at Pengarrock, his Oxford years and the history of the estate and the family. Not to mention his thoughts and views on all aspects of life and current affairs. They are a treasure trove of knowledge."

"Well, that tells me."

"Yes, it does, but I can see from your face you don't realise their worth."

"Am I that transparent?"

"At the moment, yes." I was holding my breath and staring into his eyes. I loved the little flecks of deep blue set amid the green. He was looking at me closely too. We were almost touching. His breath caressed my cheek. I fought the urge to make contact. Just one slight movement would bring my lips to his. I let the air escape from my lungs and tore my glance from his.

"Look, this is your father's journal from 2000." I handed it to him.

"Yes."

I liked the way his voice drawled out the yes, leaving me in no doubt that he didn't believe there would be anything at all interesting in there. I would prove him wrong. I liked a challenge.

"Open it."

"You know what's in here?" He turned the book over in his hands. His fingers ran along its spine.

I swallowed. "I have no idea, but I do know that your father wrote beautifully."

"Pardon me if I remain sceptical."

"You won't know until you read it." I stated my case with my eyes and focused all my determination into my look. Tristan didn't flinch. I watched his pupils enlarge and my breathing became shallow. We were talking about reading a journal, but somehow it felt like something else.

"You're not giving me any choice."

"No."

He opened the book.

"Read it."

"OK, bossy."

"Aloud."

"Aloud?" He frowned.

"Your father's prose is special."

"Now you're pulling my leg." Tristan's face broke into a grin and his eyes smiled. I caught my breath.

"Not at all. Read."

"Thirtieth of May 2000. Bluebell season. The wood appeared violet as the noon sunlight filtered through the trees not yet in leaf. The myriad blue tones never cease to amaze me. One moment it was a haze of cobalt then, looking again, a richer, almost purple-blue carpet stretched as far as the eye could see."

Tristan stopped; he was no longer looking at the diary. I could tell he was far from the room. His hand moved over the writing and I had the feeling that the loss of his father might be about to hit. With the journal in hand, he walked to a chair and settled down. Tristan needed to have this moment alone. I slipped out of the room with the image of his fingers tracing the words like a caress stuck in my head.

The smell of chocolate cake drew me from the study. What was Helen up to? She was pulling a cake out of the oven as I walked into the kitchen. "What's this in honour of?"

"You."

"Me, whatever for?" I leaned against the counter.

"Your birthday."

"What? Hold on, how did you know?" I leaned my head to the side and studied her.

She tapped her nose. "I have my sources."

"That I don't doubt, but not among those who would know it's my birthday."

"You'd be surprised." She raised her eyebrows.

"I think I might be." I couldn't think of anyone here whom I'd told it was my birthday. "Wait a minute. Did anyone call for me today?"

"Might have."

"I thought so." I ran through the possibilities. Most of my friends had been in contact by email, so who would call other than John? It certainly wouldn't be my parents. "John?"

"Who's John?" She turned the cake onto a wire rack.

"Your sources aren't that good then." I smiled.

"Well, you tell me."

"He's the old friend who visited a few weekends ago."

"The good-looking blond?" Helen watched me closely, hand on hip. I wasn't sure who was interrogating whom at this point.

"Yes, that's him." John fit that description well.

"Jenna was drooling over some man, I seem to recall." She beat the frosting.

I laughed. "Yes, that would be John. He didn't call?"

"No."

"Was it a man?" I looked at the ceiling, trying to think who it would be. The thick beams that lined the ceiling were unevenly spaced. I hadn't noticed that before.

"No."

I was about to give in and then the light dawned. "Barbara?"

"Charming woman. We had a lovely chat."

"Why does that worry me?" I turned on the tap for a glass of water.

"Wouldn't know."

"Wouldn't know what?" Tristan appeared. There was no sign of the emotion I had seen on his face a few hours ago when I'd left him reading his father's journal.

"Did you know it was Jude's birthday today?"

Tristan tapped his head. "I must confess it had slipped my mind."

"Why not come clean and admit it had never been on your mind?" I smiled.

"Does that bother you?" The corner of his mouth turned up and my stomach did a little flip.

"Not in the least."

"Children." Helen raised the wooden spoon in her hand.

"Yes, Helen?" Tristan walked over to where she was mixing the frosting and stuck his finger in the bowl. She slapped his hand.

"Judith, would you care for a birthday drink and dinner down at the Shippers?" He turned to me, licking the chocolate off his finger.

I blinked. "The what?"

"He means the Shipwright's Arms."

"Thanks for the translation, Helen. Sounds great."

"Well, that's perfect then. Stop by on the way down so the kids can sing happy birthday to you."

"Good plan." He stole some more frosting.

268

"Tristan, you might want to book. It can get a bit cool outside with a north wind blowing." She looked up from the cake.

"I'll book, and we can always change our minds."

"About dinner?" I was very confused.

"No, about whether to eat inside or out." He smiled.

CHAPTER
TWENTY-TWO

The pub was packed. It was a good thing that Tristan had booked a table inside because a light drizzle had begun to fall. As Tristan made his way to the bar the barman called out, "Hey, Tristan, your table is ready."

"Thanks, Mike." Tristan smiled at me as I was extricating myself from yet another birthday kiss. It was amazing how many people I'd met in the short time I'd been here, and how news of my birthday had spread. Tristan scanned the crowd before his eyes came back to mine. The intensity of his look made me shiver. Once at our table in the corner, I refused to dwell on the intimacy of the low light and the proximity of Tristan's body. I needed to think about other things. The old photographs on the wall were something to contemplate until I caught the eye of an old man when he wandered through the low door and winked at me.

Tristan looked at the menu on the blackboard, then turned to me. "Do you know what you want?"

I opened my mouth and then shut it and shook my head.

"I'm tempted." He glanced at me.

"Yes?" It felt like there was a tight ball in my chest.

"By the scallops to start, and then a steak. You?"

I turned from Tristan back to the blackboard. The menu held too much choice. "The crab with avocado and a steak too, I think."

"I'll go and place the order. How do you like your steak?"

"Medium rare." I watched him walk to the bar. Something felt different tonight. A line had been crossed somehow, and I needed to find a way back. The smile on his face when he returned to the table wasn't helping me find the right direction.

"Tristan, did you know that just around St Keverne alone there are about thirty places beginning with 'Tre'?"

"Can't say I'd noticed." His full attention seemed to be focused on my mouth.

"Well, there you are. There may be more." I took a deep breath.

"Yes, and what's your point?" He leaned back against the wall as the appetisers were placed in front of us.

This gave me more space, but I couldn't see the play of blues and greens in his eyes from this distance. "Well, I now know that it means something like 'family settlement' in Cornish, but from a tourist's standpoint, it would have been more helpful if they were a bit more original in their naming process."

"Cornish names are logical. Pengarrock, 'Pen' being 'head of' and 'garrock' being 'rock' or 'stone'."

"I got so lost when I first arrived." The crab was divine.

"Why does this not surprise me?" When he smiled, his eyes sparkled, reminding me of sunlight on the sea.

I rolled my eyes. "With all the 'Tre's, who could blame me?"

"There wasn't a single 'Tre' to worry about, had you taken the correct turn when you passed it."

"I know that now!" I sipped my wine. He appeared so relaxed and, well, playful. This was a completely different Tristan, and I wasn't sure how I felt about it. It was far easier when I was angry with him.

"These scallops are perfect. Would you like to try one?"

I wanted to but it would be too intimate, so I shook my head.

"I hear birthday wishes are in order." Mark came to the table and bent to kiss me.

I jumped. I'd been so focused on Tristan I'd forgotten we were in a public place.

"They are indeed." I beamed at Mark. His face seemed so open compared to Tristan's, which had just shut down like storm shutters before a hurricane.

"Care to join us for a drink?" Tristan bit out the words.

"Why don't you join me when you've finished your dinner?" Mark suggested when he saw the waiter arrive with the steaks.

"That would be great." I smiled, not sure what to do. Tristan was doing his best to be polite, but it was awkward.

"You might need to be careful with him." Tristan cut into his steak.

"Excuse me?" I stopped, a fork poised mid-air.

"I know it's not my place, but Mark doesn't have a good reputation with women."

I put my fork down. "Not to worry; I don't have a good reputation with men."

Tristan put his hands up. "Just don't say I didn't warn you."

"Don't worry, I won't." I studied the light reflecting off my wine. Why did I have to say that? Tristan knew about John, I sure didn't have to remind him. I was an ass, and should apologise to him.

"I don't want to question your sanity, but maybe you are still emotionally unbalanced after John."

"But you're going to." I put my hands on the table ready to push myself to my feet.

"Point taken." We ate the rest of the meal in silence. The sooner we got back to the house, the better.

I was about to suggest this when the kitchen staff emerged singing Happy Birthday and presented me with a candle-topped slice of chocolate cake. Our conversation had taken the joy out of the moment.

Tamsin appeared out of the crowd and handed me a glass of champagne. "Happy Birthday!"

I stood to join her. "Thanks."

She looked over at Tristan, who had moved off to talk to an older man. "It's nice to see him out. You're a good influence on him."

"Not so sure about that."

"I am." She smiled at me. "So, what about the plans for development?"

I opened my mouth, then shut it. "Is nothing in this place a secret?"

"Absolutely not. I thought you would have discovered that by now."

"I thought the goings-on at the big house were private." I looked around the room, wondering who might be listening.

"Never have been."

"What have you heard about development?"

Tamsin shrugged. "Not a lot. A friend from London called and tried to sound me out on what I thought would happen re planning permission."

"I see." I played with the stem of my wine glass, trying to be neutral about all of this but failing.

"I bet you do. Care to tell me what you've seen?"

I shook my head. "No."

Tristan walked over to us, and Mark arrived at the same time. I didn't think this would be good, as we'd all had a fair bit to drink. "So, Tristan, how much do you think you'll make out of Pengarrock?" The words didn't come out of Mark's mouth, but the man's beside him.

"Not enough." Tristan turned his back on him but the man continued.

"I've heard about the twenty houses, and dividing the house into flats."

Tristan raised an eyebrow, then glanced at me. I looked to Tamsin and she shook her head.

"I have no plans to develop Pengarrock at the moment. Now if you'll excuse me, the pub is not the place to discuss private matters."

"But it isn't private." The man moved closer to Tristan, and I thought he would punch him.

"At the moment it is."

"Tristan's right, Jim. Not now." Mark manoeuvred the man out into the fresh air.

"I think it's time to go home." I whispered to Tristan.

"Agreed." He led the way out of the pub.

As we walked in silence through the village and up the hill, the lights from the houses disappeared, To navigate I kept looking up at the sky. It was just a bit lighter than the outline of the trees that lined the road. "I love the darkness here."

"Why?"

"You can see the sky." As I glanced up again, I walked into him and he put an arm around me.

"You can see the sky everywhere."

The darkness closed around us. Just outside the house I stopped and studied the stars. "So many stars." Everything had taken on a glow, and I knew that I'd had a bit too much to drink.

"You can see the Milky Way."

"Hmm." I leaned against him, propping my not-so-steady head on his shoulder. "You can't see the stars in the city."

"Too much light." He spoke so quietly it felt like he was whispering to me.

"Growing up, I loved lying on the beach late at night."

"Did you do that often?" His words ruffled my hair.

"Not enough. The biggest problem is that you end up with your hair full of sand."

He laughed. "True."

"Have you ever lain on a beach and watched the stars?"

"No."

"Would you want to?" I glanced at him.

"Maybe."

"Why maybe?"

"It would have to be with the right person."

"That helps." I turned my head, forgetting the stars. His mouth was so close. It was my birthday and I wanted something. I kissed him. His lips tasted of chocolate and wine . . . delicious. "Thank you for a wonderful birthday dinner."

He still held me in his arms. His face was so close. It seemed so natural to kiss him again. Of course the champagne was to blame. The kissing deepened, and quickly desire fought with the little sanity I had left.

His hand fell from my back and grabbed my hand. While still kissing me he pulled me into the house. I began to tug at his shirt. My cardigan hit the floor. I felt Tristan's fingers running along the bare skin of my waist as my shirt came loose. Desire surged through me.

He drew me against his body. I wanted him now, in the hall if necessary. His mouth trailed down my neck. I shivered.

"Oh, God." I pulled away and ran to the nearest bathroom. I just made it in time. All my dinner, and then some, came up. Tristan, shirtless, stood beside me, handing me tissues. I wanted to die.

276

CHAPTER
TWENTY-THREE

"Yes!" I pumped my hand in the air.

"Are you calling me?" Helen walked into the study.

"No, sorry. I've just found Petroc's last journal. It was here in the study the whole time."

"Things are often right in front of you."

"So true." I sighed.

"How are you feeling today?"

"Much better, although I don't think I want to see another glass of wine for a while. Yesterday was a complete write-off." I really didn't want to think about it. I couldn't believe I'd kissed Tristan — no, more than that, I'd practically made love to him in the hall. Of all the stupid things to do, that had to be the worst.

"That can be good for you sometimes."

"The way I felt yesterday can never be good for you."

Helen laughed, glancing at all the boxes and piles around the room. "I take it there's some order to all this."

"Oh, yes. This side of the room is solely related to Pengarrock and is of little value elsewhere, and the other side holds things that might be of interest to the outside world."

"Outside world?"

"Did I say that?" I pushed back from the desk.

"Yes."

"Well, I guess I meant it. The rest of the world seems very far away."

"It is, but half of them are here on holiday." Helen ran a cloth around the edge of a framed map propped against a bookcase.

"How true. The beach was full yesterday."

"Yes, but the pubs and shops aren't. I guess the weather has been so lovely that everyone stays on the beaches."

"Can you blame them?"

"No, but it would be good if the community benefited from their presence."

"The holiday houses are full."

"You're right. Sue has more work than she can handle at the moment. She was telling me this morning that, on Saturday, she was flat out trying to turn the cottages around."

I stretched. "I think I'm still dehydrated. Is there any orange juice?"

"Yes, Tristan bought plenty."

"Great." I walked slowly to the kitchen, hoping that Tristan wouldn't be there. I really didn't want to face him. It was just too embarrassing. He was my employer, not my boyfriend. Not only had I removed half his clothes, he'd seen me at my worst with my head in the toilet. He'd been full of sympathy, which made it worse. I kept revisiting what could have happened, would have happened, if I hadn't been sick. My face flamed. I was so mortified, enough for a lifetime.

"How are you feeling today?" The object of my thoughts was leaning against the counter. The lips in question were smiling knowingly at me. There was a wicked glint in his eye, I was sure. I stopped walking. Maybe I could just do an about-face, pretending to have forgotten something . . . like my sanity. I didn't know whether this Tristan might be easier to take than the overly kind one of yesterday. Thinking about him passing me tissues still made me cringe.

"Much better. Thank you for your help yesterday, and sorry." I looked up from under my hair, trying to hide the blush creeping across my face. Yesterday I was too ill to be mortified.

"No problem. Don't think about it."

Easier said than done; when I looked at him I could still imagine the feel of his skin. How was I going to handle this? Could we go back to a normal working relationship after what had almost happened? "Is that coffee?"

Tristan poured a cup and handed it to me. His fingers brushed mine. I pulled away as if I'd been stung and went looking for the milk.

"Milk?"

I nodded, afraid to look at him.

"Still a bit delicate?"

"'Fraid so."

"Fancy a drink tonight?"

My head flew up and I saw the laughter in those eyes. Now I knew they looked like the Helford on a rainy day, slightly moody, sometimes stormy, but quite breathtaking. He wasn't taking this whole thing seriously, and maybe I shouldn't either, despite my embarrassment. I threw a tea towel at him. He caught it.

"I take it that means no."

"You take it right." I laughed and sipped the coffee. My eyes opened wide. "Even with milk this coffee would put hairs on your chest!"

His deep laugh sent a surge of delight through me. This was not ideal.

"Just what you need."

"I'm not so sure, but it does taste good."

"Excellent. Did I hear you shouting in the other room?"

"Was I that loud?"

"No, I just have good hearing."

"Well, it was worth shouting about. I found your father's last journal. I'm hoping he will have jotted down what his exact plans for the book were. He did this before, in a previous journal for another book."

"Are you actually missing any information?"

"Not quite. I just feel that things are not as they should be. I have sent a copy to the publishers and they will take it as it is, but I feel it isn't the work he would have wanted."

"How do you know?"

"Well, his other books are very tightly drawn. He misses nothing in his research, so the few hanging pieces in this work leave me wondering. I wouldn't want anything less than the best to go out in his name."

He poured more coffee into his cup. "Maybe I should read it."

"Might be a good idea." It was much easier to talk to him about work. If I could just keep it to that we would be fine.

"I take that to mean I should read it."

I stared at him. "Have you never read any of your father's books?"

"No. Until you put me on to his journals the other day, I had only ever read his letters to me."

I shook my head. "Wow."

"Why wow?"

"Because if my father was writing books, I know I'd want to read them."

He slipped a hand into his pocket. "Even if they were boring history stuff?"

"Hey, I resent that remark."

He laughed. "Fair enough."

"No, seriously, no matter what my father may have written I think I would have wanted to read it, except maybe a manual on, say, brain surgery. My stomach might not take that."

"OK, I'll read the book. Where is it?" He put his cup on the counter.

"I have a copy in the study. Don't look so worried! It's a pleasure to read."

"I imagine it's dry and dusty."

"Not at all. Are his journals?"

"No."

"Then you won't find this dry and dusty." We walked together to the study, and I felt his closeness unsettling. "I meant to mention it the other day. Did you receive my email about my godmother, Barbara James, who put your father and I in touch? She might be the right person to truly pull this book together. She's a fellow historian and excels at the written word."

"Is she expensive?"

I laughed. "If she were here I'm sure she'd say yes, but I think it would be very negotiable."

"Let me read the book and then I'll let you know." He stopped walking.

"Fine." I looked out to the river and saw the clouds were coming fast. I could have sworn there were none when we were in the kitchen. The air smelt different.

"Looks like some rain coming in." Tristan walked to the window.

"Feels like a storm." Which is what my insides felt like at that moment. Tristan wasn't good for me.

"You may be right. I can see some white horses out in the bay."

"White horses? Do you mean whitecaps?"

"Yes, I guess so. I think 'white horses' is much more poetic."

"Touché. Here's the manuscript. Enjoy." The rain had started pelting down and I pulled the window closed as the wind whipped up. I couldn't even see the end of the lawn, let alone the river right now. "The weather does change quickly here."

He looked at me, and his eyes were like the sea outside. Different emotions were revealed then hidden again almost as quickly. The changes left me breathless. "Yes, it can, although some days you can see it coming."

282

I looked at him, trying to read his eyes. Desire flashed in them and I flushed. I turned away. "Indeed."

Gin and Rum cantered ahead as I went through the kissing gate first. I marched off until the path opened up, leaving Tristan a long way behind. Proximity to him was unsettling, and I wasn't sure why he had to join the dogs and I on the walk. I had been trying to keep my distance.

Eventually he caught up with me. "Trying to chase away the demons?"

I swung round. That was too close to the truth. "Maybe." I closed my eyes for a moment. Every time I saw him, even in passing, I thought about the other night. It was driving me insane.

"Tristan."

"Yes."

I cleared my throat. There was no easy way to mention it but I had to say something or it would be the elephant in the room. "I am really sorry about the other night." I took a deep breath and looked at the river and not him. "It was a very unprofessional way to behave."

"Which part?"

I swung around and he was smiling. I fought the urge to hit him. He clearly found it funny. "Um, both parts."

"Apology accepted, but one wasn't required." He began walking. That was apparently the end of it as far as he was concerned, and I could have screamed with frustration. We walked on and I let the beauty of the place soothe me. How could I find him so attractive when he was such an idiot? This place was heaven on earth, and he was chosen as caretaker for such a beautiful piece of it. Could he not see?

"Every time I take this walk I think of the Du Maurier book." I pulled a long blade of grass from the ground.

"What book?" He glanced at me.

"*Frenchman's Creek.*"

"Don't know it."

I stopped walking. "How can you not know it? I can understand that you may not have read it, but not know it?"

"You wind up easily." He laughed.

"Beast." The sun was beginning to set and I was struck by how the nights were drawing in already. "Look at that wood over there." I pointed to the low hill between the river and the opposite creek.

"Groyne Point."

"Yes."

He scanned the ancient woodland of densely packed sessile oak, which appeared to fall into the water. "Its appearance is so different, looking on it from above. From the water's edge it feels mystic. There used to be good fishing at this point in the river." Tristan ran his fingers through his hair.

I decided not to interrupt his thoughts as we walked on. It sounded like he had some good memories, and if he could just tap into those maybe his eyes might be opened to what he was throwing away. We followed the path down until it came close to the water's edge. Someone rowed out of the creek, leaving it empty. The outgoing tide uncovered stretches of the banks. I spied a huge tree, which had fallen and stretched out into the creek. I stopped, then looked at him.

He raised an eyebrow. "You want to climb out there?"

"Are you chicken?"

"Certainly not. Rum, Gin." The dogs came bounding back. "Stay." He watched me scramble out on the limb none too gracefully. Once I found a comfortable spot, I sat with my legs dangling above the water.

"Can you see all the fish? We should have brought a net." I was mesmerised by the groups of grey bodies below.

"Grey mullet. Tastes like blotting paper." He made his way out onto the tree with more grace than I had managed.

"How appetising."

"Needs a very good sauce to be edible." He smiled.

"I'll try and remember that when I catch one."

"You'd be better taking a line out with you to the mouth of the river and catching some mackerel." He sat down, and the way the tree was shaped, my thigh pressed against his. This was the last thing I needed. My chest tightened. I couldn't shift even if I wanted to. Was I going to continue to be tormented with memories of what didn't happen? My mind was doing a brilliant job of taking the feel of his leg and completing some interesting scenarios.

"With JC around, it doesn't really make sense to bother fishing on my own at the moment. Maybe when I'm not under Helen's loving care I'll try it. Not too sure I'd be able to clean and gut them though."

285

"It's not hard." He motioned with his hands and I had to look away.

"No?"

"No. And what do you mean, when you're not under Helen's loving care? Are you leaving?" He sounded distressed.

"Not before the project is complete, and I don't want to leave the area."

"What?"

"I love it here." I couldn't stop the rush of longing that raced through me and made me sound so eager.

"Why? I would have thought the city would be more your scene." He turned to me.

"Maybe once, but I have never felt more at peace than here." Except when you're sitting this close to me. Peace was the last thing I was feeling at that moment.

"Not in Boston? Cape Cod? Or even Oxford?"

"Don't get me wrong. I love the Cape and Boston. Oxford was fun, but there is something that reaches straight inside me about this place. Just look in front of you. See the light on the hillside across the river. Look at the heron at the end of the creek. Peace."

"Yes, that's until the next boat comes down here." He pointed to the motorboat passing front of Calamansac on the north shore of the river.

"That's not what I mean. Can't you feel it?" I placed a hand on his arm. Mistake. Touching him was not good.

"No."

"Try. Shut your mind down. Don't let the negative voice in your head get in the way. Just be still, and open

286

your eyes to your surroundings." Tristan gave me a scornful look but I didn't back off.

"Fine, I'll try."

I'd be lucky if I could shut mine down because the sensation of his closeness was all I could feel. His scent and that of the honeysuckle were sending me mad. I forced myself to focus on the scenery. Here in the creek the light was low and the water reflected the deep green of the trees and the pale blue of the evening sky. A small boat with a red sail passed by the mouth of the creek. Beyond that lay the north side of the river where the top of the hill was still catching the evening sun. Somewhere I could hear the hum of a tractor, and the lightest of breezes reached us. Yet the warmth of Tristan's body beside me broke through the enchantment that the river was creating in my mind.

Gin's bark brought the spell completely to an end, as did the feel of Tristan's breath on my face as he turned.

"Well?" I looked into his eyes and caught my breath.

"Well what?"

"Are you telling me that it didn't speak to you? That you couldn't see and feel the beauty? The peace?"

His stare was so intent. Our lips were so close. I wasn't wrong. There was passion in his eyes. The green sparked with electricity, and it was all I could do not to kiss him. It would only complicate things more, and they were pretty messy already.

Tristan's phone rang and I saw the debate play across his face before he answered it.

"Trevillion." As he bit out the word his poker face returned and he was lost to me.

287

CHAPTER
TWENTY-FOUR

Tristan raced to reach the house phone as we walked back in.

"Trevillion." He immediately switched from the relaxed man on the walk into full business mode. "We are still in probate, as you know, but send it through." He put the phone down and looked at me. "We have an offer."

"What?" My knees wanted to give way. This was the last thing I wanted to hear.

"I hadn't told you the saga of the estate agent."

"No."

"You'll need a drink for this one. Can you face alcohol yet?"

I made a face. "Possibly. Will I really need it?"

"I did."

I frowned and followed him into the drawing room. The beauty of the room never failed to move me. The proportions were perfect.

"Wine or whisky?"

"It needs whisky?" I played with my bracelet. This wasn't good.

"I did, and still do."

"OK." While waiting for him, I opened the French windows and walked out onto the terrace. The evening was still warm. It must be quite an offer for an agent to call this late.

"Here." Tristan handed me a glass. "I've been thinking this over, and still have trouble accepting it."

I frowned, looking at the golden liquid in my glass. "Don't keep me in suspense."

"Dad put the house on the market."

"What? That can't be right. Petroc loved Pengarrock with his whole being."

"I know." Tristan shook his head and walked to a bench. "Thinking back, I knew he wasn't quite himself when he last visited me in London. He was very busy during the day, and I assumed it was with his publishers, but it turned out that he was meeting with agents and lawyers."

I pushed a stray curl back behind my ear. "Not the lawyer here?"

"No, I suspect initially it was to keep it quiet. You know what it's like here." He took a sip of his whisky.

"Yes." I turned from the river to look at the house. It was the same everywhere, except in big, anonymous cities.

"What puzzles me is his motivation. As you say, he loved Pengarrock more than life itself."

I closed my eyes. I knew why he'd done it. I didn't have any proof, but he'd done it for Tristan. He didn't want Tristan to have to carry this burden. My eyes watered and I opened them. "Are you sure you can't see why he did it?"

"No. It doesn't add up. I wonder if dementia was setting in early."

I stood up. "How can you be so blind!"

"Bloody hell, what's ruffled you?" He leaned back.

"You. He did it for you. He knew you didn't want it. And," I took a deep breath, "he hired me so that you wouldn't be faced with his stuff. I get it now. It always niggled me that a man who worked very happily on his own suddenly wanted someone else to interfere with his things."

"What?" Tristan stood.

"I think your dad thought that you had no love and no time for Pengarrock. It was a huge sadness for him, but looking back I can see he was resigned to it. That was why he wasn't developing the garden and opening it."

"Developing the garden?" He frowned. "I'm pleased it makes sense for you."

"Oh, Tristan, you are so blind in so many ways." I took a deep breath. "Your father loved you. You have no idea how much. Putting the estate on the market and hiring me were his gift to you. He was setting you free."

"No."

"Yes, but he died before he had completed everything." I was clear on that. I was very angry with Petroc and with Tristan. I'd been duped, or felt like it, and it was all Tristan's fault.

I walked down the pontoon to where the lugger I'd borrowed from Mark was tied. At the end of the pontoon there was only a foot and a half of water. There was no time to waste. The breeze was good, so I should be able to sail out through the narrows quickly.

I felt it might still be too early to see August Rock, the reef itself, but maybe not. I just wanted to view Pengarrock from the water, as Octavia's picture showed. I looked at the tide chart and each day it was getting more extreme. A splash of water hit my hand as it hung over the side of the boat. I pulled the sail tighter and the little lugger picked up its pace so that I could just sit back and enjoy being on the river on such a glorious day. My first thought wasn't a peaceful one, but one about Petroc. Had he been ill? Did he know he was at risk of a stroke? Or had he just been very forward-thinking? I wondered if Tristan could ask Petroc's doctor.

The tour boat from Falmouth was approaching, and even though they were not on course to crash, I would be swamped by its wake. A quick tack might avoid the worst of it but I'd still get wet. Joy! It was warm but there was enough wind to make the prospect unappealing.

The thought struck me that I was crazy. Here I was, out in a small boat to look at a view. What would it tell me? Most likely nothing at all. This landscape had a timeless feel about it. What could have changed since 1849? A few trees, not much more. But I needed to see it for myself. I had my camera with me to take photos so that I didn't have to rely on my memory.

As I made my way downriver, I thought about how much more there was to do. The attic was filled with trunks and boxes going back ages. The Trevillions were hoarders, from accounts to children's artwork. The only exception was Tristan. I sighed. There was a lifetime's work in the house, and I had months at most. Just

291

Petroc's journals alone were priceless for capturing the life of an estate in a time of change. But to be truthful, the estate was always evolving. It was amazing that it had held together with the same family for such a long time. Tristan's plans were criminal.

I stopped. I had a good view of the house. It sat with quiet dignity looking down on the river. I would just have to think of something to stop him. If I didn't, the whole character of this magical place could be changed for ever.

The wind switched direction as I reached the mouth of the river. The green buoy was in sight. The pace of the river had been slow and gentle, but now even in the trusty lugger I was cruising along at a good speed. Within touching distance of the buoy and despite the low tide, I still could not see the rocks yet. I released the sail and pulled the oars out. There was a slight swell, but the water was clear. If I made my way slowly maybe I could catch sight of the reef.

Three strong strokes with the oars, and then I heard a scratching noise. Pulling the oars in, I carefully knelt in the centre of the boat and leaned over. I couldn't see anything on one side, but then I felt and heard the scraping again, and this time it was different. I looked up and realised the sound was coming from the back. The rudder was down and obviously catching on something. Centring myself and pushing the boom to one side, I moved carefully to the back of the boat. The noise got worse. I pulled the rope on the tiller to raise it up.

Then I saw the tops of jagged rocks sitting just below the surface of the water. They were nasty. Well, so much for finding August Rock; I was right on top of it. The swell was increasing and so was the wind. The little lugger was dipping up and down, and I couldn't see any more than the top of the reef below. Glancing at Parson's Beach, I thought about Octavia and what might have driven her out in a small boat on the day of her wedding.

Carefully I pulled my camera out and used the telephoto lens to photograph Dennis Head and the coastline all the way to the house. Nothing looked unusual, but I couldn't study things too carefully as the boat was being pushed about by the waves and wind. I'd be able to tell more once I'd put the pictures onto the computer. Now I needed to make my way back home before the swell became much bigger.

I stood in the ticket hall watching the train approach. The last time I'd seen Barbara my life was upside down, and now it was better; well, sort of. The revelations of recent days had unsettled me. It was almost two months since Petroc's death. Until now, I would have said that things were progressing quite well, an American "quite". I'd tackled and organised the whole of the study, but the library and rest of the house remained. My problem was that now, more than ever, I knew my real role was not to organise Petroc's papers, but to stop Tristan from selling.

He seemed pig-headedly determined to go through with it. The offer he'd received was eye-watering, but I sensed he knew he'd make more from developing the estate or selling it in bits. He spoke of how nothing could be done until probate was complete, and that would take a minimum of six months, but it was looking more like eight. It gave me a little time to change things. I'm not sure why I felt I could, but I knew I would have to try. My mother's voice in my head reminded me that it was none of my business, but I'd made it mine. I loved Pengarrock. Now I just needed to make Tristan realise that he did too. Therein lay the problem.

For a moment on Frenchman's Creek I knew I'd almost made a breakthrough with him. I could feel him opening to the beauty. I could feel him full stop. The length of him against me had intensified all my senses. It would have been so easy to kiss him again, but I hadn't. Sanity had prevailed, but if I had, would it have led to a repeat of my birthday night and the madness that ensued?

The train pulled to a halt and I saw Barbara stepping down. I was so pleased that Tristan had agreed to her coming and helping. I felt like I'd won that battle.

"You're looking well." Barbara studied my face. "Very well." She laughed and leaned forward to kiss me. "It's been years since I came here last."

"How long?"

"A good twenty years since the last trip, but I was born here and lived here until I went to school."

"Really? You never mentioned it before."

"Never had any reason to, did I? Now you're here and now you know."

I smiled. There was no changing her. "Point taken. Good journey?"

"Delightful. Wonderful old lady sat beside me until Exeter, and she was a lively old thing. Gives one hope."

"Heaven's sake, Barbara, you're sounding like you're old, which you are not."

"Comes to us all, dear."

I laughed and wrestled her bag from her. We settled into the little car and made our way out of Truro when Barbara began again. "Is it the place or the man?"

"Excuse me?" I crashed a gear change.

"That riled you, didn't it? So John's been out to see you."

"OK, Barbara, you seem to have lots to ask, and you seem to know the answers before you ask the questions. Where would you like me to begin? With my answers or yours?"

Barbara threw her head back and laughed.

"With some new questions?"

"Fire away. Clearly I have no ability to stop you."

"What's Tristan Trevillion like?"

"You've caught me off guard on that one."

"Is he like his father?" She turned to me.

"That's an interesting question. How well did you know Petroc?"

"We dated."

"You *what*?"

"Don't sound so shocked. He was a friend of a friend, and we dated for a bit. He was a very good-looking man. Great mind, too."

"That all?"

"Wicked girl. I will not reveal all my past." She chuckled.

"Shame."

"But this doesn't tell me anything about Tristan."

I gripped the wheel harder than I needed to. "Tristan's very good-looking, but not as dark as his father, I would say. Did Petroc have black hair?"

"Yes, almost. Go on."

"Well, he's got green eyes with flecks of blue, but that's not important. He's stubborn, I think, or maybe focused is a better word. He doesn't have any time for his father or his work, but I'm trying to change that."

"How?"

I could see Barbara's raised eyebrow out of the corner of my eye. "Well, I have him reading Petroc's journals, for a start. They're beautiful. Were you his lover?"

"What an impertinent question!"

"Maybe, but he writes in the journals with such passion, I guess I just wondered if it carried over elsewhere." I pulled close to the hedge to let a car pass. I was getting used to this way of driving now. No longer was I filled with terror when I got behind the wheel. I saw a slight flush creep up Barbara's neck. Maybe they had been lovers.

"Might have done. Does his son have the same passion?"

"Couldn't begin to comment on that." I coughed. "Seems to run a thriving investment thing that occupies most of his time."

"You like him?"

"He's a nice guy." I pictured him sitting beside me on Frenchman's Creek, and nice was the last thing I would use to describe him.

"Nice is a bit dismissive." She stared at me.

"There's nothing to dismiss about Tristan. He's gorgeous, OK, and I find him incredibly attractive. But I am officially not in the market for a relationship. Don't do too well at those."

"You haven't really given yourself much of a chance, have you?"

"What do you mean by that?" I looked quickly at her before taking a turn.

"Well, you had a relationship with John, yes, but I can count on one hand the other boyfriends I knew about, and none of those was around for more than, let's say, a week or two."

"True." Where was she going with this?

"Quite right, too."

"You're in a feisty mood."

"Yes I don't want you hiding in the country to avoid relationships."

"I'm not." I looked at Barbara. I'd always been able to talk to her. "John is still in love with me."

"There's a surprise. You just need to love yourself."

"What?"

"It's simple." Barbara paused. "You need to love yourself before you'll accept anyone else's love. That's all there is to it."

"Maybe to you."

"It's a lesson I learned the hard way."

"Really? What happened?" I had never heard Barbara mention love when it referred to her.

"I let the right one get away." She had a faraway look in her eyes. I wondered if it had been Petroc.

"Oh, Barbara, I always wondered why you've never married. Didn't anyone else come along?"

"No, but don't worry, I wasn't ever lonely for long. Just try and learn by my mistake."

"So you think I made a mistake, leaving John?"

"I didn't say that. I said that you need to love yourself, then you can let love in."

I drove through the gates of Pengarrock. Was I trying to hide? There was no doubt that I'd escaped here, but now this place felt like home. It felt like home never had. Here I was, Jude Warren; not Judith, daughter of Charles and Jane Warren. I was me.

CHAPTER
TWENTY-FIVE

My hair was wild and bursting from its clip. I was a total mess as I walked through the big door at Pengarrock. Tristan stood at the table looking at the mail. I shoved my big sunglasses up on my head. "Tristan. This is Barbara James."

"Welcome to Pengarrock, Ms James."

"Thank you. Barbara, please." She held out a hand.

"So you're the cavalry?" Tristan smiled.

"It would appear so." Barbara's face turned serious. "I was so sorry to miss Petroc's funeral."

Tristan nodded. "Please make yourself at home."

"Thank you."

I led Barbara upstairs. My legs took the stairs with ease while she followed slightly behind. I'd put her in the Blue Room.

"Shall I leave you to settle in?" I put her bag down.

She nodded as she inspected the bookcase.

"I'll be in the study downstairs, which is to the right of the staircase."

"Fine. See you shortly." She smiled. "Tristan is very like his father, rather delicious."

"Barbara! You are wicked."

"Indeed. See you in a bit."

I was chuckling as I went to work. I laid the script out on the desk for Barbara with my notes scribbled all over it. As I'd mentioned to Tristan last night, she would have the right perspective on it. Tristan hadn't told me what he'd thought of it, but I knew all Petroc's love for the area was poured out on the pages.

"So this is where Petroc lived." Barbara walked in.

"That didn't take you long."

"Never does. Now show me this manuscript."

"It's on the desk. And before you start, I left out a notebook, one of many. It's not Petroc's work. I think it's Imogen's."

Barbara opened the book and I watched her read a few pages. "It's Imogen's work. She was a promising botanist. Due to her early death the world never benefited from her vast knowledge."

"How sad."

"Tragic." Barbara put her head down and ended the conversation.

"I can see where you're going with this." Barbara had Petroc's manuscript on her lap and a large gin and tonic in her hand.

"You can?" I was sitting on the wall looking at the view.

"Yes; this isn't like Petroc's previous work."

"No?"

"It's more like a personal memoir. A regional biography of sorts."

"I hadn't thought of it that way, but you're right. What about the holes?"

"Did the journal shed any light?" She sipped her drink.

"No. The problem is I don't know when he started this work."

"How many journals have you found?"

"Twenty, I think." I tucked a loose curl behind my ear.

"A good number."

"But aside from the current one, the more recent ones are still missing, as are some from his most productive years." I sipped my own drink.

Tristan had just walked across the lawn. His jeans were wet around the bottom, so he must have been at the beach. "That looks good. Don't suppose there is another one going."

"Coming right up." I walked into the drawing room, leaving Tristan with Barbara. I could hear them chatting. Barbara's deep, throaty laugh always made me smile. I wondered if she had been a smoker at one stage. Parts of her gave away hints of an almost secret life. When younger, I used to imagine that Barbara wasn't a lecturer but a nightclub singer. I smiled at the thought, and brought the drink out to Tristan. "How was the beach?"

"Not too busy. Someone had a good fire going, and it made me think of having a barbecue."

"Sounds good. I don't think we have anything that would work, but I could be wrong." I frowned.

"You're going to suggest a barbecue to an American, Tristan? Brave or foolish? I wonder which." Barbara winked at him.

I made a face.

"I'll go and see what we have. Before you two come to blows." He disappeared into the house.

"Bloody good-looking, on closer inspection. Different to his father, and very tasty indeed."

"Barbara!" I tried to sound scandalised.

"Just because I'm old doesn't mean I don't enjoy looking, and he's as good from the back as from the front. Superb ass."

"I'm shocked. Looking's one thing, but looking that closely is another! It's a wonder they let you near students any more."

"Yes, I eat them for breakfast."

We laughed, then I felt Barbara's scrutiny and braced myself.

"You've looked very closely indeed, haven't you?"

"What?" I drew back.

"I sensed something different about you, and now I know."

"Barbara."

"Don't 'Barbara' me, I know these things."

I shook my head.

"Jude?"

"Anyway, you know I was, could never . . ." I stopped mid-sentence.

"Oh, do tell. You could never what? Be reckless? Passionate? Allow yourself to be foolish? What could you never?"

"It's just too embarrassing."

"Dear girl, you fancy the pants off of him. You're unattached. What have you got to lose?"

"My job? My self-respect? I don't know, everything, I guess." *Most especially my heart*, I added silently.

"Bullshit. You have yourself too wrapped up. Embrace life and be the woman you are, not what you seem to think you should be. You don't have to fit someone else's desires. You need to fit your own."

I could see puffs of black smoke coming from the end of the house. "I suppose we should go help him."

"Suit yourself. The view is spectacular and the drink is perfect. Let's see what the man can produce without us, or are you just running away from the conversation?"

"Possibly I need to digest the lecture you just dished up." I took a seat. I still wondered how Barbara and Mother got on so well. Here was a woman so on top of things, and there was Mother wrapped up in a past world of the junior league and charity balls. I lived in Barbara's world much more easily than in my mother's. Why had I been so eager to please, to try and replace Rose?

"Penny for them?" Barbara studied me.

I wrinkled my nose. "How old were you when you met Petroc?"

"I was an undergraduate."

"Did you ever meet Imogen?"

"No. Heard she was a great beauty, though. Petroc loved her very much."

"How do you know that?" If Imogen was so loved, how could she have thought of straying?

"Oh, we would bump into each other at some function or other, and you could just see it in his eyes and hear it in his voice. I saw him just after he became a father. He was full of it. So in love with Imogen and the baby."

"It's funny, but I don't get the impression that Tristan had much time for his father."

"Children often don't."

I flinched. "Ouch."

"Glad to see you still can pick things up."

"I have tried repeatedly to reach them, but they never answer. Sophie tells me Dad's away fishing, which I simply can't believe."

"Agreed. Jane won't talk about it."

"That doesn't surprise me. I'm sure she says everything is fine." I pursed my lips.

"You're too hard on her."

"Am I? Why won't she pick up, or return my calls?"

"That I don't know."

I crossed my arms against my chest.

"Don't go all huffy. She loves you."

"Does she? Or am I just a reminder that she doesn't have Rose any more?" I stood up.

"That's not fair."

"I was never as good as Rose." I bit my lip. Barbara walked up to me and pulled me into her arms.

"All of you are still hurting."

"It was ages ago. We need to move on."

"I don't disagree with that. It is time to let Rose go. She would want it." Her arms tightened about me.

"True." Poor Rose would never want to be the cause of pain, let alone a rift in the family. "So how is Mother?"

304

"Not good, to be honest."

I pulled back. "Really? Health, or something else?"

"Something else."

I sighed. "Me, then."

"No, your father." Barbara picked up her glass.

My heart stopped beating. "Dad? He's not well?"

"No, he's healthy but he's not with her."

"This is my fault, isn't it?"

"No. I think this is something that has been simmering for a while, but I could be wrong. They need to work it out."

"And that isn't going to happen if Dad isn't there."

"No." Barbara sipped her drink. "Now that you know the facts, what are you going to do?"

"There's not much I can do if I can't reach them." I sat down. "I'm flying back briefly to go to Sophie's wedding. Maybe I'll discover something then."

Tristan came through the drawing room.

"Any luck with the barbecue?" I jumped up.

"Yes, found some bits of chicken and some sausages."

"Sounds good." Barbara stretched. "Need any help?"

"No, just coming to check on your drinks."

"How thoughtful." Barbara handed Tristan her glass. "What's the property market like around here?"

"Steadyish."

"You should get a fortune for this, then." She looked up at the house.

"Yes, especially if I break it up."

"Hmmm." I scowled.

"I see you're in Helen's camp." Tristan refilled my glass.

"I didn't say anything."

"You didn't have to." He smiled at me.

Barbara laughed. "You two sound like an old married couple. Shall we go round to the kitchen and keep you company?"

CHAPTER
TWENTY-SIX

Shifting on the chair, I looked at the computer screen. The Internet was dodgy in the study, and because I wanted a better connection I was forced into the billiard room where Tristan had moved the wireless router. While I waited for the computer to connect, I couldn't miss a handwritten letter sitting on the corner of the table. The address on the top was Canmere House, Sussex. It was Lady Rutherford's letter.

Dear Petroc,

Thank you so much for your generous donation to Annie's Hospice. They will be writing to you directly, but I wanted to express my personal thanks. Sebastian and I are thrilled that the paintings will be in Pengarrock. They adorned Canmere House for years, when they really should have been in Cornwall.

As you requested, I have looked through the correspondence. Peters painted mother and daughter in the summer house here at Canmere. Reading between the lines of Sebastian's great-grandmother's diary and letters, Peters and her sister Clarissa had always been in love. They had been childhood friends. I can only assume that is why she turned a blind eye to their affair.

Piecing the story together from the correspondence I have, Sebastian's great-grandmother, Anna, told her sister Clarissa to do as she was told and marry her cousin and produce an heir and then she need not worry about things too much. Basically, do her duty and be done with him.

In the diary, the tone changes. She mentions her concern at Tallan's treatment or, more precisely, mistreatment of Clarissa. I would think this is why Clarissa's visits here became more and more frequent, and how the "friendship" between Peters and Clarissa blossomed. I'm not entirely certain, but there are veiled questions about Octavia's parentage. If you wish to see the documents yourself, let me know. Although we are selling the house, we are keeping all the "history". Who knows; maybe someday the children will take an interest. Well, we can but hope.

Please do keep me updated on your research. I look forward to coming in due course to see the portraits in their new home.

Yours,

Caroline

I sank into a chair, trying to absorb the contents of the letter and the implications. The phone rang.

"I'll answer it," I heard Barbara shout from the kitchen.

"Great," I muttered, and looked again at the information on Lord Frederick Peters. He had had a successful career as a portrait artist until the *Columbia* went down.

"Judith?" Barbara walked into the billiard room.

"Yes?" I quickly shut the lid of the laptop.

"That was John on the phone. He'll ring again shortly." Barbara paused, and I didn't like the silence.

"Yes? There's more, isn't there?"

"Did you know he was working with Tristan?"

"Yes. He's helping Tristan with some US deals." I stood and walked to the French windows. The sky was cloudy and promising rain.

"A bit uncomfortable for you, I should think."

"It's OK." I stood and looked around to make sure that Tristan hadn't somehow appeared to hear Barbara's bald statement.

"He sounds on good form. Anyway, you'll hear for yourself when he rings back."

"Yes?" I wondered what Barbara was about to lead into.

"Now tell me about your lost treasure."

I sighed. "I was wondering when you were going to question me about it."

"Have I left it too long? Have I disappointed you?"

"No, it's just that I thought after Tristan's derisive comment last night you might have picked up on it sooner."

"I had the impression you would rather discuss the treasure without him."

"Right in one." I gathered up my laptop and cable. "Come into the drawing room first, and look at the portraits of the last-known owner of the jewels." We crossed the hall to the drawing room and I pushed the door open.

"My God, she is beautiful . . . almost too beautiful." Barbara shivered. "The hairs on the back of my neck went up."

"I know what you mean."

"The painter was bloody well making love to her on the canvas." Barbara stepped closer to the painting. "Tell me about her."

"Not much to tell. She disappeared in August 1846, and apparently the jewels disappeared at the same time." I looked again at the portrait. It was obvious now that Peters and Clarissa had been lovers. "She may have gone down to her death on the painter's yacht."

"How do you know this? Petroc's journals?"

"Funny you should say that. I gleaned a certain amount of information from Petroc and his work, but I've just seen the letter that arrived with the portraits. It tells a rather sad tale." I found myself becoming angry with Tristan for not sharing it with me. But then, why should he? "This is the portrait of Octavia."

"What was Petroc up to, I wonder?" Barbara went back to Clarissa's portrait.

"He was after the lost treasure."

Barbara made a wry face. "Lost treasure . . . Sounds like a wild goose chase."

310

"You are in agreement with Tristan on that."

"But not with you."

"Well, not quite. I don't think a man like Petroc would waste his time chasing fool's gold."

Barbara raised an eyebrow. "Intriguing. Well then, aside from slapping a manuscript into shape, it looks as if we have a little mystery to solve." Barbara took me by the arm and led me to the study.

Sophie's pretty face stared at me from the computer screen.

"Jude, I've tried everyone, but no one is available to stand up for me."

I took a deep breath.

She smiled. "It's because it's so quick and it's the summer, and people booked their vacations ages ago. There will only be fifty people at the wedding." She tilted her head to the side. "I know this is too much to ask, but please, please say you'll be my maid of honour."

"Sophie, I want to but you've got to realise . . ."

"I do, and I wouldn't plead like this if I could get even Mary to do it, but the only person available aside from you is my cousin, and you above all people know how I feel about that."

"Not Patty."

"Yes, Mom is saying it will have to be her."

I sighed. Despite how awful it would be for me, I couldn't let Sophie get married with the woman who had bullied her throughout her childhood standing beside her while she took her vows.

"OK, I'll do it. What do you need from me other than showing up?"

"Just you and your measurements. I promise the dress won't be awful."

I could see tears in her eyes, and mine were filling up in sympathy. I could do this for my friend, but I might need a valium or a strong drink beforehand.

"I'll email the measurements. See you soon." I was not looking forward to this.

"Jude, one more thing."

From her pained expression, I could tell what was coming next.

"John."

"No."

"He's Tim's best man." She gulped.

I pushed away from the laptop. "No way. I can't do this."

"They are like us, best friends." She held her hands up, pleading.

"That doesn't help." I looked away. The view didn't soothe me. "How can you ask me to do this?"

"Because you're my best friend, and I want you beside me."

I nodded with tears streaming down my cheeks. Sophie had been there for me during my darkest hours like no one else. "OK, but I still think John and me being there will take away from your day."

"No, it won't, and you are the best."

"Does John know?" I wiped my eyes.

She nodded.

"He's OK with it?"

"More than OK."

I didn't like the sound of that. He was still hoping we'd get back together. As I walked downstairs I wondered how I was going to do what Sophie asked. It was too hard. My foot was on the bottom step as the phone rang. "Pengarrock."

"Jude! So pleased it's you." John sounded chirpy.

"Didn't like chatting with Barbara?" I sat on the bottom stair.

"No, it's always interesting."

My mouth opened and closed.

"Come to London for the weekend."

"Oh, John," I sighed. "This isn't going to work."

"It would if you gave it a chance."

I played with the camel on my bracelet and wondered how to say this. "For so long I have followed the path expected of me."

"Was I an expectation?"

I didn't answer. That was too close, and I didn't want to probe it. I moved out of the hall and into the drawing room. "In a funny way, yes, but not in a bad way." So many glimmers of thoughts and feelings that I couldn't quite grab at swam around in my head. I picked up a small bronze figure and turned it over in my fingers. "I don't know how to explain it, but you sort of fit into the plan my life was supposed to follow."

"I don't like the sound of that." He took a deep breath. "Jude, what do you want?"

"That's a good question." Placing the bronze back down, I considered what John was still offering me: security and love.

"I want you." He was so earnest it nearly broke my heart. There was so much yearning in that statement, and I wanted to fill it, I really did. I wanted his friendship. But I didn't want . . . him.

"The best thing you can do is let go. We are no more." I took a deep breath. "Go and find the woman who's right for you."

There was silence on the other end of the line. I wondered if he had hung up on me.

"Jude, I'm here. Take your time. I'll wait."

"Don't wait. I'm not worthy of you." I bit my lip.

"Nonsense. You don't see yourself properly."

"You may be right on that one." But I knew we weren't talking about the same thing.

"I am."

I shook my head. "Such confidence."

"Absolutely."

I laughed.

"That's better, Jude. Now, let's find out when I can see you."

"No." That sounded awful. "Work is all-involving."

"Do you mean Tristan?" he asked.

"No, I don't mean Tristan." I knew I'd put too much emphasis on that.

"Are you involved with him, Jude?"

Pushing my hair back, I debated how to answer. I thought about Tristan and the estate constantly, but was I involved with him? Not in the way John meant, and just one event did not make an affair. "No."

"You took some time answering that."

"Yes, I did. Look . . ." I sighed.

314

"It's OK, Jude. Just be careful of your heart. Remember I love it."

"Don't." I paused. "Sophie and Tim's wedding."

"I know, and it will be OK."

I paced around the drawing room. "If you're sure."

"I am."

"I'm not." I just didn't see how it could end in anything but tears.

Having cleared the dinner dishes, Tristan and I walked to the pond. I kept pointing things out to him. First there was the seat carved into an old tree trunk by the pond with the graffiti on it: *Jim and Jane 1899*. He swore he'd never noticed it, but I saw a glimmer in his eyes. He was pulling my leg.

Walking slowly through the woods towards the beach, I marvelled at the estate's tree ferns and the bamboo. For a while then, silence filled the space between us. I looked intently into the woods, wondering what he was thinking. Was it more development plans, or, looking at his face, was it about his childhood? I longed to ask him to share his thoughts, but the empty beach appeared with the remains of a small fire still burning. Tristan found an old log while I went to the water's edge and prowled for sea glass.

"Yes!" I did a little dance.

"What?" Tristan looked up from the embers of the fire.

"I found some sea glass." I continued scanning the sand, hoping to find more.

"So?"

I held it to my heart. "It's my treasure."

"Your treasure? You're easy to please."

"Maybe." I laughed and walked up to the fire. "I'm not mad. It's something my sister and I did as children. Here, I've even found the elusive blue." I held out the tiny speck of glass. He glanced at it, then looked at me and pushed a wayward strand of my hair behind my ear. I held my breath. We stood very close, staring into each other's eyes until the smoke from the fire forced us to move apart.

"What do you intend to do with your treasure?" His voice was quiet.

"I keep it in a glass jar." I moved my hands in an oval shape. "Since I arrived here, I've almost filled it."

"Really?"

"Yes." Pulling a flat rock close to the fire, I sat cross-legged on it. My legs were still unstable after the touch of his hand. "Shame I haven't found the real treasure."

"It's long lost." He glanced out at the river.

"What would you do with it if you had it now?" I put my head to one side and studied him.

He sat near me. "That's a question and a half."

"Indeed, and you haven't answered me."

"I don't know, to be truthful. It would certainly give me more options." He poked the fire.

I longed to ask what those options were, but didn't dare. Looking at the sea glass in my hand and thinking of my own childhood spent in a half a dozen countries,

I wondered what it might have been like to grow up here. "Tristan?"

He was close to me but not touching me. He looked at the fire, then at me. The colour of his eyes had changed subtly. The greens had given way to blues. "Yes?"

"What was it like growing up here?"

He turned over a piece of glass that I held out to him. I hoped he didn't notice my shaky hand. "As you would expect, lots of outdoor adventure."

On the north side of the river, the last of the sunlight was catching the windows of a large house, which looked as though they were on fire as they reflected a final glorious burst of colour. "You were a typical boy — into everything, I bet."

He laughed. "And then some. I think I was under everyone's feet."

"There's an awful lot of space to avoid people."

"True, but I was everywhere." He picked up a flat stone and tossed it into the incoming tide. It skipped six times before it sank below the surface. "I was a free-range kid who dashed from fishing to troubling Helen in the kitchen. There was no part of the estate I didn't know."

"What changed?" I bit my lip. I shouldn't have asked.

A shadow passed across his eyes and the colour reverted to stormy green. "It just did." He stood and looked at the river. "Nothing remains the same, and kids grow up and learn about real life, that it's not a rural idyll."

"I know all about the growing up and doing it quickly." I stood and touched his hand. He turned to me, staring into my eyes. I didn't blink. "My sister died of kidney disease when I was twelve."

He took my hand in his and we walked up to the house together.

CHAPTER
TWENTY-SEVEN

It was hot in the attic, even with the window open. Tristan was nearby with his head in a box, and I was going through some papers by the light of the single bulb hanging from the low ceiling. I was distracted by the expanse of tanned back exposed above the waist of Tristan's jeans. I had an incredible urge to go and run my fingers over the smooth skin.

"Any luck with what you've found?" He turned to me.

"Nothing that you'd want, but interesting in its own way."

He stood and seemed to be studying me, but that wasn't it. It was desire. It was as if I was what he wanted. A tingle began at the base of my spine. If he kept looking at me that way, I might ignite.

"How about you?" I fanned myself with an old file. It had nothing to do with the stifling heat in the attic.

Tristan turned to pull a sheaf of letters out of the trunk. "These?"

I walked over, stepping carefully around the boxes that lay between us, then stood beside him. He held them out to me. They were beautifully wrapped in faded ribbon. I took them and my fingers brushed his. My mouth went dry. Was I feeling this all on my own?

His eyes revealed an invitation. Our hands remained barely touching. I moved towards him. We were so close now that I could count his eyelashes. It was difficult to breathe. He moved closer still. I could feel his breath on my mouth. In one movement, we would be kissing. His lips brushed mine and he pulled back a bit, waiting. I raised my hand and stroked his cheek. My eyes closed as his lips met mine.

This was so different than the last time we kissed. This was slower, but the same hunger was there.

"There you are." Barbara's voice echoed in the attic space. "Helen's made coffee and was going to bring it up here, but I put my foot down and said you would come to the coffee. Bring down what you've found."

We both stopped, not quite touching. My heartbeat throbbed in my ears. Barbara couldn't have chosen a worse moment to interrupt. I pulled away and turned to see her head above the top of the narrow stairs.

"We'll come down." Tristan's breath ran down my neck and I shivered. Slowly I pulled away. Tristan's fingers intertwined with mine.

"Is there anything else in there we should look at now?" My voice was husky. He released my hand and delved into the chest again, pulling out another batch of letters. He pulled me close. Everything spun around me.

"Jude." He spoke my name against my mouth, teasing me.

"Yes?"

"Are you two coming down?" Barbara called from below.

"On our way," he replied, then he kissed me quickly. On unsteady feet I made my way down the narrow staircase with Tristan close behind me. The sunlight almost blinded me on the landing. I stopped dead and Tristan collided with me. Feeling the length of his lean body against me, I gasped then stumbled forward, breaking the contact. I shouldn't become involved with Tristan, the thought hit me — it was madness.

"I'll just pick up a notebook. See you downstairs." I dashed through my bedroom door. I knew my face was flushed and I needed time to cool my thoughts. It was all becoming too complex. I wanted Tristan as I'd never wanted John. John would see that, if he ever came to Pengarrock again. Oh hell, this just wasn't going to work.

"We're all waiting to see the letters." Barbara stood in the doorway.

"Won't be a minute." I waved to her and then went to splash my face with cold water.

The letters sat on the table in the drawing room next to the silver coffee pot. Helen was back on form and instead of mugs we were being treated to silver and china, with a beautiful sponge cake decorated with sugared violets.

"They look so pretty, it's almost a shame to eat them." I took a cup.

"It would be sacrilege to cut that cake." Barbara picked up one pile of letters.

"Mind you, I'd be more worried if we didn't touch the cake. Have you encountered Helen when she's angry?" I sliced into the culinary work of art.

"Always afraid to confront the status quo." Barbara tut-tutted, and pulled on a bow.

I nearly choked on the cake in my mouth. That was unfair, but maybe it had been closer to the truth in the recent past.

Tristan wasn't saying a word as he watched Barbara open the letters. I had no idea what he was thinking. Just from their appearance I knew they were Victorian, but I didn't dare hope that they could be from Clarissa or Octavia. That would be too lucky, and how could Petroc have missed them in his search for the treasure?

"This letter is from 1840, and appears to be from an Anna to a Clarissa and it's about a miscarriage of Clarissa's."

I put my cup down and picked up the second pile. They were tied with similar ribbon. My hands shook as I opened the first one.

15th May 1845

Dearest Mummy,

I have had the loveliest day walking in the woods picking bluebells with the governess. But I miss you terribly, and when will you return? Has London been wonderful? Have you bought the new fabric for my dress that you promised? Who have you seen? How is Aunt Anna? Is my portrait finished? I can't wait to see it. Have you seen much of Lord Frederick? Will my portrait be as lovely as yours? Father will be so delighted when he sees it. He is mostly happy at the moment, but there are times when he only frowns, no matter what I do. I do wish you were home.

When the bluebells fade
And the garlic's in the glade
Will my wish come true?
I want to be with you.
Please come soon.
With all my love,

Octavia

The handwriting was recognisable as the same from the sketchbook, but more childish.

"Anything important?" Tristan stood.

"Hard to tell at this point, but maybe a clue or two about the last owner of the sapphire and what might have happened to her."

He laughed. "That bloody sapphire. It's long gone."

"That's true, but maybe we can solve the mystery and close the subject."

"As you wish." Tristan stood.

Barbara looked at him. "What was that about?"

"My father wasted the last years of his life looking for the Trevillion sapphire. If he had put half the effort into managing the estate, I wouldn't be faced with sorting and selling this mess."

"I see." She turned to me. "What do you think?"

"I can't say why, but I don't think Petroc was wrong. I think it still exists."

"A hunch then?"

Tristan walked out through the French windows.

"Sore subject." Barbara watched his retreating back.

"Yes." I frowned. "There's a painting in the dining room if you want to have another look at the sapphire." Barbara disappeared, and I sat in peace reading the letters between mother and daughter.

Not of the land
Not of the sea
Visible only
When August Rock sees

I sat up in bed. Was it just a children's rhyme, as Tristan had said, or a riddle revealing the location of the Trevillion sapphire? Clarissa and Octavia wrote riddles and rhymes to each other. There had to be more to the August Rock riddle. We were missing the rest; it must be here, in this house.

Having read the correspondence, I knew that mother and daughter were incredibly close. As I read, I felt wave after wave of jealousy. This must have been like Mother's relationship with Rose. Mother would have done anything to save Rose, but was unable to do anything other than be with Rose until the end. My mother's heart broke for ever that day, and I'd never been able to heal it.

I just knew that Lady Clarissa would not have abandoned her daughter. She wouldn't have left her to be with her lover. They were too close, and if Octavia was Peters' daughter and not Tallan's, she definitely wouldn't have left her with Tallan. Of that I was sure. But what had happened to her? Strangely, there were no letters from Anna to Octavia referring to Clarissa's disappearance. There was no record of her death. It was as if she had vanished. If I prowled around in the attic, maybe I would find more evidence. I rubbed my temples. A headache was forming. Maybe I should try and fall asleep again.

I opened my eyes wide. Children's stories . . . There was something about children's stories. I stood, walked to the door and looked along the hallway. I straightened my camisole nightgown and crept out.

"Going somewhere?"

"Damn it, Tristan! You scared the life out of me." My heart was beating so hard it felt as if it was going to come through my chest.

"Like the outfit." His glance lingered on my legs.

"You're not wearing much more." He was in jeans, no shirt. I tried not to stare at his chest.

"Well, I heard a noise and thought I'd better investigate. Where are you off to?"

I coughed. "The nursery."

"Whatever for?"

"Books."

"At this hour?"

"Come with me and find out."

He swept his hand out in the direction of the nursery and I led the way, conscious of how little I was wearing. At the door, I stopped. Tristan stood just behind me. The warmth of his body travelled quickly to mine. Trying to focus on what I had come here for and not on the feel of the man behind me, I scanned the room. Something flickered in my mind. I closed my eyes, trying to grab it. Breaking contact with Tristan, I went to the bookshelves under the window seat and pulled out the last book I had looked at in here on the day of Petroc's funeral: *A New Riddle Book or, a Whetstone for Dull Wits*.

"I remember that book." Tristan took it from my hands and sat on the window seat. "I loved it. My mother used to read it to me all the time."

"Were you the little horror that coloured it in?" I joined him on the seat.

"Guilty, but I wasn't the first. Someone had started the picture on the cover so I finished it." He laughed and opened the book. "I could almost recite the first few of these from memory, but only the first few because it was always the last book that Mum read to me at night. I don't think we ever reached the end."

I touched his hand. He looked up.

"She wouldn't have left you."

Of Merry Book this is the Chief,
'Tis as a Purging pill;
To carrying off all heavy Grief,
And make you laugh your Fill.

A tear rolled down his cheek. "I wish that were true, and that it didn't matter after all this time."

"Of course it still matters, and there is no time limit for grief." I wiped his tears away with my hand. A last one escaped me and reached his mouth. My thumb caught it on his lip. "Do you want to talk about it?"

He laughed. "Americans, and talking about it."

"Yup." I put my hand under his chin. "It can help."

"Thanks, but I'm not so sure it'll do any good to bring it all up."

"Maybe not, but with your father's death, it's bound to be close to the surface."

Tristan stood and placed the book on the seat.

"I haven't been in here in years." He walked to the table-tennis table and ran his hand over it. He looked around.

"It's a lovely place."

"Yes, I suppose it is." He turned to me. "Shall I make some coffee, and maybe then I'll talk about Mum."

I practically jumped up. "I'll just throw some clothes on." Keeping a clear head around him was hard enough at the moment, without being scantily dressed.

Tristan was pale as he sat at the kitchen table, staring but not seeing. I placed a cup of coffee in front of him and perched opposite. The morning was cool and misty. Memories of late-August mornings on the Cape filled me. I was flying to Massachusetts for Sophie's wedding tomorrow.

"Thanks." Tristan focused on me.

327

"A pleasure." I reached out and touched his hand.

"Memories can be so intense." He gave a dry laugh.

There was no delicate way to ask, so I plunged right in. "Why do you think she committed suicide?"

He took a deep breath then closed his eyes. "They argued." He opened his eyes. "That wasn't unusual for them, and it never bothered me. Mum was hot-tempered and would spark easily and, well, you know what my father was like."

I nodded.

"I didn't hear the whole conversation, but the pieces of it I heard like 'this bloody place', and 'I'm desperate' and others stayed with me as I went into the nursery to collect my bug jar." He pushed his chair back and stood. "Mum came in shortly after, looking sad, and gave me a hug. I wasn't too concerned as I had seen it before, and everything would be fine by tea. I left her sitting on the window seat and went to the beach to fish."

I could see the torment on his face and I wanted to stop him.

"I was out on the rocks fishing when I saw her rush past. I thought it was odd, but didn't call to her or go after her." He ran his hand through his hair. "She wasn't home for tea or supper. Dad went with the estate manger and walked the cliffs, but they couldn't find her. I was forced to stay with Helen. They wouldn't let me help look, even though I'd been the last person to see her. I never called out to her." He stopped and cradled his mug. "The next morning they found her scarf on a shrub halfway down the cliff face. A day later her body was discovered on a beach on the north side of the river." He put his head in his hands. "I've always wondered, if I'd chased after her . . ."

I went to him and held him in my arms.

CHAPTER
TWENTY-EIGHT

"We have been cleared for take-off. It will be bumpy, so please remain seated with your seat belt securely fastened for the whole flight."

That could be a good description of the next few days in front of me. I could see Boston Harbor below, and it wasn't the ascent of the plane or the storm clouds we were flying into that were causing my stomach to turn over. *Home.* The plane banked and the skyline looked so familiar through my window, but it was different. No, I was different, and I needed to hold onto that. I couldn't believe I'd agreed to do this. It would be crazy and emotional, but hopefully not traumatic. I would walk off the plane and straight into wedding madness. Sophie had promised me it was a small affair, and I hoped she was right.

I'd managed to make the connecting flight to Martha's Vineyard. It was weird, heading to a wedding without a dress. As promised, I'd sent off my measurements. I could only hope that whatever dress it was it would fit, as the wedding was tomorrow. Nothing like being thrown in at the deep end! I just wish I'd slept on the flight over, but my brain wouldn't shut down. Tristan had driven me to Newquay to catch the plane to Gatwick, and he had been silent the whole way. It was a silence I'd been loath to break, so I didn't. He needed time. I wasn't sure he'd ever spoken about his mother's death, and how he felt responsible for it.

The little plane hit turbulence and we jumped around. My hands tensed on the armrests of the seat. We dropped and I found myself thinking that this would be one way to avoid the next few days, but not necessarily the one I would have chosen. I adjusted the seat belt tighter and looked out the window. Clouds surrounded us, and I couldn't see beyond the wing. It wasn't a long flight, but if we continued to bounce our way along we would be doing double the distance.

The man beside me reached for the sick bag. This was not going to be pleasant. I focused on the clouds, trying to block him out. Children's books. They were the key to all of this. Petroc had been looking at them, and he wouldn't have bothered unless there was something important in them. There was only one I'd seen that Octavia might have known. There must be something in the riddle book. I would call Tristan and ask him to look carefully through it.

I walked into the little terminal and straight into Sophie's arms. "Welcome home!"

"Thanks." I pulled back. She looked amazing, the way a bride-to-be should look, not how I had just a few months ago. "You're glowing."

"You are ghostly white. Terrible flight?"

"Dire." I pulled my phone out of my bag and turned it on. Sophie linked her arm through mine and we walked to her hire car. "So, tell me the schedule." I looked at my phone, waiting for it to connect with the world again.

"We're heading straight to the rehearsal at the church, then the rehearsal dinner tonight."

"Great." I tried to sound enthusiastic. I rubbed my sweaty hands on my jeans.

"After church, I'll take you to where we're staying with Tim's aunt and we can drop off your bag."

I blinked. "OK. I hope I can stay awake."

"It's not a big deal, just a cookout." Sophie took a hand off the wheel and grabbed mine. "Thank you for coming. I know how hard this is."

I gulped, then nodded.

She parked the car and we both hopped out. Everyone was standing outside the white clapboard church waiting for us. It was all about Sophie and Tim, and it would be wonderful.

I glanced at the gathered crowd and felt faint. John was standing beside Tim. I wasn't sure I could do this. John smiled at me. I thought I might pass out. Slow, even breathing would be key. That, and focusing on other people.

"We're all here now, so let's head into the church." The pastor smiled at everyone. "Now, ushers escort your key guests to their seats." While they were doing that, he gave a little pep talk to Sophie and Tim. Sophie gave me a hug as Tim and John went to take their places. I had this awful feeling of déjà vu. Today John stood at the altar in shorts and t-shirt, not in a morning coat. I swallowed.

"You OK?"

I nodded and handed Sophie the fake flowers. I could do this. I had to, for Sophie.

"When you're ready," the pastor called as he pressed a button and the wedding march began. I fought the urge to vomit, but took a couple of deep breaths and gave Sophie a smile before I set off down the aisle. Focused on the altar, I kept a rictus grin on my face. I would not look at John. This had to be terrible for him too. He would be remembering how I'd humiliated him. My hands shook and the plastic flowers I held in them ran with sweat, but I reached the altar and didn't run. My heart was doing that for me. It couldn't be pounding any harder if I'd just completed the hundred-yard sprint in record time.

Sophie practically floated up the aisle and arrived at the altar beaming. The look on Tim's face as he watched her was wonderful and heartbreaking. He loved her so much. I knew what I would see on John's face if I looked, and knew I had to face it. I glanced up, prepared for anger and instead he tipped his head to one side and smiled. He was too good. It would have been easier to take his anger, his hurt, but he was still offering love.

"That's fine. Everybody knows what they are doing." The pastor clapped. "We then exchange vows, which you two have already practised enough. Now, Tim, you may kiss Sophie for good measure and lead your wife-to-be back down the aisle." He smiled at John and I. "John, you take Judith and follow them."

"Ready, Jude?" He held out his arm.

I tried to swallow as I placed my arm through his. My throat constricted. I could barely breathe, let alone speak. He leaned forward and placed a kiss on my temple. God, this was awful. I couldn't do this, but I must. This wasn't about John or me; it was about Sophie and Tim.

"That was brilliant, Jude." Sophie danced up to me. "Now, we need to rush in order to get ready for tonight." She waved at everyone and dragged me to the car. I closed my eyes and hoped the worst was over. I'd faced it, and tomorrow would be better.

"I'm sorry, Jude." She grabbed my hand.

"I know you are, and I'm a big girl now. I can take this, and I really wouldn't want to miss your day."

"Thanks." Sophie parked the car. "I really mean it."

"I know." I got out of the car, wondering how I would make it through the next twenty-four hours.

The morning fog had burned off and a fresh breeze blew in off the water. The weather would be ideal for Sophie's wedding. My dress lay on the bed. I just needed to complete my make-up before putting it on. It was ten. The wedding was at noon. I had a few minutes before I was needed. I'd try ringing Pengarrock again. The past few calls, I'd reached the answerphone and had left garbled messages about reading the whole riddle book because I was sure there must be something in it. Octavia might have been the first child to draw in it. I was positive that book held the answer.

"Trevillion," Tristan answered.

"Hi."

"Hello, Jude." I thought I heard a smile in his voice; I hoped I had. "Got your messages."

"And?" I pushed a loose curl back into place.

He laughed. "You were right, but I doubt it's more than a riddle that Clarissa wrote for Octavia."

"Don't keep me in suspense! What does it say?" I paced around the bed.

"OK, but it makes no sense."

"They seldom do, at first."

"That I know." He paused, then read:

Not of the land
Not of the sea
Visible only
When August Rock sees

Think of the curlew
Think of the dove
Who carries a flower
Not of peace but of love

Gone from the dinas
Lost from the world
Only at Pengarrock
Do petals unfurl

The jewel of Pengarrock
Hidden to all
Will free your heart
From duty's call

"It's dated August the 29th, 1846."

"Isn't that the day before the yacht went down?" I looked out at the boats sailing past.

"Near enough, but I can't think what it means."

"No, but it must mean something. Clarissa and Octavia used to talk in riddles to each other. It was their code, so Clarissa was trying to tell her daughter something, and I think it must be about the jewels. They were Clarissa's."

"She could have been robbed and murdered on her way to Falmouth."

"If she had been, then the jewels would have surfaced some time ago. That sapphire was too distinctive."

"Re-cut?"

"Your father looked into that possibility, and for the most part ruled it out." I played with a pen on the table.

"I think it was just a mother having fun with her daughter."

"Look at Octavia's sketches and see if there are any clues." I tapped the pen on the table, longing to be back at Pengarrock.

"I have other things to do than waste time chasing around on some treasure hunt."

I smiled. "Tristan, if we find this, it could save Pengarrock."

"Who says I want to save Pengarrock?"

I sank onto the bed. I had hoped, but obviously in vain. "No one."

"Exactly. Now forget the riddle and enjoy your friend's wedding." He rang off and I looked out to sea. I would try and enjoy today, but I wanted to be at Pengarrock more than anywhere else in the world.

CHAPTER
TWENTY-NINE

Sophie looked exquisite in a simple floor-length linen shift dress. Mine was almost the same, but in aqua instead of white. Her red hair was woven with daisies, and she was a vision of serene beauty. "You look incredible."

"You don't clean up too bad yourself, Jude. I've always loved you in aqua."

"So you've said over the years." I hugged her and looked at the two of us in the mirror. I towered over her tiny frame, but I saw two beautiful women staring back at me. The tall one did have dark circles under her eyes that concealer hadn't quite managed to cover.

Sophie's mother knocked and came in. "Don't you both look wonderful?" She smiled. "The car is waiting downstairs for us, Jude."

"Thanks." I gave Sophie a quick hug. "See you at the church." I left the two women alone. This was a huge moment for them both, and I didn't belong there. Sophie's niece was waiting by the front door. She was in a short version of my dress. Her long hair trailed down her back.

"Are you excited?" I asked her.

"Yes, but I'm afraid I'll trip."

"It won't be you doing that, it will be me."

She giggled and Sophie's mom joined us. "OK, ladies, let's head to the church."

I stared out the window on the short drive. It was a glorious late-summer day. The sun was hot but the air was cool. It was all very different from my day, and I needed to hold onto that thought. I looked at Sophie's mother; she was so relaxed. She gave me a little smile.

"I know this is hard for you."

"It's OK, really."

"You're a good friend."

I wondered if I was. Just by being here I was bringing all my baggage with me. It was as if a dark shadow followed me, and the slightest hint would destroy the beauty of this day. But I wouldn't let it. I was stronger than that. This was Sophie's day, and it would remain that way.

Tim's brother opened the car door. "Ladies." He looked very smart in a navy suit with a not-so-discreet tie covered in daisies on an aqua background. "Tim and John are in the basement awaiting the right moment to appear, in case you were concerned that they aren't here."

I flinched. I hoped that wasn't a reference to me.

"I haven't a worry in the world." Sophie's mother smiled at me and took the arm of an usher who led her to the front pew. The flower girl and I stood at the back of the church waiting for the bride and her father. As Sophie had promised, the crowd was small. A quick head count revealed about forty, but my count stopped when I saw my mother's head. My fists clenched and unclenched. This was Sophie's and Tim's day.

When the toasts and the meal were finished, I escaped to the ladies room. I locked the door behind me. A few minutes of peace, and I would be able to make it through the rest of the evening. It had all been bearable, aside from saying hello to my mother briefly in the receiving line. Everyone had gone silent every time I approached, which might not be a bad thing. As long as I kept focused on the joy of Sophie and Tim, things were fine. I stood and took a quick glance in the mirror. A little mascara had run, which I fixed before heading out the door.

My mother stood waiting.

"Hello, Mother."

"Judith."

I took a deep breath and straightened up. I knew that tone. But despite it, I leaned forward and gave her a swift hug and a kiss. She may look like she was made of stone, but I knew she was human. None of this could be easy for her either. "How are you?"

"Fine."

"That's good to hear. How's Dad?" This was what I really wanted to know.

"He's fine."

I took a deep breath. "Where is he?"

"Fishing."

"Really?"

"Yes." Mother looked around her. We stood apart like two strangers, each competing for the Best Posture award.

"You know John's mother is distraught, and thinks you have destroyed her son."

"And you agree with her." I stretched my fingers out and left them fully extended.

"That's not what I meant."

"Exactly what did you mean?" My chest tightened. This was neither the time nor the place to have an argument.

"You were so utterly heartless and unthinking with your behaviour at the wedding. I can't believe you've come back and have had the audacity to stand at the altar again with John. You've made a fool of us all again." She sucked her teeth. "You have no sensitivity."

"Not so, I just don't have yours, and it's time you realised that and accepted me for who I am. I am Jude, not Rose, nor will I ever be or want to be."

Mother stood with her mouth open and I wanted the ground to swallow me. I'd gone too far again. Not that I hadn't meant what I said. But blurting it out here and now was so wrong.

I reached out to her and placed my hand on her arm. She pulled away and walked down the hall. What had I done? I spun around, not sure whether to hide or just leave. How could I go and face the crowd with a smile?

"Jude?" John came up to me.

I jumped.

"I just saw Jane and she looked like thunder. I thought I'd better come and find you." He opened his arms, but I stood still. It wasn't right. He seemed to understand, and he led me out of the house via the front door.

"I'll go and let Sophie know that you don't feel well and I'll come back and walk you to Tim's aunt's house."

"Don't come back. I know the way, and the walk will do me good."

"Jude." He held his hand out to me.

I didn't take it. "I'm OK. It's time to let go."

He shook his head.

"It is. You need to move on, and so do I. Go ask the lovely work friend of Sophie's who has had eyes for no one but you all night to dance."

"Jude."

"John, go." I gave his hand a squeeze, then I walked down the drive. I didn't belong here any more. This place, or the world I'd known, felt alien.

Pushing open the door of the hospice, I didn't know what to expect. Just before I left Pengarrock I'd received a call from Aunt Agnes' housekeeper that she was being transferred here. Part of me didn't want to enter. I wanted to hold onto the memories I had of her as a strong but eccentric lady. I stood in the doorway. Aunt Agnes looked so little in the bed. How had this happened so quickly?

"How's my girl?" Aunt Agnes' voice was weak.

"OK." I came to the bed and sat on the edge, trying not to slip off. My aunt had brought her own sheets with her. Years ago she had told me she always slept on satin sheets, as it made her feel glamorous.

342

"Don't look so shocked. I'm ninety-four and I've tried to enjoy every day." She took a deep breath.

I nodded, unable to speak.

"Don't go all silly on me, just when I was thinking that you were finally a proper Warren after all."

I laughed. "I'll try not to."

She took my hand. "You've done well. I'm proud of you."

"Thanks."

"Remember to follow your own path, and for heaven's sake go and find out what's wrong with your silly parents."

I frowned.

"I had the strangest conversation with your father the other night. You remember he'd gone fishing?"

"Yes. He didn't come to Sophie's wedding. Mother was there on her own."

"Well, that won't hurt her." She coughed and her small body shook. "Your father didn't say what was up. He was vague, not like himself at all." She closed her eyes for a moment, and I could see how hard it was for her to breathe, let alone speak. "I know I told you not to worry about them when we last spoke, but I've changed my mind. Go and sort them out. You have far more sense than either of them."

"Not sure what I can do."

She gave my hand a pat. "I'm not either, but you must try for your sake, not theirs. Having messed-up parents interferes with your life." She coughed again. "Years of smoking. Mind you, it didn't get me until now."

"Oh, Auntie." I shook my head, fighting back the tears.

"Don't weep for me. I've had my time, more than most. Now give me a hug and go and have a good life."

I bent to her and held her small frame. It felt like I was holding the tiniest of twigs.

"Promise me to be good to yourself and true."

I nodded.

"Off to those foolish parents of yours! I love you." She gave my hand a squeeze, then closed her eyes. When she let go, I stood watching her and listening to her laboured breathing. Tears rolled down my face and I didn't want to say goodbye, but that was what this was. I didn't want to leave her, but I knew she wouldn't want me to stay. Go and have a good life, she had said. I took one last look at the frail woman that my great-aunt had become and silently promised her I would try.

There were weeds sprouting in the main flowerbed, but the grass was cut, although the edges looked messy. I bent and pulled out a dandelion and sighed. The front door was closed and I couldn't tell whether Mother was home or not. It didn't matter. Unless they had changed the locks, I still had my key. They wouldn't have done that. It was not as if I'd stolen the family silver.

I pushed open the door and called out. My voice echoed in the silence. I dropped my bag and went to the kitchen. The fridge contained some food and it was all within date, but I couldn't shake the fact that everything felt unused.

344

The light flickered on the answer machine. It was probably all messages from me, unless Mother was ignoring the rest of the world along with me. Yet she'd come on her own to Sophie's wedding. That couldn't have been easy for her, and of course I'd made it worse.

While I flipped through the mail, I brewed some coffee. There was a pile of things for me, but I had no energy to read them. I wandered out to the garden. It wasn't as bad as I feared; the front was worse. Mother had been trying to keep up, but she didn't have green fingers and it showed.

The pool was OK, and I might have a swim shortly to wake me up. I wasn't sure where I was with the jet lag, but as Mother wasn't here I might take a catnap. I stopped in the doorway of my room, not sure what I would find. I more than expected to see that I had been erased and only the memories of Rose remained.

A quick glance revealed that something had changed since I'd left. A box half filled sat by the bookshelves, and my old panda bear was down off the shelf and on my bed. I picked up the loved and battered panda and held him close for a moment before placing him back carefully. Why had she brought him down? All my other toys were tucked away, including Rose's koala.

I stretched out on the bed and a wave of exhaustion passed over me but I couldn't sleep. Every time I thought it was going to overtake me, another question came into my mind and adrenalin raced through me. In the end I gave up. I could do something positive, like help clear out this room, which someone had begun. There was so much that didn't need to be here, or anywhere. The room felt like a shrine. Rose wouldn't want that, and I certainly didn't.

I began where either Mother or maybe Dad had left off, at the bookshelves. Tucked behind the Nancy Drew Mysteries I found a stash of letters from my pen pal in Germany. I flipped through them. There was no reason to hold on to them after all these years, and I certainly didn't want to read about her teenage angst. I remembered my own well enough. I tossed them all.

Next I picked up the mysteries and put them in the box. Something fell out of one of the books. It was one of Rose's diaries. It was dated the year before I was born. I hadn't seen this one before.

January 1, 1979

I was allowed to stay up until it was New Year. It was so so funny. Auntie Barbara was drunk and so was Mommy. They gave me my first sip of champagne. It was lovely and I would have loved more but Daddy said no. He was very quiet but then he and Uncle Harry were solving the world's problems over a bottle of whiskey. I took this picture of them with my new Polaroid.

I scanned the entries about school, her best friend and the boy she liked. I could almost hear her talking. I loved her laugh. But she didn't sound happy, and she said Mother was always weepy and Dad was always travelling. I had never known them like this, but I

346

guessed Dad had been under a lot of pressure career-wise at the time.

August 20, 1979

We've been having a wonderful time visiting Auntie Barbara in Cornwall. I tried surfing but was terrible. Sometimes Mother is happy but I know she is missing Dad. I miss him too.

They took a holiday in Cornwall? This was news to me.

Dad came home for three days. He took me out rowing. I had fun but Mother didn't. I found Mother in tears again. I asked her what was wrong but she wouldn't tell me. I thought it was about me because I was sick but she said no it wasn't. She hugged me tight and said I'd be fine. Medicine was always finding new solutions. I hoped she was right. I had heard her shouting at Dad, asking why he'd given his kidney to his "good for nothing" brother who would die from the drink anyway. Dad said to leave it. Mother cried, then went on about having another baby? She pleaded. But Dad said no. What if the baby also carried the gene?

I wish they wouldn't argue about me. I know Mother wants another baby. She picks up every one she sees and has done this since I can remember. They should have a baby. If I had a choice I'd like a sister. I'd be the best big sister ever.

My tears hit the page. "You were the best big sister ever."

Why had she switched from Mommy to Mother? How old was I when I switched? I suppose I was about Rose's age in these diaries. Mother was never Mom. It was a word she didn't like.

November 29, 1980

Baby Judith is crying again and so is Mother. Daddy's been gone for months now. Judith can roll over. I overheard Mother talking to Barbara on the phone. She said, "It's my fault he left. He never wanted her. I did and I ruined it." She cried more and said she was so selfish. She didn't think of him. She didn't want Judith any more. He'd gone away because of Judith, and now there was another woman.

I dropped the book.

The sound of my own voice intruded into my thoughts.

Hi. It's Jude here. Would love to talk. Call me.
Hi. Pick up, please.
Hello? Is anyone there?
Mother, I know you are around. Either pick up or return my calls. I'm worried.
Hi, it's Jude here, trying again.

Someone was listening to the machine. I walked quietly out to the kitchen. I needed to be gentle with my mother. There was more to this than just me. Reading between the lines, there was so much more.

The answerphone was switched off and I heard the kettle settle on the stove. I paused in the hallway. I didn't know what I could say. I took a deep breath and walked into the kitchen.

"Mother, I . . ." I gulped. "Dad."

"Jude." He took a step towards me, then stopped. He didn't look like Dad. He was thinner, older and sporting a beard, a white one.

"Where's your mother?" He looked around.

"I don't know. Where have you been?"

"Away." He pulled his whiskers.

"That I know." I couldn't contain my words. "It's not the first time you've left."

He stopped moving, but then the kettle whistled and he picked it up. "Tea?"

I wanted to scream as I watched him scald the pot. Years of Mother's training had rubbed off on him too. He handed me a cup, then sat down at the table. I joined him. "Dad."

"Jude, don't." He put his hand up.

"No, Dad, listen, I need to know what happened."

"Yes, you do. I have spent this time away thinking about that." He turned his mug round and round and I could see him weighing the words. "Jude, I owe you and your mother an apology."

I nodded. All these years I felt he was blameless, but I was wrong. "I've just read Rose's journal."

"I have hurt you all so much." He looked at me with sad eyes. "There have been so many things in my life that I would have done differently if I could." He pulled on his beard again. "It's not good to have regrets. I have many, which is why I went away. Everything was too close and I needed to escape. Of course, it wasn't fair on your mother. Poor Jane has had to put up with the idiot I've been for years, and she's never complained. She simply loved me more." His eyes filled with tears but they didn't fall.

"But she loved me less." I sat back in the chair. This I still couldn't forgive her for. It hurt too much.

"I know." He dropped his head down. I wanted him to retract the words, to tell me I was wrong, but he didn't.

"It wasn't right, and I have done everything I can to try and make up for it, as I was the cause." He sighed. "She'd always wanted a big family, and I denied her that. She should have married someone else." He closed his eyes. "She could have had anyone, but she chose me."

"Dad?"

"She wanted you so much, but when I rejected you something snapped in her."

I wasn't going to cry, but it was hard. My mother had wanted me once, at least. Tears flowed down Dad's face. I hadn't seen him cry since Rose had died.

"I'd hoped that when I came back all the love I showered on you would hide her feelings. It did, until Rose died." He put his face in his hands.

I looked up to see Mother standing in the doorway. I had no idea how long she'd been there or what she'd heard. My glance broke the trance she was in and she ran forward and embraced Dad.

"Jane, I've been so stupid." Dad mumbled in Mother's embrace.

"No." Mother buried her face into his neck.

I stood up and turned away. I had to leave. They needed time alone to sort out their problems.

"Judith." Mother turned to me while safe in Dad's embrace. "I don't know what to say."

Dad reached out to me but I stood away from them, watching. "We can both begin with sorry."

"Yes." My mother looked at me, and I saw a glimmer of warmth in her expression. "I'm sorry."

"Can you forgive us?" Dad looked mournful as he gripped Mother's hand.

"I . . ." I cleared my throat. No matter how hard it was and how much it hurt, I had to be honest. There had been too many things unsaid all these years, which had just made everything worse. "I don't know." I studied the two of them. Mother flinched and Dad went pale. But they were complete again. I was on the outside, as I'd always been. I took a deep breath and looked at the pain in Dad's eyes. Mother's look was wary.

As I slowly released the air from my lungs, I knew that this family had been broken for a very long time, and that it would take time and more than a few words to begin to heal it. That was OK. My parents would survive, and so would I. I walked towards them and they both held out their hands.

CHAPTER
THIRTY

As the taxi made its way down the drive towards Pengarrock, I knew what I wanted. I wanted to try to save as much of Pengarrock as I could, even if that was only Petroc's work and his collections. On the train this morning, I'd sketched out plans for a library on gardening history. In my dreams I saw it situated in the coach house, then saw myself developing the garden to show how gardening in Cornwall had evolved through the centuries. The groundwork was in place: Pengarrock's garden already exhibited the Victorian and Edwardian eras well, and the old foundations of the medieval garden were there. It was just a case of filling in the blanks as and when money or volunteers could be found. It would be a tribute, and a lasting legacy to Petroc and his work. But I knew it was just a dream.

Walking through the door of Pengarrock, the atmosphere felt changed but I couldn't say why.

"Welcome back." Helen emerged from the drawing room, duster in hand.

"Thanks, Helen. How are things?" I kissed her cheek.

"Until today Tristan's been locked in with an architect and an engineer. Barbara has been busy with

352

Petroc's book. Other than that, we've all been missing you." She looked at me closely. "I thought they might keep you."

I frowned. My parents had their own things to sort out, as did I. "Why?"

"Because you are lovely, and they must be missing you because we did."

I laughed. "Where is everyone?" I'd noticed Tristan's car wasn't around.

"Barbara's in the study and Tristan's gone to Helston."

"Right, I'll find her." I gave Helen a quick hug. "It's good to be back."

I left my bag at the bottom of the stairs and walked into the study.

"Hello, stranger. So, they didn't keep you?"

I shook my head. "I just heard similar words out of Helen's mouth."

"Not surprising." Barbara leaned back in Petroc's chair. "It's good to be in Cornwall. I'd forgotten how much I missed it."

I pushed aside a few papers and sat on the corner of the desk.

"That was done with purpose." Barbara searched my face. "What's up?"

"Loads. Dad left us." I touched the little clock before looking at her.

"I wondered when that would come up."

"Why didn't you say? No — don't answer that, I know." I paused. "Do you think that Mother had postnatal depression, or just depression after Dad left because he felt so betrayed?"

"Probably both. I told her to seek help, but she wouldn't." She put her fingertips together. "So you've spoken to them."

"Yes, after I found Rose's diary . . ." My voice trailed off.

"Are they OK?"

"Yes, sort of." I frowned. "I always thought they were so together. I never saw the strain. I only knew that I wasn't good enough but never knew why."

Barbara stood and hugged me. "You were always wonderful. It has just taken Jane a while to see it. I always knew it."

I laughed. "Thank God I had you and Aunt Agnes."

The marinade smelt divine as I turned the meat over in it. Music blared, and I belted out the chorus to a Beach Boys' song. Barbara and I were dancing and laughing like I hadn't in ages. Wielding a pair of tongs, Barbara clacked them in the air to the beat while I sang into a large spoon. Tristan came through the door and stopped dead with a look of horror on his face.

"Care to join us?" I held out a hand.

"Not up for it then?" Barbara asked. "Scared in the face of such skill?"

Tristan laughed.

"Quite right too." Barbara smiled.

"The barbecue's waiting for you." I called from the door.

"What?"

Barbara handed him the chicken and pushed him outside. "Did you think we would take away your barbecue duty?"

"Yes."

"Shame on you. How could you think we would be so cruel?" I handed him the tongs and an oven glove.

"I don't know what came over me."

"Laziness?" I taunted, then fled into the kitchen before the oven glove could hit my retreating behind.

"Need a top-up?" Barbara asked as I joined them back outside. The scent of grilling chicken filled the air and my stomach gurgled loudly.

I held my glass out. "While I was away, did you two get anything done, or did you slack off the whole time?"

"Well, I finished cleaning up Petroc's book and sent it off this afternoon. I can't speak for certain other people." Barbara tipped her head in Tristan's direction.

"Who, me?" He flipped the chicken pieces over. "I've been busy fending off estate agents and buyers."

"Really?" I put the salad on the table.

"An old cricket bat has done the trick so far." He turned over the chicken.

"Fine. Why should I expect a straight answer from you?" I turned away.

Barbara moved closer to the grill. "Tristan, I was wondering, after your mother's death, did your father take up with any other women?"

He looked at her. She met his stare. I held my breath. I would never have dared ask such a question.

"Not that I'm aware of. I don't think there was ever anyone else for him. He loved her beyond words. I just never knew it."

Barbara put her hand on his. I watched a woman he barely knew offering him comfort for something it was clear he was only just seeing. He must have been so wrapped up in his own take on things that he never saw his father's. I'd never seen what was happening with my parents either.

"The chicken's cooked." Tristan brought the food to the table.

I passed the salad. "So neither of you solved the riddle of August Rock?"

"Well, I did look at Octavia's sketches as you asked, but it seems to me all she was doing was illustrating the riddle."

"What riddle?" Barbara looked up from her glass.

Not of the land
Not of the sea
Visible only
When August Rock sees

Think of the curlew
Think of the dove
Who carries a flower
Not of peace but of love

Gone from the dinas
Lost from the world
Only at Pengarrock
Do petals unfurl

The jewel of Pengarrock
Hidden to all
Will free your heart
From duty's call.

I stood with my mouth open as Tristan recited it off by heart. He may have said he'd done nothing, but the fact that he'd learned it implied more involvement.

"Intriguing." Barbara drew her finger around in circles on the table. "The first stanza is clear. It's a cave of some sort, only accessible when the tide is low enough to see August Rock."

"Agreed." Tristan passed the chicken. "That part is simple enough, but the rest is meaningless."

"How many times a year is the reef visible?" Barbara poured wine.

"At a guess, it happens during the really low spring tides several times a year. We're probably due one any day now. But we have so many caves, and I bet as the first part has been known for ages every single one has been searched by my father, if not every other treasure-hunter around."

"True. What about the second verse?"

Think of the curlew
Think of the dove
Who carries a flower
Not of peace but of love.

"Two types of birds found in the area. Nothing special there." Tristan smiled.

"On that you could be wrong." I found my voice. "Don't forget, this was written by a Victorian, and she would have been aware of the symbolism and superstitions associated with every animal or plant or image that she used." I paused, thinking about Octavia's book. "In the book she drew a dove carrying something. I assumed it was an olive branch, but it seems it's not."

I jumped as a loud crash echoed from above. "What was that?"

"You two go and look. I'll stay here."

"Spooked, Barbara?" I laughed at her look of horror and peered at the house.

"That doesn't sound good. Shall we go and investigate?" Tristan waited for me.

I walked up to him. "After you." He grabbed my hand and we set off into the house.

Over the past weeks, Tristan had become tanned and he looked incredibly well, but angry. Woodworm was the concern of the moment. It was the reason we were in the attic again. The loud bang of the night before was the ceiling collapsing over two bedrooms. It was as if our exploration into the attic had woken up the little beasties, but the truth was that the boxes we had moved had pushed the floor struts too far. Tristan's phone rang, and he slipped off down the stairs. It might be the builder, who had come to check out the situation this morning.

Things didn't look good. From where I stood I could see into the bedroom below. This morning, with Barbara's help, we'd cleaned up as much of the rubble as we could. But I knew this was only the beginning of the process.

Tristan joined me again and I handed him another box. His mouth was set into a grim expression.

"Dare I ask?"

He looked up at me. "You can ask, but you don't want to hear what I have to say."

"Try me."

He raised an eyebrow. "That was the builder. He's given me an estimate of fifty thousand pounds to treat all the roof space for woodworm, shore up the roof and repair the damage to the ceiling."

"Ouch."

"Too bloody right. I can't keep this place; it drains money and makes none." He closed his eyes and rubbed the back of his neck while my mind went over his words. He said *keep this place*. I hadn't thought that was even on his agenda.

"What an unholy mess," Helen commented as she came up the stairs to the attic.

Tristan turned to her, looking grim. "You could say that."

"It has made a mess, Helen, but it's fantastic. One of the boxes I saw contained some more of Petroc's journals." I smiled.

"My dear, Petroc didn't go up into the attics in ten years, if not longer." Helen shook her head. "The dust alone."

Tristan put a hand on her shoulder. "Look on the bright side, Helen."

Helen looked about at the boxes. "There's a bright side to this muddle?"

He grinned. "Yes, it will keep me occupied and delay the sale even longer."

"True, but not long enough for my liking."

I held up a household accounts book. "1756 . . . Could be interesting."

"You're impossible. You're more interested in the past than the present." He touched my shoulder.

I carefully placed the book down. "Yes, I am but the past has the answers that might help the present."

"Maybe." He gave me a wry smile.

Helen disappeared down the stairs. She was spending more time back at the house. Both Tristan and I were worried that she was overdoing it, but nothing seemed to be able to keep her away.

"The journals of your father for 1972 to 1982." I handed them to him.

"Well, we know that means Dad went up in the attic in 1982, and then never again if Helen's right."

"She wasn't here all the time."

"True, but she seems to know all things. I'll take these downstairs and have a look through them."

"Great. Let's take these last two boxes down, then I can continue with listing everything." I watched him disappear down the hall, still pondering his words. *He won't keep the house because it costs so much, but he has thought about it.* There was still hope.

I picked up my pad of paper and got back to discovering what was here. Before long my back ached from bending over the boxes.

"Your mother." Barbara handed me the phone and mouthed the words, "It won't bite."

I nodded, and thought how strange it was to have Mother calling me after all this time. I hoped there was nothing wrong at home, and this was just Mother trying to build on the small steps we'd made towards each other.

I opened the French windows to the garden. Although the morning had been damp, sunlight was breaking through and the air was fresh with the smell of newly cut grass. The deep blue of the hydrangeas jumped out from the rich green background. In the pale sunlight they seemed luminous. The sky, heavy and grey, hung low over the river, while out in the bay the sea was blue and calm. The weather was so localised. During my time here, I'd realised that it could be raining in Pengarrock, but by the time I reached Helston, just a few miles away, the sun could be baking. Today was going to be one of those days.

I sat down at my computer and hoped the wifi was working.

Not of the land
Not of the sea
Visible only
When August Rock sees

I didn't need to do any research on that, other than compare my photos with Octavia's painting. I pulled up my pictures and enlarged them. It was hard to tell. I pulled a magnifying glass from Petroc's desk — no, I corrected myself — Imogen's desk, as Tristan had told me, and studied the painting to see if Octavia had indicated on it the location of the cave, but there was nothing. The difference in the photograph and the picture didn't show any real change other than perspective.

> Think of the curlew
> Think of the dove
> Who carries a flower
> Not of peace but of love

I typed "curlew" into the search box. The first reference came from a Henry Wadsworth Longfellow poem. But with a bit of digging, I found that the curlew is a symbol of an impending storm. It is also a bird that feeds on mud or soft ground, and in winter they hang out on rocky shores. Not much of a clue there. Was Clarissa trying to reference an impending storm, or a death? Or the possibility that seeking the treasure could bring death?

I looked up as Tristan walked in. "Hi."

He came around the desk and I stifled the urge to hide what I was doing.

"A dove is the symbol of peace." He smiled.

"Yes, but more than that, I'm sure." I quickly typed in "dove symbolism". "First reference is to the Holy

Spirit." I scanned the page, quickly picking up references. "Doves always return home when released. They are used at weddings." I paused and clicked on a link. "And," I read quickly, "they are a symbol of motherhood and self-sacrifice."

"OK, but how much of that would Clarissa have been aware of?" His hand brushed my shoulder.

I focused on the screen and not on him standing so close to me. "Good question and one I can't answer, but from the few letters we have, we do know that she was well read and that she grew up here with a well-stocked library, if nothing else."

"Fine, let's assume she was well educated then. I still don't see how this is telling Octavia where to find the treasure, and most of all why she hid it. It would have gone to Octavia anyway." He sat on the desk and faced me.

"No, it wouldn't have unless she married the next Trevillion to inherit Pengarrock." I looked at him, then glanced away. Looking at him was no good for logical thought.

"Ah, you have a point there."

"Thank you." I took a breath. "I think Clarissa was trying to hide the jewels for Octavia. He must have been trying to protect her in some way. Well, financially, as everything would go to the next male Trevillion and not to Octavia, as had happened with Clarissa herself."

"What do you think happened to Clarissa?" He crossed his arms against his chest, drawing my glance there.

I pushed my hair back. "Of that, I haven't a clue. Part of me wants her to have gone off with Lord Peters and lived happily ever after, but I just can't see her abandoning Octavia." I tapped "flowers of love" into the search engine.

"That would be a red rose, wouldn't it?" He raised an eyebrow.

"For passionate love, yes, but love is a varied thing." I dared to look at him, but quickly went back to the computer screen. I scrolled down the list, hoping something would jump out at me but nothing did. On this list alone there were fifteen flowers representing love. I picked up the magnifying glass and studied the sketch. All I could tell was that one end of the stem bore a white flower. "Can you make out what the dove is carrying?"

Tristan leaned over me and took the magnifying glass. I could smell the woody scent of his aftershave. This was not good.

"No, can't help." He put the glass down and looked at me intently. "Why does this mean so much to you?"

"Because . . ." I paused. "Because it meant a lot to your father, and because I think Pengarrock is worth saving."

"Who says finding the jewels will save the estate? It will just be more money for me and more for the taxman."

"True." I took a breath. Tristan was still so close, and yet those eyes suddenly became distant. "But in your heart, do you really want to throw all of this away to someone who may not care?"

"What makes you think that's what I want to do?" His glance never left my face.

"I think," I twisted a stray curl around my finger, "that this is where you belong. You left not because you wanted to, but because you felt it was the only way. But now you know that was wrong."

"I left because there was nothing here for me." Tristan straightened and walked away.

CHAPTER
THIRTY-ONE

The road up from Helford felt steeper today. My hands had a few blisters. I might have overdone it, but I had wanted to practise once more. They had said last night in the pub that the Yank didn't have a chance of winning any of the races against the locals. I was damned if I was going to let that sort of comment go unchallenged, even if it was said in good humour. I had to hold my side up tomorrow by rowing for all I was worth. I just hoped I hadn't taken it too far today. My shoulders ached. A long bath would be the answer.

My mobile rang just as I reached the house. It was Barbara. She'd gone back to Oxford two days ago. Her job was done. I walked to the front of the house where I knew the signal was strong and perched on a bench.

"Where have you been?"

"Practising." I flexed my calf muscles and looked at the dying light on the north side of the river. The view had become so much a part of me, almost like breathing.

"Have you owned up that you rowed competitively at uni yet?"

"Absolutely not."

366

"You've changed, Jude; once so straight, and now hiding key facts. Hope no one places bets."

I laughed. "I wouldn't know, but I wouldn't be surprised."

"Have you spoken to your mother?"

I frowned. "No?"

"She's been trying to reach you."

"My phone was off when I was rowing. Are they OK?" Adrenalin surged through me.

"Yes, but your Great-aunt Agnes has died." Barbara paused. "I'm so sorry, Jude. I know how much she meant to you."

"At least I got to say goodbye." I thought of the frail woman lying in the bed. I hoped the end had been painless.

"She had a good innings at ninety-four."

"True. Thanks for letting me know. I'll call my parents." I rang off, then went through a stretch routine. I walked into the house. I could hear Tristan's voice on the phone.

"No, I'm not ready to have any viewings."

I walked towards the drawing room. I wouldn't want to be the person on the other end of the phone. I knew he was sitting on a firm offer. The figure he spoke of was large, but maybe the magic would work.

In the hallway, I glanced towards the chapel. Aunt Agnes. I would go and say a prayer. She would like that. I walked in and was again struck by the simple beauty of the place. Sunlight illuminated the kneeler at the front, and I walked slowly towards it. The glow caught the prayer books wedged into the shelf. I bent down and pulled out the first book. It was the Book of Common Prayer, a well-worn copy which gave the impression it had lived in its current location a long time. The inscription said: *To Antonia on her confirmation, 15th May 1932, Aunt Martha*. I flipped through the pages, coming to the section on death and burial. There would be some prayer here that would be appropriate.

> Most merciful Father, who hast been pleased to take unto thyself the soul of this thy servant; Grant to us who are still in our pilgrimage, and who walk as yet by faith, that having served thee with constancy on earth, we may be joined hereafter with thy blessed saints in glory everlasting; through Jesus Christ our Lord. Amen.

I looked up at the cross and smiled. As Barbara had said, she had had a good life. Placing the book back, I looked at another. It was a book of the Psalms, with no inscription. It too felt well used. I ran my hand over each book and put them back, but found they wouldn't slide in all the way.

Down on my knees, I removed the books and saw that there was something stuck at the back. I moved my fingers along the shelf, but I really needed a flashlight. The sunlight was too strong in the opposite direction to let me see. Whatever it was, it was well caught, and my fingers weren't quite long enough to get round it.

I stood and went in search of a flashlight and a screwdriver. It was probably nothing more than some elderly hymnal, but my curiosity was aroused. Walking to the kitchen, I tried to stretch my aching muscles. That bath was beckoning, but it would wait.

"How was the rowing?" Tristan stood on the bottom step.

"Fine."

"Ready to beat off all comers?"

"Not the way I feel at the moment, but I'll be ready tomorrow."

He took a few steps in my direction. "Have you got the programme? What time's your race?"

"You're coming?" I couldn't hide the surprise in my voice.

"Yes. I wouldn't miss the thrashing of the Yank for anything."

I raised an eyebrow. "Will you be rowing then?"

"Me? No, I haven't rowed in years, though I used to love it." He smiled.

"You should. You can use the lugger."

He tilted his head slightly. "Never know, I might surprise you."

"You might indeed." I liked the gleam showing in his eyes. "The regatta starts at one. Don't know what time I'm racing. Have you heard the forecast?"

"Light rain, some sun."

"Bit of everything then."

"Yes." Tristan followed me to the kitchen where I pulled out the flashlight and looked in a drawer for the screwdriver, or something else long and thin enough.

"Has something broken?"

"No, stuck." I looked up.

"Can I help?"

"Maybe." I grabbed the tools and led the way to the chapel. At the kneeler, I turned the flashlight on and looked at the back of the shelf. There was definitely something in there. Tristan bent nearer and my neck tingled from the light touch of his breath.

"Whatever made you look there?"

"My aunt passed away, and I came in to say a prayer."

"I'm so sorry." He placed a hand on my arm. It was meant as a comfort, but comforting it wasn't.

"Thank you. So when I replaced the prayer books, they didn't fit the way I wanted them to."

"Perfectionist, are we?"

I pursed my lips briefly. "Well, yes, sort of."

"I suppose that's good."

"Sometimes."

He smiled and my heart skipped a beat. "Hand me the torch."

He knelt and peered in. "There's something there." Tristan put his hand in but then held it out for the screwdriver.

"Careful. It could be fragile."

"Ever the conservationist. I'm sure it's nothing more than a mouldy old prayer book. No intrinsic value."

"You're probably right, but until we have it we don't know that."

"Point taken." He leaned closer to the shelf. "No doubt here lies the missing copy of Shakespeare's folio."

"That would be quite nice, but I don't think it would fit." There was a gentle scraping noise.

370

"Here's your precious first edition." Tristan stood up while I turned the small book over in my hand. Gold numbers glistened in the sunlight, *1984*. It was Petroc's journal from the year Imogen died. Something crawled across the back of my neck. I shook, and a folded piece of paper dropped out.

"What's that?" Tristan picked the paper up off the floor. He opened and read it. "It's Octavia's suicide note." He handed me the letter.

August 29th, 1851

I have failed. After finding Mother's riddle and note, I have tried to find the Trevillion jewels that she hid for me. She did this so that I wouldn't have to do what I'm being forced to do now, marry my cousin. She wanted me to have the freedom she hadn't had, and yet I find myself as trapped and miserable as she had been. Rather than face the same fate as her, I am leaving. I am rowing out to sea and will never return. I love Pengarrock, but not enough to wed myself to my cousin and live the hell mother had.

Octavia

My hand shook. Now we knew why Petroc had been searching, but more important for Tristan was what I held in my hands. "Tristan, this is your father's journal for the year your mother died."

CHAPTER
THIRTY-TWO

Every muscle in my body ached, which didn't make the prospect of rowing today any easier. I looked at the crowd gathering at the Shipwright's and on the river. The sun was shining for them. I would rather be asleep, but I'd made this commitment and I had to prove that the Yank could row, plus I had t-shirts, tea towels and some unnecessary umbrellas to flog along with raffle tickets. I'd better hop into the little tender I'd been given and do the job.

"Hey, Jude, ready to suffer defeat?"

I waved at one of the regulars from the pub. I couldn't remember his name, but I would show him and the rest of them. Although rowing in eights was very different, it still gave me an advantage. I needed to have something up my sleeve as I'd seen some of the competition in the Helford gig and they looked pretty fit.

Wading to the tender, I loaded it with goods. One push and I was among the spectators. Dipping the oars, I set off and each muscle complained, but it was a way to warm up. Once I'd reached the outermost boat, I began the sales patter to sell the stock and was surprised at how quickly things went. The good-natured banter from boat to boat lifted my mood. Before long I needed to head back to be ready for the start of the ladies' race.

In the throng of people standing at the Shipwright's, I saw Tristan talking to JC but looking at me. My chest tightened.

"Hi, Jude, I'll take over sales. It's time for you to go." I jumped slightly at Mark's interruption of my thoughts, but smiled at him as he climbed into the small tender. He was far too big a man to be in such a small boat.

"Thanks, Mark. Wish me luck."

"Ha, Sam will have you beat hands down." He rowed away laughing.

"Thanks for the vote of confidence." I turned and found Tristan at my elbow. "Hello." My voice sounded husky.

"Hi. Your lugger's over there. I thought I'd give you a push off."

"Thanks. I'm glad someone is supporting me."

"Your number-one fan." He smiled.

"Good." I took a deep breath. "If I win, dinner's on you tonight."

"That's a deal." There was a promise of more in his eyes, and I didn't know if my stomach was in knots because of race nerves or the thought of dinner with Tristan. It couldn't be dinner, as that happened almost every night.

The compère called for all the competitors to get to the starting line, so I jumped into the boat. Tristan pushed me out. Rowing into position, I turned to the crowd and spotted Tristan's washed-out blue shirt. The starting gun fired and I was off as old training kicked in. I pulled hard, smiling as I passed the knot of competitors. They weren't going to write off the Yank that quickly.

I was around the second barrel and on my way back with a clear lead when I heard the compère complaining that a ringer had been brought in. Something about "these foreigners" reached my ears, and then that maybe they should disqualify the Yank for being too good. I laughed as I crossed the finish line.

The cork made a satisfying pop. Tristan poured the champagne into glasses. I wasn't sure either of us needed any alcohol at this point. Yet it seemed appropriate to celebrate my first-place win in the ladies' race, and our second place in the t-shirt race. Besides, the last time I'd drunk champagne, interesting things had happened. It might work again; I could hope. "I'm beat. Would it be too decadent to take a glass of that lovely champagne with me while I have a bath?"

"Not at all." He handed me a glass.

"Here's to a successful day." I raised it.

"We still have the fireworks tonight."

"Hmmm, yes." I sipped the champagne. "I hear they should be great. When was the last time you saw them?"

"Oh, years ago when Mark nearly blew himself up trying to set them off."

"They've got a professional in now."

374

"Good thing too." We stood staring at each other, and I wondered what was going through his mind.

"Right. I'll be down in a bit. Are you coming to the fireworks?" I turned to him.

"Are you asking?"

I looked at him with my eyes wide. "Yes, I think I am."

"Then fireworks it is. Do we eat here first, or try and grab a bite there?"

"Here. It will be madness there, don't you think?"

He stepped closer to me. "Yes. I'll throw something together."

"Great." I ran before I kissed him.

The fireworks had finished, and Tristan was chatting to someone I didn't know at the makeshift bar. I leaned against a table and enjoyed the live music, one of the teens from the village singing lead. The Riverside Café and surrounds were heaving.

My head was spinning slightly — half a bottle of champagne and several glasses on top were having their effect. An older man approached me. "Are you the American working at Pengarrock?"

"Yes."

"My name is Wilf Trelawny, and I was hoping that you could help me."

The name rang a bell. "You wrote the orchid book with Imogen."

"Yes, and that's what I wanted help with." He took a sip of his beer. "You see, there was research that Immy and I were doing together and, well, I would like to see it."

I stood up straight. Was he the man Imogen had been involved with? "Imogen has been dead a long time. Why wait until now?"

He looked at his hands before he spoke. "I couldn't ask Petroc for it." He looked me in the eyes. "You see, my relationship with Immy was . . ." He swallowed. "It was above board, but only just."

"What are you saying?"

"I loved her."

"I see. Did she love you?"

He looked around at the crowds. "I always thought so. She was having troubles with Petroc, and we may have crossed a line."

I raised an eyebrow. "Were you having an affair?"

"Not quite."

I frowned. "That's an evasive answer." I looked around for Tristan but couldn't see him. "People knew of it?"

"There was talk."

"Petroc?" Was this what Imogen had been referring to in her letter?

"He guessed, which is why I couldn't ask him."

"And you think now that he's gone his son will help?"

"Putting it that way, not likely, but I do think he would like to see the work she had done acknowledged." He sighed.

"Did you have an affair with my mother?" Tristan stood beside me with his mouth hardened into a line. I reached for his hand. His grip was painful.

376

"No, she turned me down because she loved you and your father more."

The tension left Tristan's body.

"Wilf, can I reach you later about the research material?" I looked at Tristan for approval and he nodded.

"Helen knows where to find me." He looked at Tristan. "I'm sorry about your father."

"Thanks." Tristan draped an arm across my shoulder as we watched Wilf move into the crowd. "My father mentioned Wilf in that last journal. Dad never believed that my mother had cheated, but he spoke of all the gossip and the conclusions that had been drawn about her death."

"I'm so sorry."

He pulled me closer to him. "At least now I know the truth."

When I opened my eyes, there was no pain and I breathed a sigh of relief. I swung my feet to the floor then carefully raised myself up. Once sitting, I waited to see if my head was going to pound, but thankfully it didn't. I dressed and went downstairs.

Wilf's revelations last night answered the questions that had been lingering in my mind since I'd seen Imogen's letter. Tristan must be exhausted. For years he'd carried the burden of believing he could have stopped his mother's death and had listened to the rumours. He had been very silent on the way home.

There was no sign of Tristan, and I wasn't surprised. He'd had more to drink than I had, and before I'd encountered Wilf he'd kicked back like I'd not seen him do before. The way he'd spoken to people, it was like he had never left. I wouldn't say he was relaxed — that was still a step too far. Tristan was socially able, but having watched him last night I knew he was shy. Maybe it came from growing up in the big house, with everyone looking on. It couldn't have been easy.

With a large mug of coffee, I stood on the terrace and looked at the river. It was a clear morning with a light breeze. The tide was in. A yacht made its way out to the bay and I longed to join it. There was nothing like a bit of gentle sailing to blow away the cobwebs after a heavy night. As soon as the thought came into my head, I was up the stairs. I paused outside Tristan's door but there weren't any sounds. I imagined he would sleep until noon. I left a note on the kitchen table for him.

The walk to the sailing club loosened up my overused muscles and helped with the slight out-of-my-head feeling. As I reached the pontoon I realised I'd left my phone behind. I could hear Dad saying never go out onto the water without communication, but looking at how quickly the tide was going out, there was no way that I would make it to the house and back before low tide. The sky was a cobalt blue with not a cloud to be seen. I hopped in the boat and got off the pontoon before it was too late.

Once through the narrows, I could relax and let the boat do the work. Normally the river was teeming with craft on a Sunday morning, but I had it to myself. Everyone must be nursing hangovers from last night.

My stomach grumbled and I knew then that I hadn't thought this through well at all. Coming out on the river without eating breakfast and without bringing food when the tide was on its way out was silly. It was even more foolish when the twinges of hangover tummy were hitting.

I reached the bay and thought about turning around. As I sat up to tack, I saw a thick sea fog approaching. Above it and around the sky was blue. It was like a massive lone cloud descending on the river. The temperature dropped. I quickly tacked and made my way back towards the Helford. I didn't need to be becalmed in the middle of Falmouth Bay in a very small boat. I groped under the seat, hoping there were flares and such stowed away.

The sun disappeared and the fog swirled around me. Within seconds I couldn't see where I was going and the wind died. I took the sail down and put the oars in. When the mist had descended, I'd been heading west and had made it into the mouth of the river. I turned the boat south, or I hoped I had, and began to row towards the shore. Every few strokes I turned to see if anything was visible, like another boat or the jutting rocks that lined the little coves. But I could see nothing.

As suddenly as the mist had covered everything, I was through it and almost onto a tiny cove below Dennis Head. I made my way carefully to the small patch of sand and pulled the boat onto it. The wall of low cloud in front of me stretched out into the bay and upriver. Yet the sun shone clearly above it. It was extraordinary; I'd never seen anything like it. I couldn't go back on the river because it was totally obscured. In another few minutes it would be low tide. There was nothing to do but explore the cove and try to stay warm.

Most of the cliff was covered in plants, but I could see evidence of an old landslip. I walked out on the rocks looking at the mussels, thinking longingly of lunch — preferably Helen's moules marinière with crusty bread. I debated scrambling to the next cove, but thought this might prove to be a bad idea if the fog moved onshore and I didn't have my boat.

A sense of panic crept up on me as I walked back to the beach and looked up. Fog rolled down from above. I thought of my early-morning walk just after Petroc had died. I'd looked down on this very cove. I shivered. The ghostly orchid; it was a rare one. Where had I read about it? In Imogen's book. It had mentioned one that had only been found here, but was now extinct. The last one was sighted in the 1840s. I rubbed the goose bumps on my arms. I knew orchids could remain dormant for a long time until the right fungus grew to nourish the seeds. But this would be a very long time. Could it have been blooming all this time, with no one to witness it? Pacing the small stretch of sand, it came to me.

Only on Pengarrock do petals unfurl.

Fog swirled around as I looked up at the cliff. Could it be that Imogen had figured it out? Hairs on the back of my neck rose. That's what had happened.

380

Only on Pengarrock do petals unfurl.

"Pen" meaning "head of" and "garrock" meaning rock . . . Clarissa hadn't just written about the estate, but about the location. The rare orchid bloomed on the cliff, and under that cliff would be the cave. Imogen had realised this.

Closing my eyes, I could see it so clearly in my mind. Tristan had left her in the nursery when he went fishing. She must have read Clarissa's riddle at the back of the riddle book and made the connections. Her research had probably told her roughly where the orchids had been found in the past. That's why she went rushing past Tristan, perched on a rock on the beach.

Imogen must have been looking over the cliff to see the cove when she fell tragically. Or tripped when she saw the rare orchid blooming. The meticulous files in the desk were hers. The pieces were coming together now, I was sure of it. I checked my watch. It was exactly low tide. Today's tide was only marginally higher than tomorrow's extremely low one. The cave must be here.

> Not of the land
> Not of the sea
> Only visible
> When August Rock sees

Well, that would be fine if I could see more than a foot off the beach, let alone August Rock. The cave must be visible now. The normal waterline was clearly evident on the rocks, and I searched below it. Nothing jumped out, but if it had been obvious someone would have found it long before now. I walked to where the water met the cliff face and began to pull back the channelled wrack and other seaweeds that were clinging to the rocks. Would any opening remain if the landslip had happened since 1846? I ripped away, dislodging small stones until I saw a rabbit-sized hole. That couldn't be it. I peered in, but without light it was hopeless. Then I shouted in, and the noise travelled.

After frantic digging, I'd cleared the opening large enough for me to push my head through. All the time I was watching the tide rise. With one last tug, I removed a large stone, and I could then get my body through if I wanted to. Water lapped at my feet as I pushed myself through up to my waist and my hands felt around, but made contact with nothing. I came out again and widened the hole some more.

"Ouch." I pulled my hand back. Something sharp had pierced the skin on my palm. I rinsed my hand in the river and pressed against the puncture. Although it stung, I wasn't going to let it stop me. I went back to the opening. A gold pin stuck up out of the sediment. Frowning, I dug carefully around it and found what looked like a brooch. It was so covered in mud that I couldn't really see much of it. I placed it in the boat and went back to the hole. With a larger stone I bashed the opening wider. Could that piece of jewellery have belonged to Clarissa? With the opening now a bit bigger, I pushed my head through and wriggled my shoulder. I was balanced half in and half out. My hands came into contact with nothing. I pushed my feet against a rock and fell through.

CHAPTER
THIRTY-THREE

I landed with a splash in water than must have been at least two feet deep. Swiftly I righted myself and placed a hand above my head as I rose so that I wouldn't hit it. My hand didn't come into contact with anything as I stood in cold water up to my knees. Light streamed through the opening, but didn't penetrate far into the cave. I couldn't see much, yet the space felt big, very big. Something moved against my legs. I screamed. It echoed about me. I scrambled and clawed my way out.

Frantic, I ran to my boat to find it afloat and ready to set out on its own. I could barely breathe, my chest was so tight and my teeth were chattering. I clambered in, put the brooch in my pocket then rubbed my arms and legs until I felt I could row.

The fog hadn't lifted, but had rolled onto the shore. I made my way along the coastline, hugging the rocks. I was freezing. It had been foolish to go into that cave alone, but in the heat of the moment it seemed sane. Shivering like a madwoman, I rowed. The tide was still too far out to make it onto the pontoon at the sailing club. I would secure the boat on Pengarrock Beach and walk to the house, change and eat. Lack of food was causing the shakes as much as cold.

Through the fog I recognised the boathouse and knew I was on home ground. I pulled the last few strokes and waited for the boat to ground. I pulled it as high as it would go onto the beach and secured it as best I could with the rope that I had.

I was still shivering as I walked up to the house, playing with the brooch in my hands. With my thumbnail I tried to scrape the dirt off but it was like cement. I shoved it back into my pocket.

Now I needed to plan my next move. Would Tristan help me? What were the laws regarding finding treasure on someone's land? If it was in the sea, was it fair game? But what if it wasn't in the sea or on the land?

I didn't know how big the cave was, and if it was totally submerged at high tide. What I did know was that tomorrow was the last day for a few months that the mouth of the cave would be above water. Time was running out to find all this information and get someone to help me if Tristan wouldn't. I couldn't do it alone.

With my head bent down against the rain that had begun to fall, I walked straight into Tristan as I opened the garden gate.

"What the hell have you been doing?" He placed a steadying hand on my shoulder.

"I've found the cave!"

"What were you doing on the river in a fog?"

I shook my head. "It wasn't foggy when I left, and I forgot my phone."

"Stupid."

"Agreed, but I had no idea that a sea fog of biblical proportions was about to descend on the river." The last part was almost lost due to my shivering. "Did you hear what I said about the cave?"

"There are hundreds of caves along the river."

"I know that!" I tried to stop my teeth from chattering. "But I'm sure this is the one."

"How do you know?" Tristan took off his jacket and threw it over my shoulders. It smelt of his aftershave, and I snuggled into its warmth.

"You won't want to hear the answer."

"I'm sure I won't, but tell me anyway." He shoved his hands into his pockets.

"Because it all fits together."

"What the *hell* . . . ?"

"Back when your father died, I took a very early morning stroll." I pulled the jacket tighter around me.

"You would."

"Of course, and I fell and while I was on the ground I found an orchid and thought it was strange, but nothing more."

"Yes, there are wild orchids here and always have been. My mother loved them."

"She had discovered an orchid that was thought to be extinct, and it's not. I've seen it."

"Enough of that. You were out in the dark risking life and limb, so what does this orchid have to do with *the* cave?" He ran a hand through his hair.

"Your mother stumbled in her haste, like I did, but unlike me she was closer to the edge." Tristan went white. I took a breath and saw the hurt, anger and disbelief on his face. "She must have seen the orchid. She knew the riddle, and she knew how rare it was. She became distracted, and that tragically led to her fall." I could see it all so clearly in my mind. "Tristan, your mother didn't jump. She missed her footing."

"So you say."

"It's true, I just know it's true." I put my icy hand on his arm and he drew back. "She had figured it all out. The sapphire was her quest."

"We had better get you to the house and in the warm before you become ill." He marched towards the house.

I looked at the long flowerbed, noting that Michaelmas daisies had begun to bloom. "See, I told you that you wouldn't want to hear it."

"You're right there. No matter what you were after, it was utter bloody madness to go out on the water alone without your phone, and with a storm on the way in."

"That I know, thank you very much."

"You couldn't prove it today."

I overtook him and practically ran the rest of the way to the house. I was soaked through and so cold I thought I would never be warm again. I heard his footsteps behind me, and thought he could go and take a flying leap. In fact, anyplace from here. He didn't deserve this place. As the rain began pelting down on me, I looked at the flowers lining the path and sighed. Pengarrock was unique, and needed to be in the hands of someone who would love it. Not the bastard behind me, who was looking at it as a way to make money. My feet hit the ground harder and faster.

Helen was in the doorway when I arrived. Did everyone know that I'd been on the river?

"You're soaked." She stepped back.

"Yes."

"Where have you been?" She touched my dripping hair.

"Ask him." I pointed to Tristan.

"Tristan?" Helen asked.

"She's a bloody idiot, chasing after imaginary treasure."

"I'm an idiot, am I? Well, that's just fine, coming from you." I took off his jacket and threw it at him. "I'm not the one who's throwing this magic place to the wolves for profit."

"What the hell does that have to do with you going on the water in foul conditions, trying to get yourself killed?"

"Children." Helen stepped between us.

"Helen, you had better stay out of this." Tristan slammed the front door. "So just what treasure did you find in the cave, and was it worth risking your life for?"

I dug my hand in my pocket and thrust the brooch at him. "This."

"It's just a bit of junk that turns up all the time." He turned it over in his fingers. "Where did you get it? The beach?"

I clenched my hands. "No, when I dug the cave opening wider, I found it."

"You went into a cave alone?" He practically shouted.

I nodded.

"For pity's sake. You were risking your neck for what? Buried treasure?"

I stood my ground. "I know it's real."

"This is bloody ridiculous."

"No, it's not." I wrapped my arms about myself.

"This place has ruined you."

Helen coughed. I looked at her and laughed. I'd forgotten she was there.

"Quite the contrary. Coming here has been the making of me." I turned and walked upstairs, where I collapsed onto the bed. My head was spinning. Rain pelted the windows as blasts of wind hit the glass. I was lucky to be off the water. I needed a bath, and then I wanted to find out about landslips. I knew that Clarissa had been trapped in the cave and had died a horrible death there.

I was just pulling a sweater on when I heard a tap at the door. "Come in."

"I owe you an apology." Tristan held out the brooch, now totally cleaned. Flipping it over in my hand, I traced the engraving in the lapis oval. "The Trevillion crest."

"I think I'd better listen to what you have to say."

"Finally." I smiled.

CHAPTER
THIRTY-FOUR

The sea was flat and the sky blue. There was no wind at all. Yachts were heading out of the river under engine power. It was simply a perfect August day. I was perched on the bow of the dory looking intently down at the water while Tristan took charge of the boat. Along with lunch, we'd packed other useful things like long-sleeved clothes and shovels. It was so warm I had stripped down to my bikini.

We were going on a treasure hunt, but it would have to wait until after lunch because of the big swing of the tide. We had to get the borrowed boat off the pontoon long before low tide hit. I was unbelievably excited, Tristan less so, but he was going to help me so it didn't matter whether he was filled with the joys of spring or not. All that mattered was that we would find the treasure and put the mystery of Lady Clarissa Trevillion to rest.

"What do you want to do?" Tristan slowed the boat down to make himself heard over the noise of the engine.

"Why don't we anchor off the cove and wait for the tide to drop? We can eat lunch while we wait." I moved to the back of the boat to join him.

"Your cove? Will you recognise it without the fog?"

I wrinkled my nose. "Absolutely."

"Did you put an X to mark the spot?"

"Serve you right if I did and someone pinched the treasure in the night."

"Quite possible, as the river has been filled with treasure-hunters of late, seeking the lost Trevillion sapphire." He smiled and I felt slightly light-headed.

"What do you think we'll find?" I pointed. "It's that one there."

"Nothing, but I will have no further work for you on Dad's stuff if you don't get this out of your head."

I grinned. "Fair enough."

"And what's this I hear from Barbara about setting up the Petroc Trevillion Library of Garden History?"

"Oh." I looked down at my feet and wiggled my toes, admiring the newly applied red polish.

"When were you going to tell me about that bright idea?"

I looked up at him over the top of my sunglasses. "Probably never."

"Never?" He leaned back.

"It was just a dream of mine. With all the books, papers, photographs, prints, and so on that your father collected, you could easily establish a research library."

"It sounds like something that could be done with his work. Where did you propose to locate it?"

"In the stable block."

"At Pengarrock?"

"Where else but Pengarrock?"

Tristan rolled his eyes then cut the engine, and we floated into the cove with both of us looking over the side of the boat for rocks. He dropped anchor and didn't take the boat the whole way in as the cove was in the shade. I opened the picnic basket and handed him a sandwich.

"Jude, have you got sunblock on?"

"No, now that you mention it. I didn't think it would be this warm out here. Am I red?"

"Just gently pink."

"Just shy of lobster then." I studied my shoulders.

"Maybe another ten minutes."

"Right, I must have some in my bag." I dug to the bottom of the bag and handed Tristan the bottle. "Would you mind?"

"Not at all." He squeezed the thick lotion into his hand. His fingers smoothed the cold cream into the contours of my back. This was exquisite torture. His hand moved lower down my back and I gasped.

"A bit cold?"

"Mmm," I lied. The boat moved sharply to the side from the wake of a passing craft, throwing Tristan up against me. I'd lost my appetite for the sandwich in my hand. Now I wanted something else entirely.

"Tristan?"

"Yes."

I turned around. His hand remained on my waist. The boat rocked again and his body pressed against mine, making me aware of his desire. I stroked his chin with my finger.

"Jude?"

392

"Hmm, yes." I kissed him. This was madness but it was divine. His hands pulled me closer while his mouth trailed light kisses down my neck. I gasped, and the next swell knocked us both off our feet and onto the floor of the boat.

Just before low tide, we moved onto the beach where we both pulled on our jeans, long-sleeved shirts and sneakers. Tristan assessed the site. "Were you really foolish enough to go into the cave alone without knowing what you'd find?"

I put my hands on my hips and considered arguing, but having spent the last hour kissing him I felt less inclined to do so. "Yes."

He laughed as he began to clear the entrance to the cave. "Are you just going to watch?"

"Maybe." I checked the flashlights again and hoped that the ziplock bags we had would be watertight enough for them. I walked over to him. The tide had already turned. We didn't have long, maybe ten minutes, before the water would be at the opening.

"Shall I go first?" He put the shovel aside further up on a rock.

"Yes, but be prepared to fall into a hole, and it will be wet."

He frowned. "Sounds pleasant."

"Absolutely."

He got on his knees and disappeared through the opening, and I heard a splash.

I stuck my head in and could see nothing. "Are you all right?"

"Yes. This is madness. Hand me the torches." His hand came to the opening and he took them from me. "Let me have a look before you come in."

"Be quick. The water's already at my feet." I checked the boat to make sure it was still anchored properly. I turned as soon as the light from the torch caught my eye.

"Bloody hell, this is big." His voice echoed, and I could see him standing in water.

"I'm coming in."

"Careful."

This time I went in feet first and dropped with a thump, but at least I was expecting it.

"Here's a torch, but I don't think there's anything worth looking at."

I took it from him. "It's big, so how can you be so sure?"

"Because I've had a look, and I don't see anything but the odd crab."

I huffed and walked up a steep slope towards what looked like the back of the cave. From what I could see, the cave was shaped like an ellipse tilted to one side, much lower down by the opening. A large flat area at the back of the cave was empty. It looked as if the water never rose this high. I bent to touch the floor, and it was dry. With the flashlight I searched the back wall looking for an opening of some sort that Clarissa would have used to place the jewels in, but I found nothing. The desire to scream almost choked me. It had to be here. I knew it was.

"Great adventure, but no treasure. We'd best head out." Tristan stood beside me and touched my arm. "Sorry."

"It has to be here."

"It was a good try."

"Fine." I spun round and tripped over, face-planting onto the hard sand. "Shit."

"Slow down; we're not in that much of a rush." He helped me up and brushed sand off my face. "Are you OK?"

"No damage done, except to my ego. What the hell did I catch my foot on?"

"Just a rock in the sand, I expect. You didn't see it coming."

"No, I didn't." I bent to look and saw an indentation and felt something hard under it. I brushed the sand away with my fingers to reveal the edge of a metal box.

Tristan was wading back into the water. "Come on, Jude, the tide's at the opening."

"It's here. Come and look." I frantically dug with my hands and exposed the outline of a small black metal box. In seconds Tristan was beside me to help clear it from the other side. I looked up to see the water coming in over the mouth of the cave.

"Can you get it out?" I kept digging down.

"It's not budging. The sand is like cement. We need the spade."

"We haven't got time."

"Then we'll have to leave it."

"No." I stood and looked around for anything that could be used. I found a flat sharp stone and tossed it to Tristan, then sourced another for myself. I dug frantically, chipping away at the sand. The tide was flowing into the mouth of the cave and rising.

Tristan looked over his shoulder. "We'll have to leave it."

"We won't be able to get in here again until November."

"It's leave, or face the same fate as Clarissa." As he spoke the water level rose further up the slope. Only the top few inches of the opening of the cave was above the level of the tide.

"No." I stood up and stamped on the stone I'd left wedged. The box moved. Tristan grabbed it and my hand, pulling me down to the opening. I took one last breath and dived into the water and through the mouth of the cave.

"Leave it, and go and get dry. Today's the second day you've returned to the house drenched." Helen fussed. "I promise I won't open it, nor will Tristan until you are here. And for all we know it will be filled with little crabs, and I've always been afraid of them."

"But —" I looked at the box again.

"No buts, go and do as you're told and I'll make tea." She pushed me towards the door.

Tristan walked in and Helen frowned. "And you're all wet too."

"True, but we are alive." He smiled at me. "I need a shower. I'll open the box when I'm done." He left me open-mouthed in the kitchen. How could he just walk away? I looked at the battered box and longed to shake

396

it again. It was heavy and it rattled. We'd had to kill a lot of time waiting for the tide to come in far enough to get the boat onto the pontoon. It was strange how, when we were in the cave the tide moved swiftly, but while we waited without the right equipment to open the box, it took for ever. Now I was being asked to wait some more.

I ran up the stairs to my room and jumped in the shower before it had a chance to warm up. The water was cold, but no colder than what we had been in today. Slowly it warmed, and I could feel where the sun had burned me. My mind drifted to the passion in the boat, and I stopped myself by turning the cold tap on full.

I dressed with haste, then dragged a comb through my hair before I bunched it in a clip. I felt like a child on Christmas morning. I knew there were presents under the tree, and I wanted to open them now. The suspense was killing me. I took the stairs two at a time and Tristan met me at the bottom. "Slow down. You've already taken one fall today."

I laughed. "True. But without that fall we wouldn't have . . ."

He put his finger on my mouth. "Shall we go and see what's in it? See that we've found an old box filled with junk?"

I wrinkled my nose at him. I had my doubts too. "I know."

"I just don't want you to get your hopes up." He took my hand.

"They're not."

"Liar." He kissed me. "I can see the excitement in your eyes."

We walked into the kitchen. Helen was placing an array of tools and a collection of old keys beside the box. "Now that you're here, and I don't have to guard the crown jewels, I'll take the tea through to the drawing room." She was at the kitchen door when she turned. "Try the keys first, Tristan. The box is in amazingly good condition, it would be a shame to ruin it."

"Yes, Helen." He picked them up, then inspected the lock. I picked up the screwdriver with the small head. "Didn't you listen to Helen?"

I went towards the box. "What she doesn't know won't hurt her."

He rapped my knuckles with a long key, then selected a small one and tried it. It fit, but only turned part way. He tried the next one on the ring while I tapped my fingers on the table.

"Patience."

"In short supply."

"I can tell." He wiggled the key and I heard a click. I moved closer. Tristan used the key to lift the top of the box, and a small snail moved on the rim.

"Oh my God." I clapped my hand to my mouth. The box was filled with so much jewellery, but in the centre sat a huge blue stone. Although I had seen it in paintings, I wasn't prepared for it in real life. It was so much larger and bluer.

"Tristan." I whispered, and grabbed his hand. He pulled me to him and swung me around, then kissed me.

CHAPTER
THIRTY-FIVE

The dogs chased each other on the beach, and Tristan and I stood side by side, lost in thought. I imagined he was thinking about what he'd do with the treasure. The sapphire alone would bring a small fortune at auction, let alone the many diamonds and the tiara with an emerald the size of an eyeball. Petroc had been right when he said kings and queens and not the local gentry should have worn the jewels. It was an astounding collection.

A French flagged yacht left the river. My time here was coming to an end. I'd found the treasure. Petroc hadn't been mad. Imogen's quest was complete. Petroc's book would be out next summer. Now what?

"Can you show me?" Tristan turned from the water.

I jumped. "Show you what?"

"Where you found this rare orchid." His eyes held tones of grey as he looked at me.

"Yes, but are you sure?"

"I haven't walked the coastal path since she died. I think I'm ready." I could see the small boy reflected in his eyes.

I took his hand in mine and he called the dogs. Blue hydrangeas were scattered among the trees as we

399

walked in silence through the woods until we reached the copse of oak on the headland. I let go of his hand and went over the broken bit of fence, treading carefully.

"Are you certain about this orchid?" He glanced at the twisted trees. "How could any orchid grow here?"

"With difficulty, as they only flower infrequently." I ducked under the lichen-covered branches, working my way closer to the edge.

"So there is no mistaking it?"

"Yes. They are very distinctive. It has no leaves."

"None." He stopped moving.

I longed to know what he was thinking. "Careful where you step." I knelt down and crawled cautiously towards the wire. Tristan followed behind me. The roar of the waves crashing to the cove below filled the air around us.

"Please be careful. I don't want to lose you." He grabbed my shoulder.

I turned to him about to say something, when out of the corner of my eye I saw a single flower in the dark recesses. "It's there."

His shoulder pressed against mine. His breathing was ragged. "It's beautiful."

"Yes. Like she was."

"Yes." He took my hand in his. "Thank you."

We crawled away from the edge carefully. Rum poked her wet nose against mine before I stood and brushed myself off. Tristan was quiet as we walked back to the house.

400

Before we reached the house, I took Tristan's hand. "Are you OK?"

He nodded. "So much to take on board after so long pushing it all away." He looked at the house and the colour of his eyes changed again. There was a softness to them. "Thank you."

"There you two are." Helen waved from the French windows in the drawing room and tapped her watch. "If you're quick, Tristan, you'll catch this man you called about the treasure." She handed him a slip of paper and I followed Tristan to the study to collect my laptop. The Trevillion jewels were spread out on the desk. Gold shone among the stones. It was all in remarkably good condition. Light hit the sapphire, sending arcs of blue shooting across the room. It was amazing. I still couldn't believe we'd found it.

Tristan stroked the little clock while he was on the phone talking to someone about finding the treasure. But from what I'd read, I'm sure this was just a formality. He'd found the treasure that belonged to his family on his land. Lady Clarissa always intended it to be found. Unfortunately Octavia hadn't because of the landslip, which had trapped Clarissa and hidden the cave.

I walked into the drawing room and collapsed onto a chair. Glancing around the room, admiring its proportions again, I saw a pile of books on a shelf by the window. I leaped up. They looked like old diaries. I turned the pages, hoping. Time passed; what seemed like hours. My hands shook as I read. Closing the books, I wiped my eyes.

Tristan came into the room and over to me. "Are you OK?"

"Yes; I've found Octavia's journals."

"And they made you cry?" He bent down and ran his hand under my eyes, brushing the tears away.

"Octavia did. Her life was so sad."

"She had no happiness?"

"Well, yes, she did. She loved her mother, her cat, her painting and Pengarrock. She found happiness in all those things." I smiled at Tristan.

"There might be something in that."

I blinked. Something in Tristan's voice made those words sound different. I stood, stiff from sitting on the low window seat. We walked towards the door.

"I declared the find, and they want me to present the treasure to them."

"But it's yours." I stopped.

"They agreed, but this is all a formality."

We stood in the doorway together. I gave the journals to him. He turned them over in his hands before placing them on the hall table. A light breeze came through the front door, blowing my hair loose. Tristan tucked it behind my ear and trailed his finger along my jaw until it reached my lips. He lowered his head. His mouth teased mine. I raised my hands and slid my fingers round his neck and pulled him to me.

There was a not-so-discreet cough. Tristan lifted his head but held me close. I noticed that Helen didn't look at all surprised to see me in Tristan's embrace.

"Helen?" He raised an eyebrow.

"I have a message from the planning office."

"Well, out with it."

I began to pull away from him, but he wasn't letting me go. In the joy of finding the treasure, I'd forgotten about his development plans.

"Yes?"

"They've been approved." Helen twisted a duster in her hands.

My heart sank. He was still going to destroy the beauty of Pengarrock. He was leaving. My desire to run was strong, and I tried to wriggle out of his arms but couldn't escape as the door frame was behind me and Tristan's arms were around me.

He smiled. "That's good news. I hope they won't mind if I alter them again."

"Now what? What are you changing?" Helen tidied the journals on the table.

"My goals have changed."

"Dare I hope?" She looked up, her eyes shining.

"I think you might." He held me closer.

"A change of heart?" She stared at both of us.

"Rather than a change, it might be a case of finding it again." He looked at me.

Helen smiled. "Well, I shall leave you two to it then. I must say, it's taken you both long enough."

I could feel the laughter rumbling through Tristan, and it was doing wild and wonderful things to my equilibrium. He gave me his undivided attention when Helen had disappeared, smiling from ear to ear.

"You're not going to develop Pengarrock? You're going to keep it?" Hope made my voice rise.

He held me close. "I didn't say that."

I drew back.

"I will still have to sell a few things and develop others, including the Petroc Trevillion Memorial Library." Tristan took the glasses off my nose and placed them on my head. "But yes, I'm going to try and keep Pengarrock."

"Oh." My mind raced.

He bent his head towards my ear and whispered, "Does that please you?"

"Yes." A shiver ran down my spine.

"Good."

"Why?" I tilted my head back, trying to see him better.

"I want to please you, among other things." He kissed my neck. Desire spread through me.

"Hmm. I look forward to being pleased." I ran my fingers through his hair and pulled his mouth to mine.

He didn't kiss me. His mouth hovered just above mine. "Does that mean you will stay around to help?"

"Yes, a most definite yes." And I kissed him.

Acknowledgements

A Cornish Affair has been a long time in the making. The first glimmers of it began back in 2005 when Chris and I went to drinks with Richard and Christine Graham-Vivian at their beautiful home set above the Helford River. My daughter Sasha, then six, joined us. While we sat enjoying the glorious late summer evening she ran up and down the lawns and scrambled over the canons. A story idea began. So my first thanks go to Richard and Christine for sharing their perfect setting and their canons and to my beautiful daughter. Without their contribution the book never would have been born.

Special thanks go to Anne Rodell for a bit of legal understanding on estates and probate and to Dr Kate Gearing and Lesley Cookman for help on what to do when you encounter a dead body. Thanks are also due to Larry Masterson for information on hunting and fishing in Vermont and Canada.

The joy of building a house like Pengarrock from scratch in your head has to be done to be imagined. I relied on my mother-in-law's collection of books and pamphlets from houses like Godolphin and Trelowarren to create Pengarrock. But it was the helpful Tish Valva at NT Cotehele who provided me with information on the beautiful chapel at Cotehele that helped shape the chapel at Pengarrock.

My writing support network, the RNA, has kept me sane, but mostly it was the wonderful Brigid Coady who listened when I moaned and reminded me that I could do this.

Huge thanks also go to Julia Hayward who braved reading this book from its earliest stages and pulled me up on my grammar and spelling.

Without the patience of my editor, Kate Mills, this book wouldn't be here. Her incredible skill at pulling the best story out of me is truly astounding. I owe her a massive debt of gratitude. My agent, Carole Blake, has trusted me and believed in me when I no longer did . . . thank you.

A special thank you to my mother who taught me so many things, but most importantly the need to be true to myself even when it wasn't easy. Also that in love, actions speak louder than words.

Throughout this process, my husband, my children, my parents and my best friend have kept me going and reminded me that I could do this and they wouldn't let me quit. Their unshakeable belief in me was and is amazing, even when I was grumpy beyond words.

Author's Note

I have taken liberties with the landscape of Dennis Head in order to create a cave that would suit the story's purpose and to provide fertile ground for the rare "White Ghost Orchid". Cornwall is home to many wild orchids, but it is not home to the extremely rare Ghost Orchid. The cliff-top setting of Dennis Head is the last place this near-extinct orchid would appear. However its name and ghostly appearance appealed to me, along with its ability to disappear for years on end and then almost magically reappear. Cornwall is filled with many species of wild orchid and they have provided me with great joy when I have spied them on walks.

One last note before treasure-hunters begin searching the Helford River environs . . . The Trevillion treasure is purely a creation of my jewel-obsessed imagination.